The Demon

and

The Angel

Kara J Redmond

DORRANCE
PUBLISHING CO
EST. 1920
PITTSBURGH, PENNSYLVANIA 15238

Dorrance Publishing Co
585 Alpha Drive
Pittsburgh, PA 15238
Visit our website at www.dorrancebookstore.com

ISBN: 979-8-8852-7113-4
eISBN: 979-8-8852-7840-9

I want to thank all of those who helped make my dream a reality. I love you all and you will never understand how grateful I am for each of you. I'm happy you are apart of my world, all of them.
Also, for those who have always felt like an outcast, when it seems like you don't belong. You will find your place someday, never give up.

Information

Demons Appearances

Archdemon - Looks human with crimson eyes that glow when powers are used, no life in them, sharp black nails, pointed ears, sharp canines.

Goblin - Short, grass-green skin, warts, few strands of hair, smell, pointy ears, long nose, nasty teeth, deep and gargled voice, yellow and beady eyes. Wears black overalls with nothing underneath.

Imp - Smaller than a goblin, walks on all fours, black scaly skin, claws, sharp teeth, can't speak English, just gibberish, fast, small horns, naked but with no parts. (All look the same)

Jinn - Black blob, shapeshifts to be able to speak. Can turn into any person or animal.

Puck - Size of a toddler, doesn't talk, always moving, avocado skin, dark brown eyes, dead leaves as clothing, stubby hands/feet, hideous laughter.

Black Dog - Huge dog, shaggy black fur, big as a calf, red and glowing eyes.

Marching Hordes - All the same, can't think for themselves, speak gibberish. Whole body is black or red, fingers like knives. No physical ears or nose, flat face, except for a mouth filled with razors.

Succubus – Normal, sexy women up until they kill, eyes turn white, nails grow, lips turn white.

Elemental - Humanoid figure shaped by their element, telepathic.
Nightmare – Smooth, black body, tall, no eyes/mouth/nose/ears.
Blends into the darkness of night perfectly. Can speak without a
mouth.
Fury - Female, pale skin, bloody eyes, blood in teeth, sharp nails,
snakes for hair.
Oni - Hulking human figure, darker skin, black irises, dark and long
crazy hair, loincloths of tiger pelt clothing, horns, fangs, always car-
rying two thick scimitar swords.
Witch - A human but born with the gift of magic.
Demon Blade - Hilt is silver, guards are shaped like dragon heads,
killin' parts are black as night, foible has a glowing white pentagram.
When wielded, the blade ignites with black flames covering the
whole thing.
Demon Shuriken - Pentagram is carved in the middle, with the
center being the middle of the star. Must add their fire to it before
throwing.
Demon Dagger - The same design as the sword but smaller.

Angel Appearances

Archangels - All ten or more feet tall, white cloaks, wings appear when needed.

Gabriel - Dark-yellow aura, dark-yellow eyes, short curly brown hair, always big smiles.

Michael - Cobalt blue aura, cobalt blue eyes, short black hair, large arms, broad shoulders, always has a sword.

Raphael - Green aura, green eyes, long, curly red hair, female, has a little bit of meat on her bones.

Azrael - Beige aura, beige eyes, shoulder-length white hair.

Ariel - Pale-pink aura, pale-pink eyes, long blond hair, female, flower headband.

Uriel - Pale-yellow aura, pale-yellow eyes, brown ponytail, female, pencil behind ear, curious eyes.

Raziel - Rainbow aura, rainbow eyes constantly changing colors. Short black-and-gold hair, gold on the tips.

Guardian Angels - Male and female, while on duty, white T-shirt, blue jeans, white shoes, single sword strapped to their back. Off duty, can wear whatever.

Powers - White T-shirt, black jeans, white shoes, crisscross sword holster on back, two swords always in them.

Phoenix - Colorful feathers and a tail of gold and scarlet, larger than an eagle.

Pixie - Small, wingless, fairy-like, pointed ears, candy apple-red hair, joyful and mischievous, voice too quiet to hear.

Fairy - Small, pure diamond blond hair, blue eyes, wings sparkle, whole body comes across as a sparkle of light, voice too quiet to hear.

Cherubim - Taller than guardian angel, gold chest armor, golden spear, sword on hip, sandals, muscular, blazing blue eyes, gold bracelets, white pants.

Angel Sword - Hilt is gold, guards are wing-shaped, killin' parts transparent, appearing to look plastic; when wielded, lights up with bright paled turquoise light. Foible has a golden, glowing angelic symbol.

Shields - Gold and silver shield-shaped metal, handle on the back, can grow by sending out transparent walls from all sides. The center has the same angelic symbol, constantly glowing.

Spear - Staff is gold; the tip is the same as the sword's killin' parts.

Bow and Arrow - White light shaped like a bow, the string is made of gold. Arrows silver in the middle, the ends where the feathers go are wing-shaped, and the tip is a blazing white light.

Angelic Symbol - Three pointed ovals linked together with a circle going through each of them.

1

Before we start, I need you to do me a favor. Can you do that? I need you to believe, believe in the supernatural, because it is real. The Underworld, real; the place upstairs, real. Demons and angels, also real. All those scary stories you heard about when you were younger, all those malevolent beings you were afraid were watching you from the shadows, all real. Guardian angels, the archangels, are also very real. I know what you are thinking. You're thinking that I am crazy and making this all up, but I promise you that I'm not. Now you're probably telling me to prove it, asking me how I know that what I say is true. Well, the answer is simple: I know because I am a part of that world.

Hello, my name is Kalma, Kal for short. I am the daughter of the Underworld's second-in-command, Rorridun, the archdemon. I was raised in the Underworld by my father and some of the other demons. I was taught to kill and hate, to destroy, leaving nothing left when I was done. For seventeen years I was taught all of this, but there was always something in me telling me that it was wrong, that being evil was bad. I pushed those thoughts aside, trying to ignore the nagging feeling inside me until I learned something that completely changed my life.

My whole life my father told me that my mother died giving birth to me, but that was all he would say to me. I looked through his things one day while he was away at a meeting with the other archdemons. I found a picture of a woman, a human, who looked to be in her mid-twenties. The woman's hair was long, black, and beautiful. Her eyes piercing blue, her smile incredible and kind. The only thing wrong with her was her stomach bulging out from under her blue dress. The picture was taken from far away, the woman having no clue that she was being photographed. I flipped the photo over to see my father's handwriting scratched across the back.

Kalma.

That's right, I was the baby inside of that woman. A human was my mother, making me a hybrid between a demon and a human. My whole world flipped the day I found that photo. Everything changed. I changed. I wanted to learn more about the humans above.

I was told to never go up, but I didn't care anymore. I snuck out, and then up. It was the middle of the day when I came out of a crypt in a cemetery. I ran fast across the grass until I found safety in the darkness. Tall things towered over me, touching the sky above. Contraptions on wheels zoomed by on a black ground. I started walking, remaining in the dark shadows so no one could see me. After a while, the towers began shrinking until I came across a long construction that sat across the black ground from where I stood. Human children were walking all over the place. Each one of them with a smile on their face. I could hear their laughter from where I hid. I stayed where I was and watched as they all went their separate ways.

As I was getting ready to leave, I saw her. A girl who looked the same age as me walked out of the construction, laughing with others who looked the same age. That day she was wearing white shoes, dark blue jeans, a white shirt under a light-blue long-sleeve button-up shirt, with a blue bag on her back. Her smile was brighter than anything I had ever seen before. Her sand skin tone paler than those around her, with warm beige and natural tones, not a blemish in sight. Her hair and eyes being the opposite of mine. My hair short and the color of ash. Hers laid on her collarbone with layers cut in, so blond that the sunlight reflected off of it. My eyes dark red, hers sky blue. Everything about her was the exact opposite of me, and yet I couldn't take my eyes off of her. A feeling I had never felt before ached inside of me. I wanted to leave the shadows, step into the light to meet this mysterious girl. I didn't, though; I stayed where I was and watched her walk away with her friends.

I stepped farther back into the shadow, closing my eyes while taking deep breaths, her smile stuck behind my eyelids. I opened my eyes and looked down at my hands, looking at my sharp, black fingernails, my pale skin. I lifted my hands to touch the points on my ears as I rolled my tongue over both sets of my sharp canine teeth. I ran my hands through my short hair, barely able to grab a handful. As I stood there taking in all of our differences, I made the biggest decision of my life. I decided to meet her to find out why she had the effect she had on me.

I decided that I had to learn more about humanity and what they were all about, that I would make myself blend in with them so I could see more. I wanted more than anything to learn what it was like to be human. So from that day forward, every day after training, while my father was at his meetings, I snuck up to the surface, watching her as she left the same place. Some days she was with the same people, but others, she was alone, but I felt the same thing every day when I looked at her.

As time went on, I practiced blending in. I learned how to control my appearance. Making everything about me look more human. I used my mother's eye color as my fake eyes. After a few months, I had the camouflage down perfectly, so I stepped out of the shadows. The first time the sunlight hit me, it felt as if the ice inside of me melted. I felt so bubbly and happy, a feeling I had never felt before. I smiled and started walking, looking around at everything, studying everyone that I passed. I listened to their conversations, watched their interactions, soaking it all in.

A few months later, I finally gained the courage to meet her. I made sure my disguise was set before I followed her after her friends left. As I moved closer, my hands started to shake. I stuck them deep into my jeans' pockets. Part of me was screaming to turn around and go back, but the aching I had felt from day one told me to keep going. I watched as she started to cross the street, her eyes on her phone in her hands, headphones in her ears. My senses went wild as a yellow car came speeding around the corner right towards her. She didn't see it coming right for her. I took my hands out of my pockets as I pressed hard off the sidewalk. I felt the cement crack under my foot as I pushed. The car got closer to her as I did. She slowly looked up at the car; her face changed to terror. I jumped at her, wrapping my arms around her head as I pressed her against my body. We both went flying across the rest of the road. I kept her close to me, shielding her by making sure that my body hit the ground and not hers. As we laid there, I could feel her heart beating fast and her breathing quick. I gently sat up, letting her go in the process. We both stayed there on our knees. I glanced at her looking for wounds as she kept her eyes shut tight. After a few seconds, she opened them and looked at me. The moment our eyes met a sharp twinge hit me in my chest. I turned my face away to hide the look of pain. I took a deep breath and stood up. I held my hand out towards hers. I felt as her hand slid into mine, her hand warm and soft. I pulled her to her feet and looked back at her as she pulled her earbuds out. I avoided her eyes as we stood there awkwardly.

"Thank you," she said softly.

Hearing her voice made my head spin.

"I think you just saved my life." She gave me a genuine smile. Another twinge hit me, harder than the first.

Her smile disappeared. "Are you all right?"

My nerves disappeared at that moment. I turned away from her and took off running.

"Hey! Wait!" I heard her call after me.

I kept going; everything that had happened flashed in my head. I made it back to the entrance to the Underworld. I looked back over my shoulder before I went in. It has been two weeks since that day. I kept watching her but didn't go near her again. Everything changed the day

I turned eighteen, the day I was to be initiated and become an arch-demon like my father.

Our story will begin the day before my birthday. I hope you were following along and listening, because that girl is an essential part of this story. She is an important part of my story. The story about how a demon helped save the world.

2

I land hard on my butt as smoke rises from the burnt spot on my shirt.

{That almost burnt through my shirt.}

"Where is your head at Kalma? You could have easily dodged that attack." My father asks as his eyes stop glowing.

"I'm sorry, Father," I say as I stand up.

"Do not apologize to me. It will be you who will be killed one day because you were not paying attention."

I nod.

"What has you so distracted these days? The last few weeks your mind keeps wandering off."

{That girl has me distracted. Her eyes keep making their way into my head.} "It's nothing, Father."

{He can never know that I went up top. He can never know that I saved a human.} "It must be something for you to be acting this way." He folds his arms across his chest as he stares me down.

{Better come up with something quick.}

"I guess I am just thinking about what tomorrow has planned for me," I half-lie.

He stares at me for a few seconds before saying anything. "There is nothing for you to be thinking about. You know exactly what will happen. You have witnessed many rituals before."

I nod again. "I know, but it is different when it is you."

He sighs. "I thought I taught you to be fearless." He shakes his head. "You better have yourself under control for tomorrow."

{If he only knew.}

"You will be eighteen tomorrow; it is time for you to grow up. Tomorrow you will become a full-fledged archdemon like me. You cannot allow yourself to think about anything but hate or the ritual will go very badly for you."

I gulp.

{I remember what happened last time someone wasn't ready for transitioning. The blood burned until they combusted with a flare of fire, just how all archdemons do when they die.}

"Of course, Father. I will make sure to erase everything and just focus on the hatred I have built up inside of me."

He nods as he unfolds his arms. "Good, that is what I like to hear." He walks up to me until he is right in front of me. "After tomorrow, everything will change. You will finally start moving towards what you were made for."

{Made with a human.}

"Just remember that."

{Father has never shown me genuine affection like a father would.}

I nod before he turns away and walks towards the door that leads out into the hallway.

"I'm heading out to speak with the other archdemons to prepare for tomorrow. I will be back late."

"Understood."

He grabs the handle. "Don't disappoint me, Kalma."

{I'm just a tool, a puppet for him to use.}

He opens the door and walks out with it shutting behind him. I let out a deep breath. "That was close."

I look at the empty, gray room, glancing at the scorch marks on the walls and floor from previous impacts made by either Father or me. I lift my hands as I push heat into them. I stare at them as fire ignites in my palms. I watch the flames dance in my hands, the navy blue waving back and forth.

{I was young when he started training me to use my gifts, as he calls them, my quick healing, my strength, my speed, my enhanced senses, and my newly discovered camouflage power. All he wanted to work on was my firepower, making the flames bigger and hotter.}

I push more heat into my hands, the blue growing in size.

{My flames started small and red, but as I grew, the fire did as well.} I can feel the heat rising from my palms.

{By the time I was ten, the flames were blue. I learned quicker than all the other archdemon kids my age.}

I smile to myself.

{And I'm not even a full demon like the rest.}

I swing my hands forward pushing the heat out. My flames rocket from my palms soaring through the air before striking the wall hard. The fire explodes against the wall, leaving a scorch mark matching the others. I sigh as I lower my hands back to my sides.

{I'm not a full demon, and yet my body looks just like all the rest. My eyes glow just like all the other archdemons when I use my flames.}

I walk over to the door, opening it before stepping into the hall. I make my way down the hallway, stopping in front of a door. I slowly open it before stepping inside and leaning against it as the door closes. I look around my room, the walls black with tiny crack lines going up the walls, the floor gray just like the rest of the house. Two extended bookshelves line two of the walls; the wall opposite the door is an old dresser made from dark wood. Then in the center of the room is a black-and-red cushioned chair surrounded by books on all sides. I sigh as I push off the door heading towards the opposite side. I walk around piles of books before stepping up to my dresser. I grab my shirt where the burn mark lays. I frown at it.

{This keeps up I'm going to run out of shirts.}

I push heat into my hand holding the fabric. Blue flickers off my fingers as the shirt catches fire. As the flames wrap around the shirt, I hurry and rip it off, ensuring the fire doesn't get my undergarment.

{I just had to wear one of the shirts that aren't fireproof.}

I hold the burning shirt in my hand until nothing is left but ash.

{Father says demons like us do not wear soiled clothing.}

I open a drawer from my dresser, looking over all my shirts.

{Hmmm, dark blue, grey, dark red, or black?}

I reach in and grab one of the black shirts.

{I may as well stick with black for today, since that was what I was wearing before.}

I hold it out in front of me.

{We are not allowed to wear clothing with anything on it. Father says it is indecent. So, all of our apparel are solid colors.}

I pull the shirt over my head, putting my hands through the holes before pulling it down the rest of the way. I smooth it down with my hands.

{I never realized how pale my arms look while I'm wearing black.} I glance down at my dark blue jeans and black tennis shoes.

{Only dark colors for us demons.}

I look at my chair, at the dark-red zip-up hanging off the back. I sigh again as I make my way back towards my door. I walk through, closing it behind me before walking the rest of the hallway, then turning off into the living room. I look around the pretty much empty space. The only things sitting in it are a black couch and chair and a few giant bookshelves full of books.

{I think I've read every single one of those.}

I walk over to the bookshelf closest to me, glancing over the titles.

{Father wanted me to learn everything I could about demon history and the war against the angels.}

I grab one of the books, pulling it from its spot. I open it and flip through the pages until I find the page I want. I skim it over even though I know it by heart. The page talks about hybrids.

{Demons aren't the only ones who create hybrids to fight in their wars; angels do as well. Hybrids can become more potent than the being that created them if trained right.}

I shake my head as I close the book, setting it back where it goes.

{Hybrids are just viewed as weapons.}

I turn away from the books, walking over to the center of the living room.

{I am Father's weapon. He wants me to join him and the other arch-demons one day, but if I'm not strong like I am meant to be, will he still want me to? Do I still even want to now that I know the truth?}

I shake my head as I raise my hand to look at my watch.

{It's two thirty; if I go now, I'll make it up just in time to see her.}

I move to the door opening before stepping through. I close it behind me before walking down the dirt path.

{The Underworld isn't like the upside. They have houses and roads, while we have dirt paths and places to live inside the walls.}

I keep walking, passing door after door stuck inside of the rocks.

{When they say underworld, they should really say underground. We live several miles below the surface, below the city of Philadelphia. We are still inside the crust layer of the Earth but close enough to the mantle layer to feel its heat. We live in solid rocks surrounded by dirt and stone.}

I turn the corner leading towards "town," which is just a giant opening, about the size of a few city blocks, in the crust with wooden carts and small wooden shops scattered all over the place. Demons of all kinds walk all around, shopping at the different stores and carts.

{This is the Underworld's capital. Monsters from all over come here to shop or meet with the higher-ups like my father.}

In the middle of the area is a giant statue about one-story tall, made from the mantel rock beneath us, of a handsome man in a business suit with his hands folded over his chest, deep, red eyes glowing above a vicious sneer. A continuous fire burns at his feet, the white flames dancing around the statue. It can be seen from any entrance into town.

{That's supposed to be Lucifer. His power is more significant than any demon, his flames being the hottest and most powerful; that is why they are white. This statue is supposed to strike fear into all creatures, reminding them of the power that he holds. The fire at his feet is actually Lucifer's absolute fire. He keeps it burning non-stop from wherever he is.}

I begin walking towards the entrance on the opposite end of where I came from. I keep my head down and face towards the ground as I walk quickly, hoping no one will recognize me.

{The exits that I use that lead to the surface are on the farthest end of town and down a few passages. I have to be careful, or someone might see me and wonder what I am up to.}

I keep moving fast with my head still down, using my enhanced senses to avoid running into anything or anyone. I'm a little over halfway through.

"Kalma!" someone calls.

I curse under my breath as I straighten up and look back towards where the voice came from. Running towards me is Jorvexx, the son of one of my father's fellow archdemons, as well as my friend.

{I've known Jorvexx for as long as I can remember. We grew up side by side. We even trained together at least twice a week. We competed to see who was getting stronger.}

"Where have you been?" He stops in front of me. "I have barely seen you in weeks." I glance him over, noticing the small holes in his jeans and tears at the bottom of his red shirt as well as the dust sprinkled throughout his buzz-cut hair.

{I wonder why his father allows him to dress like that.}

"Oh, you know, been training like crazy to get ready for tomorrow."

He nods. "Tomorrow is the big day, huh?"

I nod.

"Are you ready?"

I shrug. "Ready as I'll ever be. I won't know until the ritual starts."

He places his hand on my shoulder. "Don't worry too much, or you'll just freak yourself out, and besides, I'll be there too."

{All of the archdemons living in our sector as well as their children will all be in attendance tomorrow.}

"If you need a distraction, just look for me and I'll help you." He smiles.

{Demons may not feel what humans do towards one another, but they still feel some kind of connection. I know that Jorvexx feels something towards me, he has for a while now, but I don't feel anything towards him.}

"Thank you, Jorvexx, I appreciate that." I give him a fake smile.

He squeezes my shoulder before taking his hand off it. "Well, it was nice seeing you, but my father is waiting for me, so I better get going," he explains.

I nod. "All right, it was nice seeing you as well."

He turns back around and starts running. "See you tomorrow!" Once he is out of sight, I look at my watch.

{Crap, I'm almost out of time.}

I turn back towards the entrance I need and take off running. I move quickly, thanks to my speed, dodging demons as I go. Once I go through the opening, I make a quick right and then left. I go straight for a little while before turning right again.

{I use the older ways to the surface, so I am not seen. I haven't seen anyone else down this way any of the times I have been.}

I take one more right before stopping inside a small square area surrounded by rock. At the opposite end of the room is a small platform big enough for one person. I make my way over to it before stepping up. As my feet settle, a small tube rises from the ground before me, stopping at my waist. An indented handprint sits on top of it.

{The reason why no one uses this one is that you have to power it up yourself. The newer ones are automatic.}

I place my hand onto the handprint. As I do, the platform lights up blue around me. I take a deep breath before pushing heat into my hand. Fire erupts around my hand before the tube starts to take in flames. The tube slowly fills up with my blue fire until it is full of swirling blue. I take my hand off the pipe right before it lowers back into the ground. The light around my feet gets brighter, and I can feel the heat under my shoes.

{I'll never get used to this no matter how many times I teleport.}

Blue flames seep out of the lights around me, slowly moving towards my feet. Fire attaches to my shoes, before climbing up my legs, covering all my body, all of me except my head.

{Here we go.}

I close my eyes as I feel the heat climb my neck and cover my mouth. Light shines on the other side of my eyelids before my body heats up.

{Just count.}

I feel the flames stick to me more.

{One.}

I clench my hands tightly into fists at my sides.

{Two.}

I can sense the teleportation start to pull at me.

{Three! Holy Sepulchre Cemetery!}

Everything is still for a second before the fire on me is gone. I carefully open my eyes to new surroundings. Beside me are two cement coffins covered in dust and cobwebs. I am inside a cement mausoleum crypt.

{No matter what teleportation we use, we will always end up in a cemetery.}

I move towards the iron gate door. I carefully open it, causing it to screech in protest. I step out and look around at all the tombstones scattered throughout the grass.

{You just have to think about which cemetery you want to teleport to.} I focus on my body, feeling my ears, nails, and teeth all change.

{The change doesn't hurt anymore like it did the first few times I transformed.} My eyes burn for a second, telling me that the color has changed. I look myself over to make sure that I appear human. I nod to myself before I take off towards the exit.

{If I hurry, I'll get there just as the bell rings.}

I feel a minor ache in my chest as I think about seeing her again.

3

I stand in my usual spot across the street from her school, waiting for the bell to ring. I glance at the school's sign.

{Springfield Township High School. What a strange name.}

I shake my head before turning back towards the doors as the bell rings. Kids and teenagers begin running out of the building with smiles covering their faces. Little groups form before each of them heads a different way, everyone walking home. I keep my eyes on the doors, not paying any attention to any of them. They swing open, and I see her. She walks out alone this time. Everything about her is the same as the first time I saw her four months ago, all except her clothes. Today she is wearing dark jeans with holes on the knees, the same shoes, a bright blue long-sleeve with white down the sides of the arms, and no bag.

{It's Friday, she never has her bag on Fridays.}

I watch as she makes her way down the sidewalk waving at people as she goes.

{We really are complete opposites.}

I follow her from the shadows.

{So then why do I feel this way when I look at you?}

I grab the front of my shirt where the aching is coming from.

{Demons can't feel towards others. We don't have hearts. That's why we only feel connections.}

I step out of the shadows when I know she is far enough away to not notice me.

{So, then what is this inside of me? Where is this feeling coming from if not a heart?}

I lower my hand, staying far behind her, but not too far, just in case something happens like before.

{If any of the others knew where I am right now and what I am doing, they'd kill me on the spot.}

I continue to follow her from a safe distance. I watch as she crosses the streets, looking both ways now. I smile to myself watching her being cautious.

{Glad that our encounter taught you something.}

We start making our way down a road with houses on both sides. I look at the road sign as we pass it.

{Biddlewoods Road. Who comes up with these names?}

She walks to the very last house in the middle of the circle that the road creates. I look at my watch.

{Thirty-one minutes every day to get here from the school.}

I watch as she climbs two steps to get onto her porch. The house is small but tall. Everything is white but the blue shutters on the windows. A swinging bench hangs from the porch. In the center of the door sits a silver knocker. From where I stand, I can see three windows, each with light-blue curtains inside them. There's no garage with the house, so sitting in the driveway is a silver vehicle with the words Ford and Taurus on the back. There isn't much of a yard, just one maple tree whose colors had changed a little over a month ago and has started to shed sits a few feet from the porch.

{When the trees started to change is when everyone started wearing longer clothing; it must have gotten colder.}

I move fast to hide behind the maple as she opens her door. "I'm home!" I hear her yell into the house.

"How was school?" another woman asks from inside the house.

"Same as always." She laughs as she shuts the door.

I sigh as I lean against the tree.

{Every day ends the same. I follow her here, just to be shut out.}

I glance over my shoulder around the tree to look at the house again.

{I don't even know her name, even after all this time.}

I shove my hands into my pockets as I stand straight and move away from her house. I walk down the road that we came from.

{I wonder if she ever thinks about me. I know that it was a while ago that I saved her, but I would hope that would be something that you wouldn't forget.}

I keep moving towards my destination, lost in thought. Replaying the scene over and over again when I had her in my arms. A painful spasm goes through my chest, causing me to flinch. I look up as I approach the gate to Holy Sepulchre Cemetery. I push open the gate and make it to the mausoleum that holds the teleportation site.

{Took me a while to figure out which cemetery was close to her house.}

I grab the door of the mausoleum, looking around to make sure no one is about before I go inside. As I close the door, my camouflage goes, feeling as my body returns to its normal state. I step into the circle; the tube rises in front of me. I place my hand on it, pushing heat into my hand. It fills with blue fire before I take my hand back. The tube moves back into the ground right before fire attaches to my body. I close my eyes as it consumes me. After a few seconds, I open them again and am back in the room from earlier. I glance at my watch.

{Crap, Father will be done with his meeting soon. If he sees that I am not in my room preparing for tomorrow... I don't even want to think about what he'd do.}

I jump off the platform and take off as fast as I can go. I run through town, swerving or jumping over the different monsters in my way. Many of them turn to yell at me but stop the moment they see who I am.

{The only good thing about Father being second-in-command is that I can pretty much get away with anything because all the other demons are afraid of him.} I'm at my door when I can hear voices echoing from the other end of the path.

{Crap, crap, crap.}

I fling open the door and bolt to my room, whipping that door open as well. I close it behind me while hearing the front door close and footsteps echo down the hall. I leap for the chair and grab a book. I use my feet to remove my shoes before swinging them over an arm and open the book, just as I hear a knock.

"Come in."

As the door is slowly opening, I quickly flip my upside-down book right-side up. My father steps into the room, the door opening the whole way. I stare at him as he crosses his arms over his chest.

{I never realized how much I look like him, not just our demon traits but other things as well. Yes, we have the same eye color, but all archdemons have red eyes, but I have his eye shape. We both have the same shade of black hair. Claws are shaped the same, same as our ears. We have different noses, though. I must have my mother's nose, and cheeks for that matter. I am built like my father but short like my mother. I'm only five foot five inches. My body is in perfect shape; my arms, legs, and stomach are built with muscle. His body is the same way. I don't know if it is from being demons or just from how often we train. I know that we do not have the same taste in clothing. I love my jeans and tees, sometimes a hoodie; he only ever wears black suits with red ties, even when we train. I don't know how he does it.}

"Have you been preparing for tomorrow?"

I nod. "Yes, Father," I lie.

"Are you working on what we talked about earlier?"

"Of course," I lie again.

He nods in approval as his eyes look around my room.

{If we could read people's minds like some of the other demons, I would be dead about now.}

"Would you like me to light your wall before I head into my room for the evening?"

{Another plus side of being a demon is that we don't have to eat if we don't want to. We can eat human food or souls or just blood, but we don't have to. We can survive without. I prefer human food when I do want to eat.}

"No, I can get them." I start to get up.

He holds his hand up. "Stay there," he commands.

I settle back as he moves over to my dresser, placing his hand at the bottom of the crack above.

{He was furious when I put the cracks in the wall, at least until he saw what they do.}

I grin as a small, blue flame jumps from my father's hand right before his flames climb the wall, filling in all the cracks throughout the whole room.

{We might be able to see in the dark, but I really like looking at my room when it is like this.}

He takes his hand from the wall and walks back towards the door. I look around at his fire dancing throughout my walls, the blue sticking out brightly compared to the dark walls.

"I put enough heat into them that it should last you until morning." I look back at him.

"This is the last thing I can do for you, Kalma. Starting tomorrow, it is all on you."

I nod.

"I cannot step in to help you. You have to learn on your own. Do you understand?"

"Yes, Father."

"I mean it, Kalma; once the ritual is complete, you live or die by your own decisions."

"I understand."

He sighs as he turns around.

{I've never seen him like this before. He has never been this concerned before.} "Be ready tomorrow by three o'clock. That is when all the archdemons will arrive."

"Yes, sir."

He grabs the handle of the door. "One more thing."

I don't say anything.

"Be ready to kill." He pulls the door closed behind him. I stare at the closed door while holding my breath.

{The last part of the ritual is to kill an innocent. I will have to kill someone to become like my father.}

I let out my breath.

"Am I ready for that?" I ask the empty air, hoping someone will answer.

4

"It is time, Kalma," Father says from the other side of my bedroom door.

I take a deep breath as I pull my hoodie on, letting it out as I take a step towards the door.

{I can do this.}

I open the door and see my father standing outside it, waiting for me. "Are you ready?"

I nod. He nods back before turning towards the living room. I follow him to the living room and out the door. We make our way down the path, and I notice multiple people standing outside their doors staring at us.

{Everyone knows what today is. They all know that another archdemon is about to be made whole.}

I continue to follow my father, lost in my head thinking about who I will have to kill.

"Here we are."

We stop outside of a hole leading into a cavern.

{Shut everything off, don't feel anything, don't think about anything but hate and destruction. I can do this.}

We walk in the entrance, to where the other archdemons and their children are waiting.

"Let us begin," my father instructs everyone.

We all nod before moving into our positions. I stand in the middle of the room as everyone stands around me, the adults closer to me, with their kids behind them. All the boys have the same haircut and are wearing the same clothing today: black shoes, pants, and shirts, while the men have slightly longer hair wearing suits with red ties to match their eyes. Allaya wears the same thing as the boys. Her hair is different, short on the sides, with the hair on top swooping into a spike above her forehead. Her mother wears a suit without a tie, her hair a perfect silky black wave down to her shoulders. I look down at my feet and see the pentagram carved out in the ground around me.

"To start the ritual, all fully developed archdemons shall give their blood to the symbol," my father explains.

I watch the adults lift an arm to their mouths before biting their wrists. Blood starts to pour from the wounds. They all hold out the arm that is bleeding, holding it over their tip of the pentagram. Behind me stands my father. Beside him on his right is Jorvexx and his father, Darixul. Next to him is Rinnixa with her daughter Allaya. By her is Thezgoth and his son Encador. Then finally, on the last tip, is Xallant with his son Vexxus.

{All archdemons and their children are required to attend a coming-of-age ritual.} Everyone's blood continues to pour from their wrists, slowly filling up the pentagon. Once the symbol is filled with blood, they pull their arms back, the wounds healing instantly.

"Next, the one in the center of the pentagram shall cover the blood with their fire without burning it."

{This is what all the training to master control was for.}

I take a few deep breaths as I hold my hands over one of the lines. I focus on my heat, closing my eyes to picture my navy fire. I imagine the blue flames dancing, waiting to be freed. I open my eyes, pushing heat into my hands and then out. Blue flies out of my hands, landing on the line of blood. I focus on the heat and power of the blast as the fire spreads throughout the whole symbol until it meets back where it started. I pull my heat back, making the flames coming from my hands stop. I look around at my fire, watching it burn above the blood.

{I did it.}

"Next, they shall drink some of the fallen angel's blood."

{Lucifer.}

I turn around as my father hands me a cup filled with dark-red liquid.

{This is the part that is the most dangerous. If the one drinking isn't ready, their blood will fight his blood, causing combustion.}

I take the cup carefully into my hands, bringing it to my chest. I stare down into the cup, focusing on turning everything off, not feeling anything. After a few seconds, I lift the cup to my lips. I feel the warm thickness enter my mouth before sliding down my throat. A strong metal taste covers my tongue as I swallow the last drop. I move the cup away from me. I stand very still, waiting for something to happen. They all stare at me, waiting for the same thing. We all wait to see whether or not my body will hold the blood. After about a minute, nothing happens.

{I don't feel any different.}

My father holds out his hand. I place the cup back into his hands.

"The final step to activate the blood swallowed is to spill an innocent's blood and consume some of it."

{So that's how it works.}

"Once the innocent blood is in the body shall the fallen angel's blood be awakened." He looks me in the eyes. "Then the weak will be strong, the youth shall be grown, and the powers waiting inside can be freed."

I take a deep breath and nod.

He waves his arm out quickly, making my flames go out.

"It is your lucky day, Kalma. Today is the day we enact our plans."

"What plans?" Jorvess speaks up.

"To help us fight back against the angels," my father answers.

{Fight back against angels?}

"Today, we start fighting to take over the world above us," he explains, "We have waited far too long to fight back, but not anymore. We are taking the fight to them. We have gathered armies to aid in this fight."

"How does one go about taking over the world?" Encador speaks up.

"We take down the oldest churches in every state's capital. Then the oldest church in the different countries around the world," Darixu answers.

"Why the churches?" Allaya asks.

"Churches give angels power. They make them stronger. So, by destroying them all, we can take down all the angels, maybe even the archangels." My father grins.

{Even the archangels? Is that even possible to do?}

"So once the churches are destroyed, we can take out the angels?" Jorvexx questions.

He nods. "For the most part."

"What do you mean?" Vexxus asks.

"Destroying the churches will only weaken full angels, not their hybrids." I tighten my fists at my sides.

"So, what do we do about them?" Allaya wonders.

"That is where all the children of all the archdemons in the world come in," Thezgoth speaks.

"What do we have to do with anything?" Encador asks.

"You all are going to kill the hybrids," Father answers.

My breath catches in my throat.

{Kill the hybrids?}

I look around at my classmates, each one with excitement in their eyes. "Killing a hybrid will be your innocent."

I look towards my father.

"The blood from the hybrid will boost the power from the blood you drank."

{It will make me stronger?}

"When do we start?" Jorvexx asks excitedly.

Darixul chuckles. "That's my boy, always ready to kill."

"Now." My father hands each of us a piece of paper. "One side is the church you will help take down once the hybrid is taken care of."

"There is only one hybrid in our area, so it should be pretty easy," Rinnixa explains.

{Gloria Dei Church is our second target.}

"On the other side, you will see the angel hybrid you all must kill first. The one whose blood you must take, Kalma."

I flip the paper over; the second I see the picture, my chest aches. On the page are the school I've visited for months, the road I have walked down hundreds of times, the address that I memorized, and the girl I have been following, the girl that I held close to protect, the girl that I saved.

{She's a hybrid?}

5

"Where do we go first, Kalma?" Jorvexx asks as I step off the platform into the mausoleum.

{Why did he have to put me in charge of going after her?}

I look at my small team, each of us armed and ready for battle. We each have black shoes, pants, and shirts on, plus black, fingerless gloves that do not burn from our flames. I am the only one who has an added piece of clothing, my red zip-up.

{Father allowed me to wear it so others would know that I am in charge of the unit.}

Each of us has a demon blade strapped across our back so that the silver hilt peeks over a shoulder. We each wear a belt with multiple shurikens stored inside a pouch on one of our hips and a small dagger on the other side. Each weapon is sharpened, ready to be used.

{I can't let them hurt her.}

"We should split up and check the two locations to see if our target is at either one," I explain to them.

They all nod in agreement.

"I'll go with you." Jorvexx steps forward.

"No," I say quickly.

They all look at me curiously.

"I mean, I can handle myself, or else I wouldn't have been made leader." I turn towards Jorvexx. "Unless you think that I am weak."

The others look at Jorvexx.

"No, of course not, Kalma." He steps back in line.

"That's what I thought."

{That was close.}

"I will go to the home while the rest of you check the school."

{It's Saturday evening, so she will be home.}

They nod.

"If you find her there, you will send a bright fireball high into the air, signaling me that you have. I will do the same if I find her. Got it?"

"Yes," all say at once. "Good, then let's get going."

I walk over to the door, opening it as I step out.

{I wanted to send them to a random cemetery, but they knew to come to this one.} "Holy Sepulchre Cemetery," Encador speaks up.

"Nice place." Allaya chuckles.

I look up and see the sun about to set.

{By the time I get to her house, the moon will be out.}

I ball my hands into fists, determination building inside of me. "All right, move it," I command.

I watch as the small group runs off towards the school.

{It takes about thirty-nine minutes while walking to get to the school from here, but with them running, it will only be about twenty-five. From here to her house takes forty-seven minutes walking. If I push and go full speed, I can be there in twenty-five minutes. Hopefully, that gives me enough time before they realize that she isn't there.}

I take off towards her house as fast as I can go. As I'm moving, my body changes into my human camouflage.

{I'm going to have to take her somewhere to keep her safe.} I keep running for quite a while, looking around as I go.

{There.}

I see a half-finished store building up the road.

{Have to make this quick.}

I move towards it, running through the building as I take my weapons off of me, dropping them all into a pile beside a stack of boxes. I keep moving until I am back on the road, still heading towards her house.

I stop on the sidewalk in front of the house trying to catch my breath. The driveway is empty, but lights are on in the place.

{She's here, but her mother isn't. That's probably for the best.} I move towards the steps.

{What am I supposed to tell her? "Hi, my name is Kalma and I am a demon hybrid, and by the way, did you know that you are an angel hybrid?"}

I take the two steps and stand in front of her door.

{"Also, four other demons are looking for you so that they can kill you."}

I sigh as I raise my hand to the knocker on the door. TAP, TAP, TAP.

I lower my hand back down as footsteps sound from inside the house. I take a deep breath as the door handle turns.

{No matter what, I am keeping her safe.}

The door slowly opens, revealing her. She is wearing dark blue jeans with her usual white shoes with a royal blue zip-up over a white tee. The familiar ache twinges inside my chest. She fully opens the door as she stares at me, her face covered in surprise.

"Uh, hi," I say trying to move past the awkwardness.

"Um, hi."

We stand there for a few seconds, just staring at one another, not knowing what to say.

{We don't have time for this.} I open my mouth.

"You're the girl who saved me from being hit by that car?"

I close my mouth and nod.

"You ran away before I could properly thank you."

I rub the back of my head. "Sorry about that."

She shakes her head. "It's all right. I'm just glad you were there when you were." She smiles at me. "I've been wondering if I would ever see you again."

Heat rushes through my whole body as my chest throbs while everything around us seems to disappear.

{Her smile.}

I shake my head.

{Not now.}

I hold my hand out. "My name is Kalma, but you can call me Kal."

She grabs my hand. "Nice to finally meet you. My name is Malak. Everyone calls me Mal."

{How ironic that her name means angel.}

I let go of her hand. "Nice to meet you as well."

"So, what are you doing here? What can I help you with, Kal?" Hearing my name coming from her lips makes my head swim.

{What is going on with me? I need to get it together.}

"I need you to listen to me and believe what I tell you no matter how obscure it sounds, okay?"

"Okay?" she asks curiously.

{I'm going to have to bend the truth for now, at least until I can get her somewhere safe.}

I take a breath. "I need you to come with me, so you can be safe."

"What?"

"There are four people who are looking for you, and not in a good way."

"What do you mean?"

"They want to hurt you, maybe worse."

She takes a small step back. "What, why would anyone want to do that? I don't understand. I'm nothing special."

{Does she not know what she is? Was she kept in the dark like I was?}

I shake my head. "I don't have time to explain it all to you right now. They could show up anytime."

"How do you know all of this?"

"I just know, okay? I need you to trust me. I want to keep you safe. I have to keep you safe. I won't let them get to you."

She studies me. "But why, why do you want to protect me?"

"I don't really know why. I just know that every part of me is telling me to save you, to protect you, just like I did that day with the car."

"You didn't hesitate to jump in front of that car for me?" She looks into my eyes. "Even though you could've gotten hit as well?"

"Not even for a second." I stare back into her eyes.

We stay like that. I study the different shades of blue in her eyes and the white specks sprinkled throughout her iris.

{I could fall into her eyes if I wanted to.} "I believe you."

I blink, breaking eye contact with her. "Really?"

She nods her head. "I always could tell when someone is kind, trustworthy, and good. I can tell from looking in your eyes that what you say is true and that you do want to keep me safe."

{Kind? Trustworthy? Good? Am I really those things?}

"I mean, it is scary to think that there are people out there who want to hurt me, but somehow, I know that I will be safe with you."

I let out a sigh of relief.

{That didn't take much convincing, which is probably a good thing. I didn't want to have to take her by force, but if she hadn't come on her own, I would have had to do anything to ensure she was safe.}

"All right, I need you to move as fast as you can. Grab a bag, fill it with clothes, and whatever else you will need. I don't know how long we will have to hide for, so just make sure you are prepared."

"What about my mom? Will they hurt her?"

I shake my head. "They only want you. The moment they realize that you aren't here, they will move on."

She sighs in relief. "Thank goodness. Is it okay if I leave her a note?"

I think it over for a few seconds before answering, "I suppose, but you can't tell her the truth, or she will worry and try to find you."

She nods in understanding.

"Go grab your things, whatever you think you will need. Move as fast as you can and meet me by the tree when you're finished, okay?"

She nods again before running back into the house. I turn and walk until I am beside the tree. I close my eyes and spread out my senses to see if the others are close.

{I don't sense them yet, just humans and animals. So either they are still at the school or just aren't on my radar. Hopefully the first one.}

I open my eyes, glancing down the street at all the lights on in the other houses.

{Each house, each family, each human, will all be destroyed within a few days. None of them realize what is to come for them. All the demons, monsters that they were all told were fake, will be hunting them down in a few days.}

I turn my head to look at Mal's house from the corner of my eye.

{If I am protecting an angel hybrid, does that mean that I am a traitor? Does that mean I am on their side? Is all of this worth being hunted by my own father?} Mal's smile flashes in my head. I smile.

{She is worth it.}

I look back towards the road.

{Is everyone else? Can I go up against my father, my kind, because one girl opened me up to this world? A world I have come to see as beautiful and wondrous. A world full of so many things that I have yet to see. A world that she cares about.}

I tighten my hands at my sides.

{I don't know what is in store for me, but for now, all I have to worry about is protecting Mal.}

I hear a door close, and footsteps hit the porch. I turn around as Mal walks up to me.

"I'm ready."

I nod as I glance her over.

{She is so calm; I don't sense an ounce of fear coming off of her at all, and the way she looks at me, it's as if she trusts me completely.}

I look at the bag half on her back.

I hold out my hand. "I'll carry that for you; you need to move quickly and it will slow you down."

"Are you sure?" She pulls the strap off and hands it to me. "It is pretty heavy."

I fling the bag onto my back and slide my arms through the straps. "I'll be all right." I spin towards the road. "Let's get moving. I picked an empty store building for us to lay low in for now, at least until I can find somewhere safer."

"I know what building you are talking about. It's like four miles from here."

"Correct."

"By the time we get there, the night will be half over."

{She's right. Even at her fastest walking speed, it will still take too long.}

I sigh as I remove my arms from the straps before placing the bag on my chest putting my arms back.

{This is the only thing I can think of so that we can get there quicker.} "Get on my back."

"Huh?"

"Just get on. If I carry you, we will get there quicker."

"How does that make any sense? You'll be weighed down more and will move slower; plus, you'll get tired faster."

I shake my head. "I'll be fine," I crouch down. "Get on."

She hesitates before I hear her feet on the ground. She carefully wraps her arms around my neck as she puts one leg on my side. I grab onto it as her other leg swings up. I hold that one too before standing. Her grip gets tighter, but not by much.

"Hold on as tight as you can, don't worry about whether you are hurting me or not. Just hold on."

"Um, okay." Her arms tighten around my neck.

{She feels so warm. I can feel her heartbeat on my back. It is such a strange feeling. I wonder what it is like to have a heart beating in your chest. All I have ever known is the empty hollow that is my core. The only heat that is in me is my fire.}

I tighten my arms on her legs.

{She is the only one who has ever made me feel a different kind of heat. What is it about her that makes her so unique, so important to me?}

I smile to myself as I take off into the night with an angel clinging onto my back.

6

"Hopefully no one will look for you here." I gently let her off of my back.

She looks around at the nearly empty room, only boxes and wood beams scattered throughout the place. Some lights hang from the ceiling. I take off her bag and place it against the wall.

"How did you move so fast?"

I look at her and see that she is staring at me.

"How did you carry me for so long without getting tired?" I turn and face her.

"How are you so strong and so fast? I've never met anyone like you before."

"You don't want to, trust me."

"What does that mean?"

"Let's just say that the others like me aren't the nicest people." She continues to stare at me but doesn't ask any more questions. "Make yourself comfortable. We may be here a while."

She nods before going to the wall that her bag is leaning on. She puts her back against it before she slides to the ground. I walk over to the same wall but put a few feet between us before leaning against it while crossing my arms over my chest.

"So, is it okay if I ask you about yourself?" I glance at her, and her eyes are on me again. "What do you want to know?"

"Um, how old are you?"

"Eighteen as of today."

"Today is your birthday?"

I look away from her as I nod.

"Happy birthday."

"Tsk, don't know what is happy about it."

"Huh?"

"Let's just say that where I come from, birthdays are celebrated a lot differently than how you celebrate them. Your celebration of birth is cake and gifts, whereas mine declares the next step in training."

"Training? Training for what?"

I shake my head. "How about you? How old are you?" I change the subject. "Seventeen," she goes along with it, "I will be eighteen in a few months."

{We're about the same age.}

"So, you obviously know where I live, what about you? Where are you from?"

"South, very, very south."

"That's so cool."

I chuckle. "Actually, it is very hot."

She gives a soft laugh. "Very true."

Her laugh makes my stomach flip. "What about your parents?"

I tighten my grip on my arms. "My mother died when I was born. It is just my father and me."

"Awe, I am so sorry."

"Why would you be sorry? You didn't kill her."

{I did.}

"I'm just sorry."

I nod. "What about you? You talked about your mom. What about your father?"

"Mom told me that she doesn't know who my father is. She always used to tell me that I was her miracle baby because she could never remember how I was conceived."

{So, she doesn't know. Her mother doesn't either.} "Did you ever go looking?"

She shakes her head. "Nah, I am happy with it just being Mom and me."

{I read that angel hybrids are conceived by an archangel coming to Earth while the mother is asleep and it places one of their feathers on her stomach so that it can slowly seep into the womb to form a baby.}

I shake my head.

{I don't understand some things, but it is what it is, I guess.} "All right, now for the real questions."

{Here we go.}

"Why are people after me?"

I sigh. "You're special, and because of it, you have to be eliminated for something terrible to happen."

"Why do I need to be taken out for something terrible to happen?"

"You are a part of a much bigger power, and as long as that power is still at play, nothing bad can happen."

"Then what is so special about me?"

"You wouldn't believe me if I told you."

"All right, I will come back to that question then."

I turn towards her. "You still won't believe it later."

She shrugs. "Maybe some more answers will prepare me for the truth." She smiles.

{That smile again.}

Heat rushes through me like last time.

"How do you know all of these things? How did you know that people are after me, how do you know that I am special, and what part do you play in everything?"

I look down at my feet. "I've always known that you were special from the first time that I saw you."

"That's not what I meant." I look back at her.

{What is wrong with her face?}

Her cheeks are bright red as her eyes are towards the floor. "How do you know, and what are you?" she asks again.

I unfold my arms as I stand up, "I need to go grab something, but I promise I will answer your questions when I return."

She stares at me, studying me. "All right."

I walk out of the room and into the one on the other side of the wall. I walk over to the boxes and grab my belt and weapons.

"I know because I was one of those sent to kill you. I am a demon," I whisper to myself.

I strap my blade onto my back and fasten the belt back around my waist. At the end of the room is a door that leads outside. I walk over and quietly step outside. I breathe in the night air as the wind blows, ruffling my hair. I look up at the moon shining bright and full.

{This world is so beautiful.}

I glance at all the stars twinkling in the black.

{Can I be one of those stars? Can I be a light that shines through the darkness, or will I just be consumed by night?}

"KAL!"

I sense them then. I feel their vile nature.

{Mal!}

I break through the door, not bothering to open it. I run through the room and slide to a stop in the one that I left Mal in.

"We were wondering where you went, Kalma," Vexxus says as I stare at them.

{I was distracted and didn't sense them until it was too late.}

I stare at Jorvexx, Allaya, Encador, and Vexxus as they form a half-circle in front of Mal standing right up against the wall.

{She looks so scared.}

"Where have you been? We went looking for you at her house?" Jorvexx asks. I stand straight.

"They all thought that you chickened out and couldn't kill the hybrid," Jorvexx explains.

Mal turns and looks at me with shock and hurt.

"I told them there is no way that she would do that. I told them that you would never defy an order from your father."

I tighten my hands.

"I mean, without her blood, you can't evolve." He smiles. She continues to look at me as fear forms in her eyes.

"Jorvexx, who are you kidding? Look at her. She looks like a human," Allaya speaks up.

"I'm sure she has an explanation as to why she looks like that and why she is hiding here with the angel," Encador explains.

Mal turns quickly to them and then back to me, understanding flashing in her eyes. "So what's going on, Kalma?" Allaya wonders.

{What am I going to do now? I can't tell them the truth; I need to get to her somehow, but I don't know if I can take them all down while protecting her.}

I let my camouflage slip, feeling my ears, nails, teeth, and eyes all return to their normal state. Mal's eyes grow as my demon appearance finishes.

"Ah, there you are." Jorvexx smiles.

{I have to fight.}

I take a step towards them all.

"So why are you holding up here with her, Kalma?" Allaya asks.

"It's not like I could kill her in her house, now, could I? I needed somewhere private where no one would hear her scream."

I step inside of their half-circle.

"Told you guys!" Jorvexx exclaims. "I know my best friend; I knew that she would never betray us or back down from an order."

{I'm sorry, Jorvexx.}

"I'm actually quite hurt that you all thought I was protecting an angel of all things. I am the squad leader, am I not?"

Mal's eyes fill with tears and confusion as she continues to stare at me.

"Yes," they say.

"Then I suggest you all back up so I can finish what I came here to do." I push heat into my hands until navy ignites.

Mal jumps in surprise, backing farther into the wall, pressing her body as flat as she can to get away from the fire. I face her entirely as I hear the others step back. I slowly move towards Mal until I'm a few inches away. Tears run down her cheeks as her body trembles.

{I'm so sorry I had to scare you and that this is how you had to learn the answers to all your questions. I really was going to tell you.}

"Duck," I whisper to her. She doesn't move. "Duck," I whisper again.

Her eyes meet mine. As we stand there, the fear in her eyes diminishes. I give her a small smile. "Duck and stay down."

I start building heat into my arms. Her eyes widen as all the fear leaves and trust builds back into them.

"What are you waiting for, Kalma? Just finish it," Vexxus demands.

"Now," I tell her.

She quickly drops down onto her butt, hugging her knees. I release all the built-up heat, shooting fire out of both my hands like a giant blue flamethrower as I spin around, blasting them all with it. They all slide back a bit as the fire presses up against them. Once the fire stops, they all stare at me with shocked expressions on their faces.

"What are you doing?" Vexxus asks.

I take a few steps away from Mal as I push more heat to my hands. I half turn back towards her as I hold my hand out with my palm facing the ground. I shoot out my flames onto the floor, moving them until there is a half-ring of fire surrounding Mal.

{That should protect her for now. We may be fireproof, but we can still get hurt by another demon's flame.}

I face them again. "I won't let any of you get to her. I won't allow anyone to hurt her."

"Kalma, what is going on? Why are you protecting that thing?" Jorvexx questions.

"She's not a thing, she is a person, and every part of me, all the way to my core, is screaming at me to protect her. To keep her safe no matter what."

"But why?" he asks again.

I shrug. "I don't really know how to explain it." I raise my hand, putting out my flame before placing it on my chest. "From the moment I saw her, something in me changed. I don't know what, but I felt it. I knew then that she was special, that she needed to be protected, and that is exactly what I did and what I am going to continue to do." I move my hand back to my side. "The same thing with this world."

"What are you talking about?" Encador speaks.

"I won't let my father and the other demons take control of this world. I will figure out a way to stop them even if it costs me everything."

Jorvexx steps closer. "Kalma, none of this makes sense. Did this angel do something to you? Snap out of it. This isn't you. Come to your senses before it is too late."

I shake my head. "That's just it, though, Jorvexx. I have come to my senses. I have come to see that this world needs protecting, that the humans on it are worth saving."

"Where did all of this come from? Why do you care for them? Why do you care about humans all of a sudden?" he asks.

I take a deep breath as the photo of my mother flashes in my head. "Because my mother was one."

All of their jaws drop in surprise.

"I'm a hybrid, just like Mal. I am as much human as I am archdemon."

"That's not possible. How would you even know that?" Allaya wonders.

"I found a photo of her in my father's files. She was pregnant in the photo, and on the back, my father had written my name."

No one says anything for a few seconds as they continue to stare at me.

"After learning the truth, I needed to learn more about humans and the world that they live in. I have been sneaking up to the surface for months, studying them and all that they care about. Learning how beautiful everything is and how unique each individual is."

Jorvexx shakes his head. "You can't do this, Kalma, you can't go against their orders. You have to kill her, and you have to help us destroy that church," he pleads.

I sigh. "No. No, I don't. I'm done following Father's orders. I'm done following Lucifer's orders. From now on, I am following what I feel is right, and allowing Hell to come to Earth isn't right."

His eyes and body language change. "They'll kill you."

"Let them try, but I'm not going down without a fight."

"Dang it, Kalma." He sighs.

{Here he comes.}

I tighten my leg muscles before launching towards him as he comes at me. We both reach over our shoulders and grab the swords on our backs. He swings his forward, the flames igniting, mine igniting as well as I bring mine around, both of them whistling in the air before they connect between us with a loud clash. I push up against his sword feeling as he does the same.

"I won't let you do this, Kalma, even if it means I have to kill you myself."

"We both know that that isn't going to happen. I have always been stronger than you, Jorvexx." I smirk.

We press harder simultaneously, causing our swords to push off of one another, sending us both back. We slide until we are back to where we started.

"Don't do this, Jorvexx. It won't end well for you," I explain sternly.

"Tsk." He launches at me again.

I tighten my grip on the handle as I move forward. I raise my blade as he swings down. They crash against one another before he lifts the sword again and swings a different way. I move quickly, using my sword to block his attack. We continue to sword fight as we move around the room, the clashes echoing throughout the room with every impact. The others just watch. I can see the other demon's disgust shine in their eyes aimed at me while Mal watches in awe and hope.

{I'll keep you safe.}

We keep moving and swinging, making it feel as if we are pirates having a sword fight. I block each of his attacks, feeling as his anger rises within him.

"I don't want to hurt you, Jorvexx, so please, all of you, just turn around and leave."

"We aren't going anywhere until both of you are dead," he tells me with venom in his voice.

He stops mid-swing before jumping back a few times. I look for Mal and see her a few feet to my right, the fire still around her. I turn back towards Jorvexx as he reaches into his pouch on his side.

{He's going to use his shuriken now.}

He pulls out a handful of metal stars with the pentagram carved on each of them.

{We can't be hurt by the shuriken themselves, but when fire is added to them, they can be deadly.}

I watch his irises light up as fire explodes in his hands, each star catching flame. I raise my sword, tightening my hands on the hilt, ready to deflect them. He grins before he throws them at me. They fly quickly through the air, heading right at me. I move my sword faster than the shurikens, knocking each aside with the blade.

{Come on, Jorvexx, you're going to have to do better than that if you want to stop me.}

"Kal!"

I turn my head towards Mal and see more shuriken flying at her.

{He distracted me to get to her.}

I push hard off the ground moving as fast as I can towards Mal. I stop in the shuriken's path, raising my sword back up. I barely have time to swing my blade to knock them off their trajectory, but not fast enough to hit them all. Two sharp, burning pains strike me on my right shoulder and my left thigh. I almost drop my sword from the pain shooting down my arm, my leg almost buckling as well. I look at the blazing star sticking half out of my shoulder and the other sticking half out of my leg.

{We've been taught to never show pain. Father would hit me with his flames over and over until I didn't react.}

I tighten my jaw as I push heat into my left hand, flames flaring around it.

{But that doesn't mean that it still doesn't hurt.}

I grab the shuriken in my shoulder and rip it out fast. Blood follows it, splattering on the ground in front of me and staining my shirt as the wound bleeds. I throw the star aside as I reach for my leg.

"She's made you weak." Jorvexx chuckles, his eyes returning to their standard shade.

I grab the one in my thigh, ripping it out as well. More blood comes from it than my shoulder.

"You should have been easily able to dodge those."

I drop the one in my hand onto the ground, watching as the fire goes out. "But you knew that if you dodged them that they would hit her."

The fire diminishes. I half turn my head to look at Mal out of the corner of my eye.

{He's right. If I had dodged, they would have hit her.}

"Being kind and protective will just get you killed."

I look back at him as the others move to stand behind him.

"I don't have any plans on dying, and I don't plan on giving up either." I smirk. They all frown at me.

"I tried, Kalma, but now we don't have a choice but to kill you," Jorvexx explains. The others pull their swords out, each one of them igniting in their black flames.

"Last chance," Allaya warns me.

I smirk. "I should be saying that to you all."

They all run at me with their swords raised, ready to strike. I grip my sword with both hands.

{Time to see if the extra training Father put me through has paid off.}

I use my thumb to press against the hilt, hearing a soft click before the whole thing splits in half.

{He wanted me to have the edge over everyone.}

My blade comes apart with half in each of my hands.

{Dual wielding. It took me a long time to use two swords at once, but now I am practically a master at it.}

Surprise shows on all of their faces as they keep running at me. I smile again as I raise both my arms.

{Keep an eye on the blades, keep an eye on their feet, and keep moving.}

I move my feet as they start swinging at me. I move my arms fast to block each of their attacks, the ringing from the swords echoing back at us. I keep moving as I keep blocking while watching their feet as best I can.

{Wait for an opening.}

Vexxus makes the first mistake of taking an unbalanced step backward. I use it to my advantage and make my move. I force heat into my right foot, slamming it down hard, pushing the fire out. Blue bursts from under my shoe, flying towards Vexxus's feet. He takes another unbalanced step back to avoid the flames.

{Sorry, Vexxus.}

I take the opportunity and swing one of my blades at him. I can feel the sword make contact with his stomach as I continue to turn. A line of blood soaks through his shirt from the wound. He falls backward as he puts his arm over where the blood is coming from. The others stop for a second to look at him before coming at me again. Their swings become more robust and quicker. My arms are barely able to keep up.

{I don't think I can keep this up much longer.}

Allaya makes the next mistake. She swings slower as she looks at Vexxus again. I raise my left arm as I make the hilt face the ceiling while blocking the other attacks. I slam my handle against the bottom of hers, causing the sword to fly into the air. She looks up at her sword while it soars through the air, no longer paying attention to me. I build intense heat into my left hand.

{Took me quite a while to be able to do this.}

My fire climbs up the blade, mixing with the dark flames as I place the tip on her sternum. A strong blast comes from the end, slamming into her. The ball of fire continues to push her until she hits the wall on the far side of the room. My fire goes out as she slides to the floor, no longer moving.

{Two down.}

I'm breathing heavily and can feel the power inside of me shrinking.

{We aren't as powerful as everyone thinks. All demons have their limits. The strength of our fire determines how long we can last. If we overuse our flames, the fire inside shrinks, causing us to become exhausted and very weak. If we keep going, the fire will eventually go out, and we will die.}

With only two of them attacking, blocking is much easier, so I decide to switch it up and go on offense. I tighten my grip on both hilts as I press hard against their swords in midair. I push them both back, making them take a few steps away from me.

{Encador and Jorvexx are almost as good as me when it comes to our swordsmanship, so we could go on forever like this. The only choice I have is to use my flames.}

I take a deep breath feeling for the fire inside of me.

{If I use this attack, my flame will be nothing but a flicker. That is why Father told me to only use this move at the beginning of the fight and never at the end because I could die from using everything.}

I quickly swing my arms together, making the two blades become one again before lifting it back over my shoulder into the sheath. I build up almost the remaining heat inside of me, pushing it all towards my hands. Jorvexx and Encador come at me again with swords raised.

{Sorry, guys.}

I kneel down and slam my hands onto the ground, sending a continuous shockwave of blue fire at them. As the flames move away from me, they lift up, causing a wave of fire. The boys stop in their tracks and stare at the tide coming for them. The room spins a little around me as a small amount of warmth pulses inside of me.

{Please hit them.}

The wave moves faster. They turn to run but don't move quick enough. It crashes down on them, completely covering them both in the fire. It continues to roll across the room until it is halfway. I stop my flames, the wave disappearing, showing Jorvexx and Encador lying on the ground covered in burns and ash from some of their clothing. Everything spins as I slowly stand up, my knees almost giving out from under me. I look towards Mal, making sure that she is all right. She is now standing inside the half-circle of flames that have grown smaller.

{The flames are going to go out. I don't have enough fire inside of me to keep them going.}

I hear feet shuffling. I turn back towards the sound to see Allaya next to Encador and Jorvexx. Vexxus is slowly moving towards them with his arm still across his stomach.

{Our fast healing doesn't work as quickly when attacked with our swords. We don't heal at all if struck with an angel blade.}

"Leave now, all of you," I order them.

Allaya and Vexxus glare at me before reaching down to their belts and placing a hand on Jovexx's and Encador's belts.

{The portals are our main form of transportation, but there is another way.} Both of their eyes flash before all four of their belts ignite in blue flames.

{Our belts, if consumed with our fire, can transport us back home, but it can be

hazardous, because they are not perfect on where you go. You can appear multiple feet in the air and have to fall however far to the ground, or the flames can seriously burn you, since they aren't carefully placed on your body. That is why they told us to only use the belt in an emergency.}

I watch as they all are slowly engulfed in fire before the flames shrink and nothing is left. I smile to myself. The room spins again worse than before. I stumble as I slowly turn around, facing Mal again, the flames around her wholly gone. She is staring at me as I carefully make my way towards her. Pain continues to shoot from my leg and shoulder, and I can feel my blood still seeping into my clothes. Her eyes look me over before they land on my eyes.

{She's not scared of me; the look in her eyes is something different.}

My fire spurts as my knees buckle and the floor comes at me. The last thing I see is Mal running towards me before the darkness.

7

"Kalma, what have you done?" my father's voice echoes all around me. "Saving a human, a hybrid! You have betrayed us all!"

{He's using his telepathic ability to get into my head. He can only do this with his special symbols in his room and for a short period.}

My whole body heats up from the inside out, my blood boiling inside of me. "I had to, Father!" I scream back into the void.

"Now you plan on saving them all?" A burning pain sears through me.

"You plan on fighting against your own? You think you can stop what is to come?" My lungs burn as if I am breathing in smoke.

"I have to."

"What happened to you, Kalma? Why are you putting yourself on the line for these humans?"

The pressure pushes against my chest. "I learned the truth."

"Why the hybrid?"

A twinge pulses in my chest.

"I don't fully understand why. I know that something in me changed when I saw her. It felt like something had awakened. From the moment I saw her, I knew she was important. I knew she was meant to be in my life."

My blood boils hotter, burning inside my veins throughout my body.

"You are not my daughter. The one I raised would never talk this way. You were raised to be—"

"Your weapon?"

"What?"

"I know what I am, Father. I know what I was made for."

"That is not possible."

"I know the truth, and thanks to that truth, I was able to meet her. I learned more about this world and the ones living in it. Something in me feels strongly about all of it, especially her. I am going to fight for them, the world, and her no matter what."

He is quiet for a moment.

{If he was actually here, he probably would have struck me by now, or worse.}

"None of that matters, you have made your choice, and now you must die."

"Not without a fight."

"Stupid child, I will kill you myself if I have to." My breath is cut off from the burning in my lungs.

"I'm no longer afraid of you. I have found light in the darkness. I have found strength. I will not be so easily defeated. Even if you come at me with everything you got, I shall not die."

He starts laughing. "I will not need to. The blood will kill you for me." His laugh echoes as it fades away.

My eyes snap open as I sit up quickly while the burning flares inside of me. I clumsily stand up, making it a few feet before my knees give out. I land on my hands and knees.

{The blood is going to burn its way out.}

Searing pain lays in my chest, threatening to burst.

{It's going to kill me.}

I can feel the blood raging inside me, getting hotter and hotter as the seconds go by.

{I'm going to die.}

"Kal what's wrong?" I hear Mal's voice behind me.

I turn my head to see her as she makes her way towards me.

{She stayed.}

I hold my hand up towards her with my palm out. "Stay back."

She stops. "What's going on?"

"I had to drink Lucifer's blood earlier, but since I am betraying him and following something else inside of me, the blood is rejecting my body. It is going to keep heating up until I combust, and I don't want you to get caught in it, so stay back."

"Why can't you just throw the blood back up?"

{Is that possible? Some has seeped into my veins, but the rest is in my stomach, waiting for more.}

I face towards the ground as pressure continues to build with the sweltering pain growing.

{Focus, force the blood out.}

I try not to scream as scorching pain climbs my throat. The boiling blood touches my tongue as I open my mouth. Dark red liquid lands on the ground beneath my face. The pain inside of me diminishes but doesn't go away completely. I stare at the steaming red in front of my face, watching the blood continue to boil with bubbles popping throughout the puddle.

{That was close. If I had held that in much longer, who knows what would have happened.}

I straighten my back while still on my knees, tilting my head towards the ceiling.

{Well, Father, the blood didn't kill me, so I guess you will try.}

Everything tilts as the strength in my body leaves.

{The blood was still able to mess with my inner flame. I can feel that it is still tiny and weak. I won't be at full strength for a while, especially if there is still some remaining blood in my veins.}

The ceiling moves farther away from me as my back falls towards the ground.

{What am I going to do in this state? I have never felt so weakened before in my life.}

Two arms press against my back as someone catches me. They slowly lower me to the ground while pulling me backward until my legs are straightened and we are near the wall. I tilt my head and see Mal's face above me.

{I have to protect her; I have to get my strength back quickly before Father and the others come looking for us.}

She pulls me a little more as she moves to my side before leaning me against the wall.

"Are you all right?" she asks as she sits beside me turned towards me.

I nod.

"Phew, I was worried."

I stare at her, stunned. "Why?"

"Huh?"

"Why didn't you run when you had the chance? Why did you stay? Why do you care what happens to me? You know what I am now."

She looks at the floor. "I couldn't just leave you. You got hurt protecting me." She looks back at me. "And I don't care that you are what you are. You are clearly not like those others." She looks into my eyes. "I can feel it when I look into your eyes." I open my eyes wide with surprise.

"There is a light inside of you. I feel calm and safe when I look into them. I've never felt anything close to what I am feeling right now." She looks away again, "I don't know how to explain it. It just feels like you are meant to be in my life, as if you are what was always missing." Her cheeks turn red.

{She feels the same things that I do.}

She puts her hand on her chest, "Something in here is telling me to stay with you, to stay by your side no matter what. Whether it's for protection or something else, I don't know." She meets my eyes again. "I don't want to leave your side either way."

I continue to stare at her, not knowing what to say.

{We are feeling the exact same things, all the way to the letter. What does it all mean?}

"I know that none of that makes sense. It doesn't even make real sense to me." She gives me a small smile. "Bottom line is, I'm not going anywhere, and somehow, even though we've practically just met, you are in here." She presses harder on her chest.

{Her heart? How am I in her heart?}

I raise my hand to my chest where my heart would be.

{Would she be in mine as well if I had one?}

"Look at me just rambling on." She chuckles.

Her laugh creates multiple pangs in my chest, causing me to flinch. She must see it because she moves her hand as she scoots closer to me.

"What, what's wrong?" She places her hand on my arm.

I shake my head. "It's nothing."

Her eyes don't leave mine. I stare into blue, feeling as if I am falling into a clear sky.

{I feel happy and a nice kind of warm when I look into yours.}

"I understand everything you just said, because I feel the same way."

She looks at me, shocked. "Really?"

I nod. "I have since I met you."

"What do you think it all means?"

"I don't know."

Her smile grows wider. "I guess we'll just have to figure it out together."

BA-DUM

I feel something beat against my hand.

{What was that?}

I press my hand harder against my chest, waiting for another thump.

{I only felt one. What was it?}

She's still smiling at me, and I can't help but smile back.

{Something inside of me changed because of her, and I am delighted it did. I like how I feel when I'm with her; I like who she has awakened me to be.}

I give her a bigger smile.

{She has become my star in the darkness, and we might not know why we feel the things we are feeling, but she's right. We will figure it out together.}

A quick chill goes through me, causing me to lose my smile.

{I just hope we survive long enough.}

8

"I see," Mal speaks slowly.

I continue to watch her as we walk side by side down the sidewalk.

{I told her everything. She now knows everything about the supernatural world that I know, including everything in it, the demons, monsters, fae creatures, and angels.}

I keep quiet, allowing her to process everything she has learned.

{She knows what I am and what I am capable of, as well as what other demons' powers are. I told her what she truly is, why the others want her dead, and what the archdemons planned.}

I look up at the midday sun.

{After I woke up, I was still too weak to move, so we stayed inside the building for a few hours until I could move again. She told me that she took care of me while I was unconscious. I guess after I collapsed, she ran to me and tried to wake me, but I didn't, so she brought me closer to the wall. She covered my wounds with gauze from the first-aid kit she brought with her. Told me that once my wounds were tended to, I was burning up; my skin was hot to the touch. So she grabbed one of her socks from her bag and used one of her bottles of water to soak it before she laid my head on her lap, placing the sock on my forehead.}

I quietly chuckle to myself.

{A sock of all things.}

I glance at her again.

{She remained calm and helped me without a second thought, even after everything that just happened.}

I look down at my feet.

{She said I was out for a few hours, that she sat there with me with my head in her lap, resoaking the sock. Said that right before I woke up, I was mumbling in my sleep, that my breathing had quickened before I started to gasp for air. Had to have been from talking to Father and the blood. She started to panic right before I jumped up and moved away from her. I knew the rest.}

I face forward again to catch a man staring at me as he walks past us.

{My human appearance is back but is draining me quickly thanks to the blood that is still inside of me, so I can't leave my weapons behind just in case I need to protect her from any more demons.}

I look around and notice quite a few people glancing at me as they continue walking.

{I was hoping that no one would pay much attention to me, considering all the craziness that goes on in this city. Philadelphia is a prominent place. Crazy things happen all the time, so I assumed the citizens wouldn't be surprised by much.}

I sigh as I jam my hands into my pants' pockets.

{I didn't want to make our way towards The Middle during the day, but everyone comes out at night there, so we didn't have a choice but to walk getting there just after sunset. I just hope we can find someone there to help us, whether it'd be a demon or an angel. At this point, I don't care; I just want her safe.}

My eyes start to burn as my camouflage starts to slip.

{Crap, I'm still too weak to keep this appearance up for too long.}

I quickly look around and see a dark alley coming up on my right. I take my hands from my pockets before grabbing her hand, ignoring the twinge when we touch. She jumps a little before her fingers clasp onto my hand. I pull her with me as I quickly move towards the alleyway feeling my ears return to normal. I turn into the alley with Mal on my heels, getting far away from the opening and the people walking. We stop as my eyes stop burning. I move my tongue across my teeth feeling my sharp canines before looking down at my hand, seeing my nails have returned.

{That was close.} "Kal?"

I turn my head as Mal stares at me, red under her eyes.

{Why is she turning red?}

Something moves in my hand. I look down and see that I am still holding her hand, my nails peeking around it.

{I still have her hand.}

I quickly let go and step back so that I am in the darker part of the alley.

"I'm sorry. I didn't mean to grab your hand like that." I shove my hands back into my pockets. "I'm sorry you have to keep seeing me like this." I move my face towards the ground.

{I could just imagine what she thinks of me when she sees me like this.}

Her foot appears on the ground where I am staring before her arm and hand move towards my side.

"I told you before." She grabs onto my wrist, slowly pulling my hand out of my pocket. "I don't care that you are a demon. Looking at you like this doesn't bother me one bit." Her hand slides down before she slides her hand into my palm, squeezing my hand against hers. "I'm just happy that I get to look at you at all."

I whip my head up quickly, meeting her eyes as she smiles at me with warmth and acceptance.

BA-DUM.

I cringe at the quick pressure in my chest but don't take my eyes off of her.

{How can she look at me like that knowing what I am; how can she look at me like that when we've just met?}

"Kal, you never have to worry about me looking at you like you're a monster because I never will. I will continue to look at you the way I am now."

I move my eyes back and forth between hers, feeling a calming warmth build within me.

"The way that you look at me."

Her cheeks turn red again.

I feel as heat rises to my face. She smiles bigger and brighter as she gives a soft laugh. Without thinking, I pull her to me, wrapping my arms around her with my chin lying on her shoulder. She freezes against me with her arms at her sides.

{What am I doing?}

I loosen my grip, but before I can pull away, Mal's arms quickly wrap around me, pressing us tightly against one another. She lays her head on my shoulder so that her face is towards my neck, and I can feel her breath against my skin. I stand there frozen for a few seconds.

BA-DUM.

{I've never been hugged before.} BA-DUM.

Ignoring the beats in my chest, I tighten my arms back around her, placing my chin on her shoulder again.

{But after what she said, I felt like I needed it.} I squeeze her a little tighter.

{She does accept all of me.}We stay like that for what seems like forever. "Thank you," I say under my breath.

"We're here," I say.

Mal stands beside me as we stand outside of the abandoned part of Kingsessing. "What is here? All I see are a bunch of run-down, old buildings and empty stores and streets."

I chuckle. "Come on." I pull her hand that is in mine, making her follow me. "If everyone could see it, then it wouldn't be very safe for our kind, now, would it?" She looks over at me, confused.

"For hundreds of years, all kinds of supernatural beings have come here to seek refuge for being different, for wanting to be something else, or for not caring about the war between dark and light. Those who come here are outside of the box; they live freely, and because of that freedom, the higher-ups want them dead. At least the demon side does. I don't know how angels deal with it."

"So what you're saying is that here everyone gets along?"

I nod. "Yep, and that's why it's the perfect place to lay low thanks to the veil; humans nor those who have any intention of harm can find this place, let alone enter it, and no one will rat us out here."

"How did you find it?"

"I protected a human."

She looks at me, shocked.

"When I decided to save you and not harm you, it opened this place up to me, because from then on I had no intention of harming anyone or anything. I guess you could say you were my doorway to safety." I smile at her.

Her cheeks turn red as she stares at me.

I face forward again. "We will be safe until I can figure out what to do next." I stop on the edge of the town circle, surrounded by buildings on all sides. "Magic protects this place, making sure that there is only one way in or out."

"How do we get in?"

I pull her closer to me. "Stay close."

She moves in closer. "Easy." She smiles.

I give her a smile before looking forward again. I raise my hand, pushing heat towards it.

{I hope I have enough energy for this. I'm still weak. It's taking longer than I thought for the blood to evaporate inside of me.}

I close my eyes, feeling her hand in mine.

{Technically, I guess you're the key to the doorway.}

I open my eyes as navy-blue flames surround my hand. I can see Mal out of the corner of my eye, watching me with fascination. I smile to myself before focusing back on my hand. I push the fire out. Blue rises straight up before curving. My vision blurs as the flame starts its descent.

{Hang on.}

The flame touches the ground a few feet away from us as more fire moves towards the earth under my hand until it touches as well. My fire creates an outline of a giant arch before lines of blue flames move towards the center from every part of the arch. My knees start to tremble as the fire on my hand flickers, the world getting dimmer as the seconds go by.

{No, not yet. I have to get her inside. I have to make sure she is safe.}
"Kal, are you okay?" Mal asks worriedly.

"It's all right."

I look at her and can tell that she's not convinced. I focus back on the arch as an opening slowly appears in the center, carefully pulling back the veil.

{Almost there.}

The archway completely opens, showing different kinds of beings walking around the once empty circle.

"Whoa," Mal whispers.

I stop my fire around my hand, quickly pulling her through the archway with me. As we cross through, it closes back up behind us, showing the road that we came from. "Welcome to The Middle."

Mal stands with her mouth hanging open in wonder. I watch her as she looks around.

{There's not a drop of fear in her.}

The world tilts.

"Kal!" Mal lets go of my hand, grabbing onto me tightly, keeping me on my feet.

{My body feels like cement. I can barely move on my own.}

I struggle to lift my head. I look around, trying to see despite the blurriness.

{He's around here somewhere; he has to stay close to the arch to protect it; he is a cherubim, after all.}

My eyes land on a golden figure standing a few feet away. "Jahoel!" I yell at the figure.

He starts running towards us. "Who is he?" Mal asks.

"He's a cherubim angel. They protect special places like this," I explain as my body grows heavier.

"Kalma?" He stops in front of us. "What's going on? I've never seen you like this before."

I shake my head. "I don't know how much longer I can keep myself conscious." As I say it, my knees buckle.

"Kal!"

Mal drops with me, still gripping me tightly. She lowers me down so that my back is leaning against her chest to sit somewhat straight. I don't have enough strength to keep myself up, so I just lie back against her.

"Your flame?" Jahoel asks frantically as he kneels.

I nod my head. "I had my ritual yesterday, but I disobeyed. I managed to spit most of his blood out, but there is still some in my body preventing my flame from growing."

"And you just used it to open the archway? Are you crazy? You could have died," he explains, sounding concerned.

I search for my internal flame, feeling a slight flicker. "Might be," I say quietly with a smile.

"What?" Mal asks, scared.

"Why push yourself so far?" Jahoel questions.

My smile grows. "To keep her safe."

I feel Mal's breath catch against my back.

Jahoel looks at me and then Mal before his eyes land back onto me.

"Jahoel, I need you to get Wanda for me." Black starts to seep into my vision. "She can help me."

Jahoel jumps back up quickly. "Right."

"And if I don't make it, if my flame goes out..."

He looks into my eyes.

"Don't let anyone hurt her. You hear me? Keep her safe, no matter what."

He looks at Mal again before nodding. "I understand." He gives a sad smile.

I watch as he takes off towards the circle, moving quickly, the moonlight reflecting off his armor. I feel my inner flame spurt, flickering between a small flame or entirely out. I look up at the moon through the veil.

{If I die now, at least it was because I was keeping her safe, but I'll never know or understand what this is between us. I'll never learn why I feel what I feel when I am with her. I won't get to stay by her side.}

I feel something wet land on my cheek, breaking me from my thoughts. I tilt my head up.

{Mal.}

"You can't die," she tells me with tears running down her face.

"Mal, I...."

She cuts me off by grabbing my hand. She raises it to her face, carefully laying it against her cheek.

"I thought we were going to be that missing piece in both of our lives."

I give her a small smile. "I thought that too, and maybe in different circumstances we would have been, because I know that every part of me wants to be with you, wants to stay by your side."

"That's all I want too, Kal. I want to be with you. So please don't die, not like this, not after I just found you."

I give a slight chuckle. "Technically, I found you." I smile up at her. The warmth inside of me from my flame starts growing cold.

"I'm sorry, Mal, but I said I would keep you safe no matter what, even if the price were my life."

"But, Kal..."

I shake my head. "It's okay. I get to leave this world while looking into those two beautiful sky eyes of yours that I can't help but get lost in every time I look at them. I feel safe lying here in your arms, I feel more content than I have ever been in my life, and that is thanks to you. I feel things when I am with you that I have never felt before, a warmth in my chest that I didn't know could ever be there."

More darkness seeps into my vision as everything goes quiet, and all I can hear is our breathing and her heartbeat.

I smile again. "It's going to sound crazy, but I thought that the feelings I got inside of my chest when I'm around you were a heartbeat."

She looks down at me, her tears falling faster.

"But demons don't have hearts. I don't have a heart."

Mal lets go of my hand before wrapping me in a hug, with her arms gripping tightly to the front of my hoodie. I sit there, feeling her body tremble from her crying, her hands balled into fists with handfuls of my hoodie inside of them. I try to talk, but nothing else comes out as my whole body goes cold and numb.

{I should have turned to ash by now.}

I barely feel as my head falls forward, my chin hitting my chest.

{Unless my human half is stopping me from combusting.}

"There's something in you," Mal says from somewhere far away. "We wouldn't feel the way that we do if there wasn't."

I fall deeper into the void.

"Kal, please come back."

A small light shines inside the darkness.

"I don't want to lose these feelings that I have for you. They are the greatest things I have ever felt in my life."

The light shines brighter as it grows.

"I don't care if we just met. I don't care that I am part angel and you are part demon."

I can see a soft hue of sky-blue shining, piercing through the light.

{What's going on?}

"Kal, I want you more than I thought a person could want someone."

{Mal, is that you?}

A calming warmth pushes out the cold as a feeling of self-awareness washes over me.

"I never thought that those things they say on TV and in the movies were true, but after meeting you, I think I believe it now."

{What things?}

"From the day you saved me, all I could think about was you, wondering who you were and if I was ever going to see you again."

{I thought those same things for months.}

The sky continues to push against the darkness.

"Then you showed up on my doorstep, and I couldn't believe that the beautiful girl that saved me was real."

{Beautiful?}

"I went with you without a second thought because my heart was telling me that it was all right. Even after everything with the other demons and finding out that you're a demon, I was still okay, because what I felt in my heart, what I felt for you, was still there. Yes, learning everything that I learned was hard, but since you were with me, I was able to accept it all and keep going."

{What could she have been feeling that made everything okay?}

"But without you, everything feels so wrong. I feel wrong. I feel empty again. I feel alone and afraid."

The soft blue light engulfs me.

"So please, Kal, please come back so I can tell you how I feel about everything."

A spark catches in the center.

"Come back so I can tell you how I feel about whatever this thing is between us."

A small flame blazes to life from the spark.

"I need you to know how I feel about you, and I need to know how you feel about me."

The royal-blue flame erupts, heat radiating off of it.

"Maybe what we feel is real. I hope that it is, because if it's not, then I don't know what is."

{I don't understand half the stuff she is saying, but something in me does. I do feel a connection unlike anything I thought was possible.}

The flame grows, shoving the sky away until all there is only royal. "Please, Kalma, wake up so we can explore this together."

{She said my real name.}

Royal blue is all there is now as the flames overtake me, filling all of me with warmth, life, and something new.

{Malak.}

9

I bolt upright, immediately checking for my internal flame, feeling its warmth dancing inside of me.

I let out a sigh of relief. "I'm still alive."

"You're lucky that you are," a female's voice speaks from the middle of the room. I turn towards the voice as a chair rumbles across the wood floor. A woman steps around the small table she is sitting at, making her way over to me. She is wearing black Converse shoes with white soles and laces, ripped navy-blue jeans exposing both of her beige knees, a white T-shirt hugging her front, with a blue-and-white plaid long-sleeve button-up with the buttons undone over the top. Around her neck hangs a pointed fluorite crystal, the lights reflecting off of its swirled blue, green, and purple surface. Her face doesn't have a single blemish on it. Her blushed, heart-shaped lips stretched out into a thin line of disapproval. A cute button nose sits in the middle of her beige face, with two piercing emerald eyes glaring at me in anger, her wavy auburn hair slightly blowing behind her as she marches towards me. "I don't know why you bother showing your bosoms like that. You know it's never gonna work on me," I joke, trying to break the tension.

She stops beside the bed I'm in, her hair resting back on its spot halfway down her back, before she crosses her arms over her chest. "I'm not in the mood for jokes, Kal."

I look at her and smile. "Awe, come on, Wanda, you know you can't stay mad at me."

Wanda continues to glare at me. "Do you know how close you came to dying? I had to summon a lot of magic and use half my stock of healing herbs to make sure that you didn't."

{Wanda is a witch who specializes in the art of healing magic, so I knew if I was going to be saved, it was going to be by her.}

"I knew you weren't going to let me die. You care about me too much." I give her a bigger smile.

She blushes at me as all of her anger slips away, her eyes losing the glare instead looking at me like she always does.

{We met the same day that I came up here. I caught her walking around outside of the barrier and from the moment we said hello we just clicked. We hung out every day since then. Outside of the barrier though since I didn't have access until a few weeks ago. Since we met, Wanda has had a crush on me even though she knew who my father was. From day one, she has been trying to get me to like her back, whether it'd be showing off her magic or wearing clothes that reveal more of her body. Sometimes she'd even try to steal a kiss.} She uncrosses her arms, but the crimson stays on her face.

{I told her time and time again that I can't feel the things that she wants me to because of what I am. I explained to her that without a heart, it could never work.} Her eyes start to glisten as she stares at me, her lip quivering as she takes deep breaths.

"Come here, you cry baby." I open my arms to her.

{But just because I can't care for her like that doesn't mean I don't care at all. We became close, we became best friends, real best friends, not like how it was with Jorvexx. Wanda and I have told each other everything. I know all of her secrets, and she knows mine. She kinda feels like an older sister, minus her liking me part.} She sniffles before jumping on the bed to wrap her arms around me. I gently settle my arms around her as she softly cries.

{I've become more human, learned how to feel because of her. Wanda is the reason I didn't lose my mind after finding the truth.}

I smile as she holds me tighter.

{Wanda, you'll never know how much you've done for me, besides just saving my life. It's because of you that I learned how to allow myself to feel more than just hatred. Without you, I don't think I ever would have opened up to...}

"Mal!" I quickly let go of Wanda, before pulling her away from me. "Where is Mal?"

Wanda sits back and wipes the tears from her face. "I thought that was who that was. She told me what her name was, but it wasn't registering at the time. She's THAT girl, isn't she?"

I nod my head. "Where is she?"

Wanda moves off the bed. "She should be back soon. I had her go into the front store and grab some things for you." She crosses her arms again. "I told her that you were as stable as you were going to be and that I needed a minute, so I gave her a list of herbs."

"But she's okay, though, right?"

Wanda looks at me, into my eyes. "Physically, yes, emotionally and mentally no."

"What do you mean?"

"She was hysterical when Jahoel brought me to where you were. She was hugging you so tightly to her as she screamed." Wanda slightly winces. "I've never heard a cry full of so much pain before in my twenty-one years. It took Jahoel and I both to get her to let you go. I held her while he ran you to my shop. Her whole body was shaking like a leaf, her face white as porcelain. I managed to pull her to her feet, but I was afraid she would break if I moved her. The look in her eyes I will never forget. It was as if someone had shredded her heart."

{She was like that because of me?} A quick stab goes through my chest.

"I had Jahoel bring you back here to the extra room behind the shop."

I look around at the wooden walls, multiple shelves lining each one I can see, each filled with jars containing different objects and creatures. The floor is a darker wood than the walls. Besides the bed, the only other thing in the room is a small, circular table overflowing with books and herbs and the chair Wanda was sitting in before pushing against it. The bed I'm in is bare. Only a thin sheet sits on it but nothing else, not even a pillow.

{Demons don't sleep, and witches barely need any, so beds are very uncommon around here.}

"Once we were all here and you were settled, I got right to work. I started mixing potions and looking up different spells."

"Where was Mal?"

"She was a statue, just staring at you on the bed with tears still dripping onto the floor at her feet. Seeing her cry made me want to as well, but I knew I wouldn't have time to save you if I wasted time on that. I told her to snap out of it. I didn't want to be mean to the poor girl, but I needed her to stop crying and help me. I had her take off your weapons belt and remove your sword. At first she was reluctant, until I told her I could still save you. Her eyes snapped back into focus as she looked right at me, her eyes boring into me as if to see if to make sure I wasn't lying. She asked me how I could save you and who I was. I told her I'd explain later. She nodded and helped me. Everything I told her to do or get, she followed each order perfectly. About two hours later, I did all that I could do to get your flame back." Wanda clenches her jaw while scrunching her face.

"What?"

"I couldn't get a spark," she explains softly.

I shake my head. "You must have, or I wouldn't be sitting here talking to you."

"That's just it, though, I have no clue how your flame was lit again. Everything I did didn't change anything. You were still gone." Her hands tighten on her arms.

"So then what changed?"

Wanda shrugs. "I honestly don't know. I don't know if it was residual magic still in the air or delayed magic, maybe something else entirely. I was sitting against the wall with my arms on my knees, my face buried, crying so hard I couldn't breathe. My heart was breaking because my best friend, the person I..." She stops quickly, looking at me with a soft hue of pink under her eyes. "You were gone, and I couldn't bring you back. As I sat there crying, I could hear Mal talking to you softly. I looked up at her, and she was sitting beside you on the bed, running her hand through your hair. She was begging you to come back to wake up. She talked about what she felt towards you and hoped that you felt the same way about her. Watching her with you..."

"What?"

She shakes her head. "I just listened to her, allowing her to say her goodbyes before I had to turn your body over."

{Supernatural creatures whose bodies don't go up in smoke or disintegrate have to be turned over to The Collector. Both sides have Collectors. No one knows what they look like or what they are. All anyone knows is to take the body somewhere deserted, draw a giant swirl with a skull in the middle, and then place the body on top. Once the body is set, they must leave for a Collector to come and take the body. Nobody knows where they take them or what they do with them. The Collectors help keep the supernatural world hidden by disposing of the bodies. This way, humans can never find them.}

"As she was speaking to you, she placed her hand on your chest and I heard her plead for you to come back. She used your real name. Then..." She stops.

"Then what?"

"You took a breath."

I stare at her as she looks down at her shoes.

{Was it Wanda's magic, or was it something else? If my flame was out for that long, then there's no way I should be alive.}

I place my hand on my chest, focusing on the heat within. A memory flashes of my flame bursting to life inside of a bright blue sky.

{Something lit my flame. Something brought me back.} I continue to look at Wanda.

{If not Wanda, then who, then what? How am I here?}

"I don't really care how you came back. I am just glad that you are." Wanda smiles at me with unshed tears in her eyes.

I give her a small smile. "I am too."

{It'd be nice to know how, though.}

"Are your powers back as well?"

I take my hand away from my chest as I pull heat from my fire and move it into my hand. Flames erupt, sending out tiny sparks into the air.

{It's different.}

Royal-blue fire dances in my palm.

{My flames were dark navy blue before. Why are they royal now? What happened to my fire?}

"They're so pretty." Wanda comes closer to the bed again. "How did you change their color?" She reaches her hand out towards my palm but doesn't touch the fire. "I thought all archdemons had the same color flames." Her eyes grow in wonder. "I thought you were all supposed to have the same hue of red when your eyes light up too."

"Huh?"

"Your eyes, they are a lighter and a much brighter red than the last time I saw you use your flames." She looks back at my hand.

"We're supposed to." I continue to stare at my palm.

{What changed? Why are my eyes and my flames different colors than before?}

"How do you feel? Do you feel weak or lightheaded?"

I shake my head. "No, I actually feel great." I close my hand, dousing my new fire. "I feel stronger, to be honest."

{My wounds.}

I touch on my shoulder where Mal had put gauze to cover the shuriken wound. I only feel a hole in my shirt.

{It's gone.}

I look down at my leg, finding only a hole there as well.

{The wounds finally healed.}

I look back at Wanda to see her looking at me with confusion and concern.

"Don't look so worried, Wanda; you saved me whether you think you did or not. I am alive because of you." I put my hand on her shoulder. "Thank you for everything." I smile at her.

A scarlet line runs across her face from cheekbone to cheekbone. I can't help but chuckle.

KNOCK, KNOCK.

"Miss Wanda, I got everything you asked for," Mal's voice says from behind the door.

"I wish she wouldn't call me that," Wanda says under her breath.

{Mal?}

I take my hand off Wanda's shoulder as the door slowly opens.

{Mal!}

I quickly jump off the bed, my shoes hitting the floor hard as I bolt towards the door. Warm pangs continue to go through my chest over and over as the door opens. I stop right outside of the door's reach as it swings the rest of the way open. Mal stands in the doorway, looking down at her arms holding multiple bags of herbs.

{She has the same clothes that she did before, but now they have dust and dirt patches all over them. Her face is paler than last I saw her, and her eyes are pinked from crying.}

"Mal," I speak carefully.

Mal's whole body jerks at the sound of my voice. She slowly raises her head to meet my stare.

BA-DUM.

I barely feel the pound as I get lost in her eyes. I watch as all the pain in them fades away, allowing joy and warmth to take their place.

"Kal? Is that really you, or did I finally drop from exhaustion?" she asks half-jokingly.

"It's really me." I smile.

Everything Mal was holding crashes on the floor as she leaps into my arms.

"Kal!"

I catch her in my arms, wrapping them around her as hers wrap around my neck. She squeezes me tightly, lifting her legs up to wrap them around me as well. I just smile as I hold onto her. I can feel her body tremble against me, her breathing quickened and her heart rate fast. I can hear her sobbing beside my ear and feel her tears on the side of my neck. My chest aches as my breathing starts to feel heavy while I listen to her crying.

{Why am I feeling like this?} She holds me tighter.

{Is it because Mal's crying? Am I feeling pain because she is hurting?}

I carefully turn with her still wrapped around me. I look at Wanda as she watches us with a smile on her face but sadness in her eyes...

{Why is she looking at us like that?}

I continue to hold onto her, and after a while Mal's breathing evens out as her heart rate slows down. Her arms and legs loosen but still stay around me.

She nuzzles her face into the crook of my neck. "You came back," she whispers to me.

I hold her tighter. "I'm sorry I left in the first place."

"You're back. That's what matters."

Her arms loosen more around my neck as her breathing starts to slow. "Just promise me you won't leave again and that we will stay together."

{Together?}

"I promise."

Mal's legs begin to lose their grip.

"Good, because I don't know what I would do if I lost you." She takes a few soft breaths. "I've never believed that the way I feel about you could happen so quickly," she half mumbles.

I don't feel pressure on my neck anymore. Her arms and head just lay on me. "What do you mean, Mal?" I ask softly.

It takes her a few seconds until she responds. "I didn't think someone would become this important to me, would sneak their way into my heart so suddenly." Her legs begin to slip.

"Kalma...I...think..." Her words become slower. "...that...I...."

Mal's legs fall. I quickly but gently move my left arm down and scoop both of her legs up. She moves as I lift her legs closer to my chest. Her left arm slips off of my shoulder, sliding down my chest until it rests on her stomach. She adjusts her head until it lays against my collarbone while her right arm slowly comes off of my shoulder before falling down to hang beside her. I stand there frozen, looking down at her fast asleep in my arms, some of her hair lying on her beautiful and peaceful face. I can't help but smile as she snuggles her face against me. BA-DUM, BA-DUM.

An incredible warmth spreads with the pulses in my chest. I hold her closer as I smile.

{What are you doing to me, Malak? Whatever it is, I don't ever want it to stop.}

10

I'm amazed she didn't collapse sooner," Wanda explains quietly as I carefully lay Mal down on the bed.

I step back, smiling as she turns on her side, bringing her knees up. BA-DUM, BA-DUM.

{The pounding keeps happening more often than when it first started.} I place my hand over top of where the pulses come from.

{What is it?}

I stare down at Mal, getting lost in my head. "Do you want to sit?"

I climb out of my thoughts and look to Wanda, who has turned away from the bed. "Sure."

I glance at Mal one last time before following Wanda to the small table. She pulls out her chair and sits.

"I'm not sitting on your lap," I joke.

Her face turns red, but she doesn't look at me as a stool slides out from under the table.

{That was completely hidden. I had no clue it was under there.} I pull the stool towards me before sitting across the table. "How long was I out?"

"Pretty much the whole night. The sun should be up in the next hour or so," she explains, still not looking at me.

"Tsk." I clench my fists hard on the table.

"What, what's wrong?" She finally looks at me.

{Her eyes are full of sadness but also happiness. What is going on in her head? She's been acting strange since Mal came back.}

"Did Mal tell you anything while I was out?"

Wanda shakes her head. "Not much, just that you guys were on the run and that you had to fight other demons and that's why you were so weak."

I sigh. "That's only part of the story."

"Kal, you're scaring me. What's going on?"

"They're making their move, my father and the others."

"What do you mean?"

"They've been planning an assault on the angels for the last few years, compiling data, doing recon, building an army, and training all of us younger demons to be ready for battle. Father told us after my ritual that they are putting their plan into action."

"Oh!" Wanda exclaims. "I know now isn't the best time, but since you brought it up I may as well get it out of the way." She starts digging into her pants pocket. "It's not much but..." She pulls a thick, black string out of her pocket, holding it out to me. Hanging from the string is a pointed crystal, the point facing down, made up of multiple colors.

"I made it myself." She smiles at me proudly. "Starting at the flat part, the silver chunks that look to be inside glass is pyrite. It helps to shield and protect you. Beneath that, the solid dark red is garnet. It will increase the power of your internal flame, making you stronger. After garnet is agate, with its mixture of black and blue, said to be the warrior stone. Then finally"—crimson runs under her eyes again—"the one on the very bottom making up the cloudy pink tip is rose quartz, said to help with the heart."

I take my eyes off of the crystal to look at Wanda as she finishes the last word. "Wanda, I don't have..."

"I know, but that doesn't mean I can't try to help whatever is in there, because there is something there. You are not like the other demons. I don't know if it's because you are part human or if it's something else, but you are kinder, you have emotions, you care about everyone, and..." She looks past me. "You can form strong connections with others." She looks back at me and gives me a sad smile. "More than you thought you could."

I just stare, not knowing what to say to her.

{Is she right? Is there actually something in me that allows me to be so different?}

I slowly reach out my hand and take the necklace from her. I hold it in both hands in front of me, studying the multiple colors.

{Shield and protect, internal flame power, warrior, and heart.}

Carefully, I pull it over my head while watching the crystal until it lands on my chest.

"Thank you, Wanda." I reach out my hand and put it on top of one of hers. "It means a lot to me that you took time out of your life to make this."

"Happy birthday, Kalma."

I smile at her. "Belated, but whatever." I chuckle, pulling my hand back.

{No one has ever given me a real gift before.}

I wrap my hand around the crystal, feeling its smoothness against my palm.

{I don't know if the crystal pieces will do what Wanda says, but I don't care.} I give it another gentle squeeze before letting go.

Wanda clears her throat. "As you were saying, though, before I—"

"Kindly interrupted," I say jokingly.

"Yeah, before that," she jokes back.

"I was saying that they've activated their plans."

"What's the plan?"

"To take out all of the oldest churches around the world to weaken the angels and archangels in order to...ya know."

"Take over the world."

I nod.

"Why the churches?"

"I don't know the full story, but I guess that the oldest churches hold a lot of holy energy in them, so by destroying them, that energy will be taken away from the angels, making them and their hold on this world weaker."

"Why now, though? This war between them has been going on since the beginning of time."

"I don't know what made them decide to move. I knew that they had to have been planning something big when Father started having meetings every day, but I wasn't expecting it to be this."

We sit for a few seconds in silence.

"Why were there other demons after you two? What did you do to get on their hit list, and what is so special about her for them to want her?"

"I disobeyed my orders, so my unit attacked me."

"What were your orders?"

"To kill an angel hybrid."

"What?! You're telling me that there's another hybrid in Philly besides you and they wanted you, out of all people, to kill it."

"Kinda."

She looks at me, confused. "The hybrid isn't OUT there."

Wanda continues to stare at me, puzzled.

"You asked what is so special about Mal for them to want her."

Her eyes grow as she looks past me again. "No way."

"Yeah, that's what I said when I first found out."

Her eyes focus back on me. "You're telling me that the girl you have been following around for months, the one that you've been obsessed with." She lowers her voice. "The girl that you've developed feelings for." She finishes so quietly I can barely make out what she said.

{What did she say?}

"Yes, Mal is the angel hybrid."

"And you don't think that's kinda weird that out of everyone in this city you could've stuck to. It was another hybrid, more so an angel hybrid?"

"I guess I never really thought of it that way. I haven't really had a chance to think about it all that much. The moment they showed us who it was, I was shocked. I couldn't wrap my head around her being like me." I let out a sad laugh as I look at my hands. "I talked about her and I being complete opposites, but I didn't realize how far it went. We are literally opposites. I am a demon, a creature of hate and darkness, while Mal is an angel, a being of love and light. How much more opposite can we be?"

I tighten my fists on the table until I feel burning from where my nails punctured the skin on my palms, the warm blood collecting in my closed hands.

"Would you have rathered it been someone else?"

I look back at Wanda. "Huh?"

"Would you rather the angel hybrid have been someone else and not Mal? Do you think her being a hybrid is what drew you to her in the first place?"

I loosen my fists, removing my nails from my palms as I turn around and look at Mal, who is still fast asleep, the familiar but strange feelings running through me that I've had since the first day I saw her.

{Would I want it to be someone else? Could it be why I was so drawn to her, why I'm still so drawn to her.}

Mal brings her knees closer to her as she tucks her hands under her head. I can't help but smile at her.

"Yes, I want someone else to be the hybrid, but not in the way that you think. I don't want it to be her because I know how much danger she is in because of it." I face back towards Wanda. "And I'd like to think that her being part angel isn't what drew me to her." I place my clean and healed hand, the blood having evaporated, on my chest, feeling the coldness of the crystal against my skin. "I think something in here did." I watch as I grab onto my shirt. "Because I know there's no way her being a hybrid has anything to do with what goes on in here when I'm around her." A strange pressure builds in my chest and throat. "I don't understand what it is, what these feelings are because I've never felt anything like them before. All I can think about anymore is her. When will I see her again, will she see me, will I finally talk to her? I literally countdown the seconds until I can see her face again. When I do see her, I just want to smile, and I don't understand why. I get so giddy when I'm around her, and I have to remind myself to stay calm. Since I've been near her, actually near her, it feels like everything will be all right. She makes everything feel so right. Even though I am a demon, she doesn't care. She accepts me for who I am. I can be my full self with her. I feel a stronger connection with her than anyone else. Sometimes when I look into her eyes, the world slips away and it's just her and I staring into each other's eyes. It might sound crazy, but something in here is telling me never to leave her, to stay with her, because everything hurts even though there are no wounds when we're apart. Then earlier, when she was crying, I felt her pain inside of me. I felt the weight of her pain. I never want her to feel like that again. I never want to hurt her like that again. I want her to be happy and safe. I've never been so protective over someone as I am of her. The second Father told us she was our target, I knew that I had to save her and protect her from anyone who wanted to hurt her even if it cost me my life, and clearly, I was serious, because I did die. I would do anything for her, be anything for her. I want to be better for her. She makes me want to be better to rise out of the darkness I have lived in my whole life to step into the light with her." I start nervously laughing again. "I don't even understand half the things that are coming out of my mouth right now. She's done something to me. She's changed me somehow, but I don't care because I like feeling this way. Is that crazy? Because I think it is. That I enjoy feeling confused with all of this inside of me that I don't understand." I grip onto my shirt tighter as my eyes start to burn, my vision becoming blurry. "I've never felt so at home but lost at the same time. It's never felt as if my world is whole but falling apart at the same time." Something wet rolls down my cheeks. "How can I be so happy when we're both being hunted and the world might be coming to an end?" I look up at Wanda, her eyes opening wider as she looks at me.

Both of my hands press against my chest to stop it from bursting.

"Wanda, I don't understand what any of the things going on inside of me means, and it scares the hell out of me."

Drops land on the table under me as I continue to grip onto my shirt, my breathing erratic while more water rolls down my face before dripping off onto the table. Wanda just stares at me with sympathy.

{What's wrong with me?}

I start to cough as I struggle to breathe, the water still streaming down my cheeks. My whole body starts to hurt as pressure continues to build. Wanda jumps up quickly, causing the chair to fall backward.

"Kal, you have to calm down," she orders as she kneels down in front of me, placing her hands on my shoulders before turning me to face her.

I still struggle to breathe, choking on the air.

"Deep breaths, you have to take slow, deep breaths."

I shake my head. "What's happening to me?" I ask through sobs.

She gives me a sorrow-filled smile. "You're crying."

{Crying? Demons don't cry. We can't.}

I shake my head at her again, but she nods hers.

"Kal, I know what crying is, and you are." She takes one of her hands and wipes some of the tears from my face. "Your body feels heavy and it hurts?"

I nod.

"Your throat is burning?" I nod again.

"Your chest feels as if someone is pressing on it?" I just stare at her as she gives me another smile.

{I'm crying.}

"Oh, Kal." She brings me closer to her as she wraps her arms around me. She holds on tight to me as my body shakes with each sob.

"Why am I crying?"

"Because of everything you just told me. You're scared because you don't understand what's going on inside of you."

I take my hands away from my chest and carefully wrap them around Wanda. "What you feel towards and about Mal are things you've never experienced before, and it scares you because you never thought that you could."

My breathing starts to slow down, and my choking diminishes with it.

"It's okay to feel how you are and to be scared because of it; everyone does at some point."

"Why am I like this?"

I can feel her shaking her head on my shoulder. "That's something you have to figure out on your own. I can't give you the answer, not this time. All I can do is be an ear when you need to talk and a shoulder when you need it." She pulls away, her emeralds meeting my stare. "Something has changed within you, Kal. I haven't even known you for a whole year yet, but I can tell that something has changed." She looks over at Mal.

I turn my head to look as well.

"I don't know if it's because she's half angel or if it's because she's the one."

{The one?}

"Either way, she has changed you. I don't know how but..." We both look at one another before she puts her hand over top of my crystal. "I think she's awoken something inside of you that you didn't know you had."

I watch as a quick tear rolls down her face.

{Wanda?}

She takes her hand away before standing back up. I wipe the remaining tears from my face.

{What's inside of me that I didn't know I had?} "Feel better?"

I nod. "I'm sorry, I don't know what—"

"Kal, it's okay."

I stand up, pulling her in quickly for a hug.

"Thank you for being an amazing friend, Wanda. I don't know what I would do without you."

I step back to look at her.

"You'd be okay." She punches my arm. "Except when it comes to human stuff, then you'd be screwed." She laughs.

I laugh with her. "True, true. You did teach me everything I needed to know about this world."

"Remember when we first met and you didn't know what anything was called?"

"Yes, that was horrible."

"Like a car, what did you call it?"

"Contraption on wheels."

She laughs harder. "And planes?"

"Metal bird."

"Oh, and my favorite, remember what you said jackhammers were?"

I sigh, placing my hand on my face in shame. "Human vibrator."

She bends over laughing.

"Hey, in my defense, I didn't know that it could destroy things." I take my hand off my face, defending myself.

"Oh, I'm sorry." She stands back up. "What would you have called it if you'd known it did?"

"The human destroyer vibrator."

"That's even better." She bends over, laughing harder.

{I don't understand why it's so funny.}

I cross my arms over my chest. "Ha ha."

She stands back up, her laughing slowing down., "I'm sorry, I'm sorry."

"It's not my fault I literally lived in a withdrawn world."

"I know, I'm sorry."

I smile before nudging my shoulder against her. "I'm just messing. I know some of my names were silly."

"Yeah, they were, but you've learned, you've grown."

"Thanks to you." I smile.

Scarlet races across her face.

"I mean it, Wanda, you didn't just save my life tonight but when I first came up here. If it wasn't for you, I would have been lost in more than one way."

"What are friends for?" She gives me a fake smile.

{I'm sorry, Wanda. I know you wish it was more.}

"Kal."

I turn around.

"Kal," Mal mumbles again.

"She's talking in her sleep," Wanda explains. "She's saying your name."

{Even when you're asleep, you're still thinking about me.}

Mal rolls onto her back, her face scrunching in panic. "Kal."

"You better go to her."

I look back at Wanda, seeing the same look in her eyes from before as she turns away.

"Yeah." I reach out and grab her before she can walk away.

{You have to know.}

I pull her into another hug, squeezing tight. "I really do care about you, Wanda, a lot."

She nods.

"Don't ever forget that." I let her go.

"I won't."

She walks over to the door, putting her hand on the side of it. "See you in a few hours?"

"Yeah. Once she wakes up, we'll be out."

"Then what?"

"I need to find out what's going on down there. I'm going to find someone who can tell me."

"How come?"

"I need to know how far along in the operation they are so I can make my plan on how to fight back."

Wanda whips her head to look at me. "Fight back?"

I nod. "I'm not going to let them destroy this world."

She stares at me for a few seconds before sighing. "Then I'm with you."

I shake my head. "No, Wanda, I can't let you do that. I don't want you getting hurt."

"You're not letting me do anything. I'm going too. You forget I'm a powerful witch. I can take care of myself." She grins. "This is my world, and I will defend it."

I sigh while shaking my head. "Guess nothing I say will change your mind?"

She shakes her head.

"Fine."

She smiles.

"First, I need to get info, and then..." I look back at Mal. "We need to find someone who can help her awaken her powers."

"Why?"

"I'm terrified that I won't make it in time and she'll get hurt. If she can use her powers, she can defend herself until I can get there."

Wanda nods in understanding. "I know you don't want to hear it, but her power could help us."

"That's what I'm afraid of." I turn back towards Wanda. "What if that is why they wanted me to kill her? What if they knew how powerful she could be and wanted her out of the way?"

"Only one way to find out."

"I just don't want her to get hurt."

"I know you don't, but at least with her powers she'll have less of a chance of getting hurt."

"I guess."

"And just think you two together, both of you able to use your powers, you'll be an unstoppable duo. Two hybrids, one from each side of the coin working together, imagine the possibilities. You guys really could be the turning point in this war."

{Could we really be that powerful? I know that hybrids are just weapons, but that doesn't always mean they become those weapons.}

"But as you said, we need to find someone who can help her before we get too far ahead of ourselves."

"I'm sure there'll be some guardian angels or Cherubims in the plaza that could help."

"I hope so, because I don't know how light powers work." I rub the back of my head as I chuckle nervously.

"Me neither." She laughs with me.

"I guess we'll figure it out together."

"Guess we will."

"Kalma," Mal mumbles. BA-DUM.

{Every time.}

I smile as I turn around, making my way towards Mal. "See ya in a bit."

"Thanks, Wanda."

I hear the door click as it shuts. I stop beside the bed and smile down at Mal as she sleeps on her back with one of her arms up beside her head and the other one lying across her stomach, her face still scrunched.

"What did you do to me, Malak?"

I reach down, gently placing my hand on the side of her face. She leans into my hand. "Kalma?"

"I'm right here. You're okay," I whisper. "Lie with me?"

BA-DUM. "What?"

"Would you lie with me?"

"Um."

She grabs my hand that's on her face, pulling it towards her as she slides over, making room for me.

{Oh boy.}

Heat boils throughout my body, including my face.

{Am I blushing? Is that even possible?}

I carefully lie on the bed beside Mal. I lie down on my back, putting my right arm behind my head. Mal takes the arm she has and pulls it around her as she moves closer, laying her head on my chest. I lie there frozen, not knowing what to do. "Just hold me."

I put my left arm on her side, pulling her up against me.

"You're so warm." She nuzzles closer, placing her leg over top of mine. My whole body feels as if it's going to burst.

BA-DUM, BA-DUM.

I look down at her face, peacefully asleep again.

{Everything is going to change when you wake up. Tonight is the last night of you only being human. When you wake up, you get to learn what it means to be an angel hybrid.}

I watch as she moves closer in her sleep.

"If you only knew what you've done to me, what you do to me, how you make me feel," I whisper. "Wanda says that you've awakened something inside of me that I didn't know I had."

I hold her closer.

{There are so many things I still don't get, but one thing is clear, and that is I don't ever want to be without you.}

"Do you know what it could be?" I ask even quieter. BA-DUM, BA-DUM.

11

Mal begins to stir against me.

{Sunrise was a while ago. I was starting to wonder if she was going to sleep the whole day away.}

"What time is it?" she mumbles.

I move my arm out from under my head to look at my watch. "About four thirty."

She quickly sits up. "Why did you let me sleep so long?"

"You needed it. You hadn't slept since the night before I came to your house," I explain as I sit up as well.

Mal lifts her arms up to stretch. "Still, though." She stretches them out in front of her. "I don't want to waste any time."

"You're not wasting time. You need rest."

She relaxes her arms as she looks at me. "I'm rested."

I nod with a smile. "Good."

She places one of her hands on top of mine. "How are you feeling?"

Heat boils inside of me as I feel her warm skin on my hand. "Depends on what way you are asking," I answer jokingly.

A puzzled expression crosses her face. "Physically?"

"I'm good, my inner flame is blazing, my strength is back to normal, and my wounds have all healed."

She nods.

"How about you? How are you doing?"

She tackles me, wrapping her arms tightly around me. "You're here and you're okay." She squeezes. "As long as those things don't change, then I am all right."

I wrap my arms around her. "Same for me. As long as you're with me and are safe, then I will be okay."

{But how long will she be safe?}

"Mal, we need to talk about what's next."

We let each other go before she sits back up. "What do you mean?"

"I told you why the others are after you and what their plans are."

"Yeah."

"Well, I need to find out if that is still their plan and what their time-table is now that they can't get to you."

"How are you going to find out?" Panic flashes in her eyes. "You're not going back down there, are you?"

I shake my head. She lets out a sigh of relief.

"There are plenty of creatures who come here that can tell me what I need to know, but that won't be until tonight."

"So we just wait around till tonight?"

"Kinda."

KNOCK! KNOCK!

"Kal, is she awake yet?" Wanda asks from the other side of the door.

"Yeah, she's up."

The door swings open as Wanda steps through wearing different clothes than what she was wearing a few hours ago. She has the same shoes on, but regular blue jeans now, with a red-and-black plaid unbuttoned button-up on with a black shirt underneath, still hugging her body tightly.

"Sorry, I know that you told me that you'd be out when she woke up, but I need to grab some stuff so I can open up soon."

"It's okay. We were getting ready to come out," I explain as I slide off of the bed. Mal slides off of the other side as I walk to the bottom.

"How are you feeling?" Wanda asks Mal.

"I'm okay, thank you." Mal stands close beside me.

"Good."

They stand staring at one another.

"You never told her who you are, did you?" I question Wanda.

She crosses her arms. "I didn't exactly have the chance to, you know, too busy saving your life and all."

Mal takes a step closer to me. "I said thank you, didn't I?"

She doesn't answer.

I sigh. "Mal, this is Wanda. She is a witch that lives and works here. She specializes in healing magic. That is why I had Jahoel bring her to me. She is very powerful and knows a lot about both worlds."

Wanda glares at me. "Didn't you forget something?"

I smirk at her. "Did I?"

"Kalma!"

Mal looks at me surprised, her cheeks flushed while her eyes light up as I laugh at Wanda's frustration.

{I love messing with her, she gets annoyed so easily.}

Wanda's hand starts to glow the same emerald color of her eyes as she takes it off of her arm. Her eyes become brighter with magic.

{She must be really pissed. She's using her magic.}

I put my hands up in surrender but don't lose my smile as I meet her angry eyes. "Come on, Wanda, you know that I'm just messing with you."

Her eyes narrow as she continues to glare at me moving her hand farther out. "You wouldn't actually hit me with that, would you?"

She smirks at me. "I might after what you've put me through last night."

{Oh crap, she is pissed. She's serious.}

Her hand glows brighter as she makes a gun shape with it before pointing it at me. I stare down the barrel of her magical pistol.

"Now, Wanda, you know what will happen if you fire your magic at me."

"What?"

I chuckle. "I'll take you down."

"Ha! You wish."

{We haven't done this since we first met.}

"It's not going to be like last time." I smile bigger.

"Nothing has changed since last time. I'm going to win again." The magic around her hand expands.

I look into her eyes.

{She's serious, but the anger in her eyes is gone. Only magic remains.} I silently chuckle to myself.

{She's testing me. She's making sure that I am ready to go back out there. She wants me to take her down.}

I reach out towards Mal, carefully pushing her backward until she is far behind me.

{I know Wanda wouldn't hurt her, but just to be safe.}

I tuck my hands into my pants pockets. "Do it."

She grins. "Cocky."

"Yep."

A green bolt of magic shoots from her pointer finger towards my feet.

{Trying to stop my mobility, huh?}

I extend my senses, quickening my reflexes in the process. I move my feet just before the magic can hit them. Wanda doesn't stop there, though. She keeps firing. I don't stop either. I keep my feet moving, turning back and forth, not allowing a single bolt of magic to hit me.

{I could stop these very easily, but it's more fun this way.}

Wanda raises her other hand, forming a hand pistol as magic surrounds it before she starts firing from that hand too.

{She's really testing me.}

I step back, running into the wall.

{The room is too small for this.}

She grins as her fingers point right at me. I see Mal out of the corner of my eye standing in front of the bed now, watching me nervously.

{Nothing to be nervous about, Mal.}

I push heat into my hands as Wanda fires two larger bolts of magical energy at me.

{We're almost done.}

I keep moving the heat into my fingers.

{I know I could just move to the right or the left, but this will be so much cooler.} The green moves closer as I take my hands from my pockets, seeing my new fire ignite around each of my fingers. I focus on making the flames move quickly around each fingertip. I swing my right hand up over my head, piercing each one of my fingers into the wall behind me. I give Wanda a cocky smile before I nimbly pull myself up using the hold I have on the wall, right before her attack can hit me. I use my arm muscles to pull and spin myself until my front side is facing the wall before stabbing my other hand into the wall as well. I feel as the energy hits the wall where I was just standing.

{I can't believe this actually worked.}

I pull my legs in until they rest on the wall above me.

{I'm literally crouching on the side of the wall upside down.}

I look up to see Wanda staring at me with her mouth hanging open and Mal's face full of awe.

Wanda shakes her head, snapping herself out of her trance. "That's my wall!" moving swiftly, I take my hands out of the wall, pushing myself off it with my feet, launching myself towards Wanda. She stares at me in shock but moves out of the way before I can grab her.

{I figured she'd move. Let's just hope this next part works. I've never done it before.}

I brace my arms and hands out, pushing myself off the floor as I hit it, doing a backflip in the air before landing back on my feet.

{Sorry, Wanda, but I win.}

I push power into both hands but create different attacks in each. I throw the first attack from my left hand towards Wanda. The multiple flaming blue spheres fly at her. I focus more fire back into my left hand, creating the same thing I hold in my right. I watch as Wanda continues to back up quickly to avoid being hit while firing her magic at them, but two more explode out of it each time one is struck.

{To be able to focus fire inside of the fire, I didn't think it was even possible.} Wanda fires faster as the burning spheres grow nearer, panic rising on her face.

{You know I'd never let them hit you.}

I swing out both my arms, opening my palms just enough for the tops of the fire whips to fly out of my hands.

{I've used these before. Father said fire whips are for cowards, so I never use them in battle, but I think they'll be of good use this time.}

I smile watching as each tip wraps around the front legs of the chair Wanda had used a few hours ago. I pull on the flaming cords, pulling the chair with them. I pull it hard enough, giving it enough momentum to move on its own. I let the flames from the whips go as I push off the ground hard, racing towards Wanda and the oncoming chair. I smile to myself.

{Gotcha.}

I reach my hand out, taking back the heat from the spheres, causing them to evaporate in the air. I don't move my hand as I continue to hold it out towards Wanda. She looks at me confused right before backing up into the chair rocketing towards me. The chair scoops her up, lifting her right off of her feet, both of them now coming at me.

{Have to have perfect timing, or it won't be as cool as it is in my head.}

I stop as I lift my knee up just as Wanda and the chair reach me. My knee slams into the front of the chair between her legs, causing the chair to stop and start to tip backward. I use my outstretched arm to grab onto the back of the chair beside her head before it can fall. I stand over her, our noses about a pen's length away with her tilted backward in the chair. She looks up at me with wonder in her eyes as she breathes heavily. We stare at each other. I watch as she looks over my whole face before landing back on my eyes, the look that she always has when she sees me returning in her eyes. The hue of magic fades from her emeralds.

I give her a warm and sincere smile. "Wanda, you are the greatest friend anyone could ever have, and I'm lucky enough to say that you are mine."

Wanda's whole face changes into an apple as she still stares at me.

I back up, carefully putting the chair legs onto the floor. I take my hand off of the chair before holding it out towards her. She glances at it before smiling and grabbing on. I pull her to her feet and into a hug.

"I know why you did all of that. I know that you are worried about me and if I am ready to go back out there and fight."

I hear her breath catch in her throat.

"I'm not mad. I'm actually thankful." I hold on tighter. "You are more than just a best friend, Wanda. You care about me as if we were family."

I pull her away to see her face. "You have no idea how much everything you've done has meant to me." I smile.

Tears glisten in her eyes as the red fades off of her face. I chuckle. "You're such a cry baby."

She quietly laughs. "I'm not the only one anymore."

"Touché."

We both laugh as we step away from one another. "So, you're Kal's friend?" Mal comes up behind me.

"No," I answer.

They both look at me shocked.

"She's my family."

A tear slides down Wanda's cheek.

{I know we can't have the relationship that you want, but what we have is what we both need.}

Wanda nods as she wipes her face. "Yeah, Kal's my family."

Mal looks at both of us as we smile before holding her hand out towards Wanda. "Nice to officially meet you. My name is Malak, and I'm an angel hybrid."

Air catches in my throat as I stare at Mal with surprise. Wanda looks at me, seeing me spun before turning back towards Mal to take her hand.

"Nice to officially meet you as well."

They take their hands back as Mal steps to be beside me, close beside me.

"Sorry about all of that." I rub the back of my head. "Wanda just wanted to make sure I was back to normal."

"You've never been normal," Wanda speaks up. Mal laughs softly.

"Ha ha."

"Just saying." She shrugs.

I shake my head. "Either way, she was making sure I was okay and ready to go back out there, because we know that out there is a battle waiting to happen."

Mal nods. "I understand."

"So, what's your next move?" Wanda questions as she moves the chair back to where it came from.

"What we discussed last night." She turns around and looks at me. "Are there any here yet?"

She nods. "There's a few in the circle hanging out before their shift."

"Good."

"What are you two talking about?"

"Remember how I said earlier that we will kinda be waiting around till tonight?" Mal nods.

"Well, what I meant was that we are going to be training while we wait around."

"Training?"

"As much as I want to be by your side twenty-four seven, I know I can't be, and during those times that I can't, I need to know that you'll be able to defend yourself against other demons or creatures."

"How am I supposed to do that? It's not as if punching and kicking will do the trick," she asks, frustrated.

I shake my head. "No, plain physical attacks won't be of much use."

"What am I supposed to do?" she panics.

I reach down and gently take her hands into mine as I turn to face her. "You've seen my fire because of my demon half."

She nods.

"Well, angels also have abilities, and since you are half angel..."

Realization flashes in her eyes. "I should have them too."

I nod. "Yes, so I'm hoping we'll be able to get an angel to help you awaken those powers and help you learn to control them."

Her eyes flicker back and forth with fear looking at both of my eyes.

"But what if I can't? What if I don't know how to use them?" She turns her head away from me. "What if you get hurt because of me? Kal, I can't..."

I cut her off, "Malak."

She shuts her mouth, swinging her head to face me again.

"Listen to me, okay? If I didn't think you could do this, I wouldn't have thought of it. You are smart and capable. I've seen your determination and your strong will. I know that there is a power inside of you waiting to come out. You don't have to worry about me getting hurt because I can take care of myself, and I will make sure no matter what happens that you won't get hurt, okay?"

She slowly nods.

"I know you can do this. I know you can do whatever your heart tells you." I smile at her. "Your heart is big, and it is pure. Those are two of the things that help to drive an angel's powers."

"How do you know that my heart is as you say?"

I smile genuinely. "Because you feel towards an evil creature like me." Her cheeks light up.

"To be able to care about a demon takes a huge heart. Not falling into darkness after everything you learned takes strength and courage. All of your honesty, your open vulnerability, your goodness, and your morality make you pure." I pull her hands closer to me, causing her to come closer as well. Our noses are almost touching as I fall into the sky of her eyes.

{I will never get tired of falling.}

"Malak, the light inside of you is the brightest I have ever seen in my life." I take a deep breath. "Your light pulled me out of my darkness," I whisper.

"Gasp!"

"You've become my light; you are the warmth that I feel..." I place her hands over my chest. "In here."

She doesn't say anything as she continues to meet my stare. "You've awakened something inside of me, Malak."

Her eyes open wider as my smile grows bigger.

"That's how I know that you can do anything as long as you keep that light inside of you shining."

{I can't believe I just said all of that.} I squeeze her hands a little tighter.

{But she needs to hear it. She needs to know the power that she holds inside of her even without using any actual abilities.}

"You really think that I can do it?"

"And so much more. I believe it with every part of my being."

Tears roll out from her eye before sliding down her face onto her smiling lips. BA-DUM, BA-DUM.

She loses her smile before her eyes quickly snap down to our hands on my chest, her eyebrows coming together in wonder.

{Why did she do that?}

She looks back up at me, studying my face. I watch as the light grows in her as her smile returns to her face.

"All right, I believe you."

I let out a breath of relief.

"Just promise me a few things."

"Anything."

"Don't ever leave me."

BA-DUM, BA-DUM.

Her smile grows.

"Never."

"And don't ever hide what you are feeling."

"Um, okay."

{Feeling? Does she mean emotions? Because I don't understand how those work just yet.}

"And don't ever stop looking at me the way that you are right now."

BA-DUM, BA-DUM, BA-DUM.

{My chest is really starting to hurt.} I nod, not knowing what she means.

"Good." She slides her hands out of mine, taking a step back, her face still blushed. I leave my hands on my chest, laying them flat against me before looking down at them.

{Why does it hurt? What is causing the pounding?} "So, what do we do first?"

I lift my head back up while taking my hands away from my chest. Mal stands with her back straight and her fists at her sides, confidence rolling off of her in waves.

{That's my girl.}

BA-DUM.

A beautiful warmth rises and boils inside of me.

{Why did I just think that?}

"Kal?"

"Um," I clear my throat. "We need to go talk to the angels and see if any of them can help us."

"Do you really think they will?" Wanda speaks up. I jump a little at the sound of her voice.

{I thought she left.} "They will," I answer.

"How do you know?" She steps into my line of vision.

"Because I'm going to tell them the truth."

She stops in her tracks, whipping around to look at me with shock. "All of it? Are you crazy?"

"If I don't tell them everything, they might not help us."

"They'll kill you if they find out who your father is, let alone the fact that you were sent to kill an ANGEL hybrid." She swings her hand towards Mal in emphasis.

I nod. "I know that they will want to, but I'm hoping that Mal being alive and well will help them see that I mean no one any harm and that I want to stop my father and the other archdemons."

Wanda lowers her hand. "You're putting a lot of faith on this."

I smile. "Faith is kind of their thing, though, isn't it?" I laugh nervously. Mal and Wanda both look at me with fear and worry.

"I'll be fine."

Wanda sighs. "I know that you can defend yourself, so I know that you will be fine."

{As long as they don't have any angel weapons with them.}

"Okay then, now that that is settled, we should head outside." I take a step towards the door.

"Um, maybe you two should clean up first."

I stop and look down at myself. I am covered in dried blood mixed with mud and dirt, plus various herbs from Wanda's spells. My shirt and pants both have holes from Jorvexx's shuriken sunk into my skin.

{How the heck did my hoodie manage to stay clean?}

I turn towards Mal as she studies herself.

{I forgot how dirty we were.}

"I have two bathrooms. You both can shower in them."

"What about clothes?" Mal asks. "I don't have my bag."

{We had to leave it behind. I was too weak to carry it all the way here.} "Kal left some clothes for herself a few weeks ago."

{Only because they got soaked and I couldn't return home with wet clothing without drawing attention to myself.}

"And I'm sure I can find something for you to wear." Wanda walks over to Mal, taking her by the hand, leading her towards the door.

Mal looks back at me nervously.

"I'll see you soon, okay?"

I smile at her.

She relaxes. "Okay."

I watch as Wanda leads her out the door. I stand there, staring.

{The battle to come is going to be brutal and deadly.}

I place my hand on my chest again, feeling the crystal under my shirt.

{Can I fight the others?}

I take a deep breath.

{Can I fight my father?}

I take a few more deep breaths.

{Will I survive?}

My knees start to shake.

{Will I be strong enough? Will my flame be hot enough?} My feet go numb as my hands begin to tremble.

{Can we really stop this war before it's too late?}

My knees give out. I catch myself with the hand not on my chest. I stay there on my knees and one hand. My breathing becomes rapid as pressure builds in my chest.

{Are these going to be the last hours for the human race? The last days for holiness on Earth? Can I save everyone?}

I grip onto my shirt tighter, balling some of it in my fist as the room slightly spins.

{Can I keep Wanda safe? Can I keep Malak safe from everyone who wants her dead? Can I save her?}

12

{**What's taking** so long?}

I pace back and forth in the hallway right outside of the room we stayed in.

{It doesn't take this long to get cleaned up.}

I look down at my new outfit. I still have the same shoes but have dark blue jeans on. My shirt is a darker gray with my red hoodie over top. The crystal that Wanda made rests on my chest. I sigh as I run my hand through my damp hair.

"Well, don't you clean up nice."

I whip my head to see Wanda standing with a smirk on her face as Mal stands next to her. She's wearing a little too big navy-blue T-shirt with regular blue jeans with her own shoes. Her hair is the same as it was before, just cleaner.

"It was all I could find that would fit her," Wanda explains, seeing me staring.

I shake my head. "No, it's okay, thank you."

"Yes, thank you," Mal speaks up as she looks at Wanda.

Wanda blushes before she turns her face away from Mal, "No thanks necessary." I laugh to myself.

{She got under your skin.}

"Well, we better get moving." They both look at me. "Need to go speak with some angels," I explain as I laugh nervously.

"You'll be fine," Wanda reassures me.

I nod. "Let's hope."

I take a step towards the front of the store, hearing Mal jog to be beside me. We leave the hallway entering Wanda's shop. There are wooden opened cases spread throughout the store, each filled with herbs, crystals, and whatever else a witch would need.

{Wanda owns the only witch shop around here, so her inventory is vast.}

Mal and I walk down the center aisle towards the door. I can see people walking around through the glass in the center of the door. I take a deep breath as I grab the handle.

{Here goes nothing.}

As I pull the door open, an autumn breeze blows through causing Mal to shiver. "Are you cold?" I slowly push the door closed again.

"Just a little, but I'll be okay."

I turn around to look at Wanda, as she leans against the checkout counter next to the old-fashioned register. I narrow my eyes to glare at her.

"What? I told you I couldn't find anything that would fit her."

I take my hand off of the door handle as I shake my head before grabbing onto my hoodie.

{I don't get cold, so I don't need this. I just like it because it looks cool and makes my eyes look more red.}

I pull my arms out of my hoodie. "Here." I hold it out to Mal.

Her cheeks blush crimson as she looks at my hoodie and then at me before looking back at the hoodie.

"You want me to wear your hoodie?"

"Yeah, you're cold and this will help keep you warm."

She gently grabs onto it before taking it out of my hand. She continues to stare at it, her face still red.

{Why is she acting so weird about it?} "Thank you," she whispers as she puts it on. As my hoodie rests on her body, she smiles.

{It fits perfectly.}

"Better?"

She nods. "Much, your hoodie is very warm." She continues to smile at me.

I nod.

"Awe, aren't you two just the cutest thing," Wanda jokes from behind the counter.

Warmth shoots to my cheeks and ears as I quickly turn around to face Wanda again. She studies me, her eyes widening in surprise with her jaw dropped.

{Why is she giving me that face?}

"We'll see you later, okay?" I ask her as my cheeks and ears cool back down. Her mouth closes as she nods her head. I bounce back before grabbing the door handle again, pulling it open.

I face towards the door and Mal again. "You ready?"

She takes a deep breath. "Ready as I'll ever be."

I reach over and give her hand a gentle squeeze. "I'll be right here every step of the way." I smile at her.

She smiles back as she nods. "Good."

I open the door more, walking through it while pulling Mal along with me. The door closes behind us as we face a giant cement fountain in the middle of everything. "If I didn't know better, this place looks just like any other village circle," Mal explains.

"It pretty much is." I start walking towards the fountain with Mal behind me. "There are stores all around here, plus a motel and a small diner. There's even a tiny library, and my favorite place is the training center."

"What's that?"

"Just a building able to withstand any attack from any creature so that they can train and hone their powers."

{Wanda and I sparred a few times there.}

"Do people live here?"

"If that's what you want to call them, then yeah. Most of them live in their businesses like Wanda, but a few have small houses farther back in the barrier."

"And you said that people from both sides live here without conflict?"

"Yep, those who come here have no hate for the other side. They all live and visit in harmony."

"That's so cool."

I look over at her as she looks around at everything in awe. I smile as I watch her, my chest aching.

"Do you want me to give you a small tour?"

She whips her head towards me. "Do we have time?"

I look around.

{I don't see the angels. They must have gone into one of the stores or something.} I nod. "We have time."

She smiles at me with her eyes sparkling with excitement. "Just around the circle, though, okay?"

She quickly nods and takes my hand, pulling us away from the fountain towards Wanda's shop.

"Start here?"

I nod. "Well, you know what this place is." I look up at the wooden sign hanging above the door. "Witchy Needs,," I read the name carved into it.

"That's a weird name." Mal chuckles.

{Just wait.}

I move towards the shop on the right of Wanda's place, Mal's hand still in mine. "This is Everyone's Diner."

We stop in front of a small, square restaurant with black tables set up in rows with chairs surrounding each one inside the building.

"Why everyone?"

"They serve food for each category of demon, supernatural being, or angel, so everyone can come here to eat."

She nods. "That's cool of them."

She pulls me to the next building, a little smaller than the restaurant. Inside the windows are figures dressed up in different kinds of clothing. Behind them in the store are clothing racks scattered throughout the place.

"This is Indestructible Clothing."

"Wait, are you serious? They have indestructible clothes here?"

I chuckle. "No, that's just their name."

"Why, then, if they aren't indestructible?"

"Have you noticed that when I used my flames, none of my clothing ever caught on fire?"

She thinks it over for a few seconds. "Now that you mention it, yeah."

"Well, that's because my clothes are specially made not to. The clothes inside this store are the same way. All creatures have an ability that could destroy their clothes, but the clothing in here won't be."

"Wow, I bet those clothes must've been tough to make."

"Maybe."

I move us on to the next building, this one taller than all of the rest. "The only motel you can find around here, The Day Motel."

The building is a few stories tall, the outside looking old and about to fall apart. In each window are blackout curtains.

"I understand why they named it that. They come out at night, so during the day, they sleep," Mal explains.

"Only some sleep. The ones that don't just hide in their rooms doing whatever until the sun goes down."

"Does the sun hurt them?"

"No, they all just prefer to avoid it." I shrug. "I never understood why, but it is what it is."

"Okay?"

I walk to the building next to us. This one is longer than the last few. Inside the windows are rows and rows of books, each one looking older than the previous.

"The History Library. Everything you could ever want to know about either side can be found in one of those books. About the creatures, demons, angels, archangels, the never-ending war, weapons, and a few books on humans."

"Have you been in there?"

I sigh. "Yes, multiple times. I needed to learn more about what I am, and my father didn't have the books that would give me those answers. Plus, I wanted to learn more about humanity, so I read all the books that they have on that subject."

"Did you learn a lot?"

"Eh, I learned more from Wanda about humans than the books."

"Wanda taught you about this world?"

I nod. "Yeah, she helped me understand and learn everything I needed to."

"She really is great, isn't she?"

{You have no idea.}

I pull her to the next building. This one is the longest out of all of them. There are no windows, just a giant metal door in the center of it.

"Give It Your All. This is the training building I was talking about."

"Where are the windows?"

"There aren't any."

"How come?"

"The glass would shatter from people's abilities. Since glass is so fragile, magic can't be worked into it to be protected from attacks."

"The place is protected with magic?"

"Yep, without the magic, the whole place would have been destroyed a long time ago."

"Cool."

I smile walking to the next building. It is square, with two big windows on each side of the door. Inside are different-sized shields, different kinds of gold and silver chest armor, and other protective gear.

"Protection is one of the most important stores in town. There is equipment in here that can help protect one from any attack."

"Really?"

"I said help protect. The user still takes on damage, just not as much as they would've without the gear."

She looks at me, confused.

"Let's say someone were to hail a fire blast at me." I point to one of the red shields on a shelf. "If I had that shield, depending on the strength of the attack, I could walk away unharmed or slightly burned."

"So nothing is one hundred percent."

"Sadly, no."

She nods with a worried look on her face.

{She was hoping something in there would keep us safe.} I look back into the shop.

{Nothing in there would protect us from my father's attacks.}

"That's the entrance." I point to the path lined with tall stone walls on the other side of a dark alley.

"I remember."

Excitement rises inside of me as I remember what the next stop is. I quickly pull her towards the pitch-black alley. I let go of her hand as I move closer to the black.

"Don't move, don't scream, and don't worry."

"What?"

"Just trust me and do as I say."

Her eyebrows come together. "Um, all right?"

I nod as I stand on the line where light meets dark.

Taking a deep breath, I whistle really loudly. The whistle echoes over and over until the sound is gone.

"Shadow! Come here, boy!" I yell into the darkness. Nothing happens for a few seconds.

"Kal?"

"Don't move."

Tiny rocks begin to bounce as the ground rumbles beneath my feet.

{Here he comes.}

I brace my legs as the rumbling becomes louder and closer. Two red dots glow through the black, moving closer and closer.

"Kal," Mal says, alarmed.

I hold my hand back at her. "Don't."

Sharp, white teeth appear beneath the dots.

{He's moving really fast.}

"Mal, step closer to the stone wall."

"Why?"

"Please."

Feet scrape across the ground before I can see her out of the corner of my eye.

{All right, Shadow, I'm ready.}

A giant, black wolf-like dog, about the size of a calf, emerges from the dark. He charges at me with his tongue flopping out the side of his mouth. I push heat into my hand as I raise it in front of me.

{All right, boy.}

Flames erupt brightly around my hand. "Stop!"

Shadow pulls his tongue in before closing his mouth. He stops running but continues to slide across the ground even as he tries to back pedal.

{I knew he was going too fast.}

I pull my fire back in as he continues to slide towards me. I stand my ground, though, knowing that he will stop obeying my orders if I show fear. I can hear his nails grinding on the cement as he inches closer.

{Please stop.}

I tense my body, making sure not to show any signs of worry or fear. Shadow begins to slow down more and more, before coming to a stop just in front of me, close enough that one of his front paws rests against my shoe.

{That was close.}

THUMP! THUMP! THUMP!

His tail smacks the ground as he looks at me, his face full of doggy joy. "Hi, buddy." I reach up to pet him. "Did you miss me?"

Shadow lowers his head so that I can reach it. I rub the top of his head before sliding to his ear to rub behind it. He tilts his head towards my hand as he closes his eyes.

"You're such a good boy." I take my hand away.

He opens his eyes, straightening his head to look at me.

"I brought someone I want you to meet." I look over towards Mal, who stands as close to the wall as she can get her eyes wide open as she stares at Shadow. "Shadow, this is Mal." I hold my hand out towards her.

She looks at me before shaking her head. "It's okay. He won't hurt you, I promise."

She looks at him again before stepping away from the wall. She slowly moves over to me, placing her hand in mine.

I pull her closer to me. "Mal, this is Shadow. He is the guard dog around here."

"Dog?"

"Well, technically, he is a black demon dog, but he acts just like a normal dog would."

Mal continues to study Shadow, her hand shaking in mine.

"You don't have to be afraid of him. He was trained to never harm an innocent, only the ones who want to cause harm or violence."

"How do you know that the training worked?"

"Because I helped train him," I say confidently.

She turns her head. "You trained him?"

"I helped train him. Demon dogs respond better to higher-up demons, those who have flames like mine."

"So that's why he obeyed when you used your fire?"

I nod. "Demon dogs have to obey whoever is the most powerful as long as they don't show any fear. He can sense fear, and he will view it as a sign of weakness. If he thinks you are weak, he will not obey."

Mal nods, turning back towards Shadow. Shadow watches both of us, looking back and forth.

"Wanna pet him?"

She whips her head back towards me. "What?" she asks panicked.

"Do you want to pet him?" I ask slower.

"Uhhh."

"I promise you it's just like petting any other dog. He's just bigger."

"And has red glowing eyes with the sharpest canines I've ever seen."

"Exactly." I smile as I lift our hands up.

THUMP! THUMP! THUMP! THUMP!

Shadow's tail shakes fast as I move our hands towards him. "Kal."

"It's okay."

She looks at me worried but doesn't try to pull her hand away. Shadow lowers his head again before I place Mal's hand on top of it. She doesn't move it, so Shadow tilts his head giving her his ear.

"He wants you to rub behind his ear."

She takes a deep breath as she moves her hand behind his ear. She rubs the back of his ear, causing Shadow's mouth to stretch in pleasure. I smile at them as I watch him lift his back leg to scratch the air.

I laugh. "He really likes that."

A giant smile forms on Mal's face as she continues to rub his ear. "You are a good boy, aren't you?" she asks in a babyish voice.

I chuckle.

{This was good for her.}

She takes her hand away. Shadow's leg stops and his mouth returns to normal while he lifts his head back up to look at her.

{And now that he has bonded with her, Shadow will keep her safe if he is near.} She steps closer to me, placing her hand back in mine. Shadow's eyes glance down at our hands before back at my face. His eyebrows rise as he stares at me.

{I swear he is looking at me like, what's going on here?} "All right, Shadow, we have to move on our tour."

"He can't come with us?"

I shake my head. "He doesn't really like to roam during the day."

"Oh, I see."

"Yep." Power moves back into my free hand. "Ready, boy?" A fireball forms in my palm.

Shadow jumps up quickly. His tail is swinging in the air as he bows down, staring at the ball.

"Go get it!" I throw it as hard as I can into the darkness.

He takes off after the blue light until both he and the light are gone. "He's cute."

I laugh. "I know."

I pull her with me as we move past the entrance to the front of the next building on the other side of the entrance's wall. This building is perfectly square with fancy steps and columns on the front. A window sits on each side of the door, but the shades are drawn, so we can't see inside.

"This is Town Hall. It is where they go to discuss different things going on here and out in the world."

"It's a beautiful building."

"It is an ancient building. Wanda told me that it was one of the first buildings inside of the barrier over a hundred years ago."

"Woah."

"I'm amazed it's still standing." She nods in agreement.

"All right, the last stop on our tour."

We move to the last building in the circle on the other side of Wanda's shop. It is long, but not as long as Give It Your All. There are four windows on the front, and in each one are dim string lights with empty wine and champagne glasses sitting in the center. The door is covered in different angelic and demonic symbols, a red carpet rolled out in front of it.

"My least favorite spot, They Come Alive. It is a nightclub that anyone can go into."

"Like nightclub nightclub? Like the ones, you know, in the real world?"

"All except for what they give them to drink. There's a dance floor, DJ, disco ball, flashing lights, and lots of beverages."

"Supernatural beings can get drunk?"

I shake my head. "Not exactly. Alcohol doesn't affect any of us."

"Then how?"

"A long time ago, a coven of witches discovered a way to make a special brew that could give them the feeling of intoxication. Nowadays, that brew is turned into a powder that the bartenders mix into the drinks. Why those witches ever looked into that is beyond me."

"I'm going to take a guess and say that you don't approve."

"Your guess is correct. I think the idea of beings not meant to be intoxicated getting intoxicated is the worst decision anyone could make. With the powers we have, the secrets we hold, and the cravings some have, who knows what could happen if someone gets too drunk. They could easily go out there and be discovered or attack a lot of innocent humans. The whole idea is stupid and not thought through, but what can you do?"

Mal nods. "Nothing you can do. Those who want to get drunk will, no matter what you tell them."

I shake my head, pulling her away from the nightclub, walking back to the spot we had started.

"Well, there you go, a quick tour of the center of town."

"There are some exciting things around here."

"You have no idea."

I look down at my watch.

{Six. The sun will set soon, and this place will be swarming with different creatures.}

I glance at Mal, watching as she looks around.

{I want to get her powers awakened before I talk to someone about what is going on down below.}

A group of guardian angels steps out of the diner moving towards the long bench between the building and the fountain. I take a deep breath in and out as my free hand shakes. I make a fist to stop the tremors.

{It'll be okay.}

13

"Hi," I say nicely as Mal and I stand in front of the angels sitting on the bench. They all stop talking to look at us.

"Hi," one of the female angels replies.

I scan each angel from left to right, all seeming to be in their early twenties. The first one is standing beside the bench with her arms crossed over her chest. She has grayish-blue eyes and is about my height. Her hair is short and black, with blue highlights mixed in. She has a slight tan. Her body is lean but with some muscle. She is wearing blue-and-white shoes, dark-blue jeans with a black belt around her waist. A blue-and-white plaid long-sleeve unbuttoned button-up over top of a white tee. I move my eyes to the next angel. Another girl, but judging from her legs, she is a lot taller than the first one. She doesn't look like she has a single ounce of fat on her, but her body looks great thanks to the muscle she does have. Her eyes are hazel, her skin a shade or two above pale. Her hair is bright red with some curls towards the bottom, which flows past her shoulders. She has on gray tennis shoes, light-blue jeans with tears throughout the legs, a rose-colored buttoned button-up under a pale-blue jean jacket.

{Nice jacket.}

I keep moving down the line to the boy sitting next to her. He seems to be tall, but his legs are not as long as the girl before him. His skin is almost the same as the girl beside him. Unlike the other two, he has some chub, but not much. The look seems to fit him perfectly. Choppy, dirty blond hair sits on his head, the bangs coming down right above his eyebrows with blue eyes sitting below them. He's wearing white shoes with dark-blue jeans, a dark-blue zip-up half-zipped, allowing the white shirt underneath to peak out. Moving on, beside him is another male. Seems to be the same height, maybe a few inches taller than the boy before him. His skin is tanner than the others before him. He is very skinny but with a bit of muscle on his arms. Short, dark-brown hair peeks out from under the gray ball cap that he is wearing. His eyes are the same hazel color as the red-haired girl. He's wearing brown work boots, dark-blue jeans, and a navy-blue tee. Another male sits beside him. This one is tanner than all of them. His legs are the same length as the guy on his left. He has more meat on his bones, though, than that guy, but just by a small amount. His body is built the same way, though, muscles shaped nicely on both arms. His hair is short and primarily black but has white specks throughout his whole head. Doe brown eyes stare at me.

{Those are some severe eyes.}

The man is wearing brown work boots with black tips, brown pants, and a white shirt. A brown cap hangs from one of his knees. The guy on the end seems the same height and build as the other two, but his muscles are slightly bigger than both of them. He is tan but not as much as the boy beside him. His almost perfectly cut black hair, but a slight curl sticks out in the front. His eyes are hazel but a darker hazel than the other two with hazel eyes. He's wearing regular white tennis shoes, regular blue jeans, a white shirt with a dark-blue dress coat over the top, making him look as if he is from the fifties or something. I scan back over each of them, taking notice of the one thing that they all have in common, the thing that all guardian angels have. The glowing tattoos on the side of their necks shaped like an angel wing.

{I read that they receive that when they become a guardian angel. It supposedly helps the lost souls or those in need find their guardians. They look for glowing wings.}

I take a deep breath. "I'm Kalma, and this is Malak." Mal steps up to be right beside me.

{I figured it was best to use our full names at first.}

"Nice to meet you," the one on the far left nods as she takes a small step closer. "I'm Jade; beside me is Summer, then Blaze, Levi, Bruce, and John."

They each give us a small wave. "What can we do for you?"

I feel my hands start to tremble again, so I lock them together behind my back, hoping that no one took notice of the shaking.

"For me to answer that, I need to tell you everything. Some of it will be hard to believe, but you have to listen, and you need to believe me."

"Um, okay?" Jade says, puzzled.

{She must be the group leader. Each squad of GAs has one.}

I look over at Mal. She turns to me and smiles. I nod, giving her a smile in return before looking back at the angels. I take a breath.

{That was everything relevant. They know what my father and the others are planning and going after the hybrids and the churches. I left out the fact that Mal and I are both hybrids. I wanted to let all of that sink in before I told them everything.}

"So you're saying that your father is the Rorridun, the second-in-command?" Summer questions.

I nod.

"And that he and the other archdemons made a plan to go after all the churches to weaken angels, including the archangels, so they can bring Hell to Earth?" Blaze asks.

I nod again.

"They're going after the hybrids because of the power they are capable of, afraid that they will stop them?" John speaks up.

I nod.

"You know all of this because they told you and your squad their plan after you finished your eighteenth-year ritual," Bruce says.

I bring my hands around to shove them deep into my pockets as fear rises inside of me. They all get quiet as they look at us and then at each other.

"Even if this is all true..." Jade turns to me. "Why should we believe you?"

"How are we supposed to believe the daughter of Rorridun? The kin of the one who made this plan?" Summer looks at me as well.

"You were literally tasked to kill an angel hybrid. How do we know that the moment we help you that you won't turn on us to make us tell you where the hybrid is?" Levi says.

"For all we know, your squad could be waiting somewhere outside the barrier just waiting to strike," Bruce explains as he puts his hat on.

"How are we to believe that a demon would want to help stop Hell from rising?" John questions.

{They all make excellent points, but I think I have the answers.}

"How are we supposed to trust you, Kalma?" Jade asks.

"You're right."

They all looked at me shocked, all but Mal, as I see her smile from the corner of my eye.

"How are you supposed to trust me? Trust a demon, trust me knowing who my father is, help me knowing what I was tasked with?" I glance at each of them. "I said that what I had to say was going to be hard to believe." I take a breath. "Well, what I just told you wasn't what I was talking about."

They each look at me with confusion covering their faces.

"I don't need to force the location of the hybrid out of you because I already know where she is."

Their eyes grow in shock.

"And my 'squad' isn't going to attack you. If they're going to attack anyone, it'd be me."

"Why?" Jade wonders.

"I disobeyed orders. I refused to kill the hybrid."

"WHAT?!" they all exclaim.

"There's no way you disobeyed an order, especially given to you from your father," Bruce questions.

"Well, I did. I tried to hide the hybrid to keep her safe, but they found us, so I had to fight them off." I chuckle. "I almost died, but I was able to get them to retreat."

"So, where's the hybrid now? If you're telling the truth and you saved her, then where is she?"

Mal steps closer to me. "She's right here." They all look at Mal.

"I am the angel hybrid, and everything that Kal has said has been true. She did come to find me and try to hide me, but she fought them all when they found us. She jumped in front of an attack for me." She looks at me. "She died for me." Her voice cracks.

"It's just not possible. Demons don't care about anyone but themselves," John explains.

"And clearly, you are lying because she is standing here. She isn't dead." Summer waves her hand at me.

Mal looks back at them. "Kal pushed herself too far during her battle with her squad. Her flame was already weakened because she disobeyed, making Lucifer's blood inside of her attack her. She didn't care, though; she wanted to save me even if she would die trying."

I look over at Mal and can see the determination and loyalty in her eyes.

{Mal.}

"Luckily, it didn't go out, but it was still feeble. She was frail, and yet she made sure that we got here so I would be safe. Opening the barrier was the final blow. She knew that it was going to kill her, but she kept going. We made it through." Her hands ball into fists. "She collapsed, and as I held her in my arms, she said to me so many things, but she told me that she swore she would protect me even if it cost her her life. Her flame went out then, her body lost all of its heat, and she stopped breathing. She was gone."

"Then how is she alive?" Summer asks again.

"Wanda brought me back," I answer. They look back at me.

"Before my flame went out, I told Jahoel to get Wanda. She specializes in healing magic, so I put all my faith in her, hoping she'd bring me back." I smile at them. "And she did."

None of their faces change as they continue to stare at us in disbelief.

"If you don't believe us, you can go ask them. Ask Jahoel or Wanda. They'll both tell you the same thing."

Jade studies me with belief flickering in her eyes. "Not good enough."

I look over at Blaze.

"Do you have any proof that something happened?" I stop smiling as I think it over.

{The only thing that changed after I woke up is...}

I quickly push heat down my arm as I take my hand out of my pocket. All of their eyes turn to fear as I raise my hand up.

"Would this be proof?" My new fire forms around my hand.

Each of them stops to stare, their eyes growing in awe and amazement. "A different color flame," John whispers.

"How's that even possible?" Bruce asks quietly.

"It shouldn't be," Jade answers.

I extinguish my flames before returning my hand to my pocket. They all regain their composure.

"So, you did die and somehow came back," Summer states. I nod.

"But how can we believe Rorridun's daughter?"

I take a deep breath, letting it out before I speak, "Because I'm not JUST his daughter?"

"What do you mean?" Levi asks.

"My mother died the day I was born. She wasn't a demon like my father or any other kind of supernatural creature."

"Then what?" Blaze speaks.

"My mother was a human." Pressure builds in the back of my throat.

"You're a hybrid too?" Jade asks.

"Pretty ironic, right? They sent a hybrid to kill a hybrid," I joke.

"The day I found out that I was half-human was the day everything changed."

They all stare at me, even Mal.

"I found my mother's picture in my father's files. She was pregnant, and on the back was my name. I always knew that there was something different about me. I've known since I was small. I couldn't block things out like the others. I couldn't not feel anything like them. There was something else in me, and I didn't know what it was until that day. Part of me is human, which means, as I'm just now figuring out, that I have emotions." I smile wider. "I can feel things that I never knew existed until after I found that picture." I quickly glance at Mal before looking back. "I went to the surface that day. I wanted to know more. I wanted to see what humans were really like, not what our books said about them. I explored, soaking everything in." I turn my head towards Mal. "That was the day I first saw her."

Mal quickly faces me, her face full of surprise.

{Part of the story I never told you.}

"It's almost been five months since that day. The day that my dark, cold world began to change."

{Why am I saying all of this right now?}

I turn entirely towards Mal. She does the same.

"From the moment I laid eyes on you, I knew that you were special. Seeing you did something to me. A calming warmth burst in my chest. It was unlike anything I've ever felt. I decided that day to learn more, to see you more. So, I did. For months I learned everything I could about this world. I wanted to know what humanity was all about. I got to see celebrations, funerals, weddings, reunions, and do you know what they all had in common?"

Mal's eyes begin to water.

"Warmth, the same kind that was growing inside of me when I saw you. Each time that I saw you, I was already thinking about when I could see you again." I softly chuckle. "When I think about it sometimes, I guess I was stalking you, sorry." She smiles as she shakes her head.

"You were all I could think about Mal, and I didn't even know your name. Is that crazy?"

Tears fall down her cheeks as she shakes her head again.

"It's because of you that I became open to this world, became open to these new feelings inside of me. They may scare the hell out of me, but I don't ever want to lose them." I take my hand from my pocket. "I don't ever want to lose you." I take her hand in mine.

Her tears start to hit the ground as we look into each other's eyes. I allow the world to slip away, the stores, the sounds from the fountain, even the angels all disappear until it's just her and me.

BA-DUM, BA-DUM, BA-DUM.

"Kal, can I tell you something?" Mal asks softly.

"Anything."

A scarlet line appears across her face. "I was going to tell you last night, but I fell asleep." She laughs nervously. "I had more bravery when I was half asleep than I do now."

I give her a warm smile. "You're always brave."

The scarlet gets brighter. "Before, I was thinking that I just thought I was feeling what I feel, that I wasn't quite sure if it was real or not, but now..."

"Now?" I scrunch my face in confusion.

She takes a step closer, our noses not even a foot apart. My blood boils inside of me as my ears get hot.

"I love you, Kalma."

BA-DUM, BA-DUM, BA-DUM, BA-DUM.

My breathing cuts off as continuous throbbing pulses in my chest, tears forming in my eyes. The warmth I was speaking of fills me up, head to toe, feeling as if it won't stop until I burst. I stare into Mal's eyes, knowing that she is serious somewhere deep inside of me. I can see the warmth and light in her eyes as she watches me.

{Is that what someone's eyes look like as they look at the one they love?} "What about you?" she asks softly.

Her voice causes my whole body to pulse.

"Do you love me?"

{Love?}

I break eye contact with her to look down at our feet. "I don't know what love feels like. I don't know how to love someone."

Her hand moves down until it is under my chin. She slowly lifts my head up until I am looking back into her eyes.

She smiles at me as her hand moves to the side of my face, her fingers pressing up against my ear. "I can help you. I'm not going anywhere, and neither is my love for you."

My tears roll over my eyelids, sliding down until they drip onto the ground, one drop after another. She looks at me in shock for a few seconds, before her smile returns bigger and brighter as she uses her thumb to wipe away some of my tears.

"I think you're feeling more than you realize," she says softly as she slowly leans in towards me.

My body reacts on its own, leaning in towards her. Our noses brush against each other as we get closer.

BA-DUM, BA-DUM, BA-DUM, BA-DUM.

"We believe you," someone speaks.

The throbbing in my chest stops as the world returns around us. Mal pulls away from me, taking her hand off of my face. We both turn towards the angels who are all watching us with eyes opened wide, understanding in each of them.

{I got so lost in her eyes that I completely forgot about them.}

I wipe my arm across my face to get the remaining tears. Mal uses her hand to do the same to her face.

"We believe you," Jade repeats.

"Why now? What changed your mind?"

"We listened to everything you said and knew that it was all true," Summer explains.

"But from watching the two of you just now, we have no doubts at all," Bruce says.

"Why?" I ask.

"No demon could ever do what you just did. You opened yourself up to her, you blushed, you cried, and you allowed her to love you."

My cheeks burn as I remember Mal saying those words to me.

"Yeah, like that." Blaze chuckles. "Demons can't do the things that you do. They can't feel the way that you clearly are."

"So we know that you do want to help protect this world, that you really do care about it and the humans on it," John speaks up.

"We can see that there's something inside of you that makes you different," Levi explains.

{That's what Wanda said. What do they all mean?}

"After all of that, we believe everything you've told us and are ready to help," Summer says confidently.

I let out a breath of relief.

{I honestly didn't think that they would believe us, let alone help us.} I put my hand on my chest, pressing the crystal against my skin.

{Is there really something inside of me that makes me so different?}

"So, what do you need from us?" Jade asks.

"Can you help Mal awaken and learn to control her powers?"

Jade scrunches her face with concern. "You haven't awakened your abilities yet?" she asks as she looks at Mal.

Mal shakes her head. "I just found out what I am, so, no."

Jade closes her eyes as she lets out a breath of disappointment. "I'll help you."

"Really?" Mal asks excitedly.

"I'm the leader of this team, so it's only fair that you get the strongest to be your teacher."

"Gloating much?" Summer says as she folds her arms.

"When do you want to start?" Jade questions, ignoring Summer's remark.

"Now." I step closer to Mal. "I want her to be able to defend herself if I can't get to her in time." I take her hand in mine. "Nothing bad can happen to her, and if she knows how to protect herself, then the percentage of that happening shrinks."

Jade nods. "Understood. Shall we head over to Give It Your All, then?"

Mal and I both nod.

"While I'm with them, I need you all to try to get a hold of one of the archangels to tell them what is going on."

"The archs?" John asks, shocked.

"They are the only ones who will know what to do," Jade tells him.

"Do you really think we'll be able to get a hold of one of them?" Levi wonders.

"You'll have to. This world depends on it," Jade says seriously.

They all stand up at once. "Right."

"I'll see you soon." Jade walks towards us.

I watch the other angels run off towards the entrance, each of their clothing turning into their standard attire of white shoes, blue jeans, and white shirts. As they leave the circle, their angle blades form on their backs.

{Good luck.}

"Ready?" Jade speaks.

"Let's do this," Mal says confidently.

We follow Jade all the way to the training building.

{This is it. Mal is going to learn how to use her powers. She is going to learn how to defend herself.}

My stomach begins to feel yucky.

{I just really hope it doesn't come down to that.}

13

"First things first," Jade explains as she and Mal stand in the center of the empty room.

The walls are gray cement with no windows. The only light source is the three giant hanging lights on the ceiling. The floor is made from a softer blue material for when someone hits the ground it won't hurt as much.

{I forgot how bleak this place was.}

"We need to awaken the angel inside of you," Jade finishes.

"How do we do that?" Mal questions.

"Couldn't tell ya."

"What?!" Mal and I both exclaim.

"You said you would help us. How are you going to do that if you don't even know how to start?" I ask angrily.

"Hey, I said I would help her learn how to use her powers, not how to awaken them," Jade explains as she looks at me. "She has to figure that part out on her own." She turns back at Mal.

{But how is she supposed to do that?}

"It's different when guardian angels get their gifts than when a hybrid does. Guardian angels receive their powers the moment we become guardians."

"When's that?" Mal wonders.

"Not long after we die."

A shocked sadness appears on Mal's face. "You're—"

"Dead? Yeah."

"How old are you?"

"I was nineteen when I died. I've been a guardian for quite a while now. That is why I am stronger than the others."

"So all the others are"—Mal gulps—"dead too?"

Jade nods.

"So is everyone who dies a guardian angel?"

"No, only certain ones. Only those who died trying to save or protect someone become a GA."

An idea flashes in Jade's eyes. Her eyes flicker to me before looking back at Mal.

{What was that about?}

"Who were you saving when you died?"

"My best friend." Jade smiles. "Our apartment building had caught on fire. As we were all running for safety outside, I realized she wasn't there, she was still inside. I knew that going back would be suicide, but I didn't care. I ran towards the building, dodging everyone who was trying to stop me. I ignored the cries of my parents as they begged me to come back. I ran into the building as fast as my legs would take me. I knew where she'd be, so I went to her apartment, avoiding the flames and falling debris as I went. I ran in screaming her name over and over again, smoke filling my lungs with each breath. By the time I got to her room, I was struggling for air. I swung open her closet door, and there she was, sitting on the floor, with her arms covering her head. I bent down and grabbed her arm. She looked at me in shock, screaming at me, asking why I came back. I asked her if she honestly thought I'd leave her there to die. She teared up, but there wasn't time. The building was starting to come down around us, and my lungs were beginning to burn for fresh air. I pulled her up and we ran for the exit. The flames had gotten bigger and hotter, making getting around them much harder. I don't know how many burns I got making sure that the fire didn't touch her. I could hear the beams around us and above us start to crack. We approached the door, but giant flames blocked the way. The cracking above us was getting louder, and I knew that it would give at any second. She looked at me, terrified, asking, 'What now?' I already had a plan, but I couldn't tell her what it was. I took off my jacket, handing it to her, telling her to hold it out in front of her so that when she went through the fire, the flames would catch the jacket and not her. She wanted to know what about me. I told her that I'd be fine, that I'd be right behind her. She was about to argue when the beam right above us snapped in half. I quickly pushed her as hard as I could through the flames and out the door. Her scream was the last thing I heard before the burning ceiling collapsed on me. Luckily, it was quick, so I didn't feel any pain. Next thing I knew, I was an angel standing with other angels, all listening to the archangel Gabriel explain what happened and what we were to do next."

Mal stares at her with glistening eyes. "What was your friend's name?" I speak up.

"Kaitlin."

"Do you regret it?" I ask curiously.

"Not even for one second. I'd do it all over again if need be."

{She's like me. Willing to die for the one we care about. We both did die, I just came back, and she became something more extraordinary.}

"But anyway, the moment I opened my eyes up there, I already had my powers. I just had to learn how to use them."

Mal sighs. "So what do I do, then, if you don't know how to help me?"

"I might be able to help you."

"Really?" Mal asks excitedly.

Jade nods. "But you aren't going to like how I go about it." Mal looks at her, just as confused as do I.

{She just said a minute ago that she couldn't help. What changed?}

"What do you mean?" Mal wonders.

"I can only think of one way to help." Jade's clothes change into GA's usual outfit, her sword appearing on her back.

{What is she doing?} "What's that?"

"By getting rid of the thing that's holding you back," Jade says coldly. My senses set off alarms just as Jade vanishes.

{Shit.}

Heat travels down my arm, quickly igniting my hand.

"I wouldn't if I were you," Jade says behind me.

Her blazing blade presses up against my throat, threatening to slice through. I put out my flame, standing as still as I can.

{I forgot how fast angels can be. I didn't even have time to defend myself.} "What are you doing?!" Mal screams as she moves towards us.

"Don't move," Jade warns her as she tilts the blade against my neck.

I feel the burn as it pierces through my skin, a small line of blood running down. Mal freezes as she looks at us, horrified.

"Why are you doing this?" I carefully ask her.

"Your demon energy is the only thing that I can think of that is preventing Mal from awakening her powers."

"What? That doesn't even make any sense."

"Makes plenty of sense. You are dark, and she is light. Darkness can snuff out the light."

"But that's not how it is with us, and you've seen that," Mal pleads.

"She's right. My darkness isn't putting out her light. Her light is pushing away my darkness."

"Maybe, maybe not. We won't know until you're gone."

"Jade, please don't do this!" Mal yells at her as tears fill her eyes. "I love her."

Jade chuckles. "Did you really think that a demon and an angel could love one another? It's not possible. Demons can't love. She might think that she does, but she can't. You two could never work, so it's better to just end it now before you get hurt."

"Killing her will hurt me. It will hurt me more than any wound ever could, so please don't do this."

"Sorry, Mal, but I don't have a choice."

She puts more weight on the sword, making it slide more into my throat.

{I'm sorry, Mal.}

"No!" Mal reaches her hand out towards us.

I close my eyes, not wanting to see the pain in hers. A bright light flashes behind my eyelids before the blade is gone and Jade's presence is no longer behind me. I slowly open my eyes to see Mal still standing where she was a second ago with her hand raised, but it is different.

{It's glowing.}

Mal stares as her hand glowing celeste blue, bringing it closer to her. Her eyes are opened wide, radiating the same blue as the light around her hand.

{She did it.}

"I did it," I hear her say softly.

"That you did," Jade speaks.

I reignite my hand as I quickly run to Mal before jumping in front of her, spinning towards Jade as she picks herself off the ground.

"That was a nice shot," she explains as she rubs her neck.

The light from Mal's hand diminishes. I turn my head and notice that her eyes have returned to their standard blue.

{Her eyes glow just like mine do when I use my flames.} I look back at Jade as she steps towards us.

I build more fire into my palm. "I wouldn't if I were you," I warn, using her words from before.

"Relax." She swings her sword over her shoulder and into the sheath on her back before her outfit returns to her street clothes, "If I really wanted you dead, you would be."

Neither one of us says anything.

"I wasn't really going to kill you. I just needed Mal to think that I was."

"Sorry if we don't exactly believe you, but you did just have a blade to my throat." I reach up with my non-fire hand to wipe the blood from my neck. I move a small amount of heat into my thumb, creating a small flame to cauterize the wound. It closes, stopping any more blood from coming out. I move my hand back to my side.

Jade sighs. "Look, I'm sorry I had to do that, but I knew that it would help Mal break the barrier that was inside of her."

"What are you talking about?" Mal asks behind me.

"I knew that you would try to save her, knowing what could happen to you if you did."

I think it over not taking my eyes off of her.

"Angels are created—"

"When you die saving someone," I finish for her as my fire goes out. Jade nods.

"But I'm not dead."

"No, but I figured that since you are a hybrid, the rules might be different for you, and obviously, I was right."

I step back to be beside Mal as I let my guard back down. "So, it was just an act is what you're saying."

"Yep." Jade grins.

I look into her eyes, searching for even a flicker of betrayal. "Not cool." I sigh, not seeing any.

Jade shrugs. "Sorry, but it needed to be done."

"So my powers are awakened now?"

I turn. "Yes, you should be able to use them at will now."

Mal lifts her hands, studying them both. Her eyes flicker quickly between normal and glowing celeste.

She lets out an annoyed breath as she puts her hands back down. "I can't get them to glow again." She looks at Jade. "How do I make them glow again?"

Jade stares at us.

"You've got to be kidding me," I say, ticked off.

"I think I know how you can reactivate them."

My body tenses up. "We are not doing that again."

Jade laughs. "No, I have a much easier way."

She walks back to the center of the room, stopping before waving for Mal to join her. Mal looks at me nervously.

I smile. "It's okay. She was telling the truth. She only did what she did to help you."

"How do you know she was telling the truth?"

"The look in her eyes. I could tell that her only intention is to help you."

Mal's eyes flicker side to side as she studies mine before nodding. She moves to the center, stopping in front of Jade.

"Angel's powers are light, right?"

Mal nods.

"Light is pure."

Mal nods again.

"What is purer than love?" Jade smiles at her. I can see as the idea connects in Mal's eyes.

"I became a guardian because I loved someone enough to die for them."

Understanding flashes in Mal's eyes.

"You unlocked your angel side because you loved Kal enough to head straight into danger."

Mal looks over at me. I give her a warm smile.

"So, love is the key?" Mal asks, looking back at Jade.

"If my logic is right, then yes, love is the key."

Mal nods before lifting her hands back up to look at them. She stares at them for a few seconds before closing her eyes. No one moves. Jade and I watch Mal intently.

{You can do it. I know you can.} I smile.

{You have too much love in you not to.}

Mal tightens her hands into fists right before the soft blue light from before bursts around them. She opens her eyes, smiling at the glowing outlining both of her hands.

{Told ya.}

Mal looks at me with a giant smile on her face, her irises matching her hands. I give her one back as a slight feeling of relief washes over me.

{She'll be able to protect herself if I'm not there. She'll be safer.}

"All right," Jade says.

Mal and I both look back at her as she folds her arms.

"Next step is to be able to use the light as an attack and defense." She grins. "Maybe even discover some other gifts along the way."

"More?" Mal asks, shocked.

Jade nods. "I have a few abilities, so being a hybrid, you should have more than I."

Mal looks back at her hands with determination covering her face. "All right, I'm ready."

"Good, but..." Jade looks at me. "You need to leave."

"Huh?" I ask, surprised.

"You are too much of a distraction. As long as you are here, she won't be able to give her full attention to her powers."

"Seriously?"

She nods. "She'll want to look towards you. She'll want to see if you're watching her. So she won't be giving it her all."

I think over her logic, knowing that she is right.

"Will you be okay if I step outside while Jade helps you?" Mal looks at me with worry mixing in with her determination. "I won't go far. I'll come running if you need me."

She lets out a deep breath. "Okay, just don't do anything stupid."

I laugh. "What me? Never."

Mal chuckles. "See you soon?"

I nod. "I'm not going anywhere, remember?"

Her cheeks turn red as her smile becomes warmer. "I love you."

BA-DUM, BA-DUM.

{I want to say it back because I know that's what you're supposed to do when someone says they love you. I wish I could shout it so loud that the moon would hear me, but I don't want to say it until I know what love feels like.}

I smile at her; she returns the smile as understanding covers her face.

{She knows that I'm not ready to say it yet.}

"I'll come for you when we're done so you can see," Jade explains.

I nod. "Thank you."

I wave at them both before heading to the door.

14

I shut the door behind me before leaning against it.

{She'll be able to protect herself.}

I let out a breath of relief as I look up into the clear night sky. The stars and half-moon shine down on the small town, onto all the civilians walking around the circle. I turn my head to face forward as I step away from the door.

{I guess while I wait I can try to gather some info on what is going on below.}

As I'm walking away from the building, two toddler-sized beings move towards me quickly. I jump out of the way before they run into me, neither one of them paying attention as they chase one another.

"Uxum! Sukir! Watch where you are going. You're going to end up hurting someone," I yell at them.

The two pucks stop and look at me.

{They've been here every night I have been. I think they live here, but I'm not positive. I don't know if they are brother and sister or just friends. I don't even know if pucks can have siblings.}

"Come here."

They both look at the ground before slowly walking over to me.

{They aren't just toddler-sized; they act like toddlers as well.} I squat down as they stop in front of me.

"You two have to be more careful. If you run into someone and hurt them, then you'll be in big trouble."

They continue to look at their feet.

{I don't know why I bother talking to them. It's not like they can say anything back.}

"All right, look." I dig into my back pocket. "How about I give you guys some money so you can get something to eat?"

Both of their heads snap up, their eyes landing on the money I hold in my hand. "But you have to swear to be more careful. I know that you two love to move around and have fun, but if you're not careful, who knows what could happen."

I look at both of them.

{Sometimes I wonder if they even understand everything that I am saying. I talk to them both all of the time. I feel bad for them. I'm the only reason that they have real clothes and not those outfits made from a bunch of dead leaves.} "Uxum?"

Uxum looks at me, his dark-brown eyes staring at me impatiently.

{Finding clothes for them was hard, but I did the best I could. Especially since they won't wear shoes or socks.}

Uxum has on toddler blue jeans and a blue shirt. In the center of the shirt says, "bad boy."

{I thought it was funny, and when I told him what it said, he did the hideous laugh that all pucks share.}

"Promise?"

Uxum nods.

"Good." I hand him some money before looking at Sukir. "Sukir?"

She looks at me with the same colored eyes as Uxum. Sukir is wearing toddler blue jeans and a pink shirt with "bad girl" written in the middle.

{It just wasn't right if they didn't match.} "Promise?"

She nods her head.

"All right." I hand her the rest of the money. "Next time I see you two running around, you better be watching where you're going." I stand back up. "Now, go eat." I smile at them.

They give me their repulsive smiles before taking off towards Everyone's Diner. "I swear, those two." I shake my head.

I start walking again, looking at all the different creatures walking around.

{It took me forever to learn all of the regulars' names. Then it took just as long to earn all of their trust.}

I move towards the fountain where all of the fairies and pixies like to hang out. As I get closer, I can see the sparkling lights floating around the fountain.

{The first time I saw a fairy light I thought it was special lighting or something. That was until I tried to catch one.}

I cringe at the memory.

{I've never heard such a high-pitched noise before. Each fairy yelled at me, but since their voices sound like bells, it was as if someone was blowing a whistle right into my ear. So, needless to say, I learned about fairies that day, as well as their cousins, the pixies.}

I sit down on the outside ring of the fountain. After a few seconds, I hear bells jingling all around me. I smile as the fairies and pixies move closer to me. The two pixies are both dressed in bright green outfits, the boy in overalls and the girl in a shirt and skirt, their candy-apple hair seeming redder because of the green. I lower my hand until it lays flat on the cement. Both of them begin to climb up my arm until they are standing on my left shoulder.

{I offered to lift them up with my hand, but it made them angry, so now I just let them climb up by themselves.} "Good evening."

They both wave at me.

"Do you have anything for us today?" someone asks as they tickle my right ear.

"I don't have it with me," I answer, trying not to laugh. "But you are free to grab some for yourselves."

The tickling stops. I turn my head and see three fairies hovering in the air beside me.

{Only certain kinds of beings can understand fairies and pixies. Those who can't only hear bells, no matter how close to the ear they get. Luckily, I am one of those who can understand them when they talk into my ears.}

Two of the fairies wear bright red and blue dresses, both of them girls. The boy fairy is wearing a bright yellow shirt and pants. Each of their wings is sparkling silver and gold, moving too fast for any human to see.

{Each fairy has a unique design on its wings. Kinda like how butterflies do.} The boy, Mihr, flies closer to my ear until it feels ticklish again.

"Why don't you have it?" he asks me before backing up.

"I've been kinda busy."

My other ear itches.

"You said you'd bring some."

I turn my head as the girl pixie, Hecca, lands back on my shoulder. "I know, but like I said, I've been swamped."

The boy pixie, Inias, folds his arms as he shakes his head with disappointment.

{One thing you never want to do is piss off a fairy or a pixie. They have very short tempers.}

"What could be so important that you forgot our promise, Kalma?" someone says in my right ear.

The fairy wearing red floats back to be beside the others.

"Agla, I swear to you that it is very important."

The other girl fairy, Dina, flies to my ear. "What is it, then?"

Dina levitates back with the others.

"I can't give you all the details, but just know that the war is coming to Earth." All five of the creatures send of an alarmed jingling sound.

I feel one of them move on my left shoulder. I shake my head before Inias can get to my ear.

"I don't have time to explain everything. You just have to believe what I am telling you."

Inias stands back beside Hecca, taking her hand into his. Fear covers all of their faces.

I sigh. "Listen, you all will be okay. Each one of you is fast and smart. You will be able to get out of any bad situation." I smile at them. "If you do want to fight, I know you will win there as well."

All of them look at me with surprise.

"You might be small, but that doesn't mean you can't be mighty, right?" Confidence fills all of the fairies' blue eyes as they jingle in agreement. The pixies tighten their fists as they nod, bravery shining through the green in their eyes.

"I swear to you all that I won't let them have this place."

Each of them smile at me brightly, all of them putting faith in me and what I said. "In the meantime, a promise is a promise." I nod over towards Wanda's shop. "Just tell Wanda to put it on my tab. Get as much crystal dust as you need."

{Pixie dust is what gives fairies their magic. It's called pixie dust because pixies put the spell inside of the dust. Without the pixies, it would just be ordinary crystal dust.}

Hecca and Inias jump off my shoulder to slide down my arm until they are back on the cement.

{Pixies are a lot tougher than people think. Each pixie is filled with magic, even more than a witch.}

Agla, Dina, and Mihr fly past me, jingling as they talk to each other on their way to Wanda's. Hecca and Inias jump off the cement, landing on the ground as a golden aura surrounds them.

{They are hard to spot, so they use their magic to surround themselves with a bright light, that way others can see them and won't step on them.}

I watch as they go into Wanda's shop through the tiny doors on the top and bottom of the big door.

{When I first saw them going towards Wanda's shop, I went to open the door for them, but Wanda stopped me and told me to watch. The fairies opened their door on top while the pixies opened theirs on the bottom. After they were through and the doors closed, you couldn't even tell that they were even there to begin with.} I chuckle to myself.

{Hard to believe all of the things I've learned these past few weeks.}

I stand up, wiping the back of my pants off as I take a step away from the fountain.

"Hi, Kalma," a silky voice whispers behind my neck. Her breath sends a cold shiver down my spine.

{Speaking of learning.}

I quickly spin around to back away from them. Three women stand together, each of them with a sly grin on their face.

{Succubi.}

Husha stands on the left, wearing her usual short light blue jean shorts showing almost all of her long tan legs. Her black shirt has a very revealing V-neck, strings crisscrossing over top of her half-exposed breasts. Her long black hair sits on her head, tied tightly into a bun. She gazes at me with her dark brown eyes. I feel as small beads of sweat collect on the back of my neck. In the middle of the group is Deseih, the leader, the one that spoke to me. She has on her favorite outfit, a skintight black dress with lace designs down her arms and back. A medium-length blond braid lays over her shoulder and on her chest. Right beside it is a bright ruby sitting in the center of her chest. Below her dress are two perfectly tan and thin legs. She is the woman every man dreams of. Deseih gives me one of her smiles as her sapphire eyes bore into me. Sweat starts to form on my forehead. The third of their group is Nestra. Her outfit of the day is white short-shorts with a white body-hugging tank top, a tan see-through shawl around her shoulders. Nestra's brown, curly hair brushes against her shoulders with every movement she makes. Her legs are long and tan but have some muscle on them. She watches me with amusement dancing in her brown eyes. My body begins to shake as each of them stares me down.

{Succubus are female creatures who prey on men. They use their abnormally good looks and their hypnotic stare to lure men to them.

Once they are alone, she transforms into her actual skin. The color and pupils in their eyes disappear, leaving only the white behind. Their fingernails turn blood-red before growing into talons. As they kiss their victims, their blush-red lips change until they are paperwhite. This kiss allows them to suck the soul from the man. It is held until there is no more soul left to take. She leaves the man's corpse as she changes back into her beautiful body, ready to find the next victim.}

"What's the matter, Kalma?" Nestra chuckles.

"Cat got your tongue?" Husha laughs with her.

I take a deep breath, focusing on here and now, not on their hypnotic eyes. Fog begins to blur away the edges of my thoughts.

{I learned that they can affect me with their glare if I'm not careful. Luckily, Wanda was there when I discovered this. If she hadn't been there, they probably would have gotten me to go with them and they would've killed me. They don't want me for my soul since I don't have one. They want me for my flame. A demon's flame, if harvested correctly, can be a potent weapon for the one who took it.}

"You're not looking too good." Deseih grins. "Why don't you sit back down?" She sits on the cement ring, before patting the spot beside her.

My legs start to move, but I fight with them, forcing them to stay still. The fog continues to fill my head, making my resistance against their glares slip.

"Come on, Kalma. We won't hurt you," Nestra explains, sitting beside the empty spot saved for me.

"No need to be so nervous," Husha says as she sits beside Nestra.

Sweat rolls down my temple. My body screams at me to move as I lose myself in the fog.

"Let us take care of you, Kalma," Deseih says sweetly. "Let us show you how much we care since no one else will."

{No one cares for me.}

"That's it." Nestra smiles as I take a step towards them. "You can do it." I take another step.

"No one else loves you as we do," Husha explains with an alluring voice.

{No one else loves me.}

I take another step. Only a step remains between us.

"*I love you, Kalma.*"

Mal's voice rings through my head, forcing all of the fog out until I am back in control of my body.

{Mal loves me.}

My eyes focus on each of them as they continue to look at me. I can see power circling in each of their eyes, but I no longer feel the pull that I did a second ago. I smile as I push fire towards my hands.

{Thank you, Mal.}

I quickly lift my arms without giving them a chance to react. I slam my hands together with mini balls of fire in each palm. As the flames connect, a blinding light flashes out from my hands, causing them to scream as they cover their eyes. I jump away but keep one arm up as I build more fire into that hand.

"This is your final warning." Flames circle around my hand.

They all blink a few more times before looking at me. Their lips curled into ugly snarls, anger burning in all of their eyes.

"Don't come near Wanda or me again." My flames glow brighter. "Actually, leave everyone who comes here alone. If I find out that you tried to lure even one of these people, I will fry each of your asses until there's nothing left except ash."

HISSS! They hiss at me as they stand up.

"How did you fight off our stare?" Deseih questions. "It shouldn't be possible."

I smile as they take a step away from me. "Someone does love me." Shock covers their faces.

"Someone loves you, loves a demon?" Nestra asks in disbelief.

I nod. "She loves me with everything she has."

Husha laughs. "She must be pretty stupid to fall for a demon."

An intense boiling begins to rumble inside of me, making my

stomach feel tense and my body stiff. Smaller flames start to spit off of the main one around my hand. Husha continues to laugh as Nestra joins in.

"No one in their right mind would ever fall for something as soulless as a demon. She must be out of her mind."

I ball my hand into a fist. The fire begins to spin faster around it as the sweltering inside of me grows more assertive.

"That girl must have a death wish or something for thinking that she loves you," Deseih speaks up.

White flickers in my vision.

"Demons can't love. They can only kill."

They all laugh so hard that they grab onto their stomachs. Flames crawl up my arm until all of it is on fire. Husha is the first one to notice. She stops and stares at me with fear. She nudges Deseih. Desieh looks at me, her eyes growing wide with terror. Nestra notices that her teammates have stopped laughing. She looks at them before following their stare to me. Nestra takes a step away from me as her body trembles.

{I've never had this much heat coming from my flames before. Is what I'm feeling causing this to happen?}

"Now, now, Kalma. You know we are just messing with you, right?" Deseih pleads as she raises her hands.

The other two follow suit, raising theirs up as well. I narrow my eyes at them, making my fire spin around my whole arm.

"You don't want to do this," Husha says softly. I open my hand back up.

"Kalma, please! We're sorry!" Nestra exclaims.

The inferno moves back towards my palm until my whole hand is consumed.

{My flames have never been this intense before. I like the feeling of holding a raging blaze in my palm. I don't know what's going on for this to happen, but I can shut these bitches up thanks to whatever it is.}

"She does love me," I whisper as I bring my arm back getting ready to fire.

As I swing it forward, a green outline appears around my arm, forcing me to stop.

{Wanda.}

I hear as she runs up behind me.

"Kal, what are you doing?" she asks, worried, as she stops behind me. She looks at me and then my hand before glancing at the succubi.

"I'll put mine away if you put yours away." She gently lays her hand on my shoulder. I turn my head just enough to see her face. Beads of sweat lay on her forehead as her eyes flicker between her usual and her lit-up emerald. The boiling continues to swelter inside of me as I turn back towards the succubi.

{I want to burn them up so badly. I want them to pay for the horrible things that they said. I have never felt so strongly about hurting someone as I do right now.} My flames push up against Wanda's magic.

"Kal," Wanda says between her teeth.

{After what they said about me.}

I can feel my fire's warmth escaping through her barrier. "Kalma," Wanda speaks a little weaker than before.

The emerald begins to flicker around my arm.

{After what they said about Mal.}

My eyes start to burn as I glare at them. Their faces turn ghost white as they take a step back. My chest begins to burn fiercely with the same searing heat as the boiling. Wanda's grip on my shoulder loosens as her barrier barely glows.

{The boiling inside of me is screaming for me to do this. My demon side is telling me to end them.}

"We're sorry. We didn't mean what we said about your lover," Deseih speaks up. The blue burns hotter.

"You have to stop," Wanda explains weakly. "Don't let your anger have control over you."

{Anger?}

Wanda's barrier vanishes as her hand slips off my shoulder. "Mal wouldn't want this," she says very quietly.

I hear as she stumbles behind me.

{Wanda?}

I turn my head to look back at her. My fire vanishes, the boiling inside of me replaced by a sinking feeling. Wanda stumbles backward, sweat covering her face and her eyes looking but are out of focus and barely open. I watch as her eyes completely close before she starts to fall.

"Wanda!" I move quickly.

I catch her before she hits the ground.

"Wanda?" I say quietly as I cradle her head in my arm.

She lays in my arms, breathing heavily with her eyes still closed.

{I made her push her magic too far.} Tears fill my eyes as I look down at her.

{I'm so sorry.}

Footsteps echo off the cement. I look up as the succubi run as fast as they can away from me.

{What have I done?}

Using my free hand, I lay both of her arms on her stomach before wrapping my left arm under her back until my hand is on her shoulder farthest from me. I move my right arm until it is beneath both of her knees. I hold on tighter to her shoulder and her legs as I carefully stand up. She makes a slight groaning noise as she rolls her head until it is pressing up against me. Tears fall onto her stomach as they escape my eyes. I lift my head and look around to see if anyone saw what just happened.

{No one saw what I almost did. Thank goodness. It took me forever to gain all of their trust, and if they would've seen all of that, I would have lost everything I worked towards.}

I pull Wanda in closer to me as I carry her to her shop. I use my back and my elbow to open the door. As it closes behind me, I hear frantic jingling. I look up and see the fairies hovering all around the store. They all fly towards me as I hold Wanda close. All of them look at her with worry covering their faces. Agla looks at me before shrugging her shoulders.

"I made her use too much of her magic. She pushed herself too far because of me and she collapsed."

Agla nods sadly before looking back at Wanda. A quiet sob escapes my throat as I start walking through the store towards the back room. Loud chiming yells at me from the counter. I stop and look at the pixies standing on top. Hecca points to herself and then at Mihr, before pointing to the fairies who come up behind me. After she's done pointing at everyone, she points to Wanda.

"You want to help her?"

Hecca nods.

"How?"

She jingles up at the fairies. Once she is done, Dina moves to be in front of me. As she hovers in the air, she reaches into her pocket. She pulls dust out and sprinkles a little bit onto Wanda. I watch as the dust gently falls on Wanda's chest. The dust flashes green before disappearing.

{Did that dust just turn into Wanda's magic?} "The dust will restore her magic?"

Dina nods as she jingles.

"Will you have enough for her and all of you?"

They jingle to each other for a few seconds before Dina nods again. I smile at them. "Thank you."

They each smile at me. I watch as the fairies fly to the pixies on the table. The pixies hand each fairy a tiny sack. The fairies nod before taking the packs. They hover over until they are levitating above Wanda. Each of them opens the bag they were given before flipping them all upside down. I watch as a ton of pixie dust sprinkles onto Wanda. As each particle of dust settles on her, it quickly flashes green before vanishing. As more and more dust disappears, I notice Wanda starting to look better. The sweat on her face dries up, and the color returns to her face. The sinking feeling in my stomach starts to disappear as she gets better. The dust stops falling. I look up at the fairies, each of them smiling down at us. Wanda slightly moves her head against me.

"Kal?" she says softly.

I whip my head down to look at her. Her bright emerald eyes look up at me, both of them filled with magic. I smile down at her.

{It worked.}

The fairies chime above us. I look back up to see them waving as they head towards the door.

"Thank you so much, you guys."

They all wave at me before leaving. I smile before looking down at Wanda.

{She's pissed.}

Her arms are folded across her chest as she glares up at me with annoyance and disappointment.

"Have anything to say?" She taps her fingers on her arm.

"I'm sorry."

She shakes her head. "Not good enough."

"Umm."

"What were you thinking, Kal? You could have really killed them."

I don't say anything, knowing that what she said is true.

"I've never seen you like that before. I've never seen you lose control like that." Tears build back into my eyes.

"You got lost in your anger. You allowed your demon side to influence you. I've never seen you so..."

"Evil?" I finish for her as tears fall on her.

She looks up at me, shocked. "Kal, I never said—"

"You didn't have to." I sniffle.

I carefully bend down as I lower my right arm until her feet are on the ground. I lift her up with my left hand until she is standing straight. Once I know that she is stable, I turn away from her, too ashamed to look at her again.

"Kal, you know I would never call you evil."

"You might not, but after what just happened, I think that I am." I lift my hands to look at them. "I've never wanted to hurt someone before, especially not like that. I've only ever hurt people when defending myself or others, and even then I didn't want to do it. If you hadn't shown up when you did, there would be three piles of ashes for someone to sweep up." I make fists. "There was so much power, so much heat that I just got lost in it. I got lost in the sweltering and the power. At that moment, I wanted nothing more than to end them."

I turn around but don't look at her face. "I didn't even care that you were pushing yourself until it was too late. You passing out was the only reason I was able to stop."

"Exactly."

I look up at her, surprised.

"You stopped. You stopped when you knew that I needed you. Would someone evil do that?"

I think about it before shaking my head.

"Would an evil person be crying right now because of what they did?" she asks softly.

I wipe my face as I shake my head again.

"You are not evil, Kal. You just lost your temper."

"Earlier, you said I was angry."

She nods. "It's the same thing."

I tilt my head to the side, confused at what she said.

"Did you feel like your insides were burning? As if something was boiling inside of you, continuing to get hotter and hotter?"

I nod.

"It filled you up until all you wanted was to let it out and do what it wanted?"

I nod.

"That is anger. Anger is intense emotion that involve a strong uncomfortable and non-cooperative response to something someone says, different kinds of hurt, or when you are threatened. When people get angry, they experience different things: increased heart rate, high blood pressure, and high adrenaline levels. Since you are half demon, though, you are affected in different ways. Increased heart rate might be the heat of your flames increasing. High blood pressure could be how fast your fire moves. Adrenaline might be the power inside of you.

I don't really know how it messes with you because there isn't anyone like you. Anger can make you do stupid things very easily. It takes over your sense of right and wrong. Most of the time, those experiencing anger are unable to stop what they are doing until it is too late." Wanda reaches out and grabs my hands. "You might have only stopped because of me, but you still stopped. Some people wouldn't have cared what happened to me, but you did. Even through all of that anger, you were able to find you." She lets go of one of my hands before laying it on my chest on the crystal. "You are not evil, Kalma, there's no way that whatever is in here"—she presses more on my chest—"is evil."

"But I—"

She shakes her head. "Everyone loses their temper. Lord knows I have." She chuckles. "It just matters how you deal with it, and now that you know what it is and what it feels like, you can be more prepared for next time it happens."

"I don't want that to happen again. I don't ever want to feel like that."

"I know you don't, but sometimes you just can't help it," she explains as she gives me a sad smile. "You're feeling more and more human emotions. Each one will feel scary, and you will feel lost, but you are not alone. Mal and I will help you learn how to manage each emotion and identify what is what. You just have to allow yourself to feel and allow us to help."

"But what if I lose myself in them like I just did?"

"You'll have to learn how to keep your sense of self through it all."

I sigh.

"Do you want to know some tips that can help with anger?" I nod.

"Remember to take deep, calming breaths, in the nose out the mouth. Understand why you are getting angry and what you can do to stop it. Remind yourself of who you are and not what the rage wants you to be. Think about something that makes you happy or calm."

"So anger is something humans feel?"

Wanda smiles as she nods.

"So I really am starting to feel as humans do?"

She takes her hand off of my chest and lets go of my hand. "Seems that way."

"But how?"

She shakes her head. "I told you, you have to figure that out for yourself."

"Always hold out on the important stuff," I mumble in frustration.

She chuckles. "Now, why don't you tell me what happened out there."

Thinking about it causes the same anger to boil in my stomach.

{Calm down.}

I take a few deep breaths, reminding myself that it's over and nothing I can do about what happened except keep my cool now.

"How did you know to come out?"

"My magic sensed your flames. I knew that something wasn't right, so I ran to find you. Luckily, you were right outside and that I was fast enough to stop your arm."

"How did your magic sense me?"

She shrugs. "Maybe because of how connected we are, I honestly don't know. That's the first time I was ever able to sense another being besides other witches."

{Because of our bond her magic can feel my flames?}

I smile. "I guess that means you really will always be there for me."

She laughs. "I told you that I would be."

"You were right, you know."

"Well of course. I usually always am, but when do you mean?" She grins.

I chuckle. "When you said that Mal wouldn't want what I was doing."

She nods.

"Mal sees the good in me. She sees what I can be and not what others want me to be. She loves me for me. If she ever found out that I hurt someone, let alone killed someone who didn't deserve it, she would never forgive me."

Wanda smiles.

"So you were right."

"Always am."

"Thank you, Wanda. Once again, you saved me."

She blushes. "I'm here for you, Kal, no matter what. I'll always be ready to help you whenever you need it. Never forget that."

I nod. "I won't."

"Now, tell me everything," she demands as she grabs my shirt, pulling me towards the counter.

I laugh as we both sit on the two stools that are behind the counter.

15

"So Jade is just helping her figure out how to use her powers and what other abilities she might have?"

I nod. "That's what she said."

"Pretty messed up how she got Mal to awaken her powers, though."

"Yeah, no kidding." I rub the cauterized scar on my neck.

Wanda chuckles. "You have to admit, though, that it was pretty clever how she figured it out."

I roll my eyes. "I guess."

"Lighten up." She nudges me with her hand. "At least Mal has powers now. That's what you wanted, right?"

"Yeah," I say quietly.

"Then does it matter how?"

"No."

"In the meantime, you can find someone with info on what is going on."

"That's what the plan was until I got distracted."

{Stupid succubus.}

"Well, it's still the middle of the night. I'm sure there is someone around who can help."

"I hope so. I only saw the succubi, Uxum, Sukir, then the fairies and pixies. Everyone else must still be out or in one of the shops."

Wanda nods. "I'm sure there are more out there now."

"Hope so."

"Yo, Wanda!" someone yells.

We look towards the door as two boys and two girls walk in, all of whom look to be in their mid-twenties.

"Oh, hey, guys." Wanda waves.

They all walk up towards us. The first one to reach the counter is Derrick. He is tall with dark ginger hair and bright blue eyes, with little specks of white scattered throughout the irises. His body is athletically built but is lean as well. Freckles are dotted all over his pale skin. He is wearing black army boots, black jeans, a white shirt with a red, black, and white plaid long-sleeve button-up on top. Around his neck is a black cord with an opal crystal hanging from it.

{Opal helps to enhance cosmic energy, making his magic stronger. All witches and warlocks wear some type of crystal around their necks to aid them in different areas of magic.}

Beside Derrick is the other boy, Chayse. Chayse is a little bit taller than Derrick, but only by an inch or two. He also has dark ginger hair and pale skin with freckles. His body is medium built with muscles mixed in. Unlike Derrick, though, his eyes are spring green.

{Derrick and Chayse are brothers. According to Wanda, they are the only sibling warlocks to be born in almost a hundred years.}

Chayse is wearing black army boots, dark blue jeans, a black shirt under a varsity jacket. The central part of the jacket is red, but the sleeves are black. Around his neck is the same cord that Derrick has but with a turquoise crystal attached to it.

{Turquoise helps improve mental state, which aids in increasing different things like sensitivity, empathy, intuition, serenity, and positive thinking. It basically helps one to open themselves up more to the world, allowing them to sense more things around them.}

Beside Chayse is Melanie. She is a lot shorter than the boys, about my height, maybe an inch or so taller. The ends of her straight, dark auburn hair touch the tops of her shoulders. Her eyes are hazel. She has olive skin and is lean but with small muscles on her legs and arms. Her outfit consists of black tennis shoes, blue jeans, a gray shirt, with a fantastic-looking black leather jacket over top. The crystal she wears is a herderite.

{Herderites are said to unify the mind and spirit. Can enhance spiritualistic abilities and psychic visions. So it can help those who have the gift of foresight to see their images more clearly.}

The last girl is Barbara. Barbara is petite in height and weight, being smaller than the others. She has hazel eyes and short, curly strawberry-blond hair with rose-pale skin. She's wearing gray shoes, black jeans, and a gray pullover hoodie. A sapphire crystal hangs from her necklace.

{Sapphire is given to those who show a lot of loyalty to those that that person cares for. It is a very high honor to be given a sapphire.}

"How have you been?" Derrick asks.

"Same old same old I guess."

{They are some of the other witches and warlocks that live around here. Derrick is the leader of their coven. They've been trying to get Wanda to join them since before I started coming around.}

"Hey, Kal," Melanie says.

I just nod in acknowledgment.

{They are nice enough but aren't particularly fond of me or the fact that Wanda and I are friends. If they knew how she felt towards me, I don't know what they'd do.}

"What are you guys up to?" Barbara asks.

"Kal was looking for someone who might have information on what is going on below."

"Oh? Why don't you just go down there real quick and check?" Chayse wonders.

"I'm not exactly able to go home at the moment." I rub the back of my head nervously. "Let's just say much has happened, and everyone down there isn't too fond of me."

They look at me confused.

I shake my head. "Too much to get into right now, but I will tell you this, be prepared."

"For what?" Derrick questions.

"A battle."

Their expressions change to curiosity. Barbara opens her mouth.

"Like I said, too much to get into."

She closes her mouth as she nods.

"So, have any of you seen someone who might have some answers?" Wanda asks them.

No one says anything as they all think.

"The only one I can think of is Frikik," Melanie speaks up.

"Have you seen him yet tonight?" I wonder.

She shrugs. "Hard to tell. We can't exactly sense jinn very easily."

I sigh. "Sorry."

"It's all right." Derrick smiles.

{Jinn are beings that can change shape and size. They can form into any living creature that they want. When they aren't shifted into something, they are giant blobs of black, moving liquid. Can see why they want to stay shapeshifted into something else almost all of the time.}

"He usually comes in here around this time of night," Wanda explains.

"Oh yeah, I completely forgot he likes to come in for different parts from various creatures to study them." I snap my fingers as I remember.

"Ew," Barbara says as she makes a disgusted face.

I shrug. "It's how they learn, I guess."

She shivers as her face stays disgusted.

"So, what did you get in that he would come in for?" I question Wanda.

"Um, I think I picked up were some goblin nails this morning."

"Goblin nails?" Chayse asks.

Wanda nods. "Some like to use the nails to bind a goblin to them. I don't like the idea of what they are used for, but I need the money. I limit how many they can have, though."

"People use the strangest things to use with binding spells and potions," Melanie explains.

"Anyway, you said he should be here soon?" I ask Wanda.

"If he's coming, yes."

"How will you know that it is him, though, if he is shifted into something or someone?"

"I can sense his aura when he has become something else."

"How?" Chayse questions curiously.

"One of the perks of being a demon, I guess."

They all give me a look.

{They really don't like to be reminded of what I am. You'd think the ears, teeth, and nails would be a giveaway.}

"Oh, I completely forgot what we came in here for," Derrick speaks up. Wanda and I look at him as he leans in.

"Have you guys heard the news?" he whispers.

{Why is he whispering? We are the only ones in here.}

"No?" Wanda says.

Melanie leans in beside him. "I guess there's a hit out on a demon and angel hybrid."

My stomach flips, instantly making me feel like I'm going to be sick. I look over at Wanda as the same pressure from a few hours ago builds in my chest, and my hands begin to shake. Wanda turns to me, immediately seeing my reaction to what Melanie said.

She puts her hand on my knee. "Deep breaths." she tells me calmly.

{We have a hit out on us? Is Father really that desperate?}

The room begins to pulse around us as the thought of the other demons coming for us runs through my mind.

{They're going to go after Mal.}

My breathing picks up as an intense feeling of danger crashes into me. I jump up off the stool, causing it to slam into the wall behind me.

"Kal." Wanda stands up.

"What's going on?" Barbara asks.

Wanda raises a hand towards all of them, before moving it back towards me.

{They're going to kill her.}

My legs start to lose feeling as my knees begin to shake.

{I thought it was just going to be my father and the others. I thought I'd be able to protect her from them, but now everyone will be after us.}

A hammer pounds in my head. I place both my hands on my head as I back away from everyone.

{What if they all turn on us when they find out who exactly the hit is for?}

"Kalma." Wanda reaches out towards me.

I flinch away from her. My breathing is frantic now. Each breath becomes a gasp fighting for more air. The room starts to shrink in on me, making me feel like I'm caught in a trap.

{Someone is going to turn us in or try to catch us.}

I start to shake my head really fast. I start choking, my lungs burning for me to slow my breathing down. The lights seem to dim, making everything darker as I hold onto my head tighter.

"Kal, you have to calm down. You're hyperventilating," Wanda warns as she takes another step towards me.

{What if Wanda turns us in?} I step back.

"Kal, it's okay." She stops but holds her hand out towards me.

As I look at her hand, I stop moving. She doesn't move as she watches me. Her eyes give me the same look that she's always given me.

{She'd never want to hurt Mal or me.}

Taking my hands from my head, I step towards her. I am still breathing quickly as the room continues to darken.

"Kal, copy me," she orders me, before taking a deep breath in and out.

I do the same thing before she does it again, and I repeat. We go back and forth until I am almost breathing normally again.

"Good." She smiles at me.

I reach out, placing my hand in hers. She gently wraps her fingers around it before slowly pulling me in.

"Everything will be okay," she whispers as she hugs me.

My body trembles up against her. My knees are still shaking beneath me. "Wanda, what's going on?" I ask quietly.

"It's called a panic attack. It happens when someone becomes very frightened. Your whole body reacts to it. Hands, feet, legs, stomach, head, chest, all of it. Everything will feel weak but strong at the same time. Your body will feel heavy as the world seems to be falling in on you."

I nod against her shoulder.

"It's normal to feel afraid of things. It's just another emotion you have to learn to live with."

"How do you handle all of these different emotions, Wanda?"

She chuckles softly. "I've had them my whole life, Kal. I had to learn just like you what they are and what they do to me. Once I figured everything out, I was able to live with them. It takes a while. I'm twenty-one, and some days I still have difficulties with my emotions."

"Really?"

I feel as she nods. "Times when I am afraid, I feel as if the whole world is coming for me and there isn't anything I can do about it. My whole body shakes as those feelings overwhelm me."

"Then what?"

"I remind myself to keep breathing. There are things out there to be afraid of, but I can't get lost in it all. I have to keep living my life, no matter what dangers are there. If I let my fear control my life, I'd never be where and who I am today." She holds onto me tighter. "Kal, I know that things are getting worse, and you have every right to be scared, but you have to remind yourself not to run away from what scares you. Avoiding it will only give it more power."

"I don't understand."

"It's hard to explain. Fear is just something you have to learn to cope with. You have to have power over it before it overtakes you. You can never allow it to control you. You have to have the bravery to control it."

"So what you're saying is that everything happening to me right now is fear, and that if I don't overcome it that it can control me?"

"Something like that, yeah."

"How am I supposed to do that if I can't stop shaking?"

She pulls me away from her but keeps her hands on my shoulders. "Kal, you can do this. You are the bravest person I know."

I don't say anything.

"You're willing to die for Mal." She grips my shoulders tighter. "You're ready to face your father, knowing what that could mean." She moves her hands from my shoulders down my arms before grabbing my hands. "Kal, you want to take all of this on by yourself because you don't want Mal or me to get hurt. You don't want anyone to get hurt."

I move my eyes back and forth, trying to look into both of her emeralds.

"Don't you see, Kal?" She smiles at me. "All of that is bravery. All of those things are examples of overcoming your fears."

My legs stop shaking as I absorb her words.

"You already know how to control your fears. You've been doing it since you met Mal, and you didn't even realize you were."

I comb through my memories, looking for the faintest feelings that I am feeling right now.

{She's right. When I saw Mal, I was afraid of what she would think of me, but I pushed it aside and decided to try anyway. I was scared every day that Father or one of the others would discover what I was up to, and I would be severely punished for it, but I kept coming up here anyway. The day I saved Mal from that car, my body was telling me to go the other way, but I ran right to her without a second thought to save her. All of those months watching, I was pushing past my fears.}

I squeeze Wanda's hands.

{Even when I met Wanda I pushed past them. I was scared that she would hate me or attack me for being what I am and whose child I am. Although every part of me was telling me it was a bad idea, I still said hello. I put myself out there, knowing all the risks that could've come with it.}

I slowly smile at her.

{Fear has always been there, even if I didn't realize it. It's been trying to get at me for months, but I was stronger. I am stronger.}

"You're right," I say quietly.

Her smile grows wider. "I told you I always am."

"Ever since that first day, I've been scared of something, but I didn't let those feelings stop me. From the first time I saw Mal, the first time I saw you."

Her eyes grow in surprise.

"All the way up till I decided I would die for her, that I would fight and die for everyone. I knew all the consequences and risks, but I pushed and pushed." Wanda nods, still smiling at me.

"I am afraid, but that doesn't mean I'll stop pushing."

My legs and arms stop shaking as I take a deep breath pushing all of the fear aside.

"I'm worried about what the future holds for all of us, but I'm going to fight to make sure that none of that happens. I will protect you and Mal and save everyone, even knowing the consequences of doing so. The idea of fighting against my father is the scariest thing of all, but I'm still going to do it. I won't let my fear win and I won't let them win, either."

I give Wanda a bigger smile as the rest of my fear shrinks and moves aside. Wanda nods at me as she gives my hands another squeeze.

{If I want to protect them and stop the demons, then I can never be afraid like that again.}

"Lovely speech, Kalma," a man says by the door.

My body tenses back up as I turn towards the door. I let go of Wanda's hands. The second they are out of hers, they blaze to life. My vision tunnels until all I can see is the figure inside the door wearing a business suit with a red tie.

"Why are you looking at me like that? I figured you would be happy to see me." He smiles, revealing his sharp canines, while his red eyes study me.

16

I protectively step in front of Wanda, using my body to shield her as my hands grow hotter.

"Kal?" she softly asks behind me.

I don't answer her as I stare him down.

{How did he get in here? The barrier should've kept him out.}

The others watch me as they stand looking back and forth between the man and me.

"Kalma, what is with the hostility? And what's with the new flames?" He grins as his crimson eyes sparkle.

"How did you get in here?" I ask coldly.

"Through the front like everyone else." He takes a step towards me.

I raise both my arms up, pushing more power into my flames. The fire covers all of my fingers and part of my palms.

{I wish I could get the same power I had when I was angry at the succubi. Even then, though, I don't think it'd be enough.}

"Easy, Kalma." He stops.

"Kal," Wanda says as she touches my back.

"Hello, Wanda." He smiles.

White flashes in my vision as blue crawls up my arms. Anger boils inside of me as fear swirls in my head.

"How do you know her name?" I ask angrily through my teeth.

He tilts his head in confusion. "What kind of question is that?" He steps towards me again.

I plant my feet firmly on the ground, blocking his view of Wanda.

{My fire isn't going to be enough, not even with this much power.} "Wanda, get out of here," I say quietly.

"What?"

"You and the others need to leave now before it's too late."

"Kal, I don't understand. What is going on? Who is that?"

I tighten my jaw as I stare the man down while he continues to walk towards us. "Kalma, I don't know what I did for you to be acting like this, but please stop before you do something we'll both regret."

I coldly chuckle. "You don't know what you did?" He stops a few feet away as he shakes his head.

"Why don't we start with the fact that you lied to me my whole life. Not telling me what I really am?"

"GASP!"

I can feel Wanda's hand on my back begin to shake.

{I hoped she would never have to see the monster that helped create me.}

"What are you talking about?" Father asks.

"Quit playing dumb. You know exactly what I mean!" I exclaim.

He doesn't say anything as he watches my flames flicker violently around my arms and hands.

I grit my teeth. "I'm just a tool for you to use whenever you want!" I yell through my teeth. "I was made to be your weapon, your daughter, the hybrid!"

His eyes grow in surprise. Out of the corner of my eye, I see the others look at me shocked.

He looks down at himself. "Now I see what is going on." He lifts his head. "Kalma, I didn't know that this was—"

"Save it! I know everything." I ball my hands, causing the flames to dance rapidly.

Father holds his hands up. "Kalma, listen to me. I'm not—"

"I'm done listening to you." I ignite my feet, getting ready to pounce. "Wanda, run!" I press hard off of the floor, making the wood splinter as I launch myself at him.

{Forgive me, Mal.}

He dodges just as I'm about to strike him. My hand goes into the shelf he was standing in front of.

"Kalma, don't make me do this because I really hate using it."

I ignore him. I swing my leg at him, my foot ablaze. He ducks backward, and I watch as my leg swings right over him. I pull my hand out of the shelf as my foot lands back on the ground. I quickly spin back around to face him.

"Kalma," he warns.

I shake my head. "I said I'd fight you no matter the consequences, and I meant it."

"I'm not the one you want to fight. Please allow me to explain."

{Please?}

A flicker of doubt flashes in my head, but I push it aside before building the flames back up around my arms.

"You're going to make me use it, aren't you?"

The floor begins to crack as more fire circles around my feet.

{Have to protect them.}

My internal flame bursts inside of me. All of my flames double in size.

{No matter what.}

He sighs. "Damnit, Kalma."

I spring off of the ground. I raise my hands, putting them together, making the fire more intense and powerful.

{I hope the others got away because this blast is going to destroy the whole place.} As I'm coming back down, I throw my hands quickly towards him.

"Sorry, Kalma, I tried to warn you."

Before I even have time to respond, both of his hands are on me. One is on my stomach, the other my chest. My flames immediately go out, but I still hover in the air above him.

{What did he just do?}

I quickly turn my head and see Wanda standing where I left her. I turn back towards my father to see him looking at Wanda as well.

{No.}

"Perfect spot." He looks back at me. "Sorry, but you know once I start this I have to complete it." He looks at his hands.

I lower my chin to look at them too. He turns both of his hands, one clockwise and one counterclockwise. Both of them start to glow black as he makes them into fists.

{This aura.}

Surprise bolts through me.

{I was so shocked by his appearance that I didn't read his aura.} His fists turn back to their original positions.

{This is going to hurt, a lot.}

He looks at me with an empathetic look before his energy slams into me, knocking the wind out of me and saliva to shoot from my mouth. I go flying backward in the air.

{This whole time, that was Frikik. If I had calmed down, I would've realized it sooner. If I had been paying attention to his words, I would have known. He was using contractions when he was speaking. Father doesn't use them.}

I keep flying through the air.

{He was trying to warn me about this, telling me to stop. I didn't listen and look where I am. Jinn have one attack, but it is very strong. A concussive blow takes in whatever energy the attacker is using and turns it against them, which I was using a lot. The only way to avoid their attack is to dodge it, but if they get their hands on you, well...}

Pain radiates from my chest and ribs as I begin to fall back towards the ground.

{Feels like he cracked a few ribs.}

I close my eyes, awaiting the impact.

{Plus whatever this landing does to me.}

"KAL!" Wanda yells as pain erupts all over my back before everything goes dark.

17

"Damn it, Frikik, why'd you have to strike her so hard?" Wanda's voice echoes somewhere in the darkness.

"It's not my fault. I tried to warn her." Frikik's voice responds.

{He doesn't sound like Father anymore.}

"Well, you didn't have to slam her into the counter," I hear as pieces of wood hit the floor.

"Yeah, that one was an accident. I was trying to aim for you. Figured you'd either catch her or use your magic to catch her."

"The counter isn't me," Wanda snarls.

"I said it was an accident, jeez."

Pressure is taken off of my stomach and chest. "Kal," Wanda says urgently.

"Crap," Frikik speaks softly.

{Ow! What is that pain?}

Burning throbs of pain come from my lower right abdominal. "She heals fast, right?" he wonders, sounding worried.

"She can't while it's still in there," Wanda explains frantically.

{Why does this keep happening to me? I swear I've been injured or weakened more in the last few days than I've ever been in my whole life.}

More wood echoes off of the floor. I feel as two hands lift my back up. My head hangs back until something soft presses up against me.

"Wanda, how bad is she?" I hear Melanie ask.

{They're still here?}

"Not too bad, but not good either," Wanda's voice explains above me.

{I'm against her.}

"How can we help?" Chayse offers.

"We need to get this big sliver of wood out of her gut so she can heal properly, or she'll bleed out."

"She's a demon. She can't bleed out," Barbara explains.

"But hybrids can," Derrick speaks up.

No one says anything.

{They all heard what I said to Frikik when I thought he was my father.} "So what can we—" Derrick starts.

"Kal!"

I hear as the door crashes against the wall.

{Mal?}

Footsteps race towards me until they stop right beside me.

"Mal, what, how did you know something happened?" Wanda asks, surprised.

"I don't know. I just had a feeling that something was wrong."

{Did her powers tell her, or was it something else? Both her and Wanda have been able to sense me. Is that what having strong bonds do?}

"What happened?" Mal asks frantically.

"It was an accident," Frikik speaks up.

"Who are you?"

"We'll explain later," Wanda interrupts. "Right now, we need to get this piece of wood out of her."

{That doesn't sound fun.}

Wanda's arms slide under my arms. "On three, we lift her."

I feel different hands slide under other parts of me. Someone stands on both sides of me, each with their hands under my hips. Two more people hold my legs. "All right, on three. One...two...three."

All the hands grab on tighter as they lift. Excruciating pain shoots from the spot on my side as it pulls. I open my mouth to scream, but instead, warm liquid shoots out.

"Kalma!" Mal yells.

Everyone stops pulling on me.

"Crap, the piece is still attached to the floor," Wanda explains. "Derrick, hurry and break it off before it does any more damage."

"Got it."

SNAP!

Some of the pulling releases, but the pain remains.

"To the bed," Wanda instructs.

I feel as they move me. "On her unwounded side."

They lay me down on the side that doesn't hurt. All of the hands disappear. "Now what?" Mal wonders.

"The not-so-fun part," Frikik answers.

"Melanie, can you go to the bathroom and grab some towels?" Wanda asks her.

"Yeah," Melanie answers.

Her footsteps quickly fade away.

"Barbara, go down the hall into the room in the back. On the dresser are a few shirts. Can you grab one?"

"Yes," Barbara says before her footsteps disappear.

RIIIIIIP!

A breeze hits my lower stomach and back.

{Did she just rip my shirt in half?}

"Frikik, I need you to hold her legs down as tightly as you can."

Hands press against my ankles.

"Why?"

"Because once I start pushing this out, she is going to want to move away from the pain, and if she moves too much, it'll cause more damage."

"What about us?" Chayse speaks up.

"Chayse, once Melanie gets back with the towels, I need you two to be ready to press them against the wound as soon as the wood is out."

"Got it."

"And me?" Derrick asks.

"How good is your control?"

"Very good," he says confidently.

"Then I need you to use your magic and try to wrap it around the splinters on the wood so none of them break off into her body. Can you do that?"

"Definitely," he says determinedly.

"All right."

"We got the stuff," Melanie exclaims, as two pairs of footsteps echo back into the room.

{Wanda really knows what she is doing. I guess that's why she's a healing witch.}

"Okay. Melanie and Chayse grab a towel and get ready. Barbara stay back until we need the shirt. Frikik, hold on tight, and Derrick focus on the splinters."

"What do you want me to do, Wanda?" Mal speaks up.

"Keep her as calm as you can."

"But she's not conscious."

"She will be once I start."

A hand gently runs through my hair. "I got you, Kalma," Mal whispers.

{This is really going to suck. Some of my body has healed around the sliver. So when Wanda pushes, everything that has healed will be ripped back open. It will feel as if I'm being impaled all over again. I wish I was utterly unconscious like I was when it pierced me.}

"Here we go." Pressure rests on the wood. "Everyone ready?"

"Yes," they answer.

"Okay, starting to push...now!"

Agonizing pain explodes in my side, making my whole body tense up. I try to pull away from Wanda, but Frikik holds my legs still. More pressure pushes against the wood, causing the first new tear. I clench my jaw so hard that it pops. Blood flows down my side from the wound.

"Barbara, grab one of those extra towels and bring it over here!"

"Got one."

"Put it under the wound and hold it there."

Fabric tickles against my back. More pain erupts as Wanda pushes more. I scrunch my face from the pain as sweat starts to form all over my face and neck.

"She's sweating," Mal says. "She's in pain," Melanie explains.

"I'm sorry, Kal," Wanda says as she pushes again.

A few more tears radiate up my body. I open my eyes. Mal crouches, her face even with mine but about a foot away as she watches Wanda. She has one hand on my head and the other on my shoulder with my shirt balled in her palm. My hands lay together on the bed in front of me. I see Mal flinching as Wanda pushes again. Everything spins as the wound continues to reopen.

{I was right...this isn't fun.}

I weakly slide my hand over to Mal until I can touch her. I run the tips of my fingers against her chin. She jumps in surprise before turning to look at me. "Hey." I smile weakly.

She moves her hand that was on my shoulder to my face, cupping my cheek in her palm. "Hey." She ruffles my hair with her other hand. "I thought I told you not to do anything stupid," she jokes.

I laugh painfully as the wood inches forward.

"Technically, I didn't." I take a deep breath. "This is all Frikik's fault."

She shakes her head with a small smile. "I'm going to put you inside of a bubble if you keep this up. You keep getting yourself hurt."

I jump as a stabbing pain shoots through my stomach. "I know, and I'm sorry."

She rubs her thumb against my cheek. "Nothing to be sorry for. I understand why you do the things you do that make you end up like this."

"Oh?" I close one eye as my body shivers with pain.

"You want to save everyone, even if it means you get hurt in the process." I open my eye surprised at her.

{She really does know.}

"But that doesn't mean I'm not serious about the bubble." She laughs.

I smile at her. "If you put me in a bubble, how can we be together? Can't exactly be in a relationship while I'm stuck inside of one."

My cheeks and ears burn as her cheeks turn red.

{Did I just say what I think I said?}

My whole body trembles while burning circles around the inside of my wound as the wood slightly moves. All the heat I had in my face disappears and is replaced by cold sweat.

"Kal?" Mal asks worriedly.

Warm fluid quickly races up my throat. COUGH! COUGH!

Red splotches land on the bed. Mal's eyes grow with fear. "Wanda."

The pressure stops for a second. "Shit."

"What's going on?" Derricks asks.

"The tip of her lung must have been nicked and the blood is seeping into it."

COUGH! COUGH!

More blood splatters in front of me. "We need to get this out, now."

My lung starts to feel heavier as the seconds pass.

{Hurry.}

"Frikik, hold as tightly as possible, even if you think you are hurting her. Derrick, I need you to focus on holding all of the splinters in. Chayse, Melanie, be ready. Barbara, don't move the towel." I hear as she takes a deep breath. "Mal, hold her down as much as you can. Keep her distracted."

Mal nods as she moves her hand back to my shoulder, gripping onto it tightly. She looks at me, worried.

"I'm sorry, Kal, but I have to push it out now before your lung fills with blood," Wanda explains.

{I know.}

She takes another deep breath. Wanda begins to force the piece to slide faster. Everything goes numb except the pain surrounding that spot. I hold my breath, trying not to scream. The room spins and flickers while Wanda keeps pushing. "Hey." Mal moves closer to me. "Keep your eyes open okay?"

I slowly nod even as my head begins to swoon.

"Can I ask you a favor?"

I nod again.

"Will you train with me later?"

I look at her, surprised.

"Jade and I have made a lot of progress, and I want to show you what I can do now." She smiles at me nervously.

{She wants me to train with her?}

As I go to answer, the wood jerks forward, and I can no longer stop myself from giving in to the pain.

"AHHHHHHHH!" I scream as I close my eyes.

{This is just as bad as the torture I received from Father while we were training.} I try to move my legs, but they are still being held, so I try to sit up, but Mal pushes me back down.

The wood slides more. "AHHHHHHHH!"

Cold sweat rolls down my face from all of the pain. "We're almost there, Kal. Hang in there," Wanda tells me.

My breathing quickens, causing more blood to shoot up my throat. COUGH!

I can feel it as it flies out of my mouth.

"AHHHHHHHH!"

"Hey, hey. Shhhhhhh. It's okay. I got you," Mal says softly as she presses her forehead against mine.

I slowly open my eyes, meeting her stare. Her sky-blue eyes invite me to fall into them to distract me from the pain.

"Shhhhhh. It's almost done," she whispers.

The sliver moves, making me want to scream, but I'm too lost in her eyes to open my mouth.

{How does she do it? Even though I'm in excruciating pain, she still makes me feel as if everything is okay.}

"It's going to be okay."

As I continue to lose myself in her sky blues, I catch a glimpse of a small ring around both of her irises.

{It's the same color as the energy she used earlier. Is it because she awakened her angelic side?}

I move my hand to the side of her face, cupping her cheek in my palm. She leans her head into my hand but doesn't take her eyes off of me.

{I thought her eyes couldn't get any more beautiful...I guess I was wrong.}

She smiles at me as I run my fingers through the hair on the back of her neck.

{You really do make the world better even at the worst of times.}

My whole body jerks just before the piece of wood crashes on the ground. "Towels. Now."

Fabric presses on my stomach as Melanie and Chayse press them against the wound the best they can without going into the hole itself.

{I'm already starting to heal.}

"All done," Mal says softly, as she takes her hand from my shoulder and puts it on top of my hand on her face.

"Thank you."

"For what?"

"Being here."

Her face lights up again. "You don't ever have to thank me for that."

"I might not have to, but I'm always going to."

The heat from my internal flame races towards my wound, slowly healing it from the inside out.

{I'd say it should take about twenty minutes tops until the wound is closed.} Wanda comes into my line of sight. Mal lets go of my hand as I take it from her face. She stands but doesn't remove her other hand from my hair.

"How are you feeling?" Wanda asks as she wipes my blood off of her hands onto a clean towel.

I nod. "Better. Thank you."

"Now, can you please stop making me worry so much? All of this stress is going to turn my hair white." She chuckles.

I laugh. "Have to keep you on your toes somehow."

"Pick a different method." She smiles at me.

I nod.

CREEAAK!

Wanda and Mal turn around, creating a small gap that I can see through. Frikik stands as still as a statue as we all glare at him. His form is different from what it was before. He looks like a typical male human with brown hair and brown eyes, wearing regular jeans and a blue shirt.

"And where is it that you think you are running off to?" Wanda throws the towel onto the bed before crossing her arms over her chest.

"Umm, just thought I'd get some fresh air." He grins nervously.

Wanda shakes her head,. "After the stunt you just pulled, you aren't going anywhere until I say you can."

I chuckle at the face he gives her.

{Frikik isn't like the other jinn. He is carefree and fun to hang around. He loves to crack jokes to make people laugh. I know that he didn't mean to do this to me. He hates having to hurt anyone.}

"I'm sorry, Frikik," I say as I slowly pull myself upright.

Mal quickly turns as she takes her hand from my hair to help me sit the rest of the way up.

"Kal, you have nothing to apologize for," Wanda tells me as she leans against the bed.

Mal sits up on the bed beside me, careful not to sit on the spattered blood. I nonchalantly wrap my arm around her, pulling her closer to me. Her face turns as red as an apple as I do so. I feel as my ears begin to burn.

"I shouldn't have attacked you."

Frikik looks at me. "It's my fault, Kalma. I shouldn't have come in looking like that. If I would've known."

"Exactly. If you would've known, but you didn't, because I never told you who my father is, and I didn't tell anyone what he looks like.

So how were you supposed to know that coming in here with your form looking like him would set me off?"

He doesn't say anything.

"So none of this is your fault. I reacted without thinking. I should have listened to you more so I could see that you weren't really him."

"Wait."

I look at Mal.

"So, what happened?"

"Frikik is a jinn. They are shapeshifters. Frikik came in to see Wanda, but his form was my father. He tried to tell me repeatedly that he wasn't who I thought he was, but I didn't listen, so I attacked. So, he did the only thing that he could do to stop me. He used his attack, which sent me flying into the counter, and well, you know the rest."

"No one knows what your father looks like?"

I shake my head. "Those who live up here, no, they don't."

Mal nods.

"Would you really attack your father like that?" Melanie speaks up.

I look over towards the group standing between Frikik and Wanda. I nod. "Without hesitation."

"But he's your dad. He may be a demon, but even demons love their kids," Barbara explains.

Memories of my father flash through my head. Of all the years of torture he put me through, the abuse I endured, the endless amounts of training, never any kind words to be said, no signs of affection. The same look in his eyes every day for years. The look that he owns me and I am his to be used however he wishes.

{I was never his daughter. I was just a weapon he could flaunt around to everyone.} I clench my hand that isn't around Mal. "I may share DNA with him, but he is NOT my father. He was never my father, and I was never his daughter."

"I don't understand. Then what are you?" Chayse asks.

"I am just a tool for him to use and control."

Everyone looks at me with sympathy covering their faces.

{Wanda is the only one who knows how he treated me.}

I give them all a fake smile. "I'm his weapon, nothing more."

{For as long as I can remember, I've only ever felt like a piece of furniture when Father was to talk about me. He would never say my name unless he had to. It was always *her* or *my daughter*. I was just something he owned.}

"His weapon, his tool, his sacrificial piece to be used whenever he sees fit, his toy. I was just a hybrid to him."

Pressure builds in my throat and behind my eyes.

{I will not cry because of him. I am stronger than that now. I have to be.}

"But you're not."

I face Mal again, putting away my fake smile.

"You are not just those things, Kalma. You are so much more." She puts her hand on my chest. "This is so much more."

"She's right, Kal," Wanda speaks up. I look at her as she smiles at me.

"You are not just a weapon or tool to be used. You are a person. An extraordinary person."

"You're not just a demon either."

I turn back to Mal.

"You're not just a hybrid. You are caring, protective, funny, brave, determined, selfless, and so much more."

"You feel just like the rest of us do," Wanda explains. "I've seen you happy, sad, scared, angry, and everything in between. You are not just a thing."

Mal presses against my chest. "A weapon, a tool would not be able to feel the things that you do." Mal smiles brightly. "I wouldn't have been able to fall in love with just a weapon."

BA-DUM.

Her smile widens. "I fell in love with you, Kalma. I fell in love with YOU."

Mal's eyes sparkle as she watches me. The warmth I've come to crave fills my chest.

BA-DUM, BA-DUM, BA-DUM.

"And you have so much more in you to find." She laughs softly.

{Huh?}

"So don't you ever say you are just a weapon, or a tool, or just a hybrid," Wanda demands. "You are my best friend, Kal. You are my family."

My head turns to Wanda to see her smiling at me brightly. My ears burn.

"Kalma."

I spin back to Mal.

"YOU are the one in my heart. If you weren't you, then you'd never have gotten in there."

Tears slip down my face.

"So please don't ever say that you are just something for someone to use, because I love you too much to allow you to say those things." Her eyes glisten. "If I have to remind you every day who you are so you don't ever feel this way again, then so be it, I will."

{Malak.}

BA-DUM, BA-DUM.

She chuckles as she presses harder onto my chest. "You are not just a thing," she whispers.

Her eyes flicker between mine as she smiles warmly at me.

"Okay?" she asks me.

I use my free hand to wipe the tears from my face as I nod.

"Thank you, Malak." I reach out and grab Wanda's hand. "Thank you both."

Wanda nods.

"My whole life, I've felt like I didn't matter. That if it wasn't what Father wanted, then it didn't matter." I squeeze Wanda's hand as I pull Mal closer against me. "Thanks to you two, I can finally feel like I matter and the things I say and do matter. I can finally start..." More tears run down as I give them a genuine smile filled with happiness.

BA-DUM, BA-DUM.

{The throbbing keeps getting stronger with every beat. What is going on inside of me?}

"Living."

Wanda returns my squeeze as Mal lays her head against my shoulder.

{Without them, I don't know where I'd be. I probably would've just stayed under Father's thumb doing everything he demanded me to do. I would've remained his weapon, fulfilling my duties as a demon hybrid.}

"Wow, that was just..." someone sniffles.

All three of us turn our heads towards the witches and warlocks. They stand there with tears on their faces. Some of them hold tissues in their hands.

"That was so beautiful," Barbara says as she blows her nose into her tissue.

"The connection that you three have is so strong," Melanie explains as she wipes her face with hers.

"A human falling in love with a demon, hybrid or not, is just..." Chayse says as he wipes his face with his hand.

"What they said is true, Kal. You are more than just a demon. I am sorry that we didn't see it sooner," Derrick apologizes as he uses his sleeve to wipe his face.

"They are all right, Kalma," Frikik speaks up.

I look at him.

"You aren't just a demon. You aren't just a hybrid. You are something else entirely." He smiles at me. "You're something special." He winks.

"That she is," Mal says before leaning farther into me.

I smile at them all as they wipe away the rest of their tears.

18

"Let's take a look at that wound," Wanda explains as she lets go of my hand.

She turns so she is facing my body. Using both of her hands, she carefully lifts the towel.

{My timetable was right.}

The inside part of the wound has healed. I can no longer see through myself anymore. The muscles and skin still have yet to recover.

"Another ten minutes or so?" Wanda asks me.

I nod. She returns my nod before putting the towel back over. Something clicks together in my head.

I turn back towards Frikik. "How did you get my father's appearance?" Everyone turns towards him as he looks at me.

"I saw him during my latest assignment."

{Frikik is a spy, if that's what you call it. He transforms into different kinds of demons and creatures to infiltrate them to learn what they are doing so he can warn those in danger.}

"What was the assignment?" Wanda questions.

"To see what all the fuss is about down below and why so many demons are coming up."

{The plan is still in motion.}

"What did you learn?" I quickly ask him.

"Nothing good. Demons worldwide are moving in on the oldest

churches in each state capital, plus the oldest ones in countries all over the world. They plan on destroying them all to weaken the angels and the archangels' hold on this world so they can bring Hell up here."

{They're really going through with it.}

"Wait," Derrick speaks up, "Kal, you said earlier to be prepared for battle. Is this what you meant?"

I sigh as I nod.

"You knew?" Melanie asks shocked.

"I was one of the first ones to know."

"Then why didn't you do anything?" Chayse wonders.

"She did," Wanda defends me. "She told the angels as soon as she could." No one says anything.

"It's not just the churches we have to worry about, though," Frikik interrupts. "They are killing all of the angel hybrids as well."

My grip on Mal tightens as I clench my jaw.

"So the hit that we heard about. That's the hybrid they are going after...?" Chayse questions.

"I guess," Frikik answers.

"Then why does it say demon hybrid as well?" Derrick asks.

Frikik shrugs.

"Because I disobeyed a direct order."

They all look at me.

"I saved the hybrid that I was sent to kill."

Mal's fingers lace between mine as she grabs my hand.

Derrick's eyes move to Mal's hand in mine before opening wide. "You're the angel hybrid?" He points at Mal.

"I am."

"So the hit is on the two of you? They want you both dead?"

I nod.

"Oh man," Chayse says.

They stand and stare as Mal continues to lean against me her hand in mine. Melanie smiles. "A demon and an angel together."

My cheeks burn.

"Who would've thought?" Barbara gives us a big smile.

"Not just together," Derrick explains, "they love each other."

BA-DUM.

I flinch at the sudden pound in my chest.

{That one hurt.}

Mal smiles at them.

"So, you're the ones they put things on hold for?" Frikik explains. Everyone's smiles disappear as we all turn back towards him.

"What do you mean?" I ask him.

"Pennsylvania is the only state that hasn't been activated. Everywhere else, the churches are being attacked."

"Why not here?"

"Because of you two."

Mal's grip tightens on my hand.

"They want you both dead before they start." He looks at me. "Your father wants you both dead."

A cold shiver runs down my spine.

{He was serious about killing me.}

"They just pressed pause on everything until they get them?" Wanda speaks up worried.

"So if we keep them here, then they won't..." Barbara starts.

Frikik shakes his head. "I guess they were only given a few days to hunt for them. After that, they have to move on with the plan."

"How long?" I sit up a little.

"They wanted to be asses about it, so they picked Hallowed End. The second it turns midnight on Hallowed End, the church will be attacked."

I can see as everyone goes still, except Mal as she looks up at me confused.

{Hallowed End. That's only a few days away. We have two full days and one whole night plus the half of night we have left tonight and the short amount of night we have before midnight. Is that going to be enough time?}

"Kal, what is Hallowed End?"

"You know it as Halloween," I numbly answer. Mal's face goes white as panic rises in her eyes.

"That's only a few days away," Wanda says, breaking from her daze first.

"We have to warn everyone," Barbara speaks.

"And tell them what?" Derrick asks. "That the whole world is about to fall under the command of Lucifer and his demons? What good would that do? They'll all just panic."

No one says anything.

I take a deep breath. "Or we can tell them to fight." Everyone's heads whip to look at me.

"You want them to fight?" Melanie questions.

"I don't want anyone to have to fight, but I know that no one wants to lose either. If we can get creatures of all kinds to help fight against the demons, then maybe we can stop them."

Derrick shakes his head. "No one will want to fight. They've spent years hiding from everyone. Avoiding violence as much as possible, living their lives peacefully."

"All of that will come to an end once the demons take over. So they can choose between running with their tails between their legs and end up losing anyway. Or help fight for the lives that they want to continue to have. At least in one of those scenarios do we have a better chance of winning."

"And if we don't?" Chayse says.

"Then, at least we know that we tried. I'd rather go down fighting for what I care about than not trying at all."

Wanda grins at me proudly.

"The moment I heard what my father and the others had planned, every part of me knew that I had to fight." I squeeze Mal's hand. "Not just for Mal but for everyone else as well. I have always planned on going out on that battlefield to fight with everything I have to give. I know that I could die, but at least I can die knowing that I didn't run.

That I stood up for what I believe in and for." I look at Mal; her eyes meet mine. "The ones I want to protect."

She smiles at me.

I look back at the others. "And I'm sure there are plenty out there who will feel the same. They will want to fight to save those they care for." Bravery and courage rumble inside of me. "I believe that when people are protecting those that they really care about, then they can become as strong as they can be. I know that I will give my full flame to protect those I care for."

Mal and Wanda are grinning at me proudly, knowing that what I speak is true. "Wouldn't you fight to try to save those who are precious to you?" I ask them. All of them stare at me.

"I will."

We all turn to see Jade leaning against the door frame.

"How long have you been there?" Mal asks her.

"Long enough to hear Kal's whole speech." She steps into the room. "She is absolutely right. People will want to fight for the ones they love no matter the consequences."

"How do you know?" Derrick questions.

Jade stops in the middle of us before turning to face Derrick and the others. "Because I know hundreds who did just that."

They look at her, shocked.

"Every guardian angel is someone who gave up their life to save the ones that they love."

{The angels wouldn't even stop to think about what to do. Every single one of them will dive into the fire to save lives.}

"Angels all over the world are doing just that right now."

"What?" I say.

"I just got word from the others. Churches are already falling. Angels are trying to stop the demons, but most of them have been wiped out and failed so far."

"So why do you think here will be any different?" Chayse asks scared.

"Because no one gave the other creatures the option to fight with them. By the time the battle had already begun, it was too late." Jade looks at me. "You want to give them the option to try to stop the demons alongside us?"

I nod.

"Then that's what we're going to do." She nods.

"But how?" Mal questions her. "We don't have enough time to warn everyone and ask them to help."

Jade grins at Mal. "Leave that to us angels." She looks at me. "Your words will be of great help."

"You want me to go with you to talk to everyone?" I ask stunned.

She shakes her head. "Not exactly." She puts her hand into her pocket before pulling something out of it. "These are hologram message receivers. These are what we use to receive messages from the archangels, and they are what allow us to talk to them and other angels."

Laying in her palm is a translucent, flat circle with wings carved into the center. "So you just have to record me and everything I say will be sent to all the other angels?"

"Yes and no."

I stare at her, confused.

"You will have to be recorded but..." She puts the disk back into her pocket. "I won't be the one recording you."

"Huh?"

"The disks can only communicate with one other disk, not multiple, and definitely not all of them."

"So how are we going to send the message, then?"

Jade folds her arms. "The only ones who can create messages that can be sent to all disks are the archs."

{The archs?}

I raise my eyebrows with surprise. "No, no, no. You're crazy if you think I'm doing that."

"It's the only way to record your words."

I shake my head. "Not happening."

"What? What does she want you to do?" Mal speaks up.

"She wants me to speak with the archangels."

GASP!

Everyone looks at Jade with shock.

She sighs. "Kal, everything you just said about how you are willing to fight even though you are a demon, even though you might die, how protecting something important can make one strong and that we should all stand up and fight, not run away. Everything you said can help ignite bravery in everyone. Hearing your words, especially coming from you, can impact them a lot."

"Why coming from me?"

"You're the daughter of the second-in-command. You are a hybrid. You are ready to lay down your life for this, and most importantly." She takes a step closer. "Once they see how unique you are, they will believe everything that you say."

"How will they see that?"

Jade smiles. "The fire you have in your eyes when you talk about defending the ones you care about and the look you get when you look at Mal."

My face heats up.

"Demons don't have feelings, Kal, but you do. You feel just like everyone else. When they see that you have something inside of you that makes you so different, they will have faith in you and will want to help you."

{Am I really followable?}

"It doesn't matter," Wanda says. We look at her.

"Kal's words are inspirational and moving, but demons can't go UP. It'll kill them." Mal jumps as she looks at me with fear.

{The heavenly light fries demons. If I go, then I'll be killed instantly.}

Jade shakes her head. "I talked to Raphael and Azrael about you."

"Wait, you told them about me?"

She nods. "When Mal disappeared to come to look for you, I gave them a call. I told them about you and about Mal. They wanted to meet you the second I told them about what you and Mal share. They've never heard of a being like you before, so they want to see you."

{The archs want to see me?}

"So Raphael and Azrael discussed whether you'd be able to go UP."

{Raphael is the archangel of healing, and Azrael is the archangel of death. Those are the ones who would know if I would survive or not.}

"They both agreed that there is a small chance that you would die, since you are half human."

"How small?" Wanda asks.

"Twenty-five percent that Kal could die."

{Twenty-five?}

"That's not that small," Frikik speaks up.

"A lot smaller than one hundred," Jade explains.

"You want Kal to risk her life just by going up there?" Wanda says furiously.

"It'd be no different than her running into battle. Either way, she is risking herself to save those precious to her."

Wanda doesn't respond.

{She's right.}

Mal looks back at me, studying me.

{I said that I'd do anything to keep her safe. I swore that I would throw myself into battle if it meant she would be okay. Risking my life to try to get us help would be the same thing, wouldn't it? It's only a twenty-five percent chance that I will die. That isn't that much. That leaves seventy-five percent that I will be okay.}

I pull Mal against me as I smile.

{I'll do whatever it takes to save her and Wanda.} "I'll go."

Wanda turns to me, shocked. Frikik and the others look at me surprised as well.

"Kal, are you sure?" Wanda questions.

I nod. "Jade's right. The percent of me dying is small. I have a higher chance of dying while fighting than going with her."

"Are you sure about this, Kalma?" Frikik says. "No demon has ever gone UP before."

"I'm sure." I smile at them. "I said I'd do anything to stop the demons and to keep the ones I care about safe. No way am I backing out of that promise."

Frikik sighs before returning my smile. Derrick and the others nod with grins. Wanda stares at me with her mouth in a straight line. Her eyes look over my whole face before landing on my eyes. We stare into each other's eyes.

{I know you know that I have to do this, the same way I see the idea of me going scares the crap out of you.}

"I'll be okay."

Wanda jumps at the sound of my voice.

"I trust that the archs know what they are talking about. Not just that, but my human side has already saved me from dying once, so I believe that it will do it again."

She looks at me, confused. "When?"

"When Lucifer's blood was rejecting me. I should have burst and turned to ash, but I didn't. I was able to throw most of it up while staying whole. I think it was because I am half human. So, I know that going won't kill me."

"Kal."

"I'll be okay. I have to do this, Wanda. Not just for Mal but for you as well."

She blushes.

"We're family, remember?" I grab her hand. "That means that you are precious to me." I give her a warm smile.

{You both make me stronger and braver.}

She looks down at my hand before meeting my stare again. Her eyes glisten, and I can see the gears turning in her head.

"Just come back, okay?" She sighs, sounding defeated.

I chuckle. "You're not going to get rid of me that easily."

"If I wanted to be rid of you, you'd have been gone a long time ago. You and your obnoxiousness," she jokes.

I stick my tongue out at her. "You know you like it when I mess with you."

She shrugs as she laughs. I squeeze her hand as we laugh together. Mal's face turns red as she watches me laugh.

"Well, that's our cue," Derrick speaks up.

Wanda and I stop laughing to turn towards the others as they head for the door. "Leaving?" Wanda asks.

Derrick nods. "We are going to deliver the message to the other covens that we know."

"Let them know to get prepared for a fight," Chayse explains.

I nod. "Good idea."

They each nod back.

"Thank you all for the help," Wanda says.

"No problem." Melanie waves.

"See you guys out there." I let go of Wanda's hand to wave at them. "Be safe."

"You as well," Barbara says before they all disappear out the door.

"I should probably be going as well," Frikik speaks up. "Let some of the demons and creatures I know what is going on. See if any of them are brave enough to fight."

"Thank you."

He nods as he moves towards the door. "And Frikik."

He turns his head.

"Sorry again for attacking you."

He shakes his head as he smiles at me. "I told you, nothing to apologize for." As he walks out the door, he sticks his hand back into wave.

"When do we leave?" I look at Jade.

"Not till morning. Still have a few hours."

I nod as I look down towards my wound before carefully lifting the towel.

{Finally.}

My skin is healed without a trace of there having ever been a wound to begin with. "Finally done healing?" Wanda asks as she looks at my stomach.

"About time too." I hold my hand out towards her. "I'd like that other shirt now, please."

They all laugh.

"I'm serious. You try having half of your top exposed. I feel ridiculous."

"Some people actually wear clothing like that," Mal explains.

"Seriously? Are they sick in the head or something?"

She shrugs. "That's fashion for ya." She chuckles.

I shake my head. "Can I just have the shirt?"

"Fine." Wanda stands up and walks over to where Barbara set the shirt down. "Don't ruin this one like you did the other one." She throws it at me.

"Um, excuse me, I'm pretty sure you are the one who ripped it in half," I say as I catch it.

"And I'm pretty sure you're the one who got themselves impaled with a slab of wood."

"Touché." I press my lips tightly together.

Wanda chuckles as she and Jade head for the door.

"I'll come to get you when it's time to head out," Jade explains.

"Thank you." I nod.

They both disappear out the door, Wanda shutting it behind her.

"I guess I better follow them," Mal says as she moves out from under my arm.

"You don't have to," I tell her as she hops off the bed.

Warmth spreads throughout my whole body, causing my ears and face to burn up. Mal looks at me, her face a bright shade of red. We both just stare at each other.

"Are you sure?" she asks quietly.

I swallow. "Yeah."

Her face turns darker as she nods. I nod back before sliding off of the bed to stand beside it. I put the shirt down as I reach over my head with both arms to grab the back of the one I am wearing.

{What am I doing? Am I really taking my shirt off in front of her?} Taking a deep breath, I begin to pull on the shirt.

{I'm not scared of what she will think of my body. I don't think I'm even embarrassed about it either. I feel safe around her. I don't want to hide any part of me from her.}

I pull the collar over my head.

{I think I'm just responding this way because I've never done anything like this before.}

I close my eyes as I pull it the rest of the way over my head, my crystal hitting my bare chest, before sliding my arms out through the holes. I drop it on the floor as I reach out to grab the other shirt.

{Where did it go?}

A warm hand lays on my bare back before sliding up to my shoulder. My eyes quickly snap open, immediately noticing that Mal and the shirt are both gone. The hand slides down to the middle of my arm before grabbing hold of it. They pull me around using that arm. Mal stands there with the new shirt in her other hand as she slides the hand she has on me back up to my shoulder. Her eyes are on my body, looking over every inch of bare skin.

BA-DUM, BA-DUM.

{What is she doing?}

She moves her hand back and forth over my somewhat muscular shoulder, watching her hand intently. I shiver as she moves her hand across my chest to where my crystal lies. Her hand stops to feel the crystal, smiling at it before moving on. I watch as she moves her hand towards my stomach. Time stops as her hand runs down the center of my breasts, across the middle of my black bra. Her eyes still stare at me, wanting more. As the tips of her fingers tickle down my stomach, the hunger in her eyes sparkles brightly. She gently traces over each indent that my abs create, my body shivering as she does so.

"You're breathtaking," she whispers.

BA-DUM.

"Looking at you now makes me want more." My face burns up from the look in her eyes.

{More? What does she mean?}

She lays her hand flat in the middle of my stomach before looking up. The way she looks at me takes my breath away. The light and warmth in her eyes brighter than I've ever seen before. Her smile is happier than I've ever seen.

"Thank you for allowing me to see you like this." Her smile widens as her hand moves back towards my chest. "You trusting me like this tells me that you are definitely feeling something inside of here," she explains, stopping her hand in the center of my chest.

{I'm definitely feeling something all right.}

Her whole face flushes as an idea flashes in her eyes. "Do you want to see me?"

I tilt my head, confused.

"Do you want to see me like how I am seeing you?" she asks, as she takes her hand off of me.

{I can still feel her warm hand on me.}

Her smile disappears as she takes a big breath before throwing my shirt back onto the bed. She grabs onto the front of the hoodie I gave her, slowly pulling it open and off. Once her arms are free, it falls to the floor. Goosebumps cover her arms as she grabs onto her sleeve, pulling her arm in through it. I stare at her in anticipation as she does the same with her other arm. Her arms push against the insides of her shirt while she raises it up and over her head. She drops the shirt onto the floor before looking back at me, her face still red.

BA-DUM, BA-DUM, BA-DUM.

The pounding inside me beats so hard on my chest that I can hear it. My eyes move all over her body, taking in every part.

{Her skin looks smooth and soft.}

Her stomach is flat, with muscle indents on both sides. The white bra she wears barely keeps in her perfectly shaped breasts.

{She's absolutely perfect.}

I start to raise my hand towards her but stop myself.

"It's okay." She steps towards me. "You can touch me," she says carefully as she grabs my hand.

My mind races as she puts my hand on her stomach. Waves of joy and exhilaration pulse through me. I carefully begin to explore her body, starting with her stomach. The tips of my fingers move all over, feeling the solid muscles beneath the surface.

{She has some muscle to her.}

A strange feeling of excitement builds in my chest and stomach as I move my hand up. I can see her watching me as my hand stops just below the bottom of her bra.

{Is this really okay?}

I look up at her. She smiles with a nod. My hand starts to move again as I look down to watch it. Careful to mimic what she did, I run my hand through the center of her breasts. She shivers beneath my fingers, causing more goosebumps to appear. As I caress her chest, a smile spreads across my face on its own. The giddiness I've held down fights its way through, making me smile even more. My hand slides up to her shoulder, before moving to her neck.

{Her skin is really soft and smooth.}

I wrap the tips of my fingers to the back of her neck, stopping my hand as I look at her face. She still watches me with contentment and a newfound peacefulness. "You're perfect," I tell her.

The crimson turns to a new shade.

"I already knew how amazing you are, but seeing you like this just confirms it. Looking at you makes me feel a different kind of excitement that I didn't know could even happen."

She smiles at me warmly.

"All I want to do is run my hands over you over and over until I have explored everything I can."

Her eyes open wider with surprise as her smile disappears. Her whole face glows so red that it looks as if it would be hot to the touch.

{What did I say?}

"Did I say something wrong?"

Mal shakes her head as she gently lays her hand back onto my shoulder. "No, not at all."

"Thank you, Mal."

"No need to thank me. This is something people do when they share the kind of connection and feelings that we do."

"This is something people do when they are in love?"

Her eyes shine with warmth as her smile returns brighter. "Yes."

{Am I learning?}

"They do other things as well," Mal says softly.

"Oh?"

She nods as she starts to pull me in closer. I don't fight her pull and allow her to take charge. Eager to find out what she means. She closes her eyes as we get closer, so I do the same. Her warm breath blows against my lips.

BA-DUM, BA-DUM, BA-DUM, BA-DUM, BA-DUM.

The throbbing hits painfully inside of me, pounding a new kind of feeling throughout my body, a really lovely feeling. Our noses brush against each other as she continues to move me closer.

{My chest feels like it's going to explode. The pounding is more intense than ever. What is happening?}

KNOCK! KNOCK!

My eyes quickly snap open, seeing that Mal's have as well. Her face is not even an inch from mine before she quickly pulls away, her eyes full of frustration and disappointment.

{What was she going to do?}

"Hey, if you two want to get some training in before morning, you better get a move on," Jade explains from outside the door.

{I completely forgot that Mal asked me to train with her.} "Okay, we'll be out." I turn to the door to tell her.

By the time I face Mal again, her shirt is already halfway back on. Disappointment runs through me as she covers herself back up.

{I could never get tired of looking at her with or without clothing. Without, though, made me feel something new.}

She bends down grabbing the hoodie, standing back up as she slides her arms through the sleeves. Her eyes not once leaving the floor. A sinking feeling flips in my stomach as a sense of worry rattles through me.

"Did I do something wrong?" I ask as I grab my shirt from the bed. Her eyes immediately look at me as I pull the shirt on.

"No, not at all," she explains, stepping closer.

"Then why wouldn't you look at me just now, and why do you look so disappointed and upset?"

My hands begin to tremble.

"Oh, Kalma." She puts her hand on my cheek. "You were perfect. You didn't do anything that I didn't want you to do."

"Then why?"

"Because I wanted to show you something special, but we were interrupted, and now I'm just sad that it'll have to wait till another time." She smiles at me sadly.

"You can still show me."

She laughs quietly. "Another time, okay?"

I study her eyes, finding the same look she always gives me.

{Is that love in her eyes? Is that why she looks at me differently than she does with everyone else?}

"Why do you look at me like that?"

She tilts her head. "Like what?"

"Warmly. Your eyes have a different light to them when you look at me. They look so calm and happy but also eager and wanting."

Her eyes sparkle as she smiles. "You know why."

I don't say anything.

"I love you."

My eyes open wider as the love in her eyes grows stronger.

{So that really is how someone looks at the one they love.} I smile back at her.

{She does love me. She always has.} "I lo—" I start.

Her hand quickly covers my mouth. "Not until you know. I don't want you to say it just because I do."

I tilt my head.

"I know that there is something inside of you that is changing and becoming stronger. I see it every time you look at me, but I also know that you don't fully understand what it means." Her hand comes off my mouth. "When everything comes together and clicks, then you can say it."

"How will I know when that is?"

She grabs my hand. "You'll just know."

{I'll know?}

"Until then, just keep on allowing yourself to feel. Don't hold anything back. Okay?"

"I won't. I want to understand all of these new feelings. I want to keep feeling what I feel when I am with you."

{I never want to lose any of this. I want everything to stay and keep getting stronger. I want to understand and know what love feels like. I want to be able to say those words back to her.}

She nods with a smile. "We better get going before Jade has a fit."

I nod. She pulls me with her as she heads towards the door.

19

"**You two ready?**" Jade asks as she leans against the wall.

Mal and I both nod as we face one another in the center of the room.

{They worked for most of the night on developing Mal's powers.} "Okay, start."

{Let's see what she's learned. I'll let her make the first move.} Mal's hands light up.

{Summoning her powers is definitely a lot quicker and easier.} Hesitation runs through her eyes.

"Don't hold back, Mal. I can take it." I grin at her.

Surprise shows on her face before the hesitation vanishes, as she nods with a deep breath.

"Better watch what you say," Jade warns me.

I turn towards her as I fold my arms. "Spectators aren't supposed to speak," I say jokingly.

She holds her hands up with a shrug. I sense as energy moves in the air towards my feet. I smile before jumping into the air, doing a backflip before landing behind her, my arms still laying across my chest.

"You are fast." She chuckles.

"What were you going to do?"

"Knock you off your feet."

"Going to have to be faster than that."

"Okay." She quickly spins around as she swings at me with angelic energy surrounding both of her hands.

I duck under her arm and slide to the side. I wink and grin with a shrug. The power glows brighter in her eyes as the energy grows on her hands.

{That's my girl.}

I uncross my arms, seeing the pulsing determination inside of her. She comes at me fast. Swinging her fists at me one after the other. I move to dodge each one, but she doesn't stop as the determination grows in her eyes. Warmth sparkles in my chest.

"How are you so fast?"

"I've always been fast. Why are you slow?"

"You think I'm slow?"

"Very," I tease.

{She is faster than any human could be, though. She's learning how to use her speed.}

"Okay then."

She moves quicker now. All of her might go into each swing.

{Jade must have taught her some hand-to-hand combat as well.}

Mal's feet brush mine as she tries to trip me. We are moving all around the room. Her fists are getting closer to hitting me, and her feet are almost catching mine. I stay on balance, though, smiling as we go. She goes for a big swing.

{Bad move.}

I look at her, giving her a big grin before ducking under her arm as I swing my leg out, catching behind one of her legs. She starts to fall, her now-powerless hand reaching out to catch herself.

{You really do make me happy and so much more.}

I slide my arm under her back and grab her outstretched one, stopping her from hitting the ground. Holding her in a dip position, I smile down at her.

"You did great."

"Who says that I'm done?" she jokes.

I laugh at her with a warm smile. Her eyes sparkle with mischief. Energy starts to glow around her irises.

{She's serious.}

Her legs lift off the ground, putting all of her body weight on my arms as energy zaps my hand causing me to let go. As she starts to fall, she pushes my other hand off of her back. Just as her back hits the floor, her legs ram my stomach fast and hard, knocking the air out of me. The force pushes me back while sliding her across the floor.

{Didn't see that coming.}

I hold onto my stomach, taking deep breaths as I watch Mal stand up, her hands lit up again.

{All right, Mal. I guess I'll play a bit more seriously.}

As I remove my hand from my stomach, power rushes down my arms into my palms, setting them ablaze.

"You sure you want to do this?" I bait her.

"Why, are you scared?" She grins confidently.

I chuckle. "You're lucky I really like you."

"I know."

She takes a deep breath before running at me. I smirk before pointing one of my hands at the floor between us. Flames shoot from my palm onto the ground, igniting the area in blue fire. That doesn't stop her. Mal quickly leaps into the air, flipping over my fire and me. My eyes follow her as she hits the ground. More energy builds into her hands right before she flings a long horizontal light beam at me. I spin around to face the power, focusing on my flames to burn them hotter and denser before sending a continuous stream in front of me, creating a wall of fire. Mal's energy crashes into the firewall, pushing the wall back against my hands.

{Strong blast.}

I stop sending heat into the wall as I step out around it. "Nice, but is that all you got?" I ask with a smirk.

She smiles at me before leaping back into the air, but as she's in the air, she holds her hands out and the energy around her hands grows.

{What're you up to?}

Multiple energy balls begin firing out of her hands, one after the other.

{Too many too quickly for me to build up more fire.}

I start dodging each one as they try to hit me. Using the fire in my hands, I smack some of the balls, each one causing my hand to burn.

{Her attacks are actually hurting.}

The attacks stop, just as my sensors go off. I turn around as Mal throws a punch surrounded by light. I lift my hand up, gathering as much heat as I can into it before her fist collides with it. My whole hand burns as celeste and royal blue energies swirl and push against each other.

"Not bad, used your energy as a distraction to get close to me for an attack," I explain, trying not to wince from the pain.

She shrugs.

"But moving close to me like this was a bad idea."

A quick wave of heat rockets down my arm, making the fire in my hand explode like a small firework.

"Ah." Mal quickly pulls her hand away.

As she is shaking her hand, I bend down and swing out my leg to trip her. She must see it coming because before my foot can touch her leg, a small, celeste barrier forms around my other foot, stopping me from twisting.

{A barrier? Not around herself?}

I look down at my foot and then at her. She winks with a smile.

{You've come far in such a short amount of time.}

Her hands shine brightly again as she reaches towards me.

{I'm proud of you but...}

Using my other leg, I quickly swing it up high, kicking her hand, making the energy she intended for me shoot up into the ceiling. While she is still looking up, I move power into both of my feet, catching them on fire. I slam my free foot down on the barrier, surrounding the other one as hard as I can while making the fire on my trapped foot flare out. The wall smashes into tiny energy particles freeing my foot. She looks back at me, surprised. I give her a smile before doing a couple backflips to put distance between us. I plant my feet firmly on the ground.

{I'm not going to make it as big or as strong, like it was when I fought Jorvexx and the others.}

Pulling more fire from my flame, I slam my hands down onto the floor, creating a shockwave of fire. The tide begins to roll towards her.

{What're you going to do?}

Mal's hands glow brighter, but the edges of the energy turn whiter as she brings her hands together.

{I see what you're going to do.}

She lays her hands flat against one another as she sticks all of her fingers out towards the fire. I smile as her energy collides with mine, slowly tearing it in half. Once I know Mal can no longer see me behind the wave, I quickly run to the side, making my way behind her, putting my hands out in the process. My attack breaks apart and diminishes as she lowers her hands back down with them glowing their standard color. She looks to where I was before, her shoulders moving quickly up and down as she breathes heavily.

{You did amazing.}

I run up behind her. Just as she starts to turn around, I slide between her legs. Once she realizes I am there, I swing my leg out and trip her. She falls fast onto her back, the energy in her palms shrinking. Before she has time to refocus her powers, I use mine. I fling my hands out, firing two small bursts of fire at her hands. The flames push her arms against the ground, holding them there while covering up her energy. She looks at both of her arms as I kneel down beside her. I grin triumphantly, as she looks at me frustrated.

"You know I was going to get you, right?"

I laugh as I let my flames go out, her energy disappearing with them. I stand back up and hold my hand down to her. She sighs before placing hers in mine.

"I'm proud of you," I tell her as I pull her to her feet.

She looks at me surprised. "Really? Even though I lost?"

"This match wasn't about winning or losing. It was about testing what you've learned, and Mal, you've learned a lot. You are as strong as I thought you could be, maybe even more."

"Yeah?" she beams at me.

I nod. "Definitely. Your control is amazing. The way you use your energy to get out of different situations is just genius. Each blast has a high power density to it that can knock down most demons. The barrier, the barrier is just...wow. I've never seen someone be able to use one on someone else like that before."

"Yeah, that was very hard to do. Not something I'm going to be able to use very often."

"As long as you can protect yourself, that's what really matters."

"Do you think she's ready?" Jade asks, coming up behind me.

I nod, turning to face her. "I'll feel a little bit better now knowing that she can defend herself. Her speed alone will outpace everything besides archdemons, but she won't be facing any of them without me." I squeeze Mal's hand. "How do you feel?"

Mal looks at me. "Stronger, faster, more powerful, and brave."

I shake my head. "Getting powers didn't make you brave, Mal, you already were." I smile.

She smiles as she lets go of my hand before moving closer to me, quickly wrapping her arms around my waist. I gently wrap mine around her.

"I'm glad you won't have to worry as much about me now."

I hold her tighter. "I will always worry about you. Even if you were invincible, I would still worry."

"I'd still worry too." She holds me tighter.

{Is worrying what people do when they love each other?} "How's your fatigue? I saw you catching your breath earlier." We let go as she takes a step back.

"I'm okay."

"Are you sure? You're not tired or need to rest for a bit?"

She shakes her head. "I don't think so."

"She's half angel, remember?" Jade speaks up. We both look at her.

"Which means she won't get tired as quickly as she used to. She'll be able to run for days with only a few hours of sleep. Same thing with food and drink." Jade looks at Mal. "You'll barely ever be hungry or thirsty."

"So what you're saying is I could survive for days without sleep, food, or water?"

Jade nods.

"That's so cool."

I laugh seeing the excitement in her eyes as she thinks about it. She looks over at me with a huge smile and joy dancing in her eyes.

"What?" I ask nervously.

"I'm even more like you now."

BA-DUM.

{I never even thought of it that way before, but she's right.} She takes my hands into hers as she steps closer.

{Her angel side being awakened has made her more supernatural than natural now. The gap between us has shrunk.}

Her smile continues to light up her face as she watches me.

{But we are still creatures from two different sides of the coin.} My cheeks burn as a smile spreads across my face.

{I don't care anymore. The fact that I'm half demon and she's half angel has nothing to do with what we feel. What we are has nothing to do with the fact that I never want to lose her.}

"You are so much more. Don't ever change, you." She embraces me tightly again.

"You either."

"Thank you, Jade," I say as I look at her.

Her cheeks light up. "Don't be thanking me. It was the right thing to do." Mal lifts her head off of me to look at Jade.

I chuckle. "Maybe, but I'm still going to thank you, because you helped make sure that Mal will be safe."

Jade crosses her arms as she quickly turns her face away from us, too embarrassed to say anything. Mal and I start laughing as a feeling of joy washes over me.

{It feels so good to be happy.}

BEEP-BEEP! BEEP-BEEP! BEEP-BEEP!

{Even if it's only for a second.}

The laughter subsides as a new feeling rushes through me, a sense of fear.

{No more playing around. From here on out, everything we do will lead to how it all ends.}

I take a deep breath as Jade pulls out her disk from her pocket. She glances down at it before looking back at us. Her shoulders square as she stands straighter before she gives us a solid nod.

{It's time.}

20

"Don't we need a church to portal up there?" I ask as we step out of the training building.

{It's already really bright out here.}

"Normally, yes, but since we are already running short on time, we are going to use a different way." Jade explains.

"How?" Mal speaks up as she walks beside me, hand-in-hand.

"I'll explain once the others get here. They should be here any minute."

{Then I have time.}

"I need to say bye to Wanda before we go."

Jade and Mal look at me. Jade with annoyance and Mal with a smile.

"Seriously? Do you have to?"

I nod. "I do. She's my best friend, my family. I want to say goodbye just in case something doesn't go right. It'll destroy her if something were to happen and she didn't get the chance to say anything."

"I told you, nothing is going to happen."

"Still, though."

Jade rolls her eyes at me. "Fine, but make it quick."

I nod. "I'll be right back," I tell Mal as I let go of her hand.

"Tell her I said bye as well."

"I will."

I turn and run towards Wanda's shop.

{The circle is empty now that the sun is up.}

As I reach the door, I slow down to grab the handle before swinging it open. "Wanda?" The door closes behind me.

She walks around the corner from the hall, "It's time, isn't it?" she asks, worried.

I nod while walking to her. "They'll be coming for us any minute."

"Then why are you here?" she wonders as I stop in front of her.

"I couldn't just leave without saying something to you first."

"Kal, I swear if you make me cry again."

I chuckle. "Not my fault you're such a cry baby."

"Ha ha."

"Seriously, though." I lay my hand on her shoulder. "I don't know what the future holds. I don't know what will happen next, so I wanted to talk to you now just in case."

"Kal."

"Please."

She closes her mouth as she nods with a sigh. "I just need you to know how sorry I am."

"Sorry? Why are you sorry?"

"I'm sorry that I couldn't return the feelings that you have for me."

"Kal..."

I shake my head, stopping her. "I've known from day one that you wanted more out of our relationship than just being friends. I told you that I am a demon, and we can't feel those kinds of things towards people. After the last few days, I now know that I was wrong. I can have feelings towards someone. I've seen the way you look at Mal and me when we are together."

Her eyes open wider in surprise.

"At first, I didn't understand why, but once it clicked, I felt awful about it. You hoped that something would change, and I would be with you, but instead, you had to watch me do the thing I said I couldn't. You have to watch the one you love..." Scarlet covers her face.

"Be with someone else. Have the feelings, the connection that you have always wanted, be for someone else. I hate that I did this to you. I hate that I put you through so much misery and pain. I tried to make it better by telling you how much you mean to me and that we aren't just friends but that we are family. The pain in your eyes didn't go away even after telling you that, and I don't know if saying any of this will help you, but I had to say something." I put my other hand on her other shoulder. "I need you to know that everything I said is true. You do mean a lot to me, Wanda. You hold a special place inside of me, just like Mal does. It might not be the same, but you need to know that you matter a lot to me. I'm still learning what it means, but I do know that the way I feel towards you and the way I feel towards Mal are similar. The feelings that I have towards you just aren't as intense as they are with Mal."

Tears stream down her face.

"Either way, I am sorry. I really needed you to know that just in case."

Wanda takes a deep breath as she raises one of her hands to wipe some of the tears away. "I don't want to lie to you. What you said is true. It does hurt seeing you with Mal. Seeing the way you look at her, the way you hold her, the way you care for her. I wanted all of those things from you, but I understood that it could never happen. I accepted that until I saw you with her. At first, I thought it was me. I thought you just couldn't love me."

"Wanda..."

She shakes her head. "My turn."

I close my mouth and nod.

"But after seeing you with her. Seeing how happy you are, the joy in your eyes, the warmth in your eyes, how easily you allowed her in, the way she looks at you, the look in her eyes, how much you both clearly care for one another. After seeing all of that, I realized that it's not that you couldn't love me. It's that you were meant to love her."

{I'm meant to love Mal. Could that be true?}

"Yes, it still hurts to see you two because of how much I wanted you." My ears burn.

"But the pain will eventually fade away. It will just take time. I'll be okay, though, because like you said, I know that I am important to you even if it's not the same way I hoped. I know that you care deeply for me, Kal. I think what you feel about me is the kind of love you feel towards family or a really close friend." She smiles at me. "You have called me both of those things so I'm pretty sure that is what you're feeling."

"There are different types of love?"

She nods. "Many different types. Each one is stronger than the last."

{So I can love Mal and Wanda just in different ways?}

"Kal, I know that you love me, whether you understand it or not." She chuckles. "I think I know more of what you're feeling than you do."

I nod in agreement.

"I'll be okay as long as you're happy. You have nothing to apologize for. You don't ever have to apologize for being happy with someone. There's this saying I hear sometimes. You love who you love."

{I love who I love.}

"You don't ever have to feel guilty for loving someone." She puts her hands on my arms. "So don't you ever apologize for it again, especially not to me." She gives me a warm smile. "I just want you to be happy, even if it's not with me."

Tears blur my vision as I nod. She nods back before pushing my arms off of her shoulders to give me a hug. We hold on tightly to each other. As we let go, it feels as if a weight has been lifted off of my shoulders. The tension that has been nagging me since Wanda first saw me with Mal fades away.

"Thank you."

"You don't need to thank me, Kal."

"I think I do. You've always been here for me, Wanda. You've never judged me even though you know who my father is. You were never afraid of me. You allowed me to open part of myself up to you. Everything you've done for me could never be repaid. So I will continue to say thank you."

She laughs. "I know how you can repay me."

"How?"

"Come back alive." My eyes open wide.

"Come back from up there alive and promise me that you will get through the battle alive as well."

{Can I make that promise?}

Her eyes stare at me, filled with worry and fear. "I'll do my best."

She shakes her head. "Promise me. I need to know that when this is all said and done that you will be here. That I will see you again."

"I'll promise if you promise me something in return."

"What?"

"If you are going to fight with us, then you will be extra careful. I don't want you getting hurt. or worse. I wouldn't be able to live with myself if something were to happen to you. Promise me that if you get into a really tough situation, you will either yell for me or you will run."

"I can't run."

"Then I can't promise that I'll make it out of this." Her eyes flicker as she thinks it over.

{I need you and Mal both to be safe. I can't go into battle with a clear head if I don't think you'll be safe.}

"All right. If things get bad, I'll do as you ask."

"Thank you."

"Now, you promise."

I sigh, "I promise."

{I hate lying to her, but if it keeps her safe, then I don't have a choice.}

"When things begin, I want you and Mal both with me. I want you both by my side as much as possible, so if you need me, I'll be right there."

"We can do that."

I nod with a light smile.

"Kal."

Wanda and I face the door as Jade's head and shoulders peek around the door. "They're here. Time to move."

"Coming."

She leaves and shuts the door.

I look at Wanda. "I guess that's my cue."

She grabs onto me and embraces me again. "Be safe, be smart. Don't go pissing off any archangels while you're up there."

I laugh. "I'll try my best."

"You'll do great," she says as she pushes me back to look at my face. "You will get them to fight with us."

"I hope so."

She lets go of me. "I'll see you soon."

"I'll find you before things really start," I explain as I start walking away.

"I'll be here."

I open the door. "Oh, Mal says bye."

Wanda chuckles. "Tell her I said bye as well."

I wave as I walk out the door. As it shuts behind me, my hands begin to tremble as pressure builds into my chest.

{I'm scared.}

Mal waves at me to come join them as she and Jade stand with the rest of Jade's team. I take a deep breath and head over to them.

21

"Hey, Kal." Summer waves as I stop beside Mal.

"Hey." I grab Mal's hand.

"Are you ready for this?" John asks.

"Ready as I'll ever be."

{My stomach is all tied up in knots. I can't shake this feeling of dread.}

"Okay, here's how this is going to go," Jade explains, holding her hand out. Bruce hands her two thick yellow wristbands.

{What are those?}

"You both need to wear one of these, and do not take it off," Jade tells us as she hands a band to both of us.

The moment it touches my hand, an intense wave of divine energy flows into me.

{That is really powerful energy. Is it from one of the archangels?}

"Once they are activated, the bands will teleport you up there, and they will keep you up there."

"What do you mean by keep?" Mal speaks.

"Where we are going is only supposed to be meant for the dead, and since neither one of you are dead, you wouldn't be able to enter or remain there. The bands are to help hide the fact that you are alive. As long as you keep them on, you will stay."

"So they are kind of like angelic backstage passes?" Mal wonders.

{Backstage passes? What the heck is that?}

Jade nods. "Yeah, I guess you could say that."

Mal lets go of my hand so she can put the band on. I put mine on as well.

{These had to have been made by one of the archs. No other angelic creature has energy like this.}

"As soon as you arrive, there will be two power angels to greet you," John explains.

"Peliel and Leo have been keeping watch for any demons who may try to get in," Blaze says.

{According to the books I've read, powers are the angels whose primary purpose is to be warriors fighting against demons. They are powerful, but there have to be at least five of them working together for them to fight an archdemon. The problem with that, though, is that there aren't that many to fight. I guess they are chosen by specific conditions. No one knows what needs or what you have to do to become one. That is probably why there aren't that many.}

"Just wait for Jade to get there, and then you'll go see the archs," Levi says.

"How long until you meet us?" I question nervously.

{If she isn't with us, then how do I know that the other angels won't try to hurt me or anything?}

"Not long, maybe a few minutes," Jade answers. "We're fast, remember?" she asks, sounding cocky. "It won't take me long to get to the church and portal up."

I nod. "Okay."

{I hope she's right.}

"Well, let's get this show on the road." She walks up to Mal and me. "Hold out your arms."

We listen and do what she stays. Fear begins to crawl up my back.

{Deep breaths. Everything is going to be okay.}

Jade places one of her hands on each of our bands. Her hand glows just before the bands begin to glow a goldish yellow color.

{They kind of look like small thicker halos.} "See ya up there." She smiles.

Before I have time to respond, my body starts to burn as it feels like it is being pulled apart.

{She didn't say how badly this would hurt.}

I close my eyes, trying to block out how much pain is radiating through me. After a few seconds the pulling stops, but the burning remains.

"Kal, are you okay?" I hear Mal's voice ask me.

I carefully open my eyes. My corneas scream at me to close them again as a beam of light sears into them. Mal stands beside me with a worried look on my face. White surrounds us. White walls, floors, ceiling, everything pure white.

{Everything is so clean, so pure, so bright. We are definitely in the right place.}

"Kal."

I meet Mal's eyes.

"Are you okay?"

"My whole body feels as if my insides are sweltering, but I'll be okay."

"Are you sure? Because I've never seen your skin look like that before."

{My skin?}

I lift my arms up to look at them.

{What the hell?}

Interlacing throughout my pale skin are dark crimson veins. I quickly grab my shirt, lifting it up to see my stomach as red veins weave all over it.

{They're everywhere.}

"How bad is it?" I ask Mal as I let go of my shirt.

"They're on your neck and part of your face as well."

Panic rises inside of me as my breathing quickens. Mal must notice my distress as she steps towards me.

"Hey, it's okay." She lays her hand gently on my cheek. "You're okay. You're still here, so that means that what Jade said was true and your human half is protecting you. I think your body is reacting like it is because your demon side is taking damage from being here, and that is why your insides are burning and probably why your veins are like this."

My chest tightens.

"But as long as you can handle the pain, then you will be okay." She smiles. "You kind of look badass like this."

Some of the pressure fades away as I chuckle. "Oh yeah?"

"Definitely."

I laugh more, pushing away all of my fear.

{How do you do it? How do you make everything better?}

"So that's what happens when a demon comes up here," a voice speaks.

Mal takes her hand from my face before we turn towards the man who spoke. Standing just inside of the doorway are two men wearing white shoes, black jeans, and white shirts. Across their chests are giant X's made from the sword holsters on their back. Over their shoulders are two golden hilts with wing-shaped guards, one on each side. They are the same build and the same height, but their hair colors are different. The one on the left has blond hair, whereas the one on the right has dark brown. They both glare at me as they move towards us.

{These must be the powers Jade told us about. Peliel and Leo. I think that is what they said their names are.}

"I'm amazed she didn't combust." Blond hair laughs. Mal balls her hands into fists.

"I guess the archs were right when they said she'd survive being up here because she's half human," brown hair explains.

{Why are they talking as if I'm not even here?}

"A demon is a demon. There's no half and half," the blond retorts.

{They hate demons, and since I am half demon, they hate me.}

They both stop in front of us. Neither one of them looks at us as they continue talking.

"What do you think, Leo?" Peliel asks.

"I agree with you. A demon is a demon, nothing more, nothing less." Leo crosses his arms. "I don't know what they were thinking by letting one up here. We don't know what she could do or if we can even trust her."

"Then I guess it's a good thing I brought these." Peliel reaches behind him before bringing his hand back around.

Anger boils inside of me as I stare at the translucent handcuffs with the angelic symbol glowing on each cuff.

"Smart thinking." Leo nods.

Peliel takes another step towards me.

"You are not putting those on her." Mal steps between us, both of her hands gleaming with power.

{Mal?}

Soothing warmth takes over the raging anger.

"This must be the angel hybrid." Leo looks down at Mal. "Tell me, darling, what is a creature of light and purity doing with an evil and vile thing like that?"

Her hands shine brighter. "She's not evil, and she's not a thing. Kalma is just as human as I am."

Peliel shakes his head. "She's got you brainwashed."

"You're the ones who are brainwashed if you think that Kal is anything like the other demons."

They both look at her, annoyed.

"You never answered my question." Leo takes a step closer. "Why are you with a demon?"

"I'm not with a demon. I am with Kal. I'm with her because I love her, and I never want to leave her side."

They look at her, shocked, before bringing their eyebrows together, both of them forming a sneer full of disgust.

"How could you ever say that?" Peliel asks angrily. "How could you ever say that you love that thing?"

"I told you, she's not a thing. And I love her because of everything she is." I can't help but smile at her response.

{She loves me for just being me.}

"That's just disgusting," Leo says. Rage builds back inside of me.

"I don't know which one of you is worse." Peliel frowns. "The demon, or you for loving it."

"I told you, she's not an it!" Mal exclaims.

"She's loyal to the thing, so maybe we need another pair of cuffs for her as well," Leo explains.

Peliel nods in agreement. "That might be a good idea."

Anger runs down my arms as Peliel moves towards us with the cuffs ready to be placed. My fingers twitch, sending off tiny sparks.

{If they touch her, I swear.}

"What's going on?" a familiar voice asks behind Leo and Peliel.

Both of them jump in surprise before turning around to face Jade as she stands with her arms crossed, looking aggravated.

The sparks on my hands stop as I cool my arms and hands back down.

{That was close. Perfect timing, there, Jade.}

Neither of the men says anything.

"I asked a question. What is going on?" Jade repeats.

"We were just about to restrain the demon and her lover to ensure everyone's safety," Leo speaks up.

Her eyebrows scrunch together with rage. "What made you think that she needed cuffs? That either of them needs them?"

"Seriously?" Peliel asks surprised. "That thing is a demon, and the other one is a traitor for falling in love with it."

Jade's arms uncross as she whips both hands out, sending short rays of turquoise energy at them. The rays knock both of them over, making them hit the ground hard on their backs. Jade moves over to Mal and me before stopping in the middle of us as she turns around. Leo and Peliel stare at Jade as they stand back up.

"If I ever hear you call Kal an it or talk about Mal that way again, I will hit you ten times harder. Are we understood?"

"But Jade—" Leo says.

"Are we understood?" she asks more sternly.

"Yes, ma'am," they respond.

"I suggest you put those cuffs away before I stick them on you two."

Peliel moves the cuffs behind his back, putting them back from where they came from.

"You're lucky that I was the one who came in here and not one of the archs. They wouldn't have been too pleased to see you two treating their special guests like that."

"Special guests?" the boys ask.

Jade starts walking towards the door, waving at us to follow. Mal and I walk quickly to catch up to her.

"Didn't you hear?" She stops just inside of the door. "These two are going to save us all."

{She can't be serious?}

I look over at Mal, seeing the same surprise on her face that I feel. Jade keeps walking, so we follow, leaving the two power angels to think about what they did.

"Thank you," I say to her as we walk down an empty white hall. "If you wouldn't have shown up when you did, I don't know what would have happened."

"There shouldn't be a reason for you to be thanking me. None of that should have happened. If I would've known that they were going to treat you two like that, then I would have made sure that they weren't the ones to greet you."

"Why did they act like that?" Mal asks.

"There are a lot of angels who hold a lot of hatred towards demons. So, there are a lot who won't trust you two and will look down on you."

"They aren't going to want to help us fight if they don't trust me."

"You'll get them to trust you."

The hallway stops a few feet in front of us. "How?"

We step out of the hall into a big, white room. "By being you."

I look around in awe. The room is circular, with other hallways all around the outside of the circle. In the middle is a giant globe with different-colored dots scattered throughout the whole thing. Under the world is a circular table with multiple keyboards and buttons built into it. A few angels stand around it frantically typing as they look up at the globe. On the opposite side of the globe are rows of tables with angels sitting typing away on their own computers. The side we are on has a round platform sitting a few feet from us. A few feet from the platform is a giant metal podium facing the platform with a few buttons on top. "Welcome to the surveillance and communication headquarters." Jade swings out her arm as she spins around. "This is where we keep track of the guardian angels on Earth and what souls really need our help, and we try to keep track of demon activity." She points to the globe. "Each colored dot has its own purpose. The white dots are angels, the yellow are those who need us, red is for demons, and then blue are the oldest churches worldwide."

{They're almost all gone. Only ten blue dots are left. Only ten churches are left.} We continue to follow Jade to the round platform.

"This is where you will stand while you give your speech."

Fear creeps up my spine as I stare at the see-through platform.

"Mal and I will be standing behind that podium." She points to the podium. "With the archangels."

Alarms go off in my head. "What do you mean with the archangels?"

"They will all be here watching. Gabriel will be the one standing at the podium. The others will just be watching."

My hands begin to shake and sweat. "But why? Why are they going to watch?"

She shrugs. "I think they are just curious about you."

"Why?"

"Because there's never been someone who is like you. There has never been a demon hybrid to ever have emotions as you do. There's never been one capable of feeling the things you do. None have had what you have towards Mal."

I look at Mal as she turns to me and gives me a warm smile.

"So, I'm guessing they want to see who you are for themselves. They want to meet you, Kal."

{Meet me?}

"I know some of them are very excited." She chuckles.

{Why is she laughing?}

Mal gapes open-mouthed at something behind me. "Jade's right," a soft female voice says.

My body goes stiff as powerful auras wash over me, setting off all of my internal warning bells, screaming at me to run.

"We have been wanting to meet you and see you for ourselves."

Pressure builds in my chest as I ball my hands into fists to try to settle the shaking. I take a deep breath as I slowly turn around.

{They're all here. They all look exactly how the texts say they do.}

Standing directly behind me smiling is Raphael, the angel of healing, with her grass green aura surrounding her and her grass-green eyes looking down at me. On her right are the archangels Ariel, Uriel, and Azrael.

{Their auras are very intense. The colors surrounding each of them are so vivid. Ariel, archangel of nature, with her pale pink aura. Uriel, archangel of wisdom and her pale yellow, and Azrael, the archangel of death with beige aura.}

On the left of Raphael are archangels Gabriel, Raziel, and Michael.

{Gabriel the archangel of communication and new beginnings, with his dark-yellow aura. Raziel, the secret keeper archangel, surrounded by all the colors of the rainbow. Then finally, Michael, the archangel warrior and his cobalt blue aura. Each archangel has their own unique gifts as well as their own aura, which match their eyes.}

"It is great to finally meet you," Raphael says as she holds her bigger than usual hand out. "We've heard a lot about you."

I stare at her hand before meeting her eyes. She continues to grin at me warmly. I swallow dryly as I force my hand to move.

"Hopefully good things." I nervously laugh as I take her hand.

"You wouldn't be here if it wasn't all good." She chuckles as we shake hands. Before turning to Mal, she lets go of my hand. "You must be the angel hybrid, Malak." Raphael holds her hand out to Mal.

Mal slowly takes her hand. "It's just Mal."

Raphael nods with a smile as she lets go of Mal's hand. "Well, it is nice to meet you, Mal. We've heard a lot about you as well."

Mal looks over at me, worried.

{She's probably scared that they are going to treat us like the power angels did.} I twitch my head, signaling her to move closer to me. She listens and steps up beside me. She takes my hand as I hold it out to her. Once her hand is securely in mine, she smiles, causing my cheeks and ears to warm up.

"So, it is true."

We look back at the archs.

"You two do share a special kind of connection," Uriel asks while staring at our joined hands.

All of them stare at us with astonishment. I tighten my grip on Mal's hand as I move slightly in front of her.

"You have nothing to fear from us, Kalma." Raphael smiles.

"We will not harm you nor judge you," Ariel explains.

"Jade was right, though," Michael speaks up. "We did want to meet you, and we do want to know more about you and what makes you different."

"There really hasn't been anyone like you before, not ever. No hybrid has been able to have any emotions. Their demon half too powerful to allow any of the humanity out. They could never feel for anything or anyone. The connection you have with your friend and for Mal was thought to never be possible for those like you," Uriel tells me.

{So I really am one of a kind.}

"Why are you like this? What happened to you?" Gabriel speaks up.

"Uh, I'm not really sure. I was like all the other demons, empty and cold. I mean, I always knew that there was something different about me. I could feel it. Something felt as if there was a piece missing." I look at Mal. "Until I saw her." Mal blushes as she meets my eyes.

"The moment I saw her, something inside of me changed."

"Jade's team told us what you told them," Gabriel explains.

I nod, looking back to them. "Then you know as much as I do. Since that day, the feelings in me, the emotions, they've grown and expanded since the beginning."

"What are the emotions that you can feel?" Raphael wonders.

"My friend Wanda helped me understand what the things are that I feel. Thanks to her, I learned that I feel happiness, sadness, fear, anger, and with Mal's help"—my face heats up—"I'm learning what love feels like."

Mal holds onto my hand tighter.

"Love?" Raziel steps closer. "You're learning to feel love?" he asks, shocked.

"She is," Mal answers for me.

"That shouldn't be possible," Raziel explains, astonished. "Not without a—"

"Heart," Mal finishes for him.

They all look at her as she smiles warmly at them. I lift my hand to my chest where my heart would be. Raziel turns to look at Raphael. They share a look before turning back towards us.

{What was that?}

"Jade told us that your flame is different as well," Michael changes the subject.

"The color changed," I explain, slowly pushing power down my arm as I take my hand away from my chest.

They stare in awe at the royal-blue flames dancing in my palm. "That's incredible," Raziel says quietly.

"I don't know what made the color change. I woke up after..." I glance at Mal to see her face drop.

I squeeze her hand, making her look at me as I give her a small smile. She takes a deep breath before returning my smile.

"My internal flame went out, and I died for a few hours. Wanda was able to bring me back, but when I woke up, my flames were this color."

"So what the team told us was true," Azrael says, "You did die?"

"For a little while, yes."

He looks at me with confused eyes.

{He's the angel of death. He knows more than anyone that I should not be standing here.}

The fire in my palm goes out as I lower my arm back to my side. "Anything else that is different?" Uriel questions.

"Um, the only other thing I can think of is the pounding I sometimes get in my chest."

"Pounding?" Raphael asks.

"Yeah, it never lasts very long. Sometimes it hurts. Other times it doesn't. I don't know what it is."

"Hmm," she hums.

"Then the warmth that spreads throughout my body."

"Warmth?" Ariel speaks up.

"It's a strange kind of warmth. It's not like the heat I feel coming off of my flame. This warmth is calming and nice, makes me feel safe and happy." I shrug. "It's hard to explain."

Raphael, Ariel, and Uriel smile at me.

"We understand." Ariel smiles brightly. I stare at them, confused.

"You are definitely a one-of-a-kind kid," Michael says.

"There is something inside of you making you different from all the others before you," Uriel explains. "I'm pretty sure I know what that something is."

"Really? What is it?" I ask excitedly.

She shakes her head. "You'll have to figure it out for yourself."

"Why does everyone keep saying that?"

Mal chuckles softly beside me.

{Does everyone know what it is except me?}

"Sir."

We all look at the angel standing behind the archs. "We're ready," he tells Gabriel.

Gabriel nods. "Thank you."

The angel nods before running back to the globe. Gabriel turns back and looks at me. "Are you ready?"

My free hand shakes as my knees feel weak. Pressure builds in my chest as my breathing picks up. They all stare at me, waiting for an answer. Their stares make the fear worse.

"Hey."

I look at Mal.

"You can do this." She squeezes my hand. "I know you can."

"What if I say something wrong?"

She shakes her head. "Not possible." She smiles. Her eyes look at me full of trust and faith.

{Mal believes in me. So maybe I should too.}

I take a deep breath, pushing away my fear. My hand stops trembling as strength returns to my knees.

"Okay."

She nods.

"Stand on the platform and we can begin," Gabriel tells me.

"Come on." Mal pulls me, leading us to the platform.

We stop right beside it. I look back and see Gabriel standing at the podium with the other archangels behind him. Jade stands farther back. She sees me looking at her; she smiles with a nod. Taking another deep breath, I put one of my feet onto the platform. Everything goes quiet. I look behind me, seeing that all the angels have stopped and are now staring at me.

{Why are they staring at me?}

Panic rises back inside of me as I turn away from them. "Don't mind them," Mal says.

"They're all staring at me. Everyone in this room is staring at me. I can't do this, Mal, I'm too afraid."

"You're suffering from what's called stage fright."

"Stage fright?"

"Yes. Stage fright is the fear of performing in front of people."

"How do I get rid of it?"

"By pushing past your fear. Pretend that there isn't anyone else here. That no one is watching you. Focus on something else."

"Like what?"

Crimson races across her cheeks. "Me."

I look at her.

"Focus on me. Block everyone else out and just keep your eyes on me. Let the world fall away until it's just you and me."

I chuckle softly. "I can definitely do that. I've done it so many times before." Her face brightens.

"Thank you, Mal."

She holds my hand tighter before letting go. "You can do this." She starts walking away. "Eyes on me."

"Okay."

{I can do this. I have to do this. I'm the only one who can.} I step the rest of the way onto the platform.

{I have to convince everyone to fight with us. To stand up against the demons, to protect what they care about.}

"Stand forward and straight," Gabriel commands me. Taking a deep breath, I do as he says.

{They have to help us. If they don't, then I don't think we can win.}

"Recording in three...two..."

The world slowly begins to blur as I stare into Mal's eyes. "One."

Mal and I are the only ones left as everything else disappears. She smiles at me with complete confidence. The warmth I just spoke of fills me up as well as determination.

22

Bright lights shoot out from the platform completely surrounding me.

{Must be how they scan me and record me to send it to the disks.}

I take a deep breath. "Hello, everyone. My name is Kalma. I'm sure you are all wondering what is happening and why a guardian angel is showing you a holographic message from a demon. The reason is that I have something vital to tell you and ask you. So please listen to what I have to say. The whole world depends on it. I'm sure by now most of you have heard about what is happening around the world. It's true. Demons are attacking the oldest churches. They're doing this to weaken the angels and the archangels so that their power over this world will diminish, and then the demons can take over to bring Hell to Earth. I know many of you aren't going to believe me and are going to ask how I know all of this. I know because I was in the room when my father Rorridun told us about the plan. Now, more of you are saying there's no way you can trust anything I'm saying because I'm the daughter of the second-in-command. Lucifer's right-hand man. I swear that you can trust me, and you need to believe me. Let me start from the beginning, then, hopefully, you will trust me and see that I want to save this world by the end. When I was younger, I knew that I was different than all the other demons. I didn't know why or how, just that I was. As I got older, those feelings grew and got stronger. How my father treated me just added to everything. He never treated me as his daughter. I was a piece of property to him. My whole life he trained me every day. He'd torture me every other day to toughen me up. He never had any signs of affection towards me, just the same look every day. The look that I was his, that he owned me. I was never his daughter. I was a weapon, a tool to be used whenever he saw fit. I came to just accept it after time until, one day, everything changed. The day started out with our usual morning training, but that morning the lesson was different." I take a shaky breath. "I was used to him using his flames on me, but that day he used his special technique on me. He used his fire blades. Two swords completely made from his flames." Mal's eyes grow. "I wasn't allowed to defend myself as he continuously stabbed me with them over and over in different spots all over my body." Tears run down Mal's face. "By the time he finally stopped, I and the floor around me was covered in my blood. I collapsed to the floor in too much pain to move. As I lay there in agony, he looked down at me and said that one day I would defend him against severe blows like those, or even a lethal one, because that was what I was MADE for. I didn't know what he meant, so I snuck into his office after I healed and cleaned up while he was out. That's when I found a photo of my mother, my human mother. That's right. I am a hybrid. The moment I learned the truth, everything finally made sense. I really was just his weapon, and I was different. I needed to know just how different, so I came up to this world to learn more about humans. That was when I met her. The second my eyes landed on her, something in me woke up. The world became brighter, warm, and full. I kept an eye on that girl while learning about humanity and what they're about. I came to really like and care about this world. I made a friend, who is now my family. She taught me a lot about humans and the other supernatural creatures that visited her. She is a witch, a mighty one. She introduced me to all kinds of creatures, and after a little while, I began to care about them like I did the humans. After months of seeing her and everything in this world, I realized how beautiful it all is. Both sides of it all, humans and the supernatural. I wanted to stay and live my life here more than anything, but I was still too afraid to defy my father even after what he did and how he lied. Until he told us the plan. Father told us about attacking the oldest churches so that the demons could rise up and take over. Every part of me knew that that plan couldn't happen or they would destroy all the beauties and warmth in the world. It wasn't until he told us what our task was that I was brave enough to go against his orders. We were tasked with finding and eliminating an angel hybrid. He showed us a photo of the hybrid. So many thoughts circled in my head, but the main one was to save and protect her, because the hybrid was the same girl I'd been watching. The same girl that changed me, the one who brought all kinds of new feelings into my life. I swore then and there that I would protect her and this world no matter what. I did just that. My team found us, and I fought against all of them to protect the girl. My flame was barely lit by the time the fight was over. That didn't stop me, though. I had to get her somewhere safe. Before all of this happened, I had just gone through my eighteenth-year ritual before we were given our orders. Lucifer's blood was inside of me, and since I disobeyed, the blood was rejecting me, slowly killing me, poisoning my flame so it couldn't grow. Even knowing this, even though I knew that if I used my fire again, I'd die." I smile warmly. "I did just that. I got her inside of one of the safe-haven barriers, using my powers to do so. My flame went out that day. I died keeping my promise to protect her no matter what." I stop smiling as I slowly raise my hand. "It's only because of my best friend that I am standing here today. She used her magic to save me." Heat rushes down my arm into my hand. "These flames are my reminder that I gave up my life for that girl and a reminder that I'd do it again. I will give my life to save her and everyone else that the demons want to hurt or, worse, kill. I will not allow them to just take this world, not without a fight." My fire goes out before lowering my hand again. "Which brings me to the question." I take a deep breath. "Will you fight with me? Will you stand and help stop them from taking this world? I understand that asking for you to fight is scary, and you probably think that you can run and hide, leaving the fighting to the GAs because it's their territory, their job to stop the demons.

You're not wrong. It is the angels' duty to fight for this world, and they are. Thousands of GAs are battling demons all over the world, trying to stop them from destroying the churches. Thousands are being killed, thousands of churches have fallen, bringing the demons closer and closer to victory. There are only a few churches remaining, one of them being here in Philly. Not for much longer, though. They're coming for it on Hallowed End, and if they aren't stopped, it is over. Everything you've built for yourselves, your lives, your peace, freedom, happiness, all of it will be wiped away once they take over. My father and the others will not look past your betrayals by remaining here and having peace with those from the lighter side. You all will be punished, or worse, they'll hurt you by hurting or taking those you care for. They will break you one way or another." I square my shoulders as I stand taller. "I know that you don't want to fight, I don't want anyone to fight, but I also know that none of you want to lose either. All that you've come to know will come to an end once the demons win. So, make a choice. Do you want to turn and run like cowards, allowing them to take it all, or help fight for everything you want to keep and protect? At least by fighting we have a higher chance of winning. Yes, there is still a chance we will lose, but I'd rather die fighting for those I care about than die not trying at all. The second my father told us, I knew, every part of me knew that I would fight. I will fight not just for that girl, who I am learning how to love." My face burns as Mal's turns red, her eyes glistening. "But for everyone else as well. I've always planned on fighting, even if I have to do it alone. I will fight with everything I have until my flame goes out if that's what it takes. I could die on that battlefield, but at least I didn't die running away. I'd die standing up for what I believe and for her. I'd take my last breath with my only regret being that I couldn't stop them, that I wasn't able to save everyone, especially her. There are many of you out there who feel the same way. You don't want to die regretting that you didn't even try protecting those you care about. Deep down, past your fears, you want to fight to save those people, to die if it means saving them. Well, you are not the only ones.

All of the guardian angels out there fighting have done just that. Guardians are those who died saving someone they loved. Even now, they are dying for all of you. They're giving their souls to save you. I'm ready to die to save her. They died to save you. When you fight for someone else, that's just incredible. You see, I believe that when people are protecting those that they really care about, then they can be as strong as they can be." My hand moves to lay on my chest. "I'll give my whole flame to protect those I care about." A smile spreads across my face. "So let me ask you again." Smile vanishes. "Will you fight to save those who are most precious to you?" I grab onto my shirt. "If so, tell the angel that is holding the message. They will tell you where and when to meet. I really do believe that if we all fight, we will win." I let go of my shirt, taking my hand off of my chest. "I hope I'll see you all out there. Thank you for listening, and if you do show up, thank you for trusting me." I give a big, warm smile, just before the lights around me go out.

23

Mal jumps on me, wrapping her arms around my neck as I step off of the platform. "You were amazing."

"Think so?" I ask as I hold her. "Definitely."

She unwraps her arms as I lower her back to the floor.

"I felt like I was going to throw up the whole time I was talking."

"You couldn't tell," Jade explains as she stops beside Mal. "That speech was—"

"Moving," Gabriel says from behind the podium.

"Most definitely. You made your point, connected with them, and opened up to them by telling them about what changed you and how you feel now," Uriel speaks from where she stands.

"Kal, was what you said about what your father did to you true?" Mal looks at me with sorrow-filled eyes.

"Everything I said was true."

"Oh, Kal," she says, heartbroken.

"He almost killed you. He could've killed you," Raphael says angrily.

"As I said before, I was just something he owned, a tool that he could bend or break whenever he wanted to."

All the archangels look at me with sympathy.

"Don't feel bad for me. I grew and got stronger because of the things he did to me, and if he hadn't done what he did that day, I never would've gone looking for answers. I wouldn't have found the picture of my mother. I never would have gone up." I reach out and grab Mal's hand. "I would never have found you."

She smiles at me as she holds my hand.

"None of this would've happened if he wouldn't have pushed me. Did what he did to me suck? Yes. Did it hurt like hell? Yes again. It made me stronger, though. I'm able to protect you and help end this war because of how hard he pushed me. Don't get me wrong, I hate him with every fiber of my being, but I don't want anyone to feel sorry for me. I told them that story to show that even though I am terrified of my father, I still betrayed him, will fight against him. I wanted them to see that you can fight past your fears."

Everyone smiles.

"You're right, Kal," Ariel speaks up. "We shouldn't pity you because of your past. We should be proud of who you are now in the present."

"And we are," Raziel explains.

{The archs are proud of me?}

I turn to Jade. She looks at me and shrugs.

Mal squeezes my hand. "I've always been proud of you." She smiles. "You've come so far in just a few days. You have learned so much about the new you. You are still learning. Even though it's hard, you allow your emotions to come through and learn what each one is. You might've been strong physically, but now you are also strong emotionally, which is just as important, if not more."

"Really?"

"To be able to understand how you feel and be brave enough to admit it are solid qualities to have," Uriel explains. "Don't ever stop doing what you are doing."

"Or you won't be able to figure out what love feels like." Raphael smiles warmly at us.

My face heats up as I remember what I said earlier. Mal looks at me and chuckles.

"Sir!" one of the angels yells behind us.

We all look at him.

"Reports are coming in from all over Philadelphia and the surrounding cities."

"What are they saying?" Gabriel asks.

I hold my breath, waiting for his answer.

"They want to fight."

{They're going to fight!}

Mal lets go of my hand to put both of hers on my shoulders before she begins to shake me. "You did it, Kal. You convinced them to help us stop the demons."

I shake my head. "I convinced them to fight for those precious to them."

"Either way, you were able to get us help," Jade explains. "Now we have an army of our own, one made up of beings from both sides. We might actually have a chance of winning this war."

Mal stops shaking me. "We will win," she says determinedly.

Jade chuckles. "We will."

"What should I tell the angels, sir?"

"We need a meeting place," Michael explains. "Somewhere that both sides can go to but also be close to the church."

"The Middle."

They all look at me.

"The Middle is hidden from the world and close to enough to the church. The barrier might need to be expanded depending on how many show, but I'm sure that won't be a problem for the archangels," I tell them.

"Will there be an area big enough to train a large number of people?" he asks.

I nod., "If we expand the barrier, there is an empty field starting behind the Day Motel stretching to the back of my friend's shop."

"That should work. All right, tell the angels to take those who are going to fight to Philly's safe haven. Have them there by tonight," Gabriel orders the angel. "Once they are all there, their commander will tell them what's next."

"Yes, sir."

Tapping from multiple keyboards echoes throughout the room. "Michael, what is the next step?" I question him.

He shakes his head. "I'm not their commander.

"Then who is?"

He stares at me. Chills run up and down my spine as anxiety sinks into my stomach.

"Oh no. You can't be serious."

"I am."

"I can't lead them. I have no clue how to lead people."

"Weren't you your team's leader?"

"Yes, but..."

"Then you know how. It's the same thing, just with more people."

"This is different! We are marching into a real battle where people could die. I can't have their lives in my hands. If I get them killed, I'll never be able to live with myself."

"Kal," Azrael says, "their lives are already in your hands."

My breath catches in my chest.

"The moment you asked them to fight with you was the moment they put their lives in your hands. You are their leader now," he explains.

"But I can't do this alone."

"You're not." Mal grabs my hand. "Part of being in a relationship is that you never have to do anything alone. I will always be here, right beside you, ready to help whenever you need it." Her face turns scarlet. "We're partners in more than one way."

"Partners?"

She nods. "We are together." My ears burn.

{Together.}

"You two are so adorable," Raphael interrupts.

We both look back at the archs as the girls stare at us with joy, and the guys look everywhere but at us.

{I always forget that there are other people around when I talk to Mal. I just get so lost in her that everything else disappears.}

"Messages have been sent," an angel explains.

"All right, thank you," Gabriel says gratefully.

"I guess we should be heading down to prepare," Michael says. Everyone nods in agreement.

"I meant to ask," Raphael starts as she looks at me, "how are you feeling being up here? By the looks of you, I can see that it is affecting your body."

{I completely forgot. I got so caught up that I didn't realize my body was still on fire.}

"There has never been any kind of demon up here, hybrid or not, that has survived the journey, let alone the stay," Azrael says.

"My body is on fire, but besides that and my veins, I'm okay. I guess my human half is stronger than those other hybrids."

"I guess so," he agrees.

"Jade, can you take them back?" Gabriel asks.

"Yes, sir, I can."

"Then we will see you down there shortly."

Mal, Jade, and I all nod.

"Follow me," Jade orders us.

Mal and I follow her to the hallway we used to come in here. None of us say anything as we walk back to the room that we arrived in.

{Things are going to move quickly once we get back. I have to stay on my toes and be ready to help whenever someone needs me.}

I hold Mal's hand that is still in mine.

{I have to keep my word. I will protect her and everyone else no matter what.} We walk into the room to see that it is empty.

"I'm glad those two aren't here," Mal says, annoyed. "The way they treated us was so ignorant that I wanted to punch both of them."

I chuckle as Jade looks at her, surprised.

"What?" Mal asks her.

Jade holds her hands up. "Nothing."

I laugh at them.

{She still makes me feel like everything is okay even though it is far from it. I don't know what it is, but I can't help but be happy and feel safe when I'm with her.}

"Stand where you two were when you arrived."

We move to stand where we started.

"You're going to feel the same thing you did when you came up here."

"Yay," I say sarcastically.

"It'll only last a second, and then the burning should stop, and your skin should return to normal."

"All right, let's get to it then."

Jade shakes her head. "So impatient."

I shrug. She continues to shake her head as she walks up to us. "Wrists."

We hold out our arms that have the yellow bands on them. Jade grabs hold of both of them at the same time.

"See ya soon." She pulls both bands off.

I close my eyes as the horrible burning I felt the first time pulses through me.

{This sucks.}

Just as fast as the pain started does it stop. I open my eyes seeing the fountain in the center of The Middle.

"We're back," Mal says.

"We are."

"What now?"

"We wait, I guess."

Mal nods.

I pull her hand to turn her so she is looking at me. "How are you doing? A lot has happened in the last few days. Things keep on getting crazier and crazier."

"You know, you'd think that I'd be having a mental breakdown or something, but I feel fine. Yes, some of it gets to me, but not enough for it to bother me. Honestly, all of this seems more real than my normal life. It's like I was dreaming all of that time, and then when you showed up at my door, it was like I finally woke up. Does that sound crazy?"

I shake my head. "Not at all. I felt the same way until I saw you."

She smiles as she places her free hand on my face. "If it weren't for you, though, if you weren't here with me, I don't think I'd be able to handle any of this. You make me feel like everything is okay."

{We really do feel the same.}

"Even after everything that has happened and everything that is about to happen, I'm still glad that you knocked on my door. I wouldn't change that for the world because I don't ever not want to know you. I don't ever want to not be with you."

"Me neither. I wouldn't change any of it either. Well, maybe one thing."

She looks at me, concerned.

"I would've come to you sooner so we'd have more time just the two of us."

A warm smile grows on her face. "Once this war is over, we will have the rest of our lives for it to just be the two of us."

BA-DUM, BA-DUM. "Really?"

"Definitely. I told you that I'm not going anywhere, remember?"

"I'm not going anywhere either."

"Then I guess we're stuck with each other." She chuckles.

"Wouldn't want it any other way."

She gently rubs my cheek with her thumb as we smile at each other. The unique warmth pulses inside of me.

"I swear you two can't go more than five minutes without doing something like this." Mal takes her hand off my face as we look at Jade.

"You're just jealous," Mal jokes, taking my hand back into hers.

Jade shakes her head. "No, not jealous, surprised, yes. The idea that you two share deep feelings for each other still blows my mind."

"Well, you better get used to it because I know I don't plan on stopping those feelings ever. In fact, I'm going to let them keep growing and get stronger."

"Same." Mal nudges me.

Jade shakes her head, trying to hide a smile. "How long until the archs get here?" I ask her.

"Any minute now. Once they get here they are going to expand the barrier, and Gabriel and some angels are going to set up a communication hub here in the center so that we can keep in contact with everyone and see what is going on."

"What are the others going to do?" Mal wonders.

"Raziel has to stay up there because of the secrets he holds. Uriel will be here helping teach everyone the different kinds of demons that we will be facing and what they can do. Raphael will scout around where the church is to see if she can make a small medic station for those wounded while fighting. Michael will go to the field and wait for people to show up there to train. Azrael has to travel around the world to track how many we've lost so far. Ariel wants to help grow different herbs and ingredients that the witches and warlocks will need for spells and potions."

"Wanda can help her with that."

Jade nods. "I figured."

"Then once everyone has arrived, the war will begin."

I take a deep breath. "I don't know what I'm supposed to do. I don't know how to lead them."

"All you have to do is be strong for them. Show them that you aren't afraid and are ready to fight for them and with them. You'll have to help with training and come up with a plan. Then when the time comes, you will have to pump them up and stir their courage to head into battle."

"Do you think I can do this?"

"I've only known you for a little over a day, but in that time, I have seen everything you are and everything you are capable of. I trust you, and I want to fight with you. All of the remaining angels do. We all believe in you, Kal. So, yes, I do think that you can do this."

"Do you think we will win?"

She doesn't say anything as she stares at me.

{Why isn't she answering?}

"In my honest opinion, I think you two are going to be what ends this war. As long as we have both of you, every part of me says that we can win."

{Why do they have so much faith in us? Why do they have so much faith in me?}

"She's not the only one who thinks that." Raphael appears beside Jade. "A lot of beings believe that now."

{They're here.}

Gabriel, Michael, Ariel, and Uriel appear out of thin air beside Raphael. "Including us," Michael says.

"No pressure or anything," I joke.

"You two are something special. You've done the impossible, so who's to say you can't win this battle?" Ariel smiles.

Mal rubs her thumb against my hand.

{As long as we're together, maybe we can stop my father and the others. Anything feels possible with her beside me.}

"Enough of that." Uriel turns away from us towards the alley between Give It Your All and Protect Gear. "We have a barrier to expand and our own tasks to complete."

"Right," Michael agrees as he walks the opposite way going in the alley between Wanda's shop and Everyone's Diner.

{The clearing should have enough room.}

The others nod before heading off in different directions. "Why aren't they all going to the same place?" Mal asks.

"They each need to be at a different point in the barrier so they can push on it so that the whole thing will get bigger, not just one spot," Jade explains.

"Oh, I see."

"How long do you think until people start to show up?" I ask.

Jade shrugs. "All depends on how far away they are."

I nod. "I'm just worried that we won't have time to get prepared. By the time everyone arrives, we will have lost a whole day. Then there's only a full night and day plus a few hours before midnight."

"We'll have time."

"I hope so."

Energy spikes all around us. The air feels heavier because of it. "Kal?"

I look at Mal surprised. "You can feel that?"

She nods. "What is it?"

"Energy. It's the energy from the archangels," I answer her.

"Your senses have gotten stronger and more sensitive," Jade tells her. "You'll be able to sense different types of energy and power, plus you will be able to feel when something is wrong or off. Your reflexes should be faster as well."

"What do you mean by something wrong or off?"

"Like how earlier I was able to sense when Jade was going to attack me and I tried to defend myself."

"You were just too slow." Jade grins slyly.

I look at her, annoyed. She holds her arms up as she continues to grin.

"The same when Wanda and I had our little sparring match in the back of the store. I could sense where she was going to fire her energy and I was able to dodge all of her magic attacks."

Mal nods. "So I'll be able to perceive things differently now?"

"That's one way to put it." Jade nods.

"If you gain better control, you'll be able to predict what is going to happen. That's how I knew Jade was going to be behind me."

"Again, too slow."

"Would you shut up?" I ask, irritated. Mal chuckles.

"I'll get you back. Just you wait." I threaten her.

"Sure." She laughs.

The archangel's power presses down on me as the barrier shimmers and goes in and out of focus.

"It's moving," Jade states.

We watch as the edges of the barrier move farther away, causing the ground to shake under our feet. The windows in the shops vibrate, threatening to break as some of the signs tremble. The door from the Day Motel swings open as some of the occupants come out looking angry but curious. A few starts pointing up at the barrier, getting others to look up. They talk to each other quickly with panic.

"Kal!"

{Wanda.}

I turn around as she runs towards us. Mal lets go of my hand as she sees Wanda still running.

"You're okay!" Wanda exclaims as she tackles me into a hug.

"Well, of course I am." I put my arms around her. "I made a promise, didn't I?"

"I saw you on the angel's disk and your body was covered in dark red veins." She squeezes harder. "I was worried."

"Nothing to be worried about. The veins were just temporary. I'm back to normal now."

She lets go of me as she takes a step back to look me over. "See, perfectly fine."

The ground stops shaking as the barrier quits moving. The group from the motel all look around before giving up and go back inside the door, shutting firmly behind them.

{Guess they're moody if woken.}

Wanda looks up at the barrier settles. "What's going on?"

"The Middle has just developed a ton of more land," I answer jokingly.

"What are you talking about?" She looks back at me. "No one can make this place bigger. The barrier is too strong to move."

"True that no ONE can do it, but multiple someones can."

"Who? Who is powerful enough to do it?"

"They are." I nudge my head, pointing to the right as Ariel comes into the circle. Wanda follows my direction. The second her eyes land on Ariel, her jaw drops in disbelief. The other archangels begin to enter the center as well. Each one is heading in our direction.

"Are those—?" Wanda starts quietly.

"The archangels? Yes, they are."

"All right, Kalma, the first step is completed," Gabriel tells me as they stop around us.

"Is the area I told you about big enough, Michael?"

He nods. "It should do."

Wanda continues to stare at them with bewilderment.

"While we wait for more to arrive, we should complete our individual tasks," Uriel explains.

The rest nod in agreement.

"Oh yeah, Raphael, Ariel." They look at me. "This is Wanda." I nudge her, making her close her mouth. "She owns the witch shop over there."

"You're a witch, I take it?" Ariel asks her.

Wanda nods, unable to speak.

"She's the one you talked about in your speech, isn't she?" Raphael wonders.

"That she is. Wanda is a witch that specializes in healing."

"You saved Kalma," Ariel states.

"I did."

"Must be pretty powerful, then." Raphael smiles.

"And you must really know your herbs," Ariel comments.

"She is really powerful, and she grows her own herbs."

"Impressive," Raphael says.

"I think she is." I smile at Wanda. "She's my best friend and my sister. I don't know where I'd be without her."

Wanda stops staring at them to look at me. I widen my smile, making her smile back at me.

"That's how I know that she can be a great help to both of you," I explain as I face them again.

"Oh?" Ariel questions.

"She can help you with knowing which herbs the witches are going to need, and Raphael, she can assist you with the different ingredients you'll need to heal the injured, plus she can heal some as well."

Both of them study Wanda as they think it over. Taking a deep breath, I walk closer to them. As I stop between them, I wave them to come closer. They step closer as they bend down so I can whisper to them.

"Please let her work with you. If she's with an archangel, then I know that she will be safe. Wanda means a lot to me, and if she gets hurt or worse during all of this..." I clench my hands at my sides. "Nothing can happen to her."

{Mal will be with me, so I can keep her safe, but I can't keep them both safe. So if Wanda is with them, then she will be.}

"Please."

"I don't think I'll ever get used to a demon caring for someone else other than themselves," Ariel admits.

"Enough to ask an archangel for help. It's just incredible," Raphael agrees. "Then again, you are special."

"You are more than just a demon. You are so much more." Ariel smiles. "All right, we'll let her help us."

"Really?" I ask.

They nod.

"Thank you." I let out a sigh of relief.

{She'll be safe.}

As I turn to walk back over to Wanda and Mal, they stand straight again. "Wanda, your help would be much appreciated," Raphael tells her.

"What did you say to them?" Wanda asks quietly as I stop beside her.

"Just the truth."

{I'm not lying to her. I did tell them the truth.} "And they want my help?"

"Guess so."

"We should get started, though," Ariel explains. "Are you ready?"

"You can help them. You have the skill and the intel that they need. You are perfect."

She studies me before turning to check the two archangels waiting for her. "I'll do what I can."

More relief washes through me. "Good."

"See you in a few hours?" she asks as she nudges my arm.

"Yep."

She nods before leading them to her shop. I watch as Raphael and Ariel duck down to fit into the door.

{Thank you, you two.}

"So, now what?" Mal asks the remaining archs.

"Hang around and wait for others to arrive," Uriel answers. "The rest of us have our own duties to complete."

"Right," Mal responds.

"Is there anything specific I should do while you are all busy?" I look at Michael.

"Just prepare yourself. Once they arrive, things are going to move quickly. Be prepared for that."

"All right, I will do my best."

"I'll be at the new opening if you need me, but"—he steps up to me and puts his giant hand on my shoulder—"you are the leader. Don't forget that."

"I won't."

He takes his hand off me as he grins. "If you feel like sparing or something, you can come join me."

"What should I do?" Jade wonders.

"Work with Mal some more," Michael answers. "Help her be faster and stronger. She's going to need to be as strong as she can be."

"Got it."

{Mal is strong, but Michael is right. She needs to be the best that she can be.} "Is there somewhere I can get information about different demons and their powers?" Uriel asks me.

"The library." I point to the building containing the library. "It's not that big, but it should have everything you need."

She nods. "I'll be there if you need me," she tells us as she moves towards the library.

"The communication equipment should be here soon, along with some angels to help me set it all up as well as run everything," Gabriel explains.

"Will you be able to get everything set up even with the fountain being in the way?" I ask him.

He nods. "The fountain is actually going to come in handy."

"How so?"

"We can have the same set up here as we do in our headquarters. The computers can sit on the cement around the fountain, and we can place the machine that projects the globe on top of the fountain so it will appear above it."

"So, everything will work out then?" Jade wonders.

"Definitely."

She nods satisfied.

Gabriel walks over to the fountain, studying it while he waits. "So, what do you want to do?" Jade asks Mal and me.

"I think you training Mal some more is a good idea."

"I agree," Mal concurs.

"Then that's what we'll do." She looks at me. "What about you?"

"Still trying to figure that out." I tensely laugh. "Trying to decide between taking Michael up on his offer of sparing or waiting around until people start to show."

"Would you like to hear my opinion?" Jade asks.

"Is it going to cost me two cents?" I joke dryly.

"Not this time." She goes along. "Seriously though, I think you should take Michael's offer."

"Oh?"

"You aren't going to find anyone better to train with than him. He is the archangel warrior. He'd be able to help you hone your skills more than you ever thought possible."

{She's right. Michael is the only one who can help me get stronger. Hopefully strong enough to take my father on.}

I nod. "You're right. Thank you. I think I will do that."

"Good idea." She smiles.

"I'll see you in a few hours," I tell Mal.

"Good luck."

I chuckle. "You too."

Jade starts walking to the training building. Mal waves before following behind her.

{Get stronger, Mal.}

I turn and start making my way to the clearing behind Wanda's shop.

{We both need to be stronger. I need to be stronger so I can protect everyone better.}

Michael stands in the center of the clearing with his arms over his chest. He grins as he sees me approaching.

{I have to be the one to take my father down and end all of this. I can't allow anyone to fight him, or they'll just be struck down.}

"I see you decided to take me up on my offer," Michael states as I stop in front of him.

"Can you make me stronger?"

"Depends."

"On?"

"The reason why you want to be stronger."

"There are multiple reasons, all of which you already know."

"Tell me."

I sigh, annoyed. "So I can do most of the fighting so that fewer people will get hurt. I need the power to stop this war, to protect those closest to me, to save Mal."

"And?"

"That's it."

He shakes his head. "I know that there is something else. If you can't admit it, then I can't help you. What are you holding back?" he asks me seriously.

I go through my head trying to figure it out. I search every part of me, digging down deep to find the answer, the answer that terrifies me.

"I need to be stronger so I can..." My hands shake, so I tighten them into fists. "I have to be stronger so I can..." I stare into his cobalt eyes. "Kill my father."

"There it is." He nods in understanding. "Now I can help you."

24

"You did better than I thought you would," Michael applauds me.

"Thanks," I respond as I am bent over with my hands on my knees, a blade in each hand.

{We've been going at it for hours while waiting for the sun to set.}

As I stand up, I put the two swords back together before lifting it over my shoulder to slide it back in its sheath.

{Even though he is weakened because of the churches being destroyed, he is still on a whole other level. I knew that archangels were notorious for their strength and powers, but damn, I don't think I wounded him even once.}

"Hey, don't make that face," He teases.

"What face? I'm not making a face."

"Yes, you are. You're making the face of someone who's thinking that after all of that, nothing was accomplished."

"Nothing was. Unless you count me learning that I have zero chance of fighting my father."

Michael shakes his head. "You really don't see it, do you?"

"See what?"

"Just how powerful you really are."

"Powerful? You think I am powerful?"

"I do." He nods. "You just need to learn how to fully tap into that power. While we were sparing, I felt the edges of that power you hold inside of you. You might not have realized it, but as we continued, you were getting faster and faster. You summoned your flames quicker each time. When you blasted your fire, they shot faster, burned hotter, and lasted longer."

{Did I really do all of that without realizing it?}

"Tell me, how do you feel? Do you feel weakened at all? Has your internal flame diminished at all?"

As if hearing him, my internal flame blazes hotter inside of me. "No, I feel fine. My flame is fine."

He nods. "As I expected." Michael steps closer to me as he kneels down on one leg so that he is almost at eye level with me. "Kal, I know that there is something inside of you waiting to break out. I could feel it with every attack you threw and with every swing of your blades or fists. That power slips out of you in small portions, helping your attacks or your strength or speed. Once those amounts seep out, your body absorbs them before settling inside of you, making you that much more powerful than you were before." He puts his hands on my shoulders. "Just think how strong you'd be if all of it was set free."

{Can there really be something like that hidden inside of me?}

"You will continue to get stronger, Kal, and once all of that is out, who knows just how powerful you will be." He grins. "Maybe even more than me."

I gape at him.

{Be stronger than an archangel? Is that even possible?}

"We told you before that we think you and Mal are going to be what ends this war."

"Does that mean...?"

"Yes. Mal has the same kind of power inside of her and the same potential to let it out as you do."

"Because we're hybrids." My voice drops.

"No, that's not why."

"Then what?"

He shrugs. "None of us knows what makes you two so special and so different from all the other hybrids before you. Raziel doesn't even know."

{Not even Raziel?}

"We feel something inside you both that we've never felt before, and we've been around for a while." He chuckles.

I can't help but chuckle with him.

He grips my shoulders a little tighter. "I'm serious, though, Kal." He looks at me, creating eye contact. "Everyone believes that you two will stop the demons, will end this war, will save us all."

My mouth goes dry.

"I understand that that is a lot to put on you two, but"—he smiles—"we all have faith that you can do it."

{Faith?}

"You and Mal need to believe that. Both of you have to pull that power sweltering inside of you out so you can be as strong as you can be." His smile brightens as he repeats my words.

"But how?" I lay my hand on my chest. "How do we force it out?"

"Sadly, I don't have the answer for that. All I know is that I, as well as all the other archangels, can see how you and Mal act towards one another and how deep those feelings go. The connection you two have is just as powerful as whatever is inside you. So all of our instincts are telling us that Mal is the key to unlocking your power, and you are the key to unlocking hers. We don't know why, and we don't know how. We just know."

{Mal is my key, and I am hers? What does that even mean?}

"You'll have to figure out how to help the other one, but we think you can do it." I look into his cobalt eyes.

{There isn't a shred of doubt in him. He truly believes that Mal and I are the answer.}

I grab onto my shirt.

{They are all putting their lives and their futures in our hands.}

A feeling of purpose slams into me. I take a deep breath as I release my shirt, making it into a fist over top of my shirt.

"Then that's what we'll do." I press my fist harder against my chest. "We will win this fight, and we will stop the demons from winning." I smile. "When I am with Mal, it feels as if anything is possible. Feels like we can do anything as long as it's together."

Michael lightly laughs as he removes his hands off my shoulders and stands back up. "Having faith in oneself is a potent thing."

I nod.

"So don't ever question yourself." He grabs the bottom of his shirt, lifting it slightly. "You are stronger than you think."

My hand falls from my chest as I gawk at the slowly healing slice above his pants on his side.

{I did that?}

Confidence rises inside of me while I watch his wound heal.

He lowers his shirt back down. "Now get going. I'm sure they've all arrived by now."

{That time already?}

I look up and see the moon shining above us, with thousands of stars sparkling across the dark canvas.

{The night sky with its moon and stars. So calming but so scary at the same time.} I face forward again before turning towards town.

"Thank you, Michael." I start running

{Wow.}

Different kinds of beings stand throughout the circle surrounding the angel's communication globe in the center.

{So many actually came.}

Taking a deep breath, I begin walking through them towards the fountain. As I pass the different groups, they become quiet to watch me as I continue moving. I take note of everyone that I see. The last line of people separates so that I can go into the inner circle. Out of the corner of my eye I see Mal and Jade step into the inner circle as well. Mal waves at me with a welcoming smile on her face. I give her a smile back but don't stop. A few of the angels see me coming, so they stop typing and move away from the fountain.

{Gotta make this look smooth and cool.}

Power rushes towards my feet as I make it to the outer layer of the fountain. Flames burst from my shoes, pushing me into the air. Using the momentum from the fire, I do a front flip before landing perfectly on the top of the fountain. My fire goes out as I carefully turn around to face everyone. Mal giggles as she watches me. Jade shakes her head with an annoyed look on her face. I grin down at them before taking a deep breath as I create a neutral look on my face. The Middle is completely quiet. The only sounds are those from the water splashing beneath me.

{I thought I had this all figured out in my head, but now that I am up here...} I glance around at them all.

{At least from here I can see everyone better and can make a more accurate count. In the front are guardian angels. I count at least a hundred of them. They must be the last of GAs. The small group beside them are the power angels and the cherubim, since I see Jahoel and those two douchebags from earlier, Peliel and Leo.}

Peliel and Leo stare up at me in shock and surprise. I can't help but smirk from the looks on their faces.

{Five power angels and two cherubim. That's not that many.} My eyes scan the next few rows.

{Right behind the angels are the witches. Seems to be ten of them, four of them being Derrick and his coven.}

They all wave to me.

{After the witches, from the aura I'm getting off them, those three must be jinn. I wonder if Frikik is one of them. Furies and succubi flank the jinn. Wonder how uncomfortable that feels. Only two furies? That's surprising.}

My stomach tenses as I scan through the succubi.

{Even though we need all of the help we can get, I was still hoping that they wouldn't show up.}

Husha, Nestra, and Deseih stand together amongst the other succubus. I glare down at them. They must sense it because they look up at me. Their eyes fill with fear before turning away again.

{At least there are five other ones.} I look at the rest of the creatures.

{Mixed together behind those bitches are goblins, imps, and pucks. Wow, twenty goblins. I've never seen so many in one place before. Never seen that many pucks together either, ten of them.}

My stomach drops as I see Uxum and Sukir standing with them.

{I was hoping that they'd avoid all of this. They aren't cut out for war.} I sigh as I count the imps.

{Five, somehow. I thought there would be more.}

Natural energy pulls me to the space between the library and the Day Motel.

{Those must be elemental beings. I've never seen one before. I never thought I'd see four in one place. From the elements circling around them, there is one for each element. Air, water, fire, and earth.}

Sparkling lights and jingling bells draw my attention. Above everyone are floating lights.

{The fairies.}

Running along the bench closest to me are two bright orbs going back and forth.

{Pixies. Why are they all here? They're just going to get hurt if they stay.}

A green flash makes me look down to see Wanda standing next to Mal. Her eyes are fading back to their usual color as she smiles up at me. I stare at her and Mal as everything hits me. Knowing that the battle is coming fast, that they've all put their lives in my hands, the fact that everyone is expecting me to be able to lead them, and most of all...

{They think I can save them.}

Panic rises in my chest, causing it to feel tight. My breathing begins to pick up as my hands start to shake. Mal and Wanda look at me, concerned. Mal turns to Wanda and says something before Wanda nods while saying something back. Mal looks back at me. Wanda's eyes flash again, telling me to look at her, so I do. Once she has my attention, she lifts her arms up to indicate a deep breath before lowering them to show letting it out. She points at me before repeating. I nod and follow her instructions taking deep breaths in and out repeatedly until the tightness is gone and my hands are no longer shaking.

{Thank you.}

I smile at her with a nod. Her eyes return to normal as her hands fall back to her sides with a grin of her own.

{Okay, I got this.}

"Thank you all for coming." Everyone stares at me.

"I'm going to make this short since you've all already heard how I feel. Everything I said during that message was the truth. All the things that I said I meant."

"Even what you said about your father?" someone yells.

{I didn't know they were going to ask questions.}

"Yes, even the part about my father."

They start to murmur and whisper to each other.

"You all saw my message. You each heard my words. I spoke of caring for all of you, just as I do the humans. I meant it. I said that I would give my life to save her to save everyone that the demons want to hurt or worse. I promised you that I won't allow them to just take this world, not without giving it my all. That's exactly what I plan on doing."

"You spoke of this girl a lot," someone explains. "Who is she?"

I glance down at Mal. She meets my eyes. She nods as a warm smile spreads across her face.

I nod back before looking back up. "Her name is Malak. She is the angel hybrid my father and the others want to kill. She is the girl that changed me, that found me in the darkness and pulled me out."

"How do we know she is real?"

{I understand why they are cautious, but I figured that they came because they trusted me.}

Mal waves at me to gain my attention. She waves me down as I look at her.

{What is she up to?}

"One second," I explain to the crowd before jumping off of the fountain to land a few feet in front of Mal.

"What's up?"

She runs up to me. "They have to see that you are genuine, that everything you say is the truth. They want to believe you, Kal, but until they have proof, they just can't. It's in their nature."

I nod. "I guess you're right."

"So let's give them proof." She beams. "Take me up there with you. Let them see that I am real, that the feelings we have are sincere."

"How do we show them that?"

"Allow them to see how you look at one another," Wanda explains. I turn to her.

"If someone can't see what is between you two, then they are either blind or stupid," Jade speaks up.

Mal turns to her.

"Do what she says, Kal," Wanda demands.

I chuckle. "Bossy, bossy."

"Just go," Wanda says, annoyed. Mal and I laugh.

{What would I do without them?} "Ready?" Mal asks me.

"Yep." I crouch down as she moves closer. "Just wrap your arms around my neck."

"Okay."

She leans against me as she slowly puts her arms around my neck. We gaze into each other's eyes as I carefully reach around her with my right arm so that it is pressing up against her back. I gently scoop up her legs into my left arm before standing back up. Her eyes threaten to pull me in as I hold her tighter against me. She smiles, causing my cheeks to burn.

"Yep, just like that," Jade speaks up.

We break eye contact to look at her as she stands with her arms folded. "Let them see you like that."

"Like what?" I ask.

She sighs as she shakes her head. "Just go." Mal shrugs as I turn back towards the fountain.

{Will seeing her, seeing us, really make them trust me?}

"I'm not going to use my flames this time. I'm just going to jump." She nods.

"Hold on tightly and try not to move more than you have to. It's a small peak, so it's hard to balance on."

"Got it."

"Here goes."

I put weight into my legs before leaping off the ground to land where I was a few minutes ago on top of the fountain. The murmuring and whispering become louder. "That wasn't so bad," Mal jokes.

I chuckle. "Not the first time I've held you like this." I squeeze her against me.

"Hopefully, it won't be the last." Her cheeks blush.

My ears heat up seeing the look in her eyes. All of the whispering and murmuring stops.

"So, it is true," I hear Deseih say.

Mal and I look out towards everyone.

{Why are they looking at us like that?}

They all stare at us in astonishment. Derrick's cult grin at us, already knowing what Mal and I share.

"That's the girl?" a voice asks.

"Yes, this is Malak."

"And you have feelings for her?" another asks me.

"I do. Ever since I saw Mal, I've been experiencing the different emotions that humans do."

"GASP!"

"A demon feeling emotions?"

"Is that even possible?"

"I've never heard of such a thing."

People begin to talk over one another as they discuss whether they think it is true or not.

"She's not lying," Mal speaks up.

They all stop talking as they gape at her.

"Kalma does have emotions. I have seen them. I've seen her sad, scared, happy, plus what she feels towards me. It is hard to believe that a demon could have emotions, but Kalma isn't like other demons. She is special."

My cheeks burn.

"You've already observed how different she is. You saw that her flames are not their normal color. You can clearly see that she can blush."

My whole face heats up as they scan me with their eyes.

"So please take everything she says to heart, because all of it is true."

"Do you love her?" Deseih questions Mal.

{The succubi said before that no one loved me and that if Mal really did, that she was either stupid or wanted to die.}

Mal's face lights up with a smile. "With everything I have." Nestra, Husha, and Deseih make eye contact with me.

{Now they see that they were wrong. That Mal really does love me, and not for the reasons they thought.}

They nod at me in apology.

{Mal loves me because her heart tells her to.}

I give them a slight nod, accepting their apologies. We break eye contact, and I notice that the angels have joined the witches and are now smiling.

{Won the angels over, but I'm sure that the archs probably talked to them about me, so it was easy to confirm their concerns. Convincing everyone else is the hard part.}

"Answer something for us," one of the jinn exclaims.

"I'll answer anything."

"This battle to save the church. We will be fighting demons, correct?" I nod.

"Archdemons?"

{I see where this is going.}

I bob my head, taking notice of Michael leaning against the wall from Wanda's shop. He watches me.

{He knows where this is going as well.}

"We will be fighting Rorridun, your father?"

"Yes."

"Our concern is that you won't be able to fight him, that you won't want to fight him because he is your dad."

{I figured.}

"I guess we just want to know if you will go up against him, if it comes to that?"

{Michael dug this answer out of me earlier. The solution that I didn't know was inside of me until that moment. I don't have to think about it because I know what has to be done.}

"I already know that it will come to that. My father wants me dead, so he will find me on that battlefield to kill me himself." I take a deep breath. "When he comes for me, I will be ready..." My resolve rings through me. "To kill him."

The jinn's eyes widen in surprise at my answer. Mal turns her head to look up at me, also shocked.

"I've been thinking about it for a while now. Wondering if I could actually bring myself to do it if given a chance. At first, there was no way I'd even consider it, but..." I tilt my head down to meet Mal's stare. "Now I know that for her to live, he must die. I care more for her than I ever did for my father." I move my head to look at Wanda on the ground. "He was never my family. I created my own family, and I will make sure that nothing happens to it." I lift my head to look back at the crowd. "So, to give you a final answer, yes, I will fight him and throw everything I have at him until his flame is no more. I told you that I believe when people are protecting those that they really care about, they can be as strong as they can be. To protect Mal and my new family, my flame will burn hotter than ever so I can kill my father and stop the others."

The jinn smile at me, as well as the furies. The goblins, imps, and pucks start to jump up and down in excitement. Bells ring loudly above us while the fairies fly quickly all around. More bells jingle on the bench where the tiny lights from the pixies dance. I look towards the elementals and notice that they moved closer to the group.

{I did it. Everyone believes in me. They are ready to fight with me.} Michael grins at me with a nod of acknowledgment.

"So, what do we need to do?" someone asks me.

"Prepare," I answer. "First, we need to know what we are up against." I scan the crowd near the library. "Uriel can help us with that."

Everyone turns around as Uriel makes her way towards me. As she gets closer, she hands one of the angels working on the keyboards one of the disks they use. The angel runs to their keyboard and begins typing quickly before laying the disk on it. The disk starts to glow.

"Need you to get down so we can use the projector," Uriel explains.

"Got it."

I hold onto Mal tightly before hopping off of the top of the fountain. We land by Wanda and Jade.

"So, how bad was it?" I ask them as I set Mal back onto the ground.

"You did great," Wanda answers sincerely.

"You were able to rally them behind you. They trust you now and want to help. Both of your speeches today have struck something inside of them."

"All I did was be honest."

"And that is why they trust you. They see that you are fighting for the same thing that they are. All of us are fighting to protect someone or something. That unites us all," Jade explains.

Mal grabs my hand. "Those who want to protect something precious to them will fight with others to make sure that it happens."

{We are all working towards the same goal.}

"All right," Uriel exclaims, "everyone, pay attention to the projector shining above me. I will be showing you what we are up against."

Mal and I face Uriel and the projector.

"After doing some recon and research, I was able to find the demons that we will be facing." She nods to the angel at the keyboard.

A giant floating image of a black demon dog appears. "It looks just like Shadow," Mal whispers.

"The same type of creature," I tell her.

"I'm sure many of you know what this is. This is a black demon dog, also known as the dog guards of Hell. The average size of these monsters is measured to be the same as a calf. Their hair is black as a moonless night. The only signs that one is hiding in the dark are its glowing red eyes. Black dogs are very fast as well as strong. Their jaws could easily bite someone in half if they were to be caught in its mouth. We want to avoid that, as well as the claws. The claws can slash through even the toughest armor, so be very careful when confronting one. The only way to defeat this beast is to either strike through the heart or pierce the skull. No other wounds will be fatal enough to kill it, only these two." Uriel nods back at the angel.

The black dog disappears, replaced by an oni demon.

"This is an oni demon. They are very skilled with their swords, can lift twice their weight, and can move quickly. Only those who are masters in sword fighting should approach them. Try to match their speed and keep moving until you find an opening. To kill them, you have to strike them down until they can no longer go on. It may sound easy, but I promise you that it is not." Another nod.

The oni vanishes, and a nightmare demon pops up. Cold shivers run down my spine as I stare up at it.

"This is a nightmare demon. Normally, it is scarce to see one of these because they hide in the darkest shadows. As you can see, nightmares do not have any features whatsoever. They are humanoid creatures whose bodies are smooth and black with nothing else. Do not let their appearance deceive you, though. Nightmares are extremely tough and fast. If one catches you, you will be slowly pulled into the void on their bodies, never being seen again. So don't let one grab you. Guardian angels, you will have to take the lead on fighting these things, since the only weapons that can harm or kill them are our blades and our angelic beams."

{I've never seen one of them before. I learned about them from Father's books.} The image changes to a marching horde.

{Those are what the higher-ups use to fight their battles.}

"This is a marching horde. Pretty scary-looking, huh? Marching hordes all look the same. They are very unintelligent creatures who blindly follow whatever order they are given. That is why they are used in high quantities to fight in battles and wars. They are speedy, especially when swinging out their arms to slash you with their claws. If they can't get you with their claws, they will use their mouths filled with rows of razor-sharp teeth. Avoid the mouth and hands at all costs. One on its own is easy to defeat. Any powerful attack or blow can do the job, but when there is a whole swarm, the task shall be much harder."

{Any of us can take them down, but like Uriel said, fighting so many at once will be very difficult.}

"Then, finally, the demons that you will really have to look out for."

The marching hordes blink away as a new photo is shown. Anger and fear mix together in the bottom of my stomach as I stare at my fellow archdemons. "These are the archdemons that will be attacking the church. We know who the adults are but not their children."

I let go of Mal's hand to step closer to Uriel. "The girl is Allaya." Everyone turns to me. "The boy on the far left is Encador, next to him is Vexxus, the last boy is Jorvexx."

"Do you know them?" Uriel questions.

"They were the unit I was in charge of until I betrayed them to protect Mal. I fought against all of them until they had to retreat."

{I didn't think that their parents would allow them to come back up after failing their mission.}

"You were able to defeat them all on your own?" someone in the crowd asks.

"Not defeat. I was only able to push them back."

"So you know all of these archdemons, then?" Uriel wonders.

"Yes, there are the archdemons of my sector. The only one not up there is my father."

Uriel looks over at the angel. The others vanish as my father comes into view. My breath catches in my chest as my knees begin to shake. His red eyes glaring down at me with rage and hate. Invisible weights press down on me, making me feel ten times heavier as my stomach flips, threatening to make me sick. I stare up at his picture, completely petrified of him.

{It's just a picture, and yet it still has this effect on me.}

My hands tremble as I take a small step away from his photo. A hand presses against mine as their fingers lace between mine. I quickly turn as Mal stands beside me. Another hand grabs my free one. I look to see Wanda standing on that side. They both look at me with warmth, understanding, and confidence in their eyes.

"Now I know that for her to live, he must die."

My previous words echo in my head.

"Yes, I will fight him, and I will throw everything I have at him until his flame is no more."

The weight lifts off of me as I remember what I said.

"To protect Mal and my new family, my flame will burn hotter than ever so I can kill my father and stop the others."

My body stops trembling as the fear evaporates. I take a deep breath as I hold their hands tighter.{Thank you.}

"This is Rorridun," Uriel tells everyone. "He is Lucifer's right hand. He is the one in charge of this operation to destroy the church here in Philadelphia. We take him out, the marching hordes will stop."

"So we just have to stop him?" a voice asks.

"No."

They all look at me.

"None of you can fight him. He's too strong. I'm the only one who stands a chance at beating him. So, leave my father to me."

"But Kal—" Mal speaks up.

"I won't allow him to hurt anyone, so I will fight him on my own."

"Are you sure, Kal?" Wanda asks.

"I am. He is my father, my responsibility, the one threatening those I care for. So please, all of you, leave him to me."

No one says anything.

"All right." I hear Michael's voice.

"Okay, Kalma."

"We will leave him to you."

"He is all yours."

"Be careful."

Different people all over begin to agree and wish me luck. "Thank you."

"Now that that is settled," Uriel says as she waves to the angel. The projector returns its typical picture of the globe.

"The other archangels also have some things they want to tell all of you. Gabriel, you first."

"Right." Gabriel emerges from the crowd.

He and Uriel trade places before Uriel stands by us while about twenty angels move to the keyboards.

"The globe above me tells us exactly what is going on around the world." The globe grows bigger and brighter so that all can see it.

{There are even fewer blue dots than before.}

"Each colored dot on the globe is for different things. The groups of red are swarms of demons. Each swarm of red surrounds a blue dot. The blue is the remaining oldest churches. As you can see, there are only five left, including the one here. Mixed in with the red are white dots, which are the guardian angels fighting to try to save those churches."

{The number of white has also shrunk since last time.}

"The demons have destroyed all the other churches, as well as killed the guardians that were protecting them. Pretty soon all of the blue will be gone except for one." The globe zooms in on the lonely blue dot.

"This is the Gloria Dei Church, the oldest church in Pennsylvania's capital. The oldest church in Philadelphia. This church will be the last one on the demons' list, so we have to defend it with everything we got."

The globe zooms back out a little, just enough to show a cluster of mixed red and white.

"This is us."

{When you look at us like that, it doesn't seem that there are that many.}

"These dots are the last of this world's defense. We will keep everyone updated on the status of the other churches and how the other guardians are doing. That is all the communication angels and I can do for now. We will be watching the world twenty-four seven. We'll be able to see when they start to head for the church."

{Good, we'll have a head start.}

"I'm sorry that I don't have good news or inspirational words like Kal did. I'm just here to make sure that you all know what is going on."

"Thank you, Gabriel," Ariel speaks as she and Raphael move into the inner circle. Gabriel nods before backing away so that the ladies can have the center stage. "These next few days, I shall be growing all the different herbs that will help with power and healing. I will make sure that all of you witches will be fully stocked with everything you need before heading into battle. So if any of you have any special requests, please do not be afraid to ask. I am here to help. You can find me in or behind Wanda's shop."

I squeeze Wanda's hand.

"I will help with healing of any kind. We found an empty parking lot around the corner from the church. Those gifted in the art of healing and I will be there trying to send healing energy through the air into the injured. As long as we are there, we hope that casualties won't be as big. Also, to the fairies and the pixies."

{What does she want them for? They can't fight?}

The floating lights levitate above Raphael as well as at her feet. "I was informed that your dust can help restore someone's magic."

{Wanda must have told her what they did for her.}

They jingle.

"Do you think you could create enough dust to help those fighting so when they run out of magic, you can refuel them?"

The fairies float down closer to the ground to jingle with the pixies.

{Making pixie dust isn't an easy task, and for the quantity we'd need, I don't know if they'd have the strength to do it, but knowing them, they'll try.}

The jingles get louder as the fairies fly back up.

"Excellent. If you need any assistance, just ask."

All of the little lights from the air and the ground disappear through the crowd.

{They aren't going to waste any time. They're going to start right away.}

"That just leaves you, Michael," Raphael says.

"Yeah, yeah, I know." Michael walks out of the crowd.

He looks over at me as he makes his way to where Raphael stands. His eyes move to my hands, which still hold Mal's and Wanda's. He grins before turning around to face everyone. Raphael stands beside Uriel.

"I'm sure that not many of you have much experience when it comes to fighting, if any. Most of you have come accustomed to the life of peace and quiet, which is okay, but right now, we all need you to be able to fight. So I am here to help teach you how, and how to defend yourself as well. Each kind of being here has a different kind of attack, and I will make sure you can use it perfectly. I have been creating warriors for over a millennium. So, believe me when I say that I can turn all of you into fighters within the time that we have. On the outskirts of the circle, the area behind Day Motel all the way to Witchy Things, that area is the training field. All of you need to go there and work with me until I declare if you are ready or not. There are no exceptions for this."

"He's being a little tough, don't you think?" Wanda asks.

I shake my head. "He's not being tough enough. If they don't learn how to fight, then what is the point in going into battle? They'd be slaughtered in minutes."

Wanda sighs. "I guess you're right."

"I'll start with the goblins, imps, and pucks. All of you head to the field now, and I'll follow you."

No one moves.

Taking a deep breath, I let go of Mal's and Wanda's hands.

"Listen to him," I command them all as I step to stand beside Michael. "I trained with him all day, and he knows what he is doing. My power has grown because of him."

He smirks as he crosses his arms.

"So do as he says, and I promise you that by the time you're done, you will feel like a completely different being. You'll be stronger than you ever thought possible. So please do what he says."

After a few seconds the imps, pucks, and goblins split from the main group and head towards the field. I let out a breath of relief.

{They have to get stronger.}

"While you train everyone, I have a job for the guardian angels." Gabriel walks up to us. "There are humans who live all around where the church is. If we don't get them out of there, who knows how many could die."

"So, what are you suggesting?" Raphael asks.

"Evacuate them. Get the ones who live about a mile all around the church."

"A whole mile?" Michael questions.

"Better to be safe than sorry," Gabriel explains.

"You're right," Raphael compliments.

"Nice thinking, Gabriel." Uriel pats him on the back.

He moves away from her hand. "I know it was. I don't need you to tell me." He grins at her.

The others laugh at them, and I can't help but smile.

{I always forget that even though they don't look anything alike, they are siblings. Seeing them like this helps remind me of that.}

"I'll send all the guardians available." Michael waves to the guardians.

"They'll have to use their angelic persuasion on the humans to get them to leave," Uriel speaks up.

{Guardian angels can temporarily brainwash humans to protect them.} "Got it." Michael nods as he moves over to the group of GAs.

{Get everyone to safety.}

All of them salute Michael before running towards the entrance. Michael walks back over to me. "I'm going to need your help training everyone."

"Me? Why not one of the other archs?"

"They trust you now. They will feel better seeing you training right along with them." He leans in closer. "And between you and me, your fighting skills are a lot better than any of theirs."

"No way."

"It's true. None of them have picked up a sword for hundreds of years, so you see, I need you."

I turn to Mal.

"He's right, Kal. Help the others," she tells me.

"But—"

She steps up to me and grabs my hands. "I know, I don't want to be apart from you right now either, but we both have different places we need to be. You go with Michael and train, and I'll be with Jade doing my own training."

I peak around Mal at Jade.

"She's getting stronger, Kal. To be honest, she has already surpassed me."

"Really?" Wanda speaks up.

Jade nods. "She is faster, stronger, and her energy control is off the charts." She meets my stare. "I promise you, Kal, that her training with me is the best thing right now."

My eyes meet Mal's again.

{All I want is for her to be safe, and I know that Jade is correct and that working with her, she can get stronger. She'll be able to protect herself better. But...}

A feeling of longing presses against my chest.

{I don't want to be apart anymore. I want to stay by her side, and it just be the two of us for a little while.}

Mal gives me a sad smile before sliding her hands up until they rest on both sides of my face. "I'm starting to be able to read you like a book." Her smile turns warm. "I want it to just be us two too, but right now we both need to be where we are needed."

I look at her sadly.

"How about this"—she pulls me in for a hug—"after the sun sets on the night of the thirtieth, we will spend those hours before battle together doing whatever you want."

My arms wrap around her tightly as fearful tears fill my eyes. I try to blink them away, but instead, I set them free.

"Kal," I hear Wanda whisper.

The archs around us take in quiet intakes of breath as my tears slide down my face.

"Malak, I'm scared," I admit. "What if these next few days are it? What if..." I hold her tighter as I begin to cry. "What if I lose you?" My voice breaks.

"Hey, hey." She runs her left hand through my hair on the back of my head, while her right presses firmly against my back.

My tears don't stop as my fear grows inside of me. Footsteps tiptoe away from us. Water continues to flow down my face while I try to catch my breath.

"Shhhh, Kalma. Everything is going to be okay."

I shake my head. "I've never been afraid to fight before. I used to love the thrill of it, but now..."

Pain shoots through my chest.

"Now I'm terrified that if we do this, I could lose you." My knees threaten to buckle. "I can't lose you, Mal, I can't. I don't understand why I'm feeling like this, but I can't stop this fear. I've tried to push it away or cover it up, but as we grow closer to battle, my terror gets stronger."

She plays with my hair.

"You are everything to me now. You are my world, my light. Without you..." I choke on a sob. "Without you, I'd die." She holds me closer.

{I wouldn't want to live without her, I couldn't}

I whimper against her shoulder. After a few minutes, I start to settle down, but tears still roll down my cheeks.

"Kalma, listen to me carefully, okay?" I nod.

"Nothing is going to happen to me because you'll be there to make sure of it. You will protect me just like you said you would. I know that you will keep me safe because I know just how much I want to keep you safe."

My tears freeze.

"All of those things that you just said, I feel the exact same way about you. I'm afraid of what could happen to you, but I tell myself that I'll be there if you need me, the same way you'll be there if I need you."

{She wants to protect me too?}

"I have faith in you." She takes her hand out of my hair as she slightly pulls away. "Do you have faith in me?"

Her eyes bore into me. I nod.

"Then neither of us has anything to worry about because we will be there for each other, no matter what, right?"

I bob my head.

She puts her hands back on my face, using her thumbs to wipe away the remaining tears. "It's okay to be scared. Sometimes that fear is what drives us." I look at her confused.

"Your fear of losing me will drive you to fight harder, and my fear of losing you will drive me to be stronger." She moves one of her hands to my chest. "This will make sure of it. Let what you feel for me fuel you." Her cheeks blush as she smiles at me. "That's what I do and look at how powerful I've become."

BA-DUM, BA-DUM.

Her cheeks redden. "Listen to it."

{Listen to what? My flame?}

She puts her hand back on my face. "I promise you that we will both walk away from this." She tilts my head down until our foreheads are touching. "Then it'll be us forever."

BA-DUM, BA-DUM, BA-DUM, BA-DUM.

My chest aches as I lose myself in her sky blues.

{Is she right? Will my fear help me protect her even more? Do we have the power to keep each other safe?}

Her eyes are full of confidence as she watches me.

{She is right about something, though. I'll use whatever I got to make sure nothing happens to her.}

I take a deep breath. "You're right." She beams at me.

"I'll protect you, just like you'll protect me. We will both walk away and live our lives together."

"Sounds like a plan."

She lets go of my face as she steps back. We stare at each other. I study her, memorizing everything I can see while remembering what she looks like without a shirt. My face and ears burn as the memory flashes through my head.

She chuckles. "What are you thinking about?"

"Nothing," I say quickly as my face gets hotter.

"Okay." She laughs.

"Malak?"

"Hmm?"

"Is being afraid of losing someone something that people do when they are in love?"

Her smile widens as she nods.

"Wanting to spend forever together?"

"Yes."

{I think I know now.}

I step closer, placing my hand on her face. She closes her eyes as she leans into.

"Thank you."

"For what?" She opens her eyes.

"Everything and more." I chuckle.

She giggles. "Always."

I take my hand off of her face. I look around to see that the circle has emptied. The only ones remaining are the communication angels and us.

{Everyone set off to prepare.} I smile to myself.

{Thank you, Wanda. I know you were the one who got the archs to leave.}

"Are you okay now?" Mal asks worriedly.

"Yes, I think that I am."

"Good."

"Guess it's time for us to go where we need to be, huh?"

"Guess so."

I take a few steps backward. "See you soon?"

"Definitely."

"Get stronger."

She laughs. "You too."

We smile before turning away from each other. I run towards the field as she moves to Give It Your All.

{We will keep each other safe. I won't allow anything bad to happen to her. I've protected her before, and I will always protect her.}

I stop on the edge of the field, observing Michael work with the goblins, pucks, and imps. Taking a breath, I step onto the field towards them. They all stop what they are doing before turning to watch me. Each of them smiles at me as I stop beside Michael.

25

{**Tonight is the night.** We've been preparing for days. Everyone has finished their training with Michael and me. They have collected the standard armor, a chest and backplate, and shields and weapons from Protect Gear. I kept my sword though since it is specially made for me. The guardian angels were able to evacuate everyone. Ariel has all of the witches and warlocks stocked full of everything they might need. Raphael, the fairies, and pixies created tons of pixie dust, ensuring that those who use magic have a few pouches full. Uriel has continued to inform everyone what our enemies' weaknesses are. She divided everyone based on skill and told them which enemy they had a better chance of beating. Jade and her team and Mal are tasked with fighting the archdemons, all but my father. He is all mine. I'm still scared about Mal getting hurt, but I snuck into the training room sometimes without her seeing me just to watch. She has grown powerful. Her level is almost equal to mine, and I couldn't be prouder. Watching her has made me feel a little better about her fighting the archdemons and their kids. With help from the angels, I know that they won't have any problem with defeating them. I took down four of them on my own, and I was a lot weaker than I am now. Gabriel informed us a few hours ago that our church is the last on the map. So now we are just waiting for the go-ahead.}

I lean against the wall beside the door into Give It Your All. I watch all of the Everyone's Diner employees set up multiple tables with a whole bunch of food laid out.

{The owner wanted to do something nice for everyone, so he and his chefs made different kinds of dishes for every other type of creature here.}

I turn my head towards the fountain. In front of the fountain is a small stage where a few creatures are setting up different instruments.

{Not sure whose idea it was to have some music and dancing before the battle, but everyone seemed to like the idea.}

People are all around the circle, some setting things up, others talking, a few practicing swinging their swords, and some just chillin' like I am.

{The calm before the storm.} "Hey you."

A smile spreads across my face as I turn to face Mal as the door closes behind her. I quickly push off the wall and grab her before lifting her into the air as I spin around.

"Kal, what are you doing?"

She laughs. "I missed you."

She puts her hands on my shoulders as I still hold her up. "I missed you too."

"I swear you need to start warning me before you do something adorable like this," Jade complains as she comes out of the building. "The cuteness is going to make me sick," she jokes, failing to hide her smirk.

Mal and I both laugh as I lower her back to the ground.

"Let them have their moment." Wanda comes up behind us. "They've worked hard. They deserve it."

"I suppose," Jade grumbles.

"Are you guys getting anything to eat?" Wanda asks us.

"Mal, you should probably eat something small," I tell her.

"What about you?"

"I'm not hungry, but if you want me to eat with you, then I will."

"Yes, please."

I laugh. "Okay."

She grabs my hand and pulls me with her towards the tables. "You two coming?" I call back to Wanda and Jade.

"Definitely. I'm starving," Wanda answers, catching up to us.

"Why not," Jade says right behind us.

"I'm sure they've made some pretty good food," I explain.

"Look, the band is starting," Mal says excitedly.

We look over as the drummer starts pounding his drums and the guitarists strum their instruments. They don't play any particular song. They just play music. "There's no singer," Mal explains, disappointed.

"Doesn't surprise me. There aren't many supernatural creatures that can play instruments, let alone sing. Those are all witches and warlocks up there now," Jade tells us.

{I didn't even realize.}

Wanda nudges me. "What about you Kal?"

"What about me?" I turn to her.

"Why don't you go up there and sing a song for everyone."

Mal whips her head to face me. "You can sing?"

"No."

"Don't let her fool you. I've heard her singing to herself on multiple occasions. Her voice is beautiful."

My ears heat up. "I don't know what you're talking about. I don't sing."

"Sure." Wanda giggles.

I roll my eyes at her before pulling Mal to the first table.

"I'll admit that was some pretty good food," Jade compliments as she sets her plate down.

"Their food is always delicious," Wanda tells her, with her plate empty on the table.

"I like their dessert," Mal explains, licking her lips.

"I can tell." I reach my hand out and slide my thumb across the top of her lip, wiping the icing off.

Her face turns red as I take my hand away. "Can't take me any-where."

"It's okay. I think it's adorable." I put my finger in my mouth to lick off the icing.

"Was the fruit any good?" Wanda asks me.

"It was. Ariel did grow it all, so of course it is good." They all nod in agreement.

"I'll take everyone's plates." Wanda stands.

"You sure?" I question her.

"Yep." She grabs mine and Mal's plates before grabbing Jade's. "I'll be right back." She walks off.

"It was a good idea to have this little quiet time. Everyone needed this," Jade says.

"I agree. This allows them to lose some of their tension and worry about what's to come. If we went to battle all tense and scared, the re-sults would've been bad." I slide my hand over to Mal's. "Doing this helps everyone calm down and brings everyone closer."

"We all need to work together in order to win," Jade explains.

I nod.

"Do you think everyone is ready?" Mal wonders.

"I trained with all of them, and I can say for a fact that they've come a long way in such a short amount of time. Everyone worked really hard to become stronger so they can protect those they care about. So, yes, I think they are ready." I glance around. "I just hope that they think that too."

Jade bobs her head in agreement.

"They need to have faith in themselves," I say.

SHRIIIIEEECKKK!

Everyone covers their ears before looking at the stage.

{What is she doing?}

"Sorry about that," Wanda apologizes as she fixes the microphone on its stand. "Just wanted to make sure this thing was on."

"Kal, what is Wanda doing up there?" Mal wonders.

{She better not.}

"I noticed that we didn't have a singer up here."

{Wanda, I swear.}

"I've found someone who can sing for us."

Everyone begins to whisper to each other as they look around. "She isn't?" Jade asks.

"She is," I answer.

Wanda points at me. "Our leader, Kalma."

Heads turn towards me with faces covered in shock.

"I'm gonna kill her," I say quietly.

Mal chuckles beside me.

Wanda continues to point at me. "Come on, Kal. Sing us a song."

I shake my head.

{Not happening.}

"Ah, come on, we all want to hear you."

"Come on, Kalma."

"Sing for us."

"Just one song."

Voices all over the circle beg me to get up there. "They're all crazy." I laugh nervously.

"I don't think they are."

I turn towards Mal as she looks at me with puppy eyes. "Not you too."

"Please sing. I really want to hear you sing." She squeezes my hand. "Sing for me." BA-DUM, BA-DUM.

{Damnit.}

"Fine." I sigh defeated.

She beams at me before letting go of my hand. "Thank you."

{I'm gonna kill Wanda for this.}

Everyone applauds as I stand up and head to the stage. "You're dead," I warn Wanda as she walks by me.

"You'll thank me later."

{She's crazy.}

I grab the microphone and look out at my small army.

{What should I sing? What can I sing that will help them?}

A light bulb goes off in my head. I turn around and move closer to the witches and warlocks.

"I know that it is a song not many people have heard but do you know 'Who's Gonna Save the World Tonight? Who's Gonna Bring You Back to Life?' by Swedish House Mafia?"

They look at each other before smiling. "Great song," the warlock drummer says.

"Figured it's perfect for our situation."

"Definitely," the witch bass guitarist agrees.

Taking a deep breath, I grab the microphone tighter and face the crowd.

{Here goes.}

The music starts.

"Into the streets, we're coming down/We never sleep, never get tired/ Through urban fields, and suburban lights."

I look over at Mal, her eyes big with amazement. "Turn the crowd up now, we'll never back down/Shoot down a skyline, watch it on prime time/Turn up the love now, listen up now, turn up the love." I smile at her.

"Who's gonna saaaaaavvvvve the wooooorrrrld tooooooniiiight? Who's gonna briiiiiing you baaaaaack to life?"

Everyone begins cheering as they stand up. "We're gonna maaaake it, yooooooou and IIIIII/We're gonna saaaaave the wooorrrrld tonight."

The band plays a few lines. The crowd moves closer to the stage.

"Aohaaoo Oah oh Oohh. Ahaaoo Oah oh Oohh. Ahaaoo Oah oh Ooh. Ahaaoo Oah oh Ooh. Ahaaoo Oah oh Oohh. Ahaaoo Oah oh Oohh. Ahaaoo Oah oh Oohh. Ahaaoo Oah oh Oohh. Ahaaoo Oah oh Oohh."

They play a few more lines. Mal stands in front of everyone, closest to the stage. "We're far from home, it's for the better/What we dream, it's all that matters/We're on our way, united."

Everyone cheers louder as they raise their hands. A smile spreads across my face. "Turn the crowd up now, we'll never back down/Shoot down the skyline, watch it on prime time/Turn up the love now, listen up now, turn up the love." I stare at Mal, my cheeks burning.

"Who's gonna saaaaaave the woooooorrld toooniiight? Who's gonna brrrriiing you baaaack to life?/We're gonna maaaaake it, yooooouu and IIII/We're gonna saaaave the wooorrrld tonight."

The instruments get louder behind me, so I sing louder.

"Aohaaoo Oah Oohh. Aohaaoo Oah Oohh. Aohaaoo Oah Oohh. Aohaaoo Oah Oohh." I pull the microphone out of its holder before moving a little closer to the edge of the stage. I sing even louder.

"Who's gonna saaaaaavvvvve?" I cup my ear.

"We are!" everyone yells.

"Who's gonna brrrrriiiiing?"

"We are!"

"We're gonna maaaaake it, yooooouuu and IIII." I point at myself, then Mal.

{We are.}

I look back out at everyone.

"Who's gonna saaaaaave?"

"We are!"

"Who's gonna brrrriiing?"

"WE ARE!"

My smile widens.

"We're gonna saaaaave the woorrrrld tonight!"

The music stops. Everyone claps and cheers, hope filling each of them.

{Now they have faith.}

I drop the microphone before jumping off the front of the stage. Mal jumps at me, wrapping her arms around me.

"That was amazing!"

"Told you," Wanda says cockily.

"Doesn't mean you are off the hook." I glare at her. She holds her hands up as she laughs.

"That song erased all of their doubts," Jade explains.

"That's what I was hoping for."

Mal lets go. "You should sing more often."

I chuckle. "Only if it's for you."

"I'd be okay with that."

CAW! CAW!

We look up to a phoenix circling above us. "What is that?" Mal asks.

"That is a phoenix," Jade answers.

The phoenix dives, heading towards me. It flaps its wings before hitting anyone as it flies over to me. It gently lands on my shoulder. Everyone watches us in anticipation.

The phoenix bends its head so that the beak is beside my ear. "They're on the move."

My body freezes.

"It's time," it whispers, before jumping off my shoulder to fly back into the sky. Mal, Jade, and Wanda watch me as heat rushes to my hand. I meet Mal's stare and give her a sad smile. Fire erupts around my hand. Shock flashes on their faces before determination takes over. I raise my hand over my head before blasting a fireball into the air, signaling that the time has come. Everything goes quiet.

{We trained for this moment.}

They all take off preparing themselves, putting on their armor and grabbing their weapons and supplies. Within a matter of minutes, everyone is ready to head out. Half stand on one side of the circle and the rest on the other half.

"You got this," Michael speaks as he appears beside me. The other archangels stand behind him.

{We all thought the archs were going to fight with us, but yesterday they told us that they couldn't. They've grown fragile because of all the churches being destroyed, and if they were to die, then it would all be over.}

"Just stick to the plan," Uriel explains.

"The healers, fairies, and pixies all know what to do," Raphael says.

"The guardians have their disks, just in case you need to get in contact with us," Gabriel tells me.

"All of the witches and warlocks are stocked up with everything they might need," Ariel informs.

{Everything is ready. We are all ready.} Mal steps up beside me.

"You two are the keys to end all of this," Raphael explains.

"So watch each other's backs." Michael hands me my sword and Mal an angel blade. I put mine in its spot on my back. Mal does the same.

"Save us all," Uriel demands.

"We will, no matter what," I promise them.

We turn around to see Wanda and Jade waiting for us. Jade has two swords on her back, plus golden chest armor. Wanda has the same armor as everyone else, with a sword hanging from her waist. They both nod at us. We nod back before walking ahead of them towards the entrance. My small army marches behind us. I tighten my fists at my side as the barrier opens. We leave the safety of the wall, making our way to the church. All of us begin to run. Mal keeps pace with me, but Wanda sits on Jade's back, and the other witches and warlocks each ride on an angel's back so they don't fall behind. The church comes into view. We stop once we are in front of it. The big group splits off into smaller clumps, getting ready to fight the creatures they were assigned to. I stand ahead of everyone. Malevolent energy begins to fil the air.

{I'm ready for you, Father. We're prepared to protect those precio to us.}

26

I look across the empty yard and driveway. "They're going to be here any second!" I yell to everyone. "Does everyone remember their targets?"

No one says anything.

"Based on Gabriel's globe and news from the scouts, there are thirty nightmares, seven black demon dogs, twenty oni, about a hundred marching hordes, and nine archdemons. One of them being my father." I turn around and face them. "Jade's team and Mal will handle the archdemons minus Rorridun. He's mine. Half of you guardian angels as well as the five pucks, four succubus, and two imps that were selected earlier will take on the nightmares. The guardians will deliver the final blows, since their weapons are the only things that can kill them. The rest of you will be their backup. The two cherubim, two power angels, and ten goblins picked to fight the black demon dogs, remember that you have to strike through their heads or hearts. Two elementals, fire and earth, plus Derrick's coven, the chosen two furies, two power angels, and three pucks. The oni demons are all yours. Jinn, you know what you all need to do. Disguise yourselves as different enemies and kill whoever you can. The rest of you were assigned to the marching hordes. The other half of the guardians, air and water elementals; three witches, Husha, Nestra, Deseih; the other succubus; ten goblins; the last power angel; three imps, Uxum, and Sukir. Marching hordes are taken down with powerful attacks or lethal blows. Healing witches, you all decided to stay near the battle so you can help the wounded faster. Stay back until you can get to someone safely."

Three witches break off running to the edge of the premises. "You too, Wanda."

She doesn't move. "Wanda."

"I'm not going."

Panic rises in my chest. "What do you mean you're not going? You going to help them was the plan, remember?"

She puts her hand on the hilt of her sword. "And I told you before that I am fighting with you." Her hand grips the top. "Did you really think that I didn't realize what you were doing by having me work with the archangels? I knew you put me with them hoping I would be safe."

I stare at her, not knowing what to say.

"I'm sorry, Kal, but I'm staying right here and fighting with you and Mal." She stands her ground.

{Damnit, Wanda.}

"Remember your promise," I tell her.

She gives a solid nod.

"You'll help with the archdemons."

"Okay."

A sinister aura appears behind me.

{They're here.}

"Be careful, be safe, stay strong, and remember what you are fighting for," I command everyone before turning around.

"Such trivial words from an incompetent child," my father sneers.

{Seeing them all together like this makes it seem as if there are a lot more.} My father stands in the center of his army. Right behind him are the other archdemons and their children. Beside them on both sides are the black demon dogs with their piercing red eyes and mouths open wide, showing all of their teeth. After the archdemons stand, the nightmares almost blending into the darkness, if it wasn't for the lights around the parking lot and grass. On both sides behind the dogs are the oni demons, with their swords already drawn, ready for battle. Then, finally, in the back are all one hundred marching hordes.

"Hello, Father."

"I see that you just continue to defy us, defy me."

"You didn't leave me much of a choice."

"A choice? You are not supposed to have choices. You are to do what I tell you to without question."

"Why, because that's what I was made for?"

He doesn't say anything as his crimson eyes study me.

"I'm not just some weapon, some tool for you to use whenever you want. I am a person." I place my hand on my chest. "I am so much more."

He starts laughing. "You? A person?" He continues to laugh.

I lower my hand, tightening it into a fist.

{I don't know why I bother. I know he will never understand.} "Who put these idiotic thoughts in your head?"

Mal and Wanda move to stand on both sides of me. He looks at them. "Sir," Jorvexx speaks.

Father turns his head. "That's her, the blonde."

"So that is the hybrid?" He faces us again.

My body tenses as he scans Mal. His eyes are moving up and down. "So, you are the reason Kalma betrayed us?"

I step in front of Mal. "I'm the reason I betrayed you."

"So, it is true? Jorvexx told me that you protected that thing. I did not want to believe him, but now that I am seeing with my own eyes." Disgust covers his face. "She is the one you spoke of the other day?"

I bob my head.

"I see." He grins. "Tell me, hybrid. Are you willing to die for her?"

Mal doesn't hesitate. "I am."

"Why? She does not care for you. She could never care about you. She just thinks that she does because that is what humans are supposed to do. She believes that since she is half human, she can be like one.

Well, I can tell you for a fact that even if she is half human, she could never have the same emotional connection to you that you think you have for her. Demons are cold and empty. We do not feel anything but darkness and hate."

"That's where you are wrong." Mal grabs my hand. "Kal isn't like that. She does feel things. She has emotions."

"Tsk, that is not possible. She played you."

"She's telling the truth," Wanda defends Mal. "I have seen Kal go through emotions. She has felt happiness, sadness, anger, panic, and she is still learning." My father glares at us.

"It is not possible," he says coldly.

"It is," I tell him. "I don't know how it happened, but I can feel the same things humans do. I can even feel a warmth inside of me sometimes, and not from my flame."

Rage builds in his eyes.

"So when you ask why," Mal says, "it's because I love her." My cheeks and ears burn.

"GASP!"

All of the archdemons gape at me as I blush.

Jorvexx is the first to regain his composure. "What are you?" he asks with rage in his voice.

"An abomination!" my father yells as his eyes glow.

{Shit.}

I quickly let go of Mal's hand before taking a step out in front of everyone, just as flames burst around his hands. I force heat down my arms. My father sends his ball of fire flying towards me. Taking a deep breath, my flames ignite around my hands. The archdemons' faces return to shock as they stare at my hands. I lock my hands together before pulling them apart vertically. As I do so, a circular wall expands between them. Just as the fireball is about to hit me, I step to the side, swinging my arms to catch the ball with the wall. The wall forms around the ball, completely enclosing it with my fire. Swinging my arms up fast, I detach the two flames from my hands, sending them into the sky. I watch as they continue to rise until all you can see is a dot. I let out the breath I was holding.

{Can't believe that actually worked.} My flames go out around my hands. "Your flames."

I look at my father.

"What happened to your flames?"

"Long story."

He shakes his head. "There is no coming back for you, Kalma."

"That's fine. I didn't want to come back anyway." Backing up, I grab Mal's hand. "I'm happy right where I am."

"We shall see what you have to say when this world is under fire ruled by demons."

"Not going to happen."

He smirks. "You sound so sure."

"That's because I am."

"And why is that?"

"Because I'm going to stop you. We're going to stop all of you."

"Is that so?"

"We are fighting for those precious to us."

"What is that supposed to mean?"

I chuckle. "You'd never understand."

He raises his hand above his head. The oni demons grip their swords tighter as the marching hordes crouch down, ready to take off; the black demon dogs begin to snarl at us; the nightmares spread their arms apart; and the archdemons pull out their swords.

{Guess the time for talking is over.}

I look back at Jade. She nods and raises her sword. My small army prepares themselves.

"In order to stop me," my father speaks.

I meet his red eyes.

"You have to kill me." He grins.

"I know."

He stops grinning.

"And I plan too."

Mal lets go of my hand so she can get her sword ready. Reaching over my shoulder, I grab the hilt of my sword, pulling it out of its sheath. As I bring it down, I grab onto it with my other hand.

{This is it.}

As I pull the blade apart to hold half in each hand, I bend my knees into a fighting stance.

"Last chance, Kalma. Stop all of this."

"Never. This world is my home now. The people I care about are here. I'm going to defend it."

He sneers at me before swinging his arm down. His army races towards us, moving around him. Taking a deep breath, I raise my blade. My army stampedes towards their targets.

{One of us is going to win, and one of us is going to die.}

I start racing towards my father as Jade, her team, Wanda, and Mal follow behind me to fight the archdemons still standing behind him.

"Be careful!" I yell to Mal over the sounds of swords clashing around us. "You as well." I look at Wanda.

"You too!" they both exclaim.

They keep going as I stop in front of my father.

"Just you and me? Do you seriously think that you can take me on?" He removes his sword from its sheath.

"One way to find out."

He shakes his head. "Would you like a slow and painful death or a fast one?"

"How about option C, none of the above." I smirk.

Mal appears about ten feet behind him, holding her own as she and Jorvexx collide blades. Wanda is a few feet beside her, using her magic against Allaya's fire, her magic pressing Allaya's flames back. I smile at them.

{They got this.}

Jade and the others take on the remaining archdemons, throwing everything they have at them. I turn my head to see the tiny individual battles going on. My army is holding its own against the enemy.

{Everyone's got this.}

As I face my father again, fire comes to life around my blades. He responds by lighting up his own sword.

{I got this.}

The flames grow as they get hotter.

"Maybe I will beat you down until you can no longer fight." My internal flame heats up my core.

"Then, once you can no longer fight, I will slowly kill that witch." Rage builds in my stomach, making my internal flame flare-up. "Then that hybrid of yours."

Flames crawl up my arms until they are consumed in fire.

"Or maybe I will kill her first." He smirks. "What do you think?"

I fly towards him as he flies at me. I focus on the flames outlining my swords. Making them thicken and glow brightly with heat. Father's blade does the same.

{I need a little more kick.}

Taking a breath, I push the fire around my arms down, my flames igniting in my hands around the hilts. I grip them tightly as my royal fire climbs up the blades mixing in with the dark flames. Both sets of fire push against the swords creating a denser flame outline.

{This should help.}

He holds his blade tightly in his hands, his eyes glow brighter. I push myself to go faster as I swing my swords.

BOOOOOOOMMMMM!

Our weapons collide. I hold myself up, making sure that my feet don't slide under the pressure. Sparks and trails of fire whip off the blades in all directions. My hands begin to burn from the intensity of our flames. I stare at my father over our weapons, his face not showing any type of effort while he pushes against me. I clench my jaw, ensuring I don't react to the pain or my arms' strain. I look into his eyes, into the darkness hidden behind the crimson. Cold chills roll down my spine from the vileness within them. Waves begin to shoot everywhere as our blades start to crack. The burning on my hands intensifies as it spreads down my arms. I watch as my skin begins to crisp and turn black.

{If I don't stop this now, my arms are going to fry.}

Focusing on my flames, I force a blast of fire to rocket up my blades to where his presses against them.

{This is going to suck.}

A bright light flashes, blinding me just as our weapons explode, shattering into pieces. The force of the blast sends us both back. I bounce hard off the ground, smacking two more times before stopping, losing my broken hilts somewhere in the process. My ears ring while I lie there trying to stop the world from spinning. My arms tingle as the burnt skin slowly heals.

{My swords are gone, but at least his is too.}

I carefully sit up as the ringing fades, the sounds of war taking over. As I stand up, I glance quickly around the battlefield. My chest throbs as I see the fallen creatures, their still bodies covered in blood, the healing witches at their sides trying to heal them, but they're too late.

{We all knew that not everyone would be walking away from this.} My hands tighten at my sides.

{Seeing them still hurts, though.}

I take notice of the numbers remaining on both sides.

{They've lost more than we have. We are winning.}

I force myself to look away from my fallen comrades. I meet my father's glare.

{I won't let any of their sacrifices be in vain.}

The sounds around me become quieter as I stare at him. I don't give him the chance to do anything as I make my move. I run at him fast, but he's ready for me.

I kick my right leg towards his head. He raises his hand and grabs my ankle. He pushes my leg, causing me to stumble back, but I don't get thrown off balance. I go at him again. Flames erupt around my fists as I swing at him, one after the other. He dodges or slaps away every attack.

{Damnit!}

He pushes out his palm, slamming it into my chest, knocking the wind out of me and forcing me back again. I stumble more this time. My hands go out before my foot ignites as I swing my leg up again. He smiles before doing the same. Our legs connect mid-kick, the fire around our feet extinguishing. I stagger back but don't stop moving. Once my foot is on the ground, I duck down, swinging it out across the floor. He jumps and rolls out of the way, landing back on his feet with a malevolent grin on his face.

{DAMNIT!}

Mal and Wanda come into view behind him. They continue to fight Jorvexx and Allaya, Mal's blade still glowing brightly as well as Wanda's magic. Both have scratches and tears in their clothing but nothing too concerning. I grin when I see the damage they've dealt their opponents. Jovexx has a giant slash down his face as well as across his chest, blood pouring out of both. Allaya's legs and arms are covered in magic burns. Blood drips from each of the blisters.

{That's my girls.}

"I do not know why you are smiling." I look back at my father.

"You will all be dead soon."

Tightening my fists, I push off the ground hard, getting through the distance between us in seconds. I throw my punch for his stomach. He's fast, though; his hand appears there with a small wall of fire above his palm. I bounce off of it, my top half being pushed back. Using the momentum of the push, I bend backward into a bridge before lifting one foot in front of the other, managing to surprise him and kick him under the jaw. The kick pushes him off the ground, causing him to fall onto his back. I continue to flip until I am back on my feet.

{Got him.}

I move towards him. He quickly spins, straightening out his legs in the process.

{Shit.}

His leg catches me on the side of my ankle, sweeping me off of my feet. As I'm about to hit the ground, he moves faster than I've ever seen before to stand beside me. He lifts his foot, ramming it hard into my gut. Something cracks before I soar across the ground, leaving a trail behind me. I grab onto my ribs once I finally stop moving.

{I should've known better. No way a minor attack like that would leave me an opening.}

My arm stings as warm liquid trickles down it. I look at my arm and see that a large piece of skin has been scraped off, and blood is oozing from the wound.

{I can feel other tears and scratches all over me as well as blood.} I press against my ribs.

{I'm too exhausted for my wounds to heal any more, and I need to use whatever I have left against Father.}

I get onto my hands and knees to get up. "You stupid child."

I flinch in surprise as I quickly look up at him. Before I can do anything, he slams his knee into my stomach, lifting me off the ground.

"ACK!" Blood shoots out of my mouth.

"Did you honestly think that you could beat me?" His elbow jabs into my back, sending me back to the ground hard.

My head smacks, causing the world to go black for a few seconds. "I taught you everything you know."

I carefully open my eyes. Everything spins as the light hurts my pounding head. Blood rolls down my eyebrow before running over my eye. I move my hand to my forehead, where my hairline is. My hand immediately becoming soaked. I bring it down and see blood covering my fingers.

{He split my head open.}

I use the back of my hand to wipe the line of blood off of my eye before slowly placing them firmly on the ground. As I push myself up. I notice the small indent that the impact created. Blood drips off of my head and out of my mouth as I push myself up. As I stand, the world tilts, threatening to knock me back down, but I plant my feet. Father watches me as I stand. I wipe my mouth off as I breathe heavily, allowing everything to settle around me.

"Still not done?" he asks, annoyed.

"Never." I spit blood out of my mouth.

He shakes his head. I move before he has the chance to raise his defense. I swing out my right hook. As he goes to block my attack, I switch my plan. Using the small amount of strength I have left, I put it into my leg to quickly turn behind him. I lift my leg with my foot already ablaze.

{Dodge this!}

He sighs before swinging his leg at the leg still on the ground. I barely manage to move out of the way, but he is moving faster now. The moment my feet are steady, I swing again. He slightly shifts his head to the side to dodge my fist.

{What?!}

Before I have the chance to pull my arm back, he grabs it tightly. "I told you." My arm cracks as he squeezes harder. "You will lose."

He lifts me off the ground as he pivots before flinging me hard and fast. I fly above the battles going on below as I head towards the church. I see Wanda blasting a weaponless Allaya with her emerald magic.

{I might not win against you, Father, but they'll win against everyone else.}

Mal stands a few feet away from Wanda, slashing across Jorvexx's chest from shoulder to hip. Jade and the other guardians are fighting Thezgoth, Vexxus, Rinnixa, Darixul, and Encador. Each archdemon is in the same position as Jorvexx and Allaya.

{We're winning.}

I collide into the side of the church with extreme force.

"ACK!" Blood flies out of my mouth as my back cracks almost as loud as the bricks I hit.

I fall from the indent left in the wall all the way to the ground. My head is spinning and pounding too hard to catch myself. As my stomach impacts the floor, my wind gets knocked out of me, and more blood shoots from my mouth. I try to breathe, but everything screams at me to not move. My lungs burn as I spit out more blood. I carefully tilt my head so my chin is lying on the ground. Everything blurs and spins as more blood rolls back over my eye. A shadowy figure appears inside of the blur moving towards me.

"What happened to all of that bravado from before?" Father asks as he stops in front of me.

My body fights against me as I get to my knees. I look up at him, my eye focusing on his vile grin.

"This is how it should be."

{I don't think I can move anymore.}

"You kneeling at my feet. You were only made to obey my will." He grabs my hair, lifting my head up to meet his eyes. "Right now, my will is for all of this to stop." His knee slams into my chest. Blood fills my mouth as my bones break. The world turns as he lets me go. I fall onto my side, choking on the blood in my mouth and leaking into my chest. I struggle for air as I lie there.

"From the look of you, I think my will shall be fulfilled soon."

He bends down and grabs a handful of my shirt under my chin. He lifts me off the ground. My arms and legs are hanging useless. I try to breathe but can only manage to cough up blood.

"Once I finish with you"—fire ignites around the hand holding my shirt—"all that is left is that hybrid that you are so fond of."

My body goes cold as all the pain fades into the background. "Do not worry, I will make it quick," he sneers.

"No," I struggle to say.

He chuckles before his fire burns brighter, and I am airborne again. I silently scream as my broken and burnt body soars through the air.

CRASH!

Rubble falls from the sky back to the ground around the small crater my landing created. I lie there, not able to move, barely breathing. The sounds of everyone fighting continues around me, quieter than it was earlier. My internal flame flickers inside of me, waiting to go out.

"Kalma!" I hear Wanda's voice scream.

{Wanda?}

Rocks move beside me as footsteps get closer. "Oh my! Kal!"

{Where's Mal?}

"It's okay, Kal. Everything is going to be okay." Wanda sniffles as hands softly grab onto me, causing more pain to shoot through me.

{Where's Mal?}

"There's so much blood," Wanda says to herself. "So many bones broken."

I cough, spitting up blood.

"Kal?"

Light slowly shines into the eye not covered in blood, with Wanda sitting in the middle of it.

"Stay with me, okay, Kal? Stay with me and I'll heal you." Tears stream down her face.

"Where's...Mal?" I struggle to ask.

"She's all right. We were both able to defeat our opponents." Her hands start to glow. "The war is almost over. The archdemons are gone. We're winning, Kal."

"Where's...Mal?" I repeat.

"She's okay."

"Where?" I sit up, with my body cracking in the process.

"Don't move."

I meet Wanda's eyes. "Where?"

She sighs before pointing behind me. I turn around, blood rolling out of my mouth as I do so. Mal stands alone with demon ashes surrounding her. Her blade still glowing and her spirit blazing. A sinister aura rushes over me.

{No.}

"Kal, what are you doing?!" Wanda hollers at me as I push myself off the ground. My broken body tries to weigh me down more and more with each step I take. I force my feet to keep going, no matter the amount of pain yelling back at me. Blood continues to flow from my mouth and head as the broken bones creak inside of me. The aura moves closer to Mal.

"I'm sorry," I whisper.

I step in front of Mal, her eyes widening in surprise. I smile at her as fire rips through my back to my chest, striking through my flame. Mal stares at me in shock, with my blood now splattered all over her shirt.

"Kalma...what did you—?" she asks quietly.

We both look at the fiery tip sticking out of my chest.

"Stupid child," my father says behind me. "You just had to interfere." He pulls his fire out of me.

Blood seeps from the wound. Mal drops her sword before placing her hands over the top of the wound, trying to stop the bleeding.

"Kalma!" Wanda wails. Sounds fade around me.

"Oh no," I hear Derrick say.

"Kal, no," Frikik speaks.

"Kalma," Jade says.

Mal's eyes fill with tears as she watches the blood still flowing. "Why are you crying, child?" Father asks.

Mal's eyes glow brightly as she lifts her head to look at him.

"She is nothing worth shedding tears over. She is just a thing, after all." He laughs.

Her eyes glow brighter as she lifts one of her hands ablaze with the same light. "You're wrong." She blasts him.

I hear his impact far behind me.

"Get him," Jade demands.

Multiple sets of footsteps move towards where my father landed. My flame shrinks, making my body grow colder. I cough more blood onto Mal's shirt as my knees give out.

"Kal." Mal grabs me, slowly lowering me to her lap.

She lays me on her arm as her other hand presses back against the wound. Blood seeps through her fingers. I stare up at her through my good eye.

"I'm sorry."

She shakes her head. "You promised you wouldn't leave me."

I put my hand on top of hers on my chest. "I also promised not to let anything bad happen to you even if it cost me my life."

Wanda comes up behind Mal, her face turning white when she sees me. Mal must hear her. "Wanda, do something."

Wanda doesn't say anything as more tears fall. "Wanda!"

"I can't."

"What do you mean you can't? You healed her before. Just do it again."

"I don't know how I did it last time. I honestly don't think that it was me who healed her."

"Then who?"

She doesn't answer.

"So there isn't anything you can do?" Mal asks scared.

"Her body is too damaged. Her flame is going out." Wanda falls to her knees. "I'm so sorry."

{Don't be sorry, Wanda.}

Mal meets my stare. "You can't die, not again." Tears roll down her face. "Not like this. Not after everything between us." Her tears fall onto me.

"I'm sorry, Mal." Blood flows from my mouth. "I'm sorry for everything." My vision blurs with tears. "I wish none of this—"

"Don't say it," she cuts me off. "If none of this happened, then we never would've met." She moves her hand out from under mine and wipes the blood from my mouth.

I smile. "You know that you are the light in my life. You woke something in me that has grown stronger every minute that I've been with you. The calming warmth that comes when I'm next to you has completely taken over, and I'm glad that it did." I wipe the blood off of my eye so I can see her better. "You make everything feel all right even when it's not. When you're with me, the sun is brighter, colors are vibrant, music sounds more beautiful. My world changed because you are in it." More tears drip onto my shirt as she smiles sadly down at me.

"You do know what love feels like," she explains quietly.

My eyes grow in astonishment.

{I've known what it was all this time?}

My flame begins to diminish as the world fades around me and my breathing slows.

{I've always loved her.}

I lift my bloody hand and lay it on Mal's cheek.

"I understand what love feels like now, and Mal..." I smile brightly at her. "I've always felt like this since the day I saw you."

Her eyes sparkle with surprise and love. The world grows darker until Mal is all that remains. My breathing becomes shallower with each breath.

"Malak," I'm barely able to say.

I move my hand to be behind Mal's ear before pulling her closer. I use the last of my strength to sit up a little until our foreheads are touching. Warmth spreads throughout my whole body, pushing away the pain.

{I think I know what that other thing was you wanted to show me before.} I close my eyes, pushing more tears out. "I love you."

Drops fall onto my face, mixing in with mine. "I love you too."

I pull her closer until her soft lips gently press against mine. Bright, magical colors explode in my head as a new kind of heat pushes out all the cold inside of me. My insides begin to warm up, the blood in my veins growing hotter. My wounds tingle as my bones shift back into place. I push my lips harder against hers as she moves closer to me. The colors continue to swirl and explode in my head, the royal mixed in glowing brighter and brighter. Mal's energy grows as our lips desperately explore the others. Pressure builds in my chest, but not like all the other times. This time the beating feels natural.

BA-DUM, BA-DUM, BA-DUM, BA-DUM, BA-DUM, BA-DUM, BA-DUM, BA-DUM.

The pounding doesn't stop as it beats away inside my chest. Each beat brings more warmth, love, and power. My injuries close up as my bones finish settling. My internal flame bursts back to life inside of the beating, igniting with even more passion, a power greater than anything I've ever felt before. Mal holds me tightly to her.

"Disgusting." A rough hand grabs the back of my neck before yanking me away. I don't resist as I allow the new power to settle inside of me.

"A demon and angel should never share intimacy towards one another." My father's hand tightens around my neck, trying to choke me.

"Let her go," Mal demands.

{Mal's energy is different. It feels more potent, more powerful. Does she feel it?} I listen as she and Wanda stand up.

"Or what?" He laughs. "She is almost dead anyway."

My right eye burns as I smirk before grabbing my father's wrist. "Still have some fight left, huh?"

"You made a huge mistake, Father." I ignore his comment.

"Oh, and what is that?"

My eye stops burning. I tighten my grip on his wrist. CRACK!

His wrist snaps, causing him to let go of me. I land perfectly on my feet with my new power attaching to me.

"You never should've gone after Mal." I open my eyes to give him a death glare.

He takes a small step away from me, still holding onto his wrist. His eyes are full of terror. I tighten my hands into fists.

{This warmth, it's the same heat I feel when I'm with Mal. It's just more robust now.}

I lift my head and look over at Mal. She looks at me with a giant smile on her face.

{Did she cause this?}

"Your eyes?" my father exclaims.

{My eyes?}

I turn back towards him. "One red, one blue. How?"

I lift my hand to my right eye.

{It's blue?}

"You are completely healed? Your flame should have gone out. You should be dead," he explains with a hint of horror in his voice. "What are you?"

"She's who she's always been," Mal answers as she appears beside me. "A demon-human hybrid whose human heart"—she looks over at me—"now beats."

I quickly move my hand to my chest, immediately feeling the pounding inside.

{That's my heart?}

"I have a heart?"

"I think you always have. It just wasn't beating," Mal answers. I look at her confused.

"I know that you've felt it beat before. You had to because I have." She smiles.

{All of those times. That was my heart?}

"But how? Why now?"

"You're half human, Kal," Wanda speaks up. "There has always been a heart inside of you, waiting."

"Waiting for what?"

"For you to feel love," she explains.

Mal takes my hand. "The love you have for me woke it up." She squeezes. "Each time your heart has beaten was because of love."

Memories flicker through my head.

"I don't care that you are a demon. Looking at you like this doesn't bother me one bit." Her hand slides down before she slides her hand into my palm, squeezing my hand against hers. "I'm just happy that I get to look at you at all."

I whip my head up, quickly meeting her eyes as she smiles at me with warmth and acceptance.

BA-DUM.

{She accepted me, and I loved her for it.}

Mal's arms quickly wrap around me, pressing us tightly against one another. She lays her head on my shoulder so that her face is towards my neck, and I can feel her breath against my skin. I stand there frozen for a few seconds.

BA-DUM.

{I'd never been hugged before, and when she wrapped her arms around me, I liked it. I wanted her to hold me}

I stand there, frozen, looking down at her fast asleep in my arms, some of her hair laying on her beautiful and peaceful face. I can't help but smile as she snuggles her face against me.

BA-DUM, BA-DUM.

{Holding her in my arms like that, the feelings I had while looking at her were so strong.}

I hold her closer and smile.

{There are so many things I still don't get, but one thing is clear, and that is I don't ever want to be without you.}

BA-DUM, BA-DUM.

{Lying beside her, holding her in my arms. I felt complete.}

Tears roll from her eyes before sliding down her face onto her smiling lips.

BA-DUM, BA-DUM.

She loses her smile before her eyes quickly snap down to our hands on my chest, her eyebrows coming together in wonder. She looks back up at me, studying my face. I watch as the light grows in her as her smile returns to her face.

{You felt it then, didn't you?}

"Don't ever leave me."

BA-DUM, BA-DUM.

Her smile grows.

"And don't ever stop looking at me the way that you are right now."

BA-DUM, BA-DUM, BA-DUM.

{I never want to leave you. Back then, I didn't know what you meant when you said don't stop looking at you that way, but now I get it. You didn't want me to stop looking at you with love.}

{That's my girl.}

BA-DUM.

A beautiful warmth rises and boils inside of me.

{Knowing that she was mine made my stomach flutter.}

I allow the world to slip away, the stores, the sounds from the fountain, even the angels all disappear until it's just her and me.

BA-DUM, BA-DUM, BA-DUM.

{When the world fell away and all I could see was her. I can't even begin to explain what I felt.}

"I love you, Kalma."

BA-DUM, BA-DUM, BA-DUM.

{Hearing those words from her was the best moment of my life. I never thought that someone would ever say that to me.}

My body reacts on its own, leaning in towards her. Our noses brush against each other as we get closer.

BA-DUM, BA-DUM, BA-DUM, BA-DUM.

{That was the first time we almost kissed, and I guess my heart knew it.}

"I wouldn't have been able to fall in love with just a weapon."

BA-DUM.

Her smile widens. "I fell in love with you, Kalma. I fell in love with YOU."

Mal's eyes sparkle as she watches me. The warmth I've come to crave fills my chest.

BA-DUM, BA-DUM, BA-DUM.

"And you have so much more in you to find."

{She helped me see that I am more than what I always believed. She showed me that I am someone who can be loved. The warmth her words filled me with, I couldn't get enough. You knew that I had to find my heart to see who I really am.}

BA-DUM, BA-DUM.

She chuckles softly as she presses harder onto my chest.

{You loved it when my heart would beat.}

"Not just together," Derrick explains, "They love each other.

BA-DUM.

I flinch at the sudden pound in my chest.

{He was right. I did love you.}

Her eyes are on my body, looking over every inch of bare skin.

BA-DUM, BA-DUM.

{What is she doing?}

"You're breathtaking," she whispers.

BA-DUM.

"Looking at you now makes me want more."

{I didn't understand why you wanted to see more of me until I saw you.}

She drops the shirt onto the floor before looking back at me, her face still red.

BA-DUM, BA-DUM, BA-DUM.

The pounding inside of me beats so hard inside my chest that I can hear it.

{Seeing you like that, I understood why you wanted more, because that's all I wanted too.}

She closes her eyes as we get closer, so I do the same. Her warm breath blows against my lips.

BA-DUM, BA-DUM, BA-DUM, BA-DUM, BA-DUM.

The throbbing hits painfully inside of me, pounding a new kind of feeling throughout my body, a really lovely feeling.

{We almost kissed then. I wonder if my heart would've stayed beating if we had. It felt like it would've.}

A warm smile grows on her face, "Once this war is over, we will have the rest of our lives for it to just be the two of us."

BA-DUM, BA-DUM. "Really?"

"Definitely. I told you that I'm not going anywhere, remember?"

{All I wanted was to be with you forever. To love you forever.} *Our foreheads press against each other. "Then it'll be us forever."*

BA-DUM, BA-DUM, BA-DUM, BA-DUM.

My chest aches as I lose myself in her sky blues.

{Every part of me screamed yes.}

"Your fear of losing me will drive you to fight harder, and my fear of losing you will drive me to be stronger." She moves one of her hands to my chest. *"This will make sure of it. Let what you feel for me fuel you."* Her cheeks blush as she smiles at me. *"That's what I do and look at how powerful I've become."*

BA-DUM, BA-DUM.

Her cheeks redden. "Listen to it."

{You meant my heart. You told me that it would make me stronger and that my love for you would make me more powerful. You reminded me to listen to my heart because you knew that it was there.}

I smile. "You were right."

Mal looks at me confused.

"You told me that my heart would make me stronger. That if I allowed it to fuel me that it would make me stronger."

She smiles.

"You were right about everything."

"I knew that your heart was trying to start, and I wanted you to see that as well."

I nod. "I do now. Thank you."

"For what?"

I give her a big smile. "Allowing me to love you." Her face lights up.

"Letting me kiss you."

My face burns.

{The kiss is what filled my heart full of love, allowing it to beat and stay beating. Without you, Mal, I would be dead right now, in more ways than one.}

I stop smiling as I look back at my father.

{He would've killed me if it wasn't for you loving me and you letting me love you in return. He would've killed me months ago if not for you. Finding you saved me from losing myself in his darkness. You saved me more than you could ever know, Mal.}

"It is not possible," my father says. "No hybrid has ever had a beating heart. Their human heart always remained dead."

"No other hybrid found the one they're meant to be with either." I hold Mal's hand tighter. "It's because of her that it lives, that I live." I let go of Mal's hand as I step towards him. "It's because of her that now you will be the one who dies."

Fear flashes through his eyes, but he quickly regains his composure. He stands tall as his face returns to being neutral.

"Really, Kalma? Are we going to have this conversation again?" he asks annoyed.

I shake my head. "There's no need to." My eyes burn as fire bursts around my hands.

{The flames are different again. They are brighter and hotter. They feel lighter somehow.}

Everyone stares at my flames as they dance around my hands. "They're beautiful," I hear Mal whisper.

I grin.

"There's no need to talk because you've already lost," I explain. He glares at me.

"Your army has fallen. All that remains are a few marching hordes and you. My comrades are still standing ready to fight, ready to win."

He grins. "Hahaha," he laughs sinisterly. I frown at him.

"That is where you are wrong." He raises his hand. "My army still stands." He snaps his fingers.

All around us marching hordes shimmer into view.

{How was he hiding them? Cloaking that powerful is almost unheard of.} I grit my teeth as I look around at my father's new army.

{There's at least a hundred, maybe more.} I scan over my remaining troops.

{A little over half of the guardian angels remain, plus Jade and her team. The healing witches are still going around healing who they can. The cherubim are still alive. Only one power angel remains. A few goblins, pucks, and imps can still fight.

All of the jinn are alive, but I don't know how much help they will be now. The earth and air elementals can still fight. Most of the remaining witches can still fight. Both of the furies are gone, and only two succubi are still alive.}

I glance at Wanda, scanning her, taking notice of her wounds.

{She's exhausted, whether she'd admit it or not.}

I look at Mal, immediately feeling the new power that she holds. I move my head to look at my hands as the flames continue to dance. Michael and my conversation from the other day plays in my head.

"We told you before that we think you and Mal are going to be what ends this war?"

"Does that mean...?"

"Yes. Mal has the same kind of power inside of her and the same potential to let it out, just as you do."

He grips my shoulders a little tighter. "I'm serious, though, Kal." He looks at me, creating eye contact. "Everyone believes that you two will stop the demons, will end this war, will save us all.

"The connection you two have is just as powerful as whatever is inside of you. All of our instincts are telling us that Mal is the key to unlocking your power, and you are the key to unlocking hers."

{Is this what they meant? Is that why both of us have gotten a great deal stronger? Did we unlock each other's power?}

"Do you feel it?" I ask Mal.

She doesn't say anything at first. "I think so."

"Your power? My power?"

She nods. "What happened? Where did it come from?"

"When I was training with Michael, he mentioned this. He told me that there was power inside of both of us, just waiting to come out. That we would be each other's keys to unlocking it, and I think he was right. That kiss, our kiss unlocked this power."

"What kind of power?"

"Just think how strong you'd be if all of it was set free."

"You will continue to get stronger, Kal, and once all of that is out, who knows just how powerful you will be."

"Maybe even more than me," Michael's words echo in my head.

"Power great enough to end this." I look back at her. "The archangels, no, everyone. They all believe that you and I are going to stop the demons, will save everyone." Her eyes glow.

"They all believe that we are going to end this war."

Blue celeste aura bursts to life around her hands. My jaw drops in awe as the energy climbs up her arms before spreading to cover her whole body. I gawk at the celeste cloak radiating around her.

{She really looks like an angel now.}

I close my mouth before smiling at her. "I love you."

{I'm never going to get tired of saying that.}

Scarlet covers her face, really popping out against the blue. "I love you too."

My fire grows. "No one else has to die. We can end this now." I hold my hand out towards her.

She nods before taking my hand. The second her hand is in mine, power pulses inside of me. The weight of it takes my breath away for a few seconds until my body adjusts to it.

"Did you...?" Mal starts.

"Yes, I felt that."

"What was—?"

Before she can finish, my flames and her aura begin to expand. My fire slowly envelopes my body, just like her aura covers her.

{Wow.}

It doesn't stop there, though. The fire attaches to Mal's hand. Panic pokes at my chest watching it climb up her arm, afraid of her being burned. Her face doesn't show any signs of pain, though. The flames spread to cover her whole body. Now both of our powers surround her.

{What's going on?}

Mal's energy slides across our hands, carefully making its way all over me until I have the same cloak as Mal.

{Our energies are mixing together. They're harmonizing. How is that even possible?}

We both look at ourselves and each other.

"The connection you two have is just as powerful as whatever is inside of you."

{This must be what Michael meant. Our connection is making us more powerful.}

A safe, calming feeling washes over me. I glance over at Mal, watching her continue to study the cloak around us. My favorite kind of warmth fills me up.

{We really are meant to be together.} "What is happening?" my father exclaims.

We both look at him with our hands still joined.

"How are you doing that? Your flames should be burning her, and her energy should be destroying you."

I hold Mal's hand tighter.

Rage boils off of him. "You both are abominations. Creatures from opposite sides should never be able to share power like this, not without one of them dying. Hybrid or not."

{He's losing it.}

Father's eyes shine dark red. "Just the sight of you makes me sick. Neither of you should exist. Whatever kind of thing you two are does not belong in this world."

{I can't tell if he's more upset with how much power we have now or by the connection that we share.}

"Forget the church for now."

The marching hordes turn away from the building.

"I have a duty to make sure that you two do not leave here." His army turns and faces Mal and me.

"Lucifer would have my head if he found out I allowed"—he waves one of his hands at us—"this to go on. He is already upset with me for allowing my property to run amuck and cause problems for us. If he knew about this..."

{He wants to strike us down to correct the wrongs that he and Lucifer see. He's going to use everything he has to do so.}

"Everyone," I say, "get back."

"What?" Wanda asks.

"All of you, get behind us."

"Kal, you can't honestly think that you two can take them all on by yourselves?" Jade questions.

{Right now, with Mal beside me and our hands together, I feel like we can do anything.}

"The guardian is right, Kalma," my father agrees. "No matter what power you two now possess, there is no way you can take them all down." He points at us.

The horde begins to sprint towards us. "Get behind us, now!" Mal demands.

"But—" Wanda starts.

"NOW!" Mal and I exclaim.

Everyone moves quickly until they are all behind us. "You feel it too?" I ask.

"That we can do this?"

I nod.

"Yep."

I smile. "When I'm with you—"

"It feels like we can do anything," she finishes my sentence.

I laugh. "Man, do I love you."

"I love you too." She chuckles.

We face the oncoming enemy, our cloaks becoming brighter. "Ready?" I ask.

"Let's finish this."

We raise our free hands, facing our palms towards the oncoming herd. We take a deep breath, and I can feel our energies building up inside and around us. The air surrounding us begins to crack from the intensity of it all. The ground shakes beneath us as our hands glow.

{One blow.}

The marching horde is about ten feet away. "Let's end it!" I exclaim.

Demon fire and angel energy blast from our palms, continuously growing until the stream is as wide as the army. The blinding ray of power overwhelms the marching horde, covering all of them. We watch as each horde blows up before turning into ash and the ash blowing away with the wind. I pull my fire back as the last one disintegrates. Mal pulls hers in as well before we lower our arms. The aura enveloping us slowly diminishes until it is just her and I standing there with our hands still together.

{We got them all.}

My internal flame dances inside of my heart as my heart beats with relief. I smile as I look at the almost empty space.

{Only one left.}

"It's over, Father. Your army is gone, and soon, you will be too."

His eyes beam with wrath. "Just because my army is gone does not mean this is over. I am still standing, and I can take you all on by myself. I am Lucifer's right-hand man for a reason." Flames come to life around his hands.

Taking a deep breath, I let go of Mal's hand before stepping towards him.

"Kal."

I stop to look at her.

"Are you sure?"

I nod. "I have to. He is my father, so he is my responsibility. I have to be the one to stop him. I have to be the one that kills him."

She nods in understanding. "I'll be here."

"I know." I give her a smile.

"So, you want to go another round?" he asks me.

"This won't be like last time." I march towards him.

"No, it will not. This time, I will make sure to finish you off."

"Maybe even more than me."

{Michael said I could be even stronger than him, so that means...}

I stop a few feet away from my father. He glares at me with hatred and bloodlust.

{That I am stronger...}
My fire reignites around my hands.
{Than you, Father.}

27

{**My power isn't** the same level it was when I was with Mal, but it is still really high. I'm much stronger than when I was fighting him earlier.}

I smile to myself.

{There's no way I'm going to lose this time.} "Don't worry, Father, I'll make this quick."

"Tsk."

I quickly bend down, slamming my hands onto the ground. A giant wave immediately appears, rolling towards him.

{I can use the big, flashy attacks now without draining myself.}

Father lifts his hands before blasting a ray of fire at the oncoming wave. Our flames collide, causing a giant inferno as the royal and navy flames push against each other.

{Wonder how fast I am now.}

The fire around my hands disappears, but the wave stays as I stand up. The pressure from my foot creates a small crater as I push off of it. My feet move quicker than ever, and I am behind him within two seconds.

{It's as if I teleported, that's how fast I moved.}

His shoulders tense before his hands go out. Both sets of fire attacks vanish as he turns around. I swing, but he dodges before I can hit him.

So, I bend down, grabbing his ankle before pulling. As he lifts off the ground and flips, I kick him hard in the stomach.

{Pay back from earlier.}

I can hear as the air is forced out of him before he goes sailing through the air. He lands on the ground, sliding a few feet before stopping.

"Is that all you got?" He stands back up. "If so, then you will never beat me."

{There's more, believe me, but I'm trying to figure out how much power I have.} He launches towards me. I allow him to come to me. He throws a punch at my face, but I move to the side before kneeing him in the ribs. Some ribs crack against my knee. He flinches from the pain but keeps going. I remove my knee before quickly spinning around. I swing this time. He pushes my arm away as his fist slams into my chest.

{That barely even hurt.}

I throw another punch without hesitation. My fist nails him in the face, making him slide back some.

"How is this possible?" Blood drips from his mouth. "You should not be able to injure me." He wipes his hand across his lip.

{I actually made him bleed.}

"I'm going to do more than just that."

"Cocky little—"

My fist stops him from finishing as it sinks into his stomach. "ACK!" He spits blood.

"Not so fun when it's you spitting up blood, is it?" Energy rolls down my hand into my fist. "Neither is being blasted."

Fire explodes from my hand. Father goes flying into the air, farther this time, before smashing into the ground. He coughs as he lies there. I walk over to him, watching as he continues to spit up more blood.

{Paybacks a bitch, isn't it, Father?}

The coughing stops as I make it to him. His leg kicks out, connecting to the side of my leg, causing it cave in. I fall forward as he jumps up.

{Not going to work this time.}

Using the momentum of the fall, I roll to the side before he can get another attack in. As I jump back onto my feet, he throws another punch.

{Let's see if he remembers this one.}

His fist moves closer to my head, but before it strikes me, I move my head to the side to dodge it. His eyes widen in shock. I smirk at him before turning a little while watching his arm straighten out in front of me. I grab onto his arm squeezing it hard.

CRACK! CRACK!

"Ah!" he exclaims as both of the bones in his arm snap. Holding on tight, I lift him up and pull him over my head.

"It's over! I'm going to break every bone in your body!" I scream as I use all of my strength to swing him back down.

BOOOOOMMM!

The impact echoes all around us as pieces of the pavement fly all over the place and dust fills the air.

{No matter how strong he is, there's no way he's walking away from that anytime soon. I used every bit of muscle in that swing.}

The dust clears, and I can see the body-shaped hole in front of me.

{That hole is at least three feet deep.}

I step closer to see down into it. Father lies at the bottom, with multiple streams of blood leaking from his mouth, nose, and ears.

{I thought so.}

"I told you that I'd make it quick," I tell him as I kneel down.

"How did you?" he struggles to ask before he starts coughing.

"You know how. You just don't want to believe it."

{I have to finish this before he can heal.}

"Kalma, no matter what I have done, I am still your father. You cannot kill me."

I sigh. "I might share some of your DNA, but we both know that I was never your daughter." Fire blazes around my hand. "My whole life, you only ever treated me as a thing, a weapon, a tool. To you, I was never anything more."

The light from my flames shines into the hole, showing the panic on his blood-covered face.

"Every day, for as long as I can remember, you tortured me."

"I was making you stronger so that you could defend yourself."

I shake my head. "No, you were making me stronger so I could defend you." I smile sadly down at him. "You wanted me to be able to defend you against excruciating blows, or even a lethal one." My hand shines brighter. "Because that's what I'm made for, right?"

He doesn't say anything as he stares at my hand.

"For years, I believed that. I believed that I was just a tool for you to use. You never treated me as anything else. Not a single word of affection, no kind words. The only time you spoke my name is whenever you were flaunting me around to everyone, showing off your hybrid."

His eyes narrow.

"I was your weapon, your tool to be used and controlled, your hybrid." My fire slowly grows into a straight line.

"You told me that that was what I was MADE for." A hilt made of flames forms in my fist.

"But even after everything you put me through and all the horrible things that you said and did to me, I still have to thank you."

A bewildered expression forms on his face.

"If you wouldn't have treated me like that, then I never would've felt different. I never would've questioned what I am, who I am. Without you, I wouldn't have searched through your things and found the picture of my mother. None of this would have happened if it weren't for you, Father." I beam down at him. "Because of you, I came up here and saw how amazing it all is. I learned about humans and everything they are about. I made a best friend who became my real family. Most of all, it's because of you that I found the one I'm meant to be with. I found the love of my life."

My heart beats faster as I think about Mal. He looks up at me now with rage and hatred.

"Bottom line is, you are what made all of this possible, and I want to thank you for it." The fire sword solidifies in my hand. "Thank you."

"You are wrong! I raised you to be evil, to be vile, to be a demon. I had nothing to do with any of this!" he hollers at me.

"You might believe that, Father, but we all know the truth."

{I want him to die knowing that he made my life better, that he is the reason I found happiness.}

I slowly stand up, my blade dancing in my hand.

{Because knowing that he'll see that his life's work was for nothing.}

As I step closer to the hole, I flip the sword around to face down the tip.

{I have to strike his flame.}

"Stop, Kalma!" he yells as he tries to move but can't.

"Goodbye, Father." I swing down.

"Not so fast there, Kalma," a voice says.

Extremely sinful energy flies towards me. My flames go out before I jump into the air, doing a few backflips before landing on my feet. White flames strike the spot where I was just standing.

{No, it's not possible. He can't be up here. Not all of the churches have been destroyed. There's still heavenly influence on the Earth.}

My hands and knees shake as sweat rolls down my neck. My heart pounds quickly in my chest with dread as his presence rolls over me.

"Kal?" I hear Mal say.

I hold my hand out, motioning her to stay still and quiet.

"I'm very impressed with your new power, Kalma," the voice says again.

White flames slowly rise from the ground. The beating gets faster as the fire continue to increase.

"Can't say I'm too happy with how you received them, though," the voice explains, coming from the fire.

The fire stops rising before taking shape. I let out a small sigh of relief but a tiny one.

{It's just his flaming astral projection.} The flames form into a humanoid shape.

{Still have to be careful, though. Even if it's not actually him, those flames are still dangerous. I don't know if I'd be able to defend against them, even being as strong as I am now.}

"I've been watching you, Kalma. I've been watching for quite some time now." Alarm runs up and down my back, my mouth becoming dry.

"Your father is right when he said that you are an abomination and should not exist in this world."

My heart falls into my stomach as I feel all the blood leave my face. "Don't worry, I'm not here for you or that angel hybrid."

I instinctively step back and in front of Mal to protect her.

"I said not to worry. You two are not my concern." The humanoid head turns towards us. "At least not today."

{What does that mean?}

"Right now, I am only here for your father." The figure steps closer to the man-shaped hole.

{Why is he here for him? Did he come to save him?}

"Rorridun, look at yourself. How could you allow this to happen?"

"I am sorry, sir. I was not expecting this many to show up to fight, and I definitely was not expecting the power from the hybrids."

"Clearly."

"I swear to you, though, that I will finish my task. The last church will fall."

The white shape shakes its head. "I have a feeling that no matter how many troops we send to tear this place down, those two will just destroy them."

{Got that right.}

"Then what would you have me do, sir?"

"You? Nothing."

"What do you mean?"

"You're done. You failed me. A church still stands. Our hybrid joined the other side, which allowed her to start her human heart, making her more powerful than any demon."

{Any demon?}

"And with the angel hybrid by her side." It shakes its head. My hands tighten at my sides.

"Sir, I am sorry. I will make it up to you."

"It's too late."

"Sir."

Energy presses down on me as the white flames flicker faster.

{Is he going to?}

"Goodbye, Rorridun."

"NOOOO!"

The figure dives into the hole. "AHHHHHHHHHHHHH HHHH! AHHHHHH! AHH H HHHHH!" my father howls in pain.

I cringe at the sound as he continues to wail.

"KAAAAAAALLLLLLMMMMMMMAAAAAA!" My heart skips at the sound of my name.

"KAAAAAALLLLLLMMMMMMMAAAAA! PLEASE HELP ME!" Pressure builds behind my eyes.

"MAKE IT SSSSSTOOOOOOOOOOOOP!"

Tears stream down my face as my body trembles.

{Why am I crying over him after everything he did?} "KAAAA-ALLLLLLMMMMMMAAAAA! AHHHHHHHHHH!"

{I was prepared to kill him. I was about to kill him, so why am I responding like this?}

A hand gently slides into mine. I turn and see Mal standing beside me. "AHHHHHHHHH!"

She holds on tighter as she stares at the hole where my father continues to burn. "KAALLMMAA!" His howls become quieter.

{Is it because I was going to make his death quick and this isn't? This is torture. No one deserves to die like this, no matter how evil.}

The yelling stops. Tears roll down my face before dripping onto the ground. "Goodbye, Father," I say softly.

The white flames jump back out of the hole before retaking the humanoid shape. "That took a lot longer than I thought. I must be losing my touch."

Anger flickers inside of me.

"Don't look at me like that, Kalma. I did you a favor."

I don't say anything as I glare at it.

"You didn't have to kill your own father. You should be thanking me."

"He didn't deserve to die like that," I finally speak.

"Maybe, maybe not. I had to set an example so everyone knows not to fail me." The figure looks around. "Speaking of which." It raises one of its hands before white fires start popping up everywhere.

I quickly look to watch as flames burn the corpses lying on the ground from both sides.

"Can't have anyone seeing any of these, now, can we?"

"Stop!" I exclaim as I let go of Mal's hand, stepping closer. "Their loved ones need to say bye to them."

It chuckles. "That's such a human thing to do."

"They've lived with humans for years. They've picked up on some of their ways."

I take another step as my hands ignite. "So stop."

The figure turns towards me but doesn't stop as the fire patches spread out everywhere.

"I'd watch who you are talking to like that, and I'd definitely be careful of who you are threatening with those."

My hands keep blazing as I stare at the head. Neither one of us moves or puts out our fires.

"My body might not be here, but believe me, I still have enough power to kill you."

I swallow a gulp of air but stand my ground.

After a few seconds, "You got guts, kid, I'll give you that, but..." The small fires grow and burn faster. "I don't take orders from anyone."

"NO!" I yell as the corpses turn to ashes.

My hands go out, as I fall to my knees with even more tears.

"Let me give you some advice." The figure walks towards me. "Don't allow your new emotions to get the better of you, or you'll regret it." It stops in front of me.

I look up at it with hatred roaring inside of me.

"Like that anger you are feeling right now, it's telling you to attack me, isn't it?"

I don't respond.

"Well, if you listen to it, then you'll probably die, but if you don't, then you'll live to see another day."

I hear feet shuffle behind me. I turn my head a little to look back at Mal as she watches us terrified.

"I don't think your hybrid would like it very much if I'd kill you."

I face towards it again to see the head facing Mal.

{Why does it seem like he knows more about Mal and me than he lets on?}

"Lucifer?"

"Hmm?" The head looks back down at me.

"You've been around since the beginning, right?"

"Correct."

"Can I ask you something?"

"And why should I answer your question?"

"You owe me." I slowly stand up.

"Oh? How so?"

"You said you don't like those who fail you and that they must die for doing so."

"Yeah? Your point?"

"We killed this whole army. We killed everyone that failed you."

It doesn't say anything.

"So, technically, we did your dirty work."

"Hahahaha! You really do have guts, kid."

I stand taller.

"All right, I suppose you're right. What is your question?"

{How do I ask this?}

"It's a two-parter."

"Go on."

"Are Mal and I really the first hybrids to fall in love?"

"Hmmm, yes, I believe so. Usually when two hybrids from opposite sides meet, they want to kill one another. So yes, you and she are the first."

{So the archs were right.}

"Do you know where this new power came from?"

"Didn't you ask Raziel these questions?"

I nod. "He didn't know the answers."

"Figures." It chuckles again. "I don't know the exact reason. All I can tell you is that you were right about love being what woke everything up. The love you have for her is what started your heart, and that kiss allowed both of your powers to be unlocked. A long time ago, there was talk about something like this happening, but after eons, it never happened, so it was discarded."

"What was said?"

"Something like when two hybrids meet, and the angel falls in love with the demon, and the demon returns those feelings will their true selves be awoken."

{True selves?}

"An angel is a being of pure light, which can also be described as pure love. So when one can love a creature with no soul or warmth, a demon, they awaken the brightest light, becoming the angel that is inside of them."

{So, wait, does that mean Mal is now more angel than human?}

"The demon being something that could never love being able to love and awaken their heart, as you know, but it also brings them to life."

"Brings them to life?"

"The moment your heart stayed beating was the moment you literally started living. You are alive now. You are no longer the cold, dark, empty creature. Real heat flows inside of you. It's that real heat that makes you stronger. Your internal flame feeds off that heat, which makes the flame bigger, stronger, hotter, and more powerful. So, the more you love, the stronger that heat will become."

{My heart makes my flame stronger.}

"So when that happens to a demon hybrid, they become a being of pure love as well, just like an angel, but clearly, you aren't an angel."

"What am I?"

"You are a demon who not only has the powers of a demon but also has the energy of pure light inside of you." It sighs. "Kalma, I'm only going to tell you this not because I want to help you but because I want to see what comes from it…"

"Okay?"

"The information said that when a demon hybrid has power from both sides, of light and dark, they can become more powerful than all of the archangels."

"All of them?"

"Even Raziel."

My head spins with this new information.

"When you two used your powers together, your flame got amplified, and your light energy combined with her light energy, making your powers ten times stronger. That's why you were able to evaporate the whole army in seconds."

{So I was right. When Mal and I are together, we really can do anything.} "Does that answer your questions?" it asks, annoyed.

"I think so."

"Good, then it's time I leave. I hate being up here too long, even just my astral self."

{Lucifer hates humans.}

"One more thing before I go." It holds its hand out towards me. "Just a little taste of what's to come."

Energy fills the air around us, the white flames spread over its hand. My eyes grow with fear.

"This won't kill you, just going to hurt like hell." The fire blasts into my chest. The front of me screams as my skin burns while I fly through the air. I hit the ground hard, smacking the back of my head in the process.

"Kal!" Mal and Wanda exclaim.

"See you soon, Kalma," Lucifer says before everything goes black.

28

"Lucifer!" I yell, sitting up fast.

"Hey, hey, you're okay." Mal jumps onto the bed to sit next to me. "He's gone. Everything is all right."

The familiar room comes into view around me.

{We're back at Wanda's place?}

"Mal, what happened? How did we get back here?" I rub the back of my head. "The last thing I remember is getting blasted by Lucifer."

She nods as she slides her hand to mine. "After he attacked you, you hit your head really hard off of the ground, knocking you unconscious."

{His flames must have done more to me than just hit me, because I never would've been knocked out by something like that.}

"Once we were sure he was gone, we regrouped before heading back here." A slight hue of pink appears on her cheeks. "I carried you on my back all the way here."

I look down at myself, noticing the new clothing I have on, and the blood on my arms and hands is gone.

{She cleaned me up.} "So everyone is here?"

She looks at me with sad eyes. "Those who survived, yes."

Grief strikes my chest. "How many?"

"A little less than half of the guardian angels managed to survive, but only one power angel made it."

"Leo. I remember seeing him."

"Yeah, he's the one."

I nod, telling her to go on.

"Both cherubim lived."

{Jahoel made it.}

"Half of the goblins, two imps, and four pucks."

{I hope two of them are Uxum and Sukir. I've watched over them for weeks. I couldn't imagine them just being gone.}

"The jinn all managed to make it through, with barely a scratch on any of them."

{Sneaky little bastards. Good job, Frikik.}

"Only two succubi returned with us."

"Which ones?"

"Um, I don't know their names, but one has brown, curly hair and the other a blond braid."

{Husha didn't make it.} "Who else?"

"The earth and air elementals survived, but they didn't come back with us. They went off somewhere."

"Elementals use strong elemental magic to heal. They can only do that from where they came from."

"Oh, okay."

"Anyone else?"

"None of the furies survived."

{That's surprising, even if there were only two. Furies are very hard to kill. The only way for them to die is to be decapitated.}

"And then Derrick's coven and two of the healing witches."

"Only two? What happened to the third?"

"I guess she went into the center of the battlefield to heal a fallen succubus, but as she was doing so, a nightmare grabbed her."

{She ran in there knowing that it was the most dangerous area. She still went to help even though she knew it could cost her her life.}

I ball up a handful of bed sheets in my free hand.

{So many lost. So many gave their lives for people they didn't even know. Each of them died with honor and selflessness.}

"Their deaths will not go unnoticed. Each of their sacrifices is why we were able to win." I look at Mal. "Their names will not be forgotten."

She smiles at me. "I agree."

{I'll make sure of it.}

"So, you're awake?"

We turn towards the voice to see Jade and Wanda standing just inside the door. "Hey." I wave.

Anger flashes behind Wanda's emeralds.

{Oh shit.}

She starts running towards me. Mal quickly lets go of my hand before jumping away from the bed. I look over at her with a look of betrayal. She holds her hands up as she tries not to laugh. Magic pulses in the air. I face towards Wanda, just as she leaps onto the bed with her magic in tow. She knocks me onto my back right before the green aura rams into me.

CRACK!

The bedframe snaps under us, the broken frame causing it to collapse with us on top of it.

"Oof!" I breathe as the mattress hits the ground.

{She's really pissed.}

"You have been upset with me for days for ruining your place because of the holes I put in the wall and the counter I fell into, but you can just come in here and break the bed." I joke. "I'm calling double standards."

Wanda's eyes continue to radiate green, while her magic continues to press against me.

{I could break out of this in a second, but I know she needs this.}

She lifts her hand.

SLAP!

My head is turned to the side with a handprint stinging on my cheek.

{And that.}

I turn my head to look back up at her. Some of the magic fades from her eyes, being replaced with concern and love.

{I really scared her this time.}

Guilt fills my stomach as she stares down at me. SLAP!

My other cheek burns, with my head turned the other way now. I slowly face forward again as all of her magic fades away. She brings her hands together over my chest as she sits on me. Tears lay in her eyes, ready to fall.

"You made a promise, remember?" she asks me, dead toned.

"Promise me that you will get through the battle alive as well.

"Promise me. I need to know that when this is all said and done that you will be here. That I will see you again."

"I promise."

{I knew when I made that promise that I wouldn't be able to keep it. I knew that I would likely die while fighting my father.}

"And I kept it."

"Only because of some new power, not because you tried to." I sigh, knowing she's right.

{I'd be dead right now if it wasn't for Mal and my heart beating.}

"You looked me in the eyes and promised me that you would survive that battle, that you would come back when it was all done and I'd see you again."

"And I did. You are seeing me. I'm alive, Wanda."

"NOT BECAUSE OF YOU!"

The frustration and pain in her scream takes my breath away.

"Did you forget that I'm the one who found you in that crater? I saw the blood, the broken bones, and I felt your flame. You were dying, you were dying fast, and I was so scared that I wasn't going to be quick enough to save you."

"Wanda."

"No, my turn," she cuts me off. "Just as I was about to heal you, just when I thought I could save you this time, you ran away." The tears finally break free. "You ran to die."

Feet shuffle beside us. Mal stands there with her arms crossed tightly across her chest.

"You knew what was coming, you knew what your father was going to do, and you still kept going."

A small speck of anger pulses. "If you want me to apologize for saving Mal's life, you can forget it."

Wanda looks down at me, shocked by my sudden outburst.

{I've never gone off on her before.}

"Yes, I knew that he was going to try to kill her, and yes, I knew what technique he was going to use to do so." Angry tears slide down my temples. "I'm sorry, Wanda. I'm sorry that I broke my promise. I'm sorry that you had to see me like that and had to watch as I slowly died again. I'm sorry that I have repeatedly hurt you time and time again by doing stuff like that, but I will never apologize for jumping in front of that attack."

My flame rumbles inside of my heart while it pounds harder.

"I'm sorry, Wanda, but I will always take the fatal blow for someone I care about, for someone I love." My anger softens. "Including you."

More tears fall onto me.

"I really am sorry that you had to see all of that. I never wanted either of you to see me like that." I take a breath, trying to contain my tears. "I see now just how much that has hurt you, has hurt both of you." I pause, making sure Mal is listening. "That's the last thing I want, to hurt either of you." I gently put my hands over Wanda's.

"I can't do this anymore, Kal. I can't keep watching you die or coming close to it. It's destroying me."

I don't say anything.

"I love you too much."

My heart races faster.

"Whether I can be with you or not, I still love you, Kal, and I think I always will. Whether it'll be romantically or not, I will still love you. And just as you can't allow anyone to hurt us, I can't sit back and watch it happen to you either." She cries harder.

{Oh, Wanda.}

I quickly sit up and wrap my arms tightly around her. She shakes and trembles with each breath as she cries into my shirt.

"I'm so sorry, Wanda. I never wanted this. I never wanted any of this. If I would've known how much I'd come to hurt you, I would have stayed away."

She pulls her arms out from between us, pushing me back so she can see my eyes. "I'd never want that." She slowly lays her head on my shoulder. "The pain of not having you in my life would be more unbearable than the pain of watching you get hurt."

"I don't understand. You're hurting because of me, but you'd also hurt if I left?"

She nods.

"Then what can I do to stop you from hurting? Tell me, and I'll do it."

{I just want Mal and you to be safe and happy. I'll do whatever it takes to make sure of it.}

"I couldn't help you, Kal," she says softly.

"What?"

"When you really needed me, I couldn't help you. All I could do was sit there and watch you die. Mal begged me to heal you, to fix you like I did before, but I couldn't. I don't think I ever could."

"You said something like that before. What did you mean?"

She sighs. "Since that day, I've been replaying it over and over in my head. There's no way my magic could've relit your flame. It had already been out for too long."

"If not you, then who?"

Wanda lifts and turns her head.

"Me?" Mal speaks up.

Wanda nods. "The idea crossed my mind many times, but after listening to what Lucifer said, I knew it was true." She lays her head back on my shoulder. "He said that when Mal fell in love with you, and you being a demon, she awakened the brightest light."

"Okay?"

"Well, my first theory was that she healed you without knowing she was doing it." Mal and I look at each other.

{Could she have?}

"My second theory." We look back towards Wanda. "That even though Kal hadn't yet awakened her heart, she still felt love. So there was a small spark of that light energy in you that he was talking about, and it was because of that small spark that when Mal was holding your hand that day talking to you, your energies combined, which would've amplified your flame."

"Restarting it, as well as changing the color and making me stronger," I finish for her.

{It makes sense. I remember seeing a beautiful blue hue in my head just before I woke up.}

I look at Mal. I look at her eyes.

{The blue was the same color as her eyes.} I chuckle.

{How did I not notice that until now?}

"I think you're right." Wanda lifts her head.

"It just makes sense. If you honestly think that your magic isn't what reignited my flame, that it was something else, then this is the something else."

I meet Mal's stare again. "There was love inside of me that day."

Mal smiles brightly.

"So, if you loved me, then..."

"I did," Mal answers quickly. We both laugh.

"I did," she says more calmly.

"Then the light energy inside of you two connected, just enough to bring Kal's flame back," Wanda explains.

"So Mal is the reason Kal's flames changed colors?" Jade speaks up.

"Technically, we both are the reason," I tell her.

{Our love saved me A LOT more than I thought.} "So you see, Kal..."

My eyes land on Wanda's.

"I couldn't save you then, the same way I couldn't save you last night." Realization clicks.

{You're not just mad at me, are you?}

"I'm useless." She cries more. "I couldn't heal you, I couldn't help you, and now I definitely won't be able to help you. You're too powerful now to ever need my help."

{You're mad at yourself too.}

"What are you going to need me for now? Mal can heal you, teach you about this world, and be there for you. There's nothing I can do for you anymore, Kal. You don't need me anymore." She becomes hysterical.

My chest aches as she bawls.

{Is that really what she thinks?}

I turn my head to see Mal. She meets my eyes, before nodding with a smile, knowing what I'm thinking.

"You couldn't be more wrong." My hands lay on both sides of Wanda's head. "How could you ever think those things?"

Her eyes study mine.

"Because..."

"No, there's no universe where that would ever happen." She doesn't say anything.

"Do you honestly think those are the reasons I hang out with you? If you do, then you must not know me as well as I thought you did."

Shame fills her eyes.

"Damnit, Wanda. After all these months of us being friends, you can really sit there and say those things?" Now tears fall from my eyes. "How many times do I have to repeat myself, huh?" I pull her in closer till our heads touch. "You are my family."

Her eyes fill up again.

"It's not because you taught me pretty much everything I know about humanity, not because of your healing magic either. You're my family because you were the first one to accept me for me. You allowed me to be who I am without any shame. Wanda, you opened your arms and heart to me, even though you knew what I was and who I was re-lated to. Every day I came to see you, you always greeted me with a smile." More tears roll down my face. "You care about me, you want what is best for me, you always have my back, you're there to catch me if I fall, you are the person I look up to most."

Crocodile tears stream down her cheeks.

"You love me Wanda, and yes, it's not the same way I love you, but it's still there. Without you being in my life, I don't think I would've survived." I give her a sad smile. "The day we met, I was so lost and confused. I didn't know what to do. I didn't even know..." I take a shaky breath. "If I wanted to keep going."

Mal takes a quick breath as Wanda gapes at me.

"When I found out what I was and what hybrids are used for, I didn't want to live and be used as a weapon. Even after seeing Mal, the thoughts were still in my head, fighting with me to just end it." I push Wanda away so I can look directly into her eyes. "Then I met you, and you were so kind and so caring towards me. I wasn't just a hybrid to you. I was a person. I was someone worth caring for. So, I decided to visit you every day because I enjoyed being around you. You made me happy and let me forget about my father and the others while we were together. Not long after we met, I decided to keep living because of everything you did for me." I smile warmly. "So you see, Wanda, you were the first one who saved me."

"Kal, I..." she says.

"I know, it's okay." I pull her into a tight hug. "Just don't ever repeat those things."

She nods against my shoulder.

"You're my family, Wanda. I'm not going anywhere." She squeezes me harder. "I love you, Kal."

"I love you too, Wanda."

I look over at Mal to see her beaming brightly at us.

{You really can love two people in different ways.} After a few minutes, Wanda finally settles down. "Are you okay now?"

"Yes."

She lets go of me before slowly getting off of me to stand up. Once she is off, I stand up also.

"I'm sorry for slapping you." I chuckle.

"It's all right."

"And for everything I said."

"Make it up to me by never thinking those things ever again."

"I won't, I promise."

"Good."

"Would you really have done it?" Jade questions me.

{Always has to make things awkward again, just as it settles down.} "Yes." I sigh.

Mal rushes past me before slamming into Wanda. "Thank you." She hugs her.

Wanda looks down at her, shocked. "For what?"

"Saving Kalma."

No one says anything. Wanda looks over at me with her cheeks all red. I shrug with a smile.

She smiles as her arms wrap around Mal. "You're welcome." Loving warmth fills me up as I watch them.

{Those two are my whole world.}

They let go of each other, smiling before Mal turns back towards me and rams into me with a hug. I can't help but laugh as she buries her face into the crook of my neck.

"Don't you ever leave me," she orders.

"Not planning on it."

She lets go, stepping back. "I love you."

My internal flame roars inside my heart. "I love you too." We start leaning towards each other.

"Are you guys done yet?"

We stop to look at the door.

"How long have you been standing there?" Jade asks.

"Long enough," Frikik answers.

My face heats up as Mal's turns crimson.

"They're waiting for you," he tells me.

"Who is?"

"Everyone."

He turns and walks away.

"I guess that's your cue," Jade says.

"I guess."

Mal takes my hand as she squares her shoulders. "Ready?"

"As I'll ever be."

"Then let's go," Jade orders before heading out the door. Wanda shrugs before she follows. We follow behind her.

Wanda's store door closes behind me.

{It's night again. I was unconscious for a whole day.} I look around. {Who are all of these people?}

Different creatures fill up the circle. Some I recognize from my small army, but the rest are strangers.

"They are the families of the fallen," Frikik explains seeing me looking around. Guilt sits in my stomach seeing all of the families and loved ones.

"They've been waiting to hear from you."

"Why? What do they want me to say?"

He shrugs. "I don't know. All I can say is, what would you want to hear after losing someone you love?"

I glance at Mal and Wanda.

{I don't even want to think about something happening to them, but he's right.} "You can stay here if you want. You don't have to face them if you don't want to," I tell Mal.

"I know. I want to go with you."

"All right. Wanda?"

"I'll come too."

I nod before heading towards the fountain. As the groups see us, they part so that we can get past them. We make it through everyone. I stop in front of the fountain and face them.

"I'm sorry to have kept all of you waiting."

"Where is my wife?" someone yells.

The question shocks me.

"Didn't anyone tell them what happened to the bodies?" I ask Jade.

"No. Everyone thought it'd be better to hear it from you."

"It doesn't matter who the information comes from. They're still going to be upset."

She shrugs.

"Well?" the voice asks.

"I hate to have to tell you all this, but your loved ones' bodies were turned to ash."

Everyone starts talking quickly and loudly, all of their voices sounding upset.

"What do you mean turned to ash?" someone else asks. "Only demons turn to ash when killed."

"Normally, yes, but in this case, someone burned them."

"What do you mean someone burned them?"

"Who would do something like that?"

"I'm guessing no one informed them about Lucifer either?"

"Nope," Jade responds.

"Great." I stand taller. "Lucifer, Lucifer burned them until they were nothing but ash."

They all stop talking.

"You expect us to believe that?"

"Lucifer can't come up here. Not as long as there is a church still standing."

"He might not be able to, but his fire astral projection can, and it did."

"If that is true, why did he bother sending one up here?"

"He wanted to finish off my father. He set my father on fire and slowly burned him alive."

"But why? Why do that when you were going to kill him anyway?"

"Because my father failed Lucifer, so he had to make sure that he suffered and died by his hand so everyone would know not to fail him."

"So, Lucifer was really there?"

"Yes."

"Why did he burn the bodies?"

"He said so humans wouldn't discover them, but I think the real reason was to show off some of his power."

"Why didn't you stop him?"

"How could you allow him to do that?"

"We wanted to say our goodbye properly, and now we can't."

"I know that, and that is why I was prepared to fight Lucifer to get him to stop."

Someone scoffs loudly, "You expect us to believe that you were going to fight Lucifer?"

"She's telling the truth."

I glance towards where the voice came from.

"She was going to fight him, but he turned up the heat on his flames, turning them all to ash within seconds," Deseih defends me.

"That's right," Leo exclaims. "Her hands were ablaze with fire as she stepped closer to him, demanding him to stop."

"Kalma was prepared to go up against the Prince of Darkness in order to bring your loved ones back," One of the jinn explains.

"She really was going to fight for them." a warlock says.

No one says anything for a few seconds.

"But why? Why would you ever consider fighting him, just to save the bodies of those already dead?"

"Because I'd want to be able to say goodbye to someone I love. To be robbed of that opportunity is heinous, and I didn't want that to happen to all of you."

"It doesn't matter. They are gone, and now we don't have anything to remember them and their sacrifices."

"That's where you are wrong."

"What do you mean?'

"I have a way to honor them and to make sure no one ever forgets what they did for all of us."

"How?" Wanda asks me curiously.

"Do we have a list of all of those that didn't make it?"

"Yes," Jade answers.

"Get it."

Jade nods before running off.

"I wanted to make sure that their names would always be remembered and would always be seen." I move closer to the fountain.

"I got it." Jade runs up to me and hands me a piece of paper.

I scan down the page, memorizing each name listed. "Thanks." I hand her the paper back.

"What are you going to do?"

"You'll see." I let go of Mal's hand before facing the fountain. "Their names will forever be written in stone."

{Hope this actually works.}

Fire ignites around my arms. I push the flames down into my hands as I place them on the outer ring of the fountain.

{Each name, no one will be forgotten.}

I close my eyes, picturing the list of names. My flames burn hotter before sinking into the cement. I force the heat from the fire to cover the whole circle.

{Focus. Use the flames to carve into the cement.}

Small chipping sounds come from around the fountain as I keep forcing flames and heat out of my hands.

{I won't allow any of them and what they did be forgotten. I know everyone thinks that Mal and I are the reason we won, but the truth is, it was because of them. They fought and gave their lives to make sure that we won. It's only because of their sacrifices that we did.}

The last name finishes burning into the stone.

{Need to say why their names are here.}

I move the heat to the side of the outer ring facing the entrance. Fire starts carving. I smile as the last letter finishes. All of my energy returns to my hands before taking them off and opening my eyes.

"Now everyone will see their names and know what they did for all of us." Everyone moves closer to the fountain. Some cover their mouths as tears fill their eyes, while others stand still, trying not to cry. The group circles the whole fountain to find the name of their loved one.

"How did you know you could do that?" Mal asks.

"I didn't. I just knew that I had to."

She laughs. "That makes absolutely no sense."

I shrug before taking her hand and pulling her to the front of the fountain. "So, what do you think?" I point.

"To those who fought and died to save us all. May their names forever be remembered as those who ended the war," she reads the engraving. "They deserve the credit more than we do."

"I agree. I love it."

"There's one more thing I want to do so that people will look at it. But I need your help to do it."

"What do you need me to do?"

"Be a hybrid with me."

She chuckles. "Easy."

Both of our energies burst around us, doing the same thing they did on the battlefield. Everyone stops to stare at us in awe. We place our free hands onto the fountain. Mal follows my lead as I pull a tiny part of my core flame out of me into my arm, then to my hand. I feel as Mal does the same thing with her core light. Our energies unite before fusing with the fountain.

{Thanks for the idea, Lucifer, but this one will be a symbol of love, not fear.}

The water evaporates before my flames and Mal's energy starts flowing out of it, just as the water did.

"This fountain will forever flow with our power, making sure no one ever forgets."

29

"So, what's the next step?" I ask the archs as we sit at one of the new tables set around the fountain.

{It's been a few days since the war. Everything is slowly returning to normal. Everyone went back to their homes to mourn with their families, satisfied that their loved ones would never be forgotten.}

I look around the table.

{Michael, Gabriel, and Uriel came back down yesterday to check in with us and see what needs to be done now that we know Lucifer isn't going to be sending any more troops up.}

I grin.

{Thanks to Mal and I, he knows that there's no point, because we'll destroy them in an instant.}

"We've been studying some things," Uriel speaks up.

{I've been so anxious since they arrived, waiting to hear what they have to say.} I glance at Mal sitting beside me.

{All I want is to start our lives together. Now that the war is over, we can finally just be us.}

"Our research shows that the heavenly energy isn't getting any better," she explains.

"What do you mean it's not getting any better?" Jade asks, concerned.

"There's still only a small amount of energy, and that is because of the church here in Philly still standing," Gabriel answers.

"But since the other churches are destroyed and demons have claimed the lands the churches used to be on as their own, divine energy can't build back up," Michael says.

"So what has to happen for it to build back up?" Jade questions them.

{I have a bad feeling about where this is going.}

"The churches must be rebuilt, and the demons have to either be destroyed or scared away so that their vile energy doesn't block the heavenly." Uriel clasps her hands together as she puts her elbows on the table.

"As each church is reclaimed and built, more and more energy will be restored. Then once all are back, the energy will be as well," Michael tells us.

"So all of the churches around the world have to be cleared of demons and rebuilt?" Wanda asks.

"Yes." Gabriel nods.

{Have an awful feeling.}

"How do we do that?" Jade puts her hands on the table. "After the battles all around the world, the number of guardian angels is deficient. There's no way they'll be enough to recover all of the churches."

"We're aware of that," Uriel explains. "That's why we came here."

Michael, Gabriel, and Uriel look at Mal and me.

{I knew it.}

"You want us to go around the world and clear out the demons so the angels can rebuild the churches?" I sigh.

They nod.

"How long do you think that would take?" Mal wonders.

"Depending on how fast you move and how long it takes to destroy the demons. It could take anywhere from eight to twelve months, maybe more."

{A year. A year of traveling and fighting.} Mal nods. "I see."

I study her, trying to figure out what she is thinking.

{Do you want to do this, Mal? I'll do whatever you want to do.}

"How would they get around?" Jade asks.

"We were hoping that you'd be their transportation," Michael answers. Mal and I turn to Jade, surprised.

"You want me to go with them?"

Michael nods. "Your transporter would be of great help to them, and you could signal us, telling us when we can send angels down to start building."

Jade thinks it over. "What about my team?"

"Jade, you know that the transporter can only take four and that we need as many guardians around helping people as we can get. Your team will follow their normal duties while you are away," Gabriel says.

She nods. "I understand."

"Wait," Wanda exclaims. "Did you say four?"

"Yes, why?" Gabriel responds.

Wanda looks over at me.

{I know that look.}

"Would it be possible for me to go with them?"

They all look at her with bewilderment.

"You'd want to go with them even though of the dangers and the time period?" Uriel gapes at her.

Wanda nods. "It's not like I have anything better to do, and who knows, maybe I could be of help to them."

I smile at her.

"Besides, Kal is my family, and I don't think I can handle being away from my family for that long. I'd rather go with them than sit here alone."

"You'd really come with us?" Jade asks, stunned.

"I would."

"Kal."

I look at Michael.

"You haven't said anything. What do you think about all of this?"

{I don't know what to think. I understand that the churches need to be restored for the heavenly influence to retake control over the world again, but I also know that I just want things to be calm so that Mal and I can start our lives.}

"I know what you're thinking," Mal speaks before I can answer. "I told you that after the war was over that it'd be you and me."

I nod.

"But I also said that we have the rest of our lives for it to just be the two of us."

I nod again.

"So, what is a year to forever?"

{She's right. A year is nothing compared to forever. Significantly, since now that I'm eighteen, I won't age any more thanks to those hybrid genes. This means once Mal turns eighteen, she'll stop aging as well. So we literally will have eternity together.}

Love builds in my chest as I smile. "You're right. A year is nothing compared to eternity."

She smiles back at me.

"So, then you'll do it?" Gabriel asks. "You'll travel the world taking care of all the demons?"

"You two are the only ones powerful enough to do this," Michael explains.

"We know," I say, "We also know how important it is to get things back to normal."

"That's why we'll do it," Mal tells them.

They smile at us.

"What about you, Jade?" I ask her. "Gonna join us?"

"Tsk. Not like I have much of a choice. I can't trust you two to do it on your own. You'd get distracted with all of your lovey-dovey stuff and screw everything up." We all laugh.

"Are you sure about coming Wanda?" I look at her.

"Definitely. I can't go a year without seeing that goofy face of yours." She chuckles.

"Hey, just because my eyes are two different colors now does not make my face goofy."

"If you say so." She smirks.

I stick my tongue out, making her to laugh even more.

"I have a question before we make plans," Mal explains.

"What is it, Mal?" Uriel wonders.

"How bad would it be if we waited a few months to start?" We all stare at her.

"It's just that I graduate in May, and I've put years of hard work into my schooling. I kind of want to see all of that hard work pay off."

Uriel turns to Gabriel for a few seconds before facing forward again.

"Nothing will get worse. It will still be the same as it is right now," Uriel explains.

"The energy won't go down any further, so I suppose waiting till then will be okay," Gabriel says.

"So, I can graduate first?"

They nod.

Mal beams brightly. "Thank you."

"So I guess you all will have a few months to prepare yourself for the challenges ahead. Once Mal finishes school, you will head out immediately," Michael orders.

"Got it." Mal, Wanda, Jade, and I say.

"Well, we have to head back, but we will keep in touch. You get in contact if anything changes," Gabriel explains as he stands up.

"Thank you again." Mal stands up. "This means a lot."

"It's the least we can do after everything you've been through. Your whole life literally got turned upside down. We can understand why you want some normal before everything stays paranormal," Uriel says.

"Yeah."

"Good luck and have fun." They wave before vanishing.

"So, what now?" Wanda asks.

"We continue on with our lives until the day comes for us to leave," Jade answers. "These next few months are going to be long," Wanda complains.

"They'll go by faster than you think," Jade tells her.

"I hope so. I hate waiting."

They turn away from us, heading towards the shop, lost in conversation.

{Those two seem to be getting along.}

"Kal." I turn.

"Could you do me a favor?"

"Of course. What's up?"

"Well, we're together, right?"

I grab her before planting a passionate kiss upon her lips. "You tell me." I step back again.

She smiles, her face red. "Well, since we're together and I'm going to be graduating, that means that my human life has to return to some kind of normal."

"Okay?"

"Which means I have to go home."

"I know," I say sadly. "I knew one day that you'd have to go back to your life, and I wouldn't be able to see you for a while."

She looks at me alarmed. "You are not getting pushed out of my life, not ever."

"How...?"

"You're going to meet my mom."

Panic stabs my chest. "What?"

"You are going to meet my mom."

"My human self, you mean?"

She shakes her head. "No. YOU are going to meet my mom."

"Are you crazy? I can't meet your mom like this. She'll totally freak, and then who knows what."

"She's probably already freaking out. I've been gone for a long time. At least when she meets you, I'll be able to tell her what really happened."

"You want to tell her everything?"

"I have to. I'm not going to make you hide who you are. I love you too much to do that. Plus, if we are going to be leaving for a year, she needs to know why, and I hate lying."

{Angel part.}

"Is this really what you want to do?"

She nods. "If we're going to spend forever together, then you have to meet her."

I sigh with a smile. "Let's go."

She quickly grabs the front of my shirt before yanking me towards her. Her soft lips press against mine. We stay like that as her lips hungrily search mine. Fireworks continue to go off in my head as I allow her to explore. My heart races as my breath catches in my throat. Her tender lips kiss me over and over again. She stops herself. I can feel her warm breath hit my lips as she breathes quickly. "I wish we could do that forever," she says breathlessly.

"We do have forever."

"True." She pecks my lips before backing up. "Ready?" I nod as I take her hand.

{Mal's house is very lovely.}

I sit on her couch with Mal beside me and her mom across from us in a chair. Their living room is average sized, lined with white walls covered in family photos and paintings. The carpet is a grayish color. The couch and chair are tan, with side tables sitting next to them all.

{It looks like the pictures of homes I saw in some of the magazines Wanda had me look through to help me learn things.}

Her mom gawks at us from her chair with her eyes open wide.

{Mal and her have almost the same colored eyes, Mal's are just lighter.}

Her mom is averaged height and slightly above normal weight, with gray-streaked short brown hair. She has laugh lines covering her face but no blemishes in sight. The brown sweater she is wearing makes her look even more pale than she already is. Blue jeans and white socks lay comfortably on her legs and feet.

{Mal just finished telling her everything that happened. She hasn't seen my proper form yet, though. Mal wanted to wait until her mom knew everything.}

"Mom?"

Her mom regains her composure. "Malak, I don't know why you thought telling me all of that would get you out of trouble. Making up a story like that just to hide whatever it was you were really doing. I'm very disappointed in you."

{Figured this was how the conversation was going to go. No human would ever believe in the world that I'm from.}

"Mom, I'm not lying. Everything I said is the truth."

"So, what you're telling me is that you're an angel hybrid, and your friend here is a demon hybrid. That you two are in love and because of that love, her heart started beating, which saved her from dying. That you two fought in a war against demons and evil creatures, and that's where you met Lucifer."

Mal nods.

"And the stuff about witches, warlocks, fairies, pixies, and all of that is true too?"

"Yes."

"So, you met the archangels as well?"

"I did."

Her mom shakes her head. "Malak, if you don't knock it off this instant, I'm calling an ambulance to come to get you and take you to the psych ward. Do you understand me?"

"What's a psych ward?" I whisper to Mal.

"It's where they send the mentally ill people."

"Oh, I see."

"Is she the reason you believe all of this stuff happened?"

"No!" Mal exclaims.

"Did she give you drugs or something?"

"No, Mom."

"What did you do to my daughter?" She stands up looking at me angrily. "I suggest that you leave right now and never come near her again, or I will call the police." I look over at Mal.

"Don't you dare look at her." She steps closer. "I don't know how you put all of this stuff in her head and made her think that she's in love with you, but I promise you that this is the end of whatever is going on."

"She didn't do anything to me, Mom, and I do love her. All of me loves her, all the way to my soul." Mal grabs my hand tightly. "I know that this all sounds crazy, but I'd never lie to you, especially not about something this important."

Her mom's face turns red with rage. "Don't you touch her." She grabs onto my arm, ripping my hand out of Mal's.

Anger pulses in my stomach. Mal must sense it because she takes a deep breath. I copy her to calm myself down.

"Please, Mom, I need you to believe me, because after graduation, Kal and two of our friends and I are going to travel all over the world to kill hordes of demons so that the guardian angels can rebuild the churches."

{I don't think laying more and more information on her is going to help any.} "You're doing what?"

"I'm leaving for a year to help Kal."

Her mom trembles with hate and anger as she glares at me.

{Oh boy.}

She reaches down and grabs my shirt with both hands before pulling me off the couch.

{Strong for an older human.}

She turns us so my back is towards the door. "My daughter is not going anywhere with you. She won't be going anywhere near you ever again." She shoves me hard. "Leave now!"

"MOM!" Mal jumps up.

"Don't you move, Malak!"

I stand there staring at both of them.

Mal sighs. "She's not listening." She looks up at me. "Go ahead."

"You sure?"

"Go ahead with what?! What do you think you're going to do?!"

Mal's mom quickly snatches a letter opener from the stand beside the couch. She raises it up. "Get out, or I'll use this."

354 Kara J Redmond

{Violent for someone who gave birth to a half angel.} "Do it, Kal. It's the only way she'll believe us."

"Okay."

Terror fills her mom's eyes. She swings the letter opener at me.

{Guess she's going to see two unbelievable things.}

She steps back as the letter opener sticks out of my stomach.

{Human weapons can't hurt me.}

I grab onto the handle before pulling it out of me. My skin immediately heals. The only evidence that something happened is the hole in my shirt.

"How? Why are you not bleeding?" her mom studders as she steps away from me.

"Mal told you how, you just don't want to believe it, but after this, you won't have a choice."

My body slowly transforms back into my original form. My teeth sharpen as my ears point. My nails return to normal as my one eye burns.

{That's better.}

Mal's mom's face is ghost white as she stares at me in shock. "So, do you believe us now?"

The light leaves from her eyes.

{Crap.}

I move quickly to the chair before sliding it over so that she lands in it. Mal comes up behind me as she looks at her mom.

"Well, when she wakes up, I guess the real conversation will start."

"Should be fun." I nudge her.

She pushes me back. "Want to see my room?"

"Definitely."

"Come on."

I follow her up the stairs.

"Are you sure you're ready? Because once it's out, it's out," Wanda warns me.

"I know, and I'm sure. I've been waiting months for this, and since we are leaving tomorrow, it has to be tonight."

{Jade was right when she said the months would go by fast. The last few months have been amazing, though. I've never been happier. Every day after school, I'd be outside waiting for her so we could walk together and talk about our days. We'd either go to her house or The Middle. It took a while for her mom to warm up to me, but we became really close once she did. She sees how much Mal and I genuinely love each other, and she said she'd never stand in the way of that. So, I was allowed over there whenever I wanted and for as long as I wanted.}

My face heats up as memories of some of our nights together flash through my head.

{Those nights were terrific. The first time was the night of her birthday. It was her birthday present. Seeing Mal like that, I'll never forget. When we weren't at her house or visiting Wanda, we went on actual dates. I had to hide my appearance, of course, but it was worth it. I told Mal that it didn't bother me as long as I spent time with her. We spent all those months, when I wasn't at home with Wanda, acting as an average couple would. Becoming closer and closer as the days went on. The love I have for her now is so much greater than it was months ago, and in a few more months, it'll be even more. I love Mal more every day. We kept up with our training as well by sparring with Wanda and Jade. All of us had to keep our strength up to prepare. Needless to say, we're ready. We leave in the morning, but for now, we're focusing on Mal's graduation.}

Wanda sits on one side of me with Jade beside her, and Bonny, Mal's mom, sits on the other. We sit in the front row of the many rows behind us. Each seat is filled with friends and family of the graduates.

{Today is a critical day.}

"Oh, it's starting," Bonny says excitedly.

The band starts to play as the graduates march down the aisle.

{I saw Mal right before she went to get ready. I told her just how proud and happy I was for her. That this was really important to her, and I'm glad that she got the opportunity to graduate. I kissed her deeply before she ran to get her gown.}

"I sense her energy before I see her. "She's coming."

"How do you know? Can you see her?"

"I can sense her." I smile.

"Oh."

"She's coming out...now."

Mal walks out the door with her hair gently touching her shoulders, the sun reflecting off her sky-blue eyes. She smiles brightly with so much joy as she marches. She must sense me because she looks right at me. I give her a big smile before blowing her a kiss. She giggles before blowing me a kiss back. She walks by us onto the stage where she stands with her classmates. We sit there as each student's name is called, and they are handed their diploma.

"Malak Serenity Giffin."

I'm up faster than anyone else, clapping my hands hard and quickly as she steps away from the group. She shakes the principal's hand as he hands her diploma. I feel her energy spike with happiness, and I can't help but chuckle. She walks to the edge of the stage before raising her diploma up high. I clap harder as my eyes fill with joyful tears. She turns around and rejoins the group. We sit back down.

"Are you sure?" Wanda asks me again.

"Definitely."

"Where are you taking me?" Mal laughs.

Her eyes are closed tight, with me standing behind to guide her to where I want to go.

"We're almost there."

"I hope so. We've been walking up for a while now."

"Tired?"

"Ha, ha, very funny."

"Just be patient."

"You should know by now that that is one thing I'm not."

I laugh. "Fair enough." I stop moving. "All right, open your eyes."

She opens them. "Kal, this is beautiful."

I watch as she walks to the edge of the cliff overlooking nothing but forest. "Figured we could gaze up at the stars. The night is perfectly clear, and the moon is full."

She turns around and walks back over to me. "I love it." She pecks my cheek. "I'm glad."

I lead us closer to the edge. A giant rock sits a foot away. I walk over to it and grab the blue blanket hidden there.

"Sneaky. Hid the blanket here so I wouldn't get suspicious."

I chuckle. "Only way to make sure you didn't figure it out." I open the blanket and lay it down on the grass.

"After you, madam." I bow to her.

"Why, thank you." She sits down on the blanket.

My hands start to shake, so I shove them in my pockets before sitting down. "You looked beautiful today."

"Thank you."

"Then again, you look beautiful every day so..." I smile.

She nudges me. "Stop."

We stare up at the stars in silence for a few minutes. My heart pounds hard inside of me.

{I hope she can't hear that.}

"Are you ready for tomorrow?" she asks.

"I don't want to talk about tomorrow. I just want to focus on here and now."

"I can agree to that."

She leans over until her head is on my shoulder. We watch the stars.

{Come on, you can do this.}

I take a nervous breath. "Can I show you something?"

"Of course." She sits up.

"I've been working with explosions from my flames, and I discovered something really cool." I stand up and move to the edge.

"What?"

"Just watch."

Flames burst around my hands. I face towards the clearing as I concentrate on the shape of my fire. I throw the ball into the sky. We watch as it soars up and up. BOOM!

The ball explodes. The flames move in the sky until they create a star shape. "Wow! How did you do that?"

"Lots of practice."

I throw another ball. BOOM!

This time it creates angel wings. "Beautiful."

Two more. BOOM! BOOM!

A shooting star and rainbow.

{I got this.}

"Come closer."

"Okay."

She gets up as I step to the side so she is closer to the edge. Two bigger balls.

BOOM! BOOM!

Two figures form in the sky. One looks at the other with longing. "Is that you and me?"

"Yeah, it's the first day I saw you." Three more big ones.

BOOM! BOOM! BOOM!

The exact figures reappear, but my figure is running towards Mal's as a cab moves towards her.

"That's the day you saved me."

"Yep."

Three more.

BOOM! BOOM! BOOM! Me, her, and a door.

"The day you came to my house." BOOM! BOOM! BOOM!

Me standing in front of her with my arms spread wide, with Jorvexx standing in front of me.

"When you protected me against Jorvexx." BOOM!

Mal hugging me. "Awe."

BOOM! BOOM! BOOM!

Me on a bed, with Mal sitting with me. "Is that when I healed you?"
"Yes."
BOOM! BOOM!
Mal snuggled in my arms. BOOM! BOOM!
Us staring at each other intently.
"When the world fell away," she says in awe. BOOM! BOOM!
BOOM!
Jade holding me hostage as Mal's hands glow. BOOM! BOOM!
Me standing without a shirt in front of her. BOOM! BOOM!
Us sparring.
BOOM! BOOM! BOOM!
Me standing on a platform staring at Mal. BOOM! BOOM!
Mal standing in front of me with her hand on my chest. "When I
told you to listen to your heart."
BOOM! BOOM! BOOM!
Me standing on a stage with a microphone and Mal on the ground
in front of me. BOOM!
Mal holding me in her lap as we kiss. BOOM! BOOM!
Us standing with our hands together and energy surrounding us.
BOOM! BOOM! BOOM!
Mal hugging Wanda as I smile at them. BOOM! BOOM! BOOM!
Us telling her mom the truth.
BOOM! BOOM! BOOM! BOOM! BOOM! BOOM! BOOM!
Multiple scenes appear. Me waiting outside of her school. Us walk-
ing together. Us hanging out at her house and The Middle with Wanda.
Dinner date, movie date. My face burns as the last one takes shape.
Mal and I lying in bed together. BOOM!
Mal holding her diploma.
"Wow, Kal, that was really amazing."
"I'm not finished."
"What do you mean? You're all caught up."
"Just keep watching."
"Okay."

BOOM! BOOM! BOOM!

A giant K and M inside of a heart with FOREVER written inside. "Forever."

I reach into my pocket before sending out the last two. BOOM! BOOM!

I get down on my knee behind her as the figures take shape. Me down on my knee, holding a box out to her.

"Kal?"

I hold the box up just as she turns around. Her eyes grow in shock as she stares at me.

"I know that it's only been a little over a year, but Malak, I can't imagine my life without you anymore. I want it to be us forever and always. I want to be able to say, 'Yeah, she's my wife.' I always said that I wanted to spend our lives together; well, when I said that, I meant TOGETHER." I open the box to show her the silver, flat crystal ring.

{Wanda made this special for me. She created a crystal that won't be destroyed when Mal uses her energy or when our energies combine. She had to make the ring flat, though, so the crystal would stay denser.}

"Will you marry me, Malak?"

She doesn't hesitate. "Yes! Of course, yes!"

My heart flutters as I pull the ring from the box before sliding it onto her finger. She jumps at me the moment it's on, knocking me over onto the grass.

"You are all I want forever, Kalma."

"And that's what you shall have. Me. Forever." She smiles before kissing me.

{She said yes!}

"Are you sure you guys have everything?" Uriel asks us for the hundredth time.

"Yes," we answer.

"I'm just making sure."

Michael chuckles. "She's a worrywart."

"We'll be okay, Uriel," Jade assures her.

"I know. I just worry."

Wanda slides over to me. "Well, how'd it go?"

"How'd what go?"

"You know exactly what," she says, annoyed.

"You mean this." Mal appears behind me as she holds her hand over my shoulder.

A giant smile spreads across Wanda's face. "Congratulations!" She wraps us both in a hug. "I'm so happy for you."

"Hey, what's going on over here?" Jade questions.

"Nothing much." Wanda lets go of us. "Just Kal and Mal getting married."

"What?!" Jade, Michael, and Uriel exclaim.

They come running over to see Mal's ring. "When did this happen?" Uriel wonders. "Last night," I tell her.

"How did you ask?" Michael asks.

"I—"

"It's a secret," Mal interrupts me. "Something just for Kal and me." I beam.

"All right."

"So when is the big day, or haven't you decided yet?" Jade ponders. "Actually, we do have a day," Mal tells her.

"Oh?"

"The day I first saw Mal."

"That's so romantic." Uriel smiles.

"It works out really well because it's right around the time we'll get back after completing this mission," I explain.

"That's perfect. Must just be meant to be." She smiles bigger.

"Don't worry, time will fly by," Michael says.

"I hope so," Mal and I say.

We look at each other before laughing.

"Speaking of time, it's time for us to go," Jade commands.

"You know, just because you have the transportation thing doesn't mean you're in charge," Wanda tells her.

"Yeah, yeah," Jade mouths.

I laugh softly.

{Definitely something there.}

I pull my bag onto my back as Mal does the same. "Ready for this?"

She nods. "Let's get this over with so we can come back and get married."

"Agreed."

"Get over here, you two. You all need to be touching me for you to get teleported." Mal and I walk over and put our hands on Jade's shoulder as Wanda has hers on Jade's head with a smirk on her face.

"Where to first?" Jade asks.

"Paris!" Mal exclaims.

"Ugh, seriously?"

"May as well celebrate our engagement while fighting demons, right?"

Jade rolls her eyes. "Fine, but I swear, if I see you two making out while we're busy kicking ass, I'll be kicking both of your asses."

"Good luck," Michael, Uriel, Wanda, Mal, and I say.

"Wow, okay, that's just rude."

She pushes the button on the disc. The Middle disappears, everything becoming bright before we stand in front of the Eiffel Tower. We take our hands off of Jade as we look around. Mal gawks at all of the lights. I smile at her.

{Day one. Three hundred and sixty-four to go.} I sigh.

{I really do hope this goes by fast. I'm ready to get married.}
"Church is this way." Jade points.

Mal's hand slides into mine. I look up at her, seeing nothing but love in her eyes.

{Three hundred and sixty-four.}

We follow Jade.

Epilogue

"Aren't you ready yet?" Wanda pounds on the door.

"It's not my fault these things are so damn hard to do," I complain as I mess with the blue bow tie around my neck.

"Are you decent?"

"No, I'm standing in here naked with just a bow tie on." The door opens. "You think you're funny, don't you?"

"As a matter of fact—"

"Shut it."

{Over the last year Wanda and I have really become sisters. She no longer has the feelings for me that she had before, and I'm glad, because I know how much it was hurting her seeing Mal and me together.} "Now come here."

I stand still as she grabs onto the fabric. "You don't look too bad in a tux."

"Where's your dress?" I ignore her comment.

"I'll get there."

"When? Are you waiting till everything starts? Because that's in like ten minutes."

"I said I'll get there."

"Okay, but don't come crying to me when she kicks your ass."

"Ha, ha, now hold still."

{Mal and Wanda have also grown close. It's nice to see the two people I care most about getting along as if they're family.}

"There." She steps back. "Now, don't touch it."

{Because soon, they will be.}

"Yes, sir," I salute.

"You know ever since Mal and you started really dating, you've been even more of a smartass."

"What can I say? She makes me happy, which in turn makes me funnier." I laugh.

"Only place you're funny is in your head."

"Jade thinks I'm funny."

"No, I really don't." Jade appears in the doorway.

"Awe, come on. Not even a little?"

She walks up and stops beside Wanda. "Not even a teeny bit."

"You guys suck," I grumble.

"Serves you right." Wanda leans over and kisses Jade's cheek. "You should know by now that she doesn't lie."

{The reason Wanda no longer has feelings for me is that she developed them for somebody else.}

"There's no point in lying. You know me too well and would be able to tell that I am."

"True."

{I saw the chemistry there long before they did, so when they finally decided to give them a try, I bragged for days that I saw it coming.}

"Where's your suit?" I ask Jade.

"I'll get there."

I sigh with frustration.

"You two are perfect for each other."

They both grin.

"Well, while you two GET THERE, I have to head to my spot. We're going to be starting soon." I walk around them. "Oh, and thank you, guys." I keep walking.

{They helped plan all of this even while we were traveling. I owe them a lot.}

I make my way through the back of Wanda's shop before going out her back door into the giant field behind the building.

"Hey, Kal." Melanie comes around the building. "Don't you look nice."

"Thanks, you do too."

"Do I? I've never worn a dress before, so it feels kind of weird."

I glance over the celeste-colored strapless dress with a white lace shawl over her shoulders.

{I've never understood the appeal in dresses, but I guess these ones are okay-looking.}

"Yeah, you look good."

"Well, thank you. I'm going to go get ready, talk to you later."

I wave as she heads through the door. Anxiety twists my stomach, making me feel as if I'm going to puke.

{Deep breaths, Kalma. This is what you wanted, remember? You got this.}

{Is this really happening?}

I stand in front of everyone seated in the chairs laid out in rows on the grass on both sides of the white rose petal aisle.

{Mal loved the idea of using rose petals.}

Everyone stares up at me. In the front row is Uxum, Sukir, some goblins, a few imps, and all of the fairies and pixies share a chair. Sitting in the chair closest to the aisle is Bonny. She waves to me.

{We slowly introduced her to the creatures of the supernatural world until she learned each kind and that they wouldn't hurt her. Now she treats them as if they were regular people.}

Behind them sits Nestra and Deseih, who both wore regular clothing via my request so that none of the male guests would be stunned by them. Scattered throughout the chairs are some of the family members of the ones that fell in battle. Also in the audience are some of Mal's friends.

{It took the witches a while to temporarily spell them into seeing everyone here as humans. But they did it because they knew how much it meant to Mal to have them here.}

The rest of the people here are guardian angels and the archangels.

{They were all able to come today, which is great because we were able to talk Raziel into marrying us.}

"Are you ready?" a voice asks.

I jump in surprise before turning to see Raziel. "I've been ready since the day I saw her."

He smiles. "Well, okay then."

The music starts, "I Knew I Loved You" by Savage Garden. The back door of Wanda's store swings open, as Jade and Wanda appear with their arms wrapped together.

{They cleaned up nicely. Why was it so hard just to get dressed earlier?}

I watch them as they walk down the aisle towards me. Wanda has the same dress as Melanie. Jade wears the same style suit as mine, but she has a black bow tie, whereas mine is royal blue. They continue walking until they make it to the front. They split, with Jade coming to my side and Wanda to Mal's.

{Jade is my best woman, and Wanda is Mal's maid of honor.}

The next couple emerges from the building. Melanie and Bruce walk the same way that Wanda and Jade did. When they split, Bruce comes to my side, and Melanie goes to the other. Next are Barbara and John. Barbara goes to Mal's side and John to mine. Summer and Blaze follow behind them. Blaze moves to my side as Summer goes to Mal's. Levi walks out, looking very nervous as Raphael has her arm wrapped through his.

{They shrunk themselves down, so they weren't towering over everyone today.}

Levi joins my side, Raphael moving to Mal's. Ariel appears with a very scared Chayse on her arm. He about runs to his spot on my side as Ariel casually walks to hers. Then finally, it's Derrick and Uriel.

{He's the only one not afraid of the archangel he was paired with.}

The music becomes quieter, and everyone stands up.

{My heart is going to break through my chest.}

The music continues to play, but no one comes out the door. Everyone starts to whisper to each other.

{What's going on?}

Wanda moves closer to me. "She told me she was afraid to walk down the aisle alone. I didn't think she wasn't going to do it."

I look back at the door and smile.

{That's all?}

I step down off the platform and make my way to the door.

{She's just afraid of being alone, not of marrying me.}

I stop on the other side of the door before I turn and lean my back on it. "Hey," I say quietly.

"Kal?"

"Who else?"

"What are you doing?"

"What am I doing? What are you doing? I'm getting married today," I joke with her.

"I can't do it. I can't walk out there with all of the different beings staring at me."

"What beings? All I see are a bunch of empty seats."

"Not funny, Kal."

"I'm serious. I don't see anyone." I push the door open with my back. "The only one I see...is you."

My cheeks burn as well as my ears when I look at her. Her celeste dress fits her body perfectly, the lace on it shaped like wings, the blue halo floating about her head glowing with energy.

{It was a gift from the archangels. They said every angel needs a halo. It's made from natural energy and is actually floating.}

I smile at her as love fills me head to toe.

{So beautiful.}

"What?"

I hold out my hand to her. "Come on."

She looks at my hand and me as if I'm crazy. "Just me and you."

She smiles at me as she slides her hand into mine. "Always," I whisper as I pull the door open.

Everyone standing at the podium sends warm smiles our way as we walk down the aisle.

"See, nothing but empty seats."

"Kalma."

"The only ones I see are our friends who care about us." She looks up at those waiting for us.

"You're right. They are all I see."

I lead her the rest of the way and up the podium before we stop to face each other. The music stops, and everyone settles back into their seats.

"Thank you, everyone, for coming to this memorable occasion. We are here today to join these two in holy matrimony. I'm not going to even bother asking if anyone has any reasons why these two should not be wed because we all know that they are meant for each other. These two are the true definition of soulmates. I knew from the moment I saw them together that it was meant to be, and I know a lot of things."

I chuckle quietly.

"So I know that all of you feel the same way."

{Does everyone really see how much we belong together?} "All right, I was told that you two prepared your own vows."

"Yes," I answer.

He nods. "Go ahead."

"Mal," I say quietly.

"Oh, me first, um, okay," she panics.

"Deep breaths, it's okay. Just you and I remember?"

She nods as she takes a deep breath. "Kalma, the day we first met, you saved my life. The second time you asked me to trust and believe you, I did. I believed this strange girl that appeared on my porch telling me a bunch of crazy things. I don't know what it was, but every part of me told me that I could trust you and put my life in your hands, and that part of me was right. You saved my life again that night. You protected me against multiple enemies, and you did it without a second thought. You told me that you'd save me even if you died in the process. I couldn't understand why someone who had just met me could say something like that. Maybe you were just saying that to make me feel safer, but when you did die to save me, I knew that this girl was the real deal. As I watched you die, it felt as if a part of I didn't know existed broke. The pain I felt was unlike anything I had ever felt before. I begged for you to come back. I wanted you. I needed you. Somehow, I knew that I loved you even though we had just met. It felt as if I was always meant to love you. As I spent more time with you, I learned about who you really were. You are kind, protective, determined, and will always protect those precious to you. I am one of those people. I don't know how many times you've saved me since the day we met. Between the archdemons and the demons we fought during our mission, you saved me so many times that I lost track. Sometimes I would be angry with you for doing so because you'd end up hurt in the process or worse. You jumped in front of your father's attack for me. You allowed him to strike right through your flame for me, to save me. It felt as if my world was crumbling around me as I had to watch the life drain out of you."

The memory of that day hits me, and guilt washes over me.

{I put her through so much pain.}

"But just like a fairy tale, my kiss brought you back." She smiles at me. "My love saved you, just as yours saved me. That's what I want. I want the love that we share to keep each other safe. I want to keep you safe, just as much as you want to keep me safe. So that is why I vow to continue to love you every second of every day. I vow to protect not just your body but your heart as well. I am the one who started it, after all, so it should be my responsibility to keep it safe, right? I want to take care of your heart. I want to make you happy, make sure that you know you are loved. I want to be the one you can tell anything to and be whoever you want to be. I want to do these things and so much more. I love you, Kalma. I always have, and I always will."

Tears stream down my face as my heart races with love and my flame blazes with warmth.

"Kalma," Raziel says.

I wipe my face. "Not sure how I'm supposed to follow that, but here goes. I'm going to tell you something that we've both known for a while now. You were always the one. There could never be anyone but you. When we met, I had never felt love before. I didn't even know there was such a thing. At the time, all I knew was that there was a strange, beautiful warmth and a strange beating inside of me that would go off when I was with you. Even though I didn't know what love felt like, I still knew that I felt something towards you, which continued to get stronger when I was with you. I've told you time and time again how you changed my life. How you brought light into my life and changed me. I meant every word each time I spoke them. Malak, your light saved me from my darkness. I only ever thought I was a tool, a weapon, that my father and the other archdemons could use whenever they liked. When I saw you though, something inside of me told me that that was wrong. Seeing you set me on the path that I followed to get here. If I had never met you Mal, I know that the darkness would have consumed me. Without you, I would've been lost forever. I almost was lost. My flame went out, and I was surrounded by nothing but an empty abyss. Your light found me and pulled me out. Your love reignited my flame. So when you say that I've saved you over and over, well, you have saved me just as much. You brought me back to life, yes, but you also saved the person that I am today, the person I was always meant to be. I never would've found myself if not for you. The emotions I have now never would've developed. The self-worth that I never had, you brought that to life. You brought me to life, Malak. The heart that you brought to life"—I put my hand on my chest—"belongs to you and will only ever belong to you. I vow to always love you, always take care of you, always stand by your side, and will always fight to remain by your side. I promise to stay with you forever. Because of you, it is a lot harder to kill me, so I can keep that promise." I smile. "There is no other love like ours. Malak, I promise

irdest questions. You listened and always answered me no matter
w strange the answer. You helped me dive deeper into the supernat-
l world, thank you.

To those who stuck by me and helped me through the tough times,
uldn't be more thankful. It was a struggle, but you all helped me
back on my feet and encouraged me to not give up but to write as
Grandma, you don't know what I write about, but you are still
ng to read it anyway. We've grown closer this past year; I couldn't
ine not having you to talk to. I love you, Grandma, love you,
dpa. My brother Chayse and his fiancé Angel, thank you for al-
g me to hide at your place and use your computer whenever I
d it. Angel, thank you for reading small sections of my book and
you for keeping it a secret and for telling me whether something
fixed or if it was good just the way it was. Even if one of the
s made you feel uncomfortable, you still read on, thank you.
, even though you don't like to read you still pushed me to go
with this, so I thank you for not giving up on me. Dad, you
big part in making sure that I could get this book published.
u for everything, thank you for reconnecting. Mom and Bruce,
th done so much for me this past year. You supported me and
e through everything. The doctors, the tests, the unanswered
s. If I were to write everything you've done for me, I'd run out
So, I'll just say this: Bruce, we might not be blood but that
ped you from treating me as your daughter. You fought for
a father would and I love you for that even if I don't say it
Mom, you've been with me my whole life. Not just as a par-
a friend as well. Life hasn't been easy, we've been through
od and bad, but we remain us. You've always had my back
you knew when I was making a mistake. You wanted me to
self, but you were there when that mistake came back and
down. Mom, I know that you don't understand why I like
do but you've never made me stop. You might make com-
you've never taken any of it from me. Thank you for

to protect that. I love you more than I thought anyone could love someone." I take her hands in mine. "I know I'm mostly just rambling now,
but there's so much that I want to say to you that I want you to hear."

"Then I guess it's a good thing we'll have forever." She smiles
warmly.

"Even forever wouldn't be enough time with you."

Tears run down her cheeks.

"Wow," Raziel says.

The world comes back around us.

{I didn't even realize that they all disappeared.}

Sniffles sound from all over the audience as well as the podium. I
look over at Wanda to see as she wipes her face.

"Your rambling was beautiful," Raziel tells me. "Does that end your
vows?"

"For now. As Mal said, we have forever."

"All right, if that concludes the vows, the rings, please."

I turn around as Mal does too. Jade hands me a ring. I spin back
around, just as Mal does.

"Malak Serenity Giffin, do you take this woman to be your wife for
all eternity?"

"I do."

She holds the ring out. I lift my hand, so she can slowly slide it up
my finger.

{These rings are made out of the same material as the engagement
ring. These won't be destroyed when we use our powers.}

The cold metal presses against my finger.

{It feels so right.}

"Kalma."

{Demons don't have middle or last names.}

"Do you take this woman to be your wife for all eternity?"

"I do with every part of my soul."

"I do would've been just fine."

"Sorry, I do."

Mal raises her hand as she chuckles so I can slide her ring onto her finger. We hold both of each other's hands.

{After everything we've been through. With all of the fights, the pain, the struggles, the deaths, and the fear, we are finally getting our happy ending.} "Then by the power vested in me..."

{There may be more fights in the future, but we will face them together. As long as we're together, we can do anything.}

"I now pronounce you married."

{Forever.}

"You may now kiss your bride."

I wrap my arms around her. "I love you."

"I love you too."

We lean in towards each other. I quickly dip her as a dancer would. She laughs as she smiles up at me, her eyes sparkling. I smile down at her as I move in closer. Her lips press against mine, sending warmth down my body and setting off the fireworks in my head. We continue to kiss, turning our heads as our lips smack with passion and yearning.

{You're all I want.}

We pull apart just enough for our foreheads to touch. I fall into her eyes, allowing everything to disappear around us.

{You are all I'll ever want.}

"I'm never letting you go," I whisper.

"I never want you to," she whispers back.

{So, this is a happy ending?}

I close my eyes; my love for her swirls and burns in my chest. Strength builds inside of me as my love for her does.

{Lucifer might think he understands what this is between her and me, but he couldn't be more wrong. The power I'm feeling from our love right now...could be just as powerful as his. We can do anything together, so bring it on Lucifer.}

I smile. "My wife."

The End....is just the beginning

Acknowledgments

People say that whenever something bad happen[...] good. That's what I did this past year when the [...] corner. For as long as I can remember I've alway[...] thor, I just never had the time or the resources. [...] when an unexpected illness struck, leaving m[...] the time. I looked towards the brighter side and [...] I was stuck at home to write, and this book is [...] This book and those who helped me along th[...]

I want to start off by thanking those wh[...] lowed me to afford to publish my book. With[...] who you are, all of this wouldn't have been [...] the bottom of my heart. To those who help[...] ferent things, thank you so much fo[...] commitment. The time we spent togeth[...] we might have lost our tempers a few tim[...] it back. We didn't just make things, we [...] gether and that was the best.

Next, to my friends and family tha[...] to take my characters in. Some of you [...] it was even sent. You gave me feedb[...] better story. My brother Derrick, I bu[...] mons and angels should be like. [...]

to protect that. I love you more than I thought anyone could love some-one." I take her hands in mine. "I know I'm mostly just rambling now, but there's so much that I want to say to you that I want you to hear."

"Then I guess it's a good thing we'll have forever." She smiles warmly.

"Even forever wouldn't be enough time with you."

Tears run down her cheeks.

"Wow," Raziel says.

The world comes back around us.

{I didn't even realize that they all disappeared.}

Sniffles sound from all over the audience as well as the podium. I look over at Wanda to see as she wipes her face.

"Your rambling was beautiful," Raziel tells me. "Does that end your vows?"

"For now. As Mal said, we have forever."

"All right, if that concludes the vows, the rings, please."

I turn around as Mal does too. Jade hands me a ring. I spin back around, just as Mal does.

"Malak Serenity Giffin, do you take this woman to be your wife for all eternity?"

"I do."

She holds the ring out. I lift my hand, so she can slowly slide it up my finger.

{These rings are made out of the same material as the engagement ring. These won't be destroyed when we use our powers.}

The cold metal presses against my finger.

{It feels so right.}

"Kalma."

{Demons don't have middle or last names.}

"Do you take this woman to be your wife for all eternity?"

"I do with every part of my soul."

"I do would've been just fine."

"Sorry, I do."

Mal raises her hand as she chuckles so I can slide her ring onto her finger. We hold both of each other's hands.

{After everything we've been through. With all of the fights, the pain, the struggles, the deaths, and the fear, we are finally getting our happy ending.} "Then by the power vested in me..."

{There may be more fights in the future, but we will face them together. As long as we're together, we can do anything.}

"I now pronounce you married."

{Forever.}

"You may now kiss your bride."

I wrap my arms around her. "I love you."

"I love you too."

We lean in towards each other. I quickly dip her as a dancer would. She laughs as she smiles up at me, her eyes sparkling. I smile down at her as I move in closer. Her lips press against mine, sending warmth down my body and setting off the fireworks in my head. We continue to kiss, turning our heads as our lips smack with passion and yearning.

{You're all I want.}

We pull apart just enough for our foreheads to touch. I fall into her eyes, allowing everything to disappear around us.

{You are all I'll ever want.}

"I'm never letting you go," I whisper.

"I never want you to," she whispers back.

{So, this is a happy ending?}

I close my eyes; my love for her swirls and burns in my chest. Strength builds inside of me as my love for her does.

{Lucifer might think he understands what this is between her and me, but he couldn't be more wrong. The power I'm feeling from our love right now...could be just as powerful as his. We can do anything together, so bring it on Lucifer.}

I smile. "My wife."

The End....is just the beginning